ROSIE EDWARDS

by

Hilda McKenzie

HEADLINE

17816

First published in 1990
by HEADLINE BOOK PUBLISHING PLC

10 9 8 7 6 5 4 3 2 1

British Library Cataloguing in Publication Data

McKenzie, Hilda
Rosie Edwards.
I. Title
823.914 [F]

ISBN 0-7472-0251-6

Typeset in 11/13½ pt Times
by Colset Private Limited, Singapore

Printed and bound in Great Britain by
Richard Clay Ltd, Bungay, Suffolk

HEADLINE BOOK PUBLISHING PLC
Headline House
79 Great Titchfield Street
London W1P 7FN

To my late Mam and Dad, Annie and Jim Smith, in gratitude for a happy carefree childhood.

And to my son, John, for all his interest and help. And to
my husband, Reg, and my daughter, Judith, for listening.

Acknowledgements

My grateful thanks to the following:

Mr Geoffrey Rich, Editor of the *South Wales Echo*, for allowing me to use their source material, and for letting me see 'Bombers Over Wales'.

Mr John Humphries, Editor of the *Western Mail*, for news stories of the period.

E. W. Thomas, Nursing Officer of the Whitchurch Hospital, for advice on the treatment of depression in the 1930s and on nurses' uniforms of the period.

The staff of Local Studies at Cardiff Central Library for all their help, especially Mr Tom Davies and Mr Bryn Jones.

My friends of the Cardiff Writers' Circle for all their encouragement.

And my editor, Jane Morpeth.

Chapter 1

Her skinny arms taut with effort Rosie Edwards pushed the deep-bellied pram up the slight incline of Wesley Street. She was small for her ten years; a mass of curly chestnut hair tucked into a floppy woollen tam framed a heart-shaped face whose most striking feature was a pair of wide brown eyes. Now they wore an anxious expression as she hurried past the narrow grey stone houses, their tiny front gardens confined by spiked iron railings.

'Wanna go, Rosie?' cried one of the children playing hopscotch on the opposite pavement.

'Our mam's waiting,' Rosie shouted back without stopping. Albert needed changing an' all, she could smell him.

The houses in Wesley Street, one of the many streets branching off Broadway, had been built in the second half of the nineteenth century when Cardiff was an up-and-coming industrial town. Now in the bright autumn sunshine of 1928 many of the houses looked drab, but at number forty-two, where Rosie stopped to push open the gate, the front door had been newly painted green, and knocker and letter-box glowed from a recent application of Brasso and elbow grease.

Opening the gate wide and manoeuvring the pram up the four yards of path to the front door, Rosie groped through the letterbox for the key on the end of the string.

'Is that you, Rose?'

'Yes, Mam.' Carrying Albert under one arm she went through to the kitchen.

Her mother was sewing at the scrubbed wooden table. Two pieces of striped coconut matting almost covered the flagstoned floor, and in front of the range lay a colourful rag mat which was Rosie's handiwork.

1

Rosie looked up anxiously at the china clock on the high mantel-shelf. 'Our Albert's poohed, I'd better change him 'fore I go to school,' she told her mother, taking off the faded blue coat and navy tam and dropping them on the sofa.

'Oh Rose! Couldn't you just say Albert needs changing?' Laura Edwards was a pale thin woman in her early thirties, the violet blue of her eyes heightened by dark shadows beneath. An abundance of silky fair hair drawn back into a loose bun seemed too heavy for her head.

Rosie brought bowl, some soap and a towel and spread the towel on a mat in front of the range – she was used to her mother's little niceties.

'Ych-y-fi,' she said, smiling down at seven-month-old Albert, using the phrase she'd learnt from Nana Edwards. The baby, free from his nappy and freshly washed, kicked and babbled contentedly.

She watched anxiously as her mother lowered herself slowly into the wooden armchair in front of the guard and put out her arms to receive the now freshly nappied Albert.

'Shall I stay home and help you, Mam?'

'No, love, we don't want the school inspector round again, do we?' As Albert was put on her lap she gave her daughter a warm hug; ever since the baby's birth she had been weak and listless, but Rose had coped wonderfully with her five young brothers.

Ernie, two years Rosie's junior, had already taken six-year-old Willie and four-year-old Bobby to school.

'Where's our Teddy, Mam? Is he next door?'

Laura nodded. 'I don't know what I'd do without Ada – he loves going in there.'

Ada Jenkins was one of those women who is a treasure in any street. Always ready to help, it was Ada who willingly lent a hand at births and the laying in, and when there'd been a bereavement it was she who was called upon to see to the laying out. She was a stout little woman with warm brown eyes and plump rosy cheeks that dimpled easily into a smile.

Teddy at two was into everything and too much for Laura to handle in her present state of health. But he adored the motherly

Ada Jenkins, and was very happy to spend hours playing, and being spoilt, next door.

Rosie put her coat back on and set off. Outside the school gate her cousin Vi was waiting. Despite being tall, Vi had a dainty look, with her pink and white complexion, neat features and big blue eyes. Her long, straight, honey-coloured hair was drawn tightly back into a tortoiseshell slide.

'Can you come to see my new doll after school?' Vi asked. Aunty Mabel, her mam's sister, Uncle Ted and Violet lived with Grandma Hughes in the large, four-bedroomed Victorian house where Mam had been brought up.

Rosie wasn't interested in dolls – she'd had far too much of the real thing – but Grandma's house was a place of wonder with its deep red Turkey carpets and gleaming brass.

'I should go straight home, Vi.'

'It won't take long, Rosie, then you can run all the way.'

Stanley Road School stood in a leafy road flanked on either side by tall old houses with long gardens. It was a large building, solidly built of grey stone now glinting silver in the sunshine. Tall windows were set at intervals along the frontage, and above the wide entrance doors now open ready for afternoon school the legend 'Girls Junior School' was carved in ornate curly lettering.

The girls' part of the school was divided from the boys' by a high brick wall. Rosie blushed, remembering yesterday. Clad only in navy-blue gym knickers and cream school blouses her class had been exercising in the yard when she noticed two boys were sitting astride the wall watching them. Grinning broadly, they had disappeared quickly when they caught Miss Williams's outraged attention.

Rosie and Vi had just entered the playground when a teacher began ringing the bell, and in a matter of moments children who had been skipping, running and chasing one another were forming neat lines ready to enter school in class order as soon as they heard the whistle.

Remembering that the English composition results would be given this afternoon Rosie couldn't get into class quickly enough. She loved writing essays. Even her dismay at the subject 'A Day at the Seaside' hadn't lasted long. She knew she had been taken once, before Ernie was born, but had no memory of it, and there'd been the slides on the magic-lantern at Band of Hope. But it had been Vi who had helped her by describing it to her so vividly. 'I can tell you about it but I'm hopeless at writing it down,' Vi had added.

When the class had settled down she waited anxiously while Miss Hopkins shuffled the stack of exercise books on her desk and began to put them in order. Rosie, from her seat nearest the playground, watched impatiently the specks of silver dust whirling endlessly in wide ribbons of sunlight that streamed through the windows.

Miss Hopkins had a pale complexion and mousy brown hair pulled back into a loose untidy bun. She wore sagging skirts and baggy jumpers but her grey eyes were bright with interest as she rapped the desk for their attention.

She took ages going through the merits and faults of each essay in detail before picking up one exercise book and holding it aloft.

'This is easily the best,' she told them. 'Here—' She tapped the book with her pen. 'Here you can smell the sea, hear the receding waves sucking at the shingle, touch the glossy seaweed, feel the warm sea breezes, hear the seagulls' cries. Well done, Rose Edwards!'

Rosie had to go to the front of the class and take the Five Boys chocolate bar that was her prize, then, blushing with embarrassment, she was told to read her composition aloud to the class. When she'd finished they all clapped her and Vi clapped louder and longer than anyone else.

After school, the bar of chocolate safely tucked into her pocket until she could share it amongst the younger boys, Rosie hurried with Vi across the Newport Road to the wide, tree-lined road where Vi lived.

Lifting the burnished lion's-head knocker Vi rapped twice. The door was opened by Grandma Hughes wearing a dainty muslin apron over her pale grey afternoon dress. Grandma's blue eyes lit up with pleasure as they rested on Rosie, and her thin, rather serious face broke into a welcoming smile.

'How is your mama today, Rose?' she asked, stepping back for them to enter the wide hall, its gilt mirror reflecting the brass bowl of chrysanthemums on the hall table.

'Rosie's composition came first, Grandma,' Vi broke in excitedly, and Rose had to go into the kitchen, take the exercise book from her schoolbag and read it to Grandma and Aunty Mabel. With their praise echoing in her ears, she followed Vi back to the hall where the ornate brass stair-rods gleamed as ever against the thick red carpet. She gave a deep sigh of satisfaction, having long ago made up her mind that one day she would have a house just like this, with its big comfortable kitchen and long dining room with the dark polished furniture.

At home, the scrubbed kitchen table stripped of its green chenille cloth was used for many things besides eating. On Saturday mornings she put down newspapers on which to clean the knives with bathbrick, or in the evenings laid an old flannelette sheet for the ironing, heating the heavy flat-irons on the range.

'Come on, Rosie!' cried Vi, waiting impatiently on the stairs. As they reached the landing Aunty Mabel called, 'Come and have some hot chocolate and Welsh cakes before you leave, Rose.' And Rosie's mouth watered in anticipation of the creamy drink and feather-light cakes with their coating of caster sugar.

'Isn't it lovely?' sighed Vi, lifting the baby doll from its cot. It was dressed in an embroidered gown and Grandma had knitted a bonnet and shawl in fluffy white wool. But Rosie was gazing longingly around the bedroom, at the beautiful walnut wardrobe and dressing table, at the brass bed, its pink satin cover sprigged with rosebuds, at the pretty curtains and the deep, cream-coloured carpet square, at the shoes on a stand by the bed. Her eyes opened wide – there were now three pairs of shoes and a pair of rose velvet slippers with matching satin bows.

After admiring the doll the girls went downstairs and sat either side of the kitchen fire while Aunty Mabel, plump and dimpled, her brown hair cut in the new fashionable bob, poured chocolate and passed the Welsh cakes.

Rosie looked around the room with her usual appreciation, first at the large dresser filled with willow-patterned china, then at the pretty mosaic-tiled floor partly covered by matching rugs and at the row of gleaming copper pans on the high shelf.

'You haven't told me how your mama is, Rose. It's too much for her, you know, all the children and so much to do.'

'Come, Mother! You know that Rose does most of the work. Laura's very lucky that way,' Mabel said quickly.

'When I think what her life might have been,' Grandma Hughes sighed deeply. 'Well, child. How is she?'

'Mama's fine,' Rosie assured her. 'She's just tired. Teddy's a handful but Mrs Jenkins minds him a lot and Dada helps all the time when he's home.'

'I told you, Mother there's no need to worry. Rosie can cope until Laura feels better.'

Grandma Hughes tutted impatiently. 'I'd be around there myself,' she said tartly, 'but I know *he* wouldn't want me there.'

'We can manage fine, Grandma, really,' Rosie assured her again, knowing only too well that she was right. Dada wouldn't want her there.

All too soon she had to leave, clutching a basket of goodies for Mama.

'See that she has the calf's-foot jelly, Rose, and the honey. She needs to build up her strength, poor girl.'

Grandma Hughes made no secret of the fact that she deeply regretted her elder daughter's present circumstances. There was no love lost between her and Dada, and he was as bad, making an awful fuss if he found any presents from Grandma in the pantry.

'It's just that his pride is hurt,' her mother had explained after one particular row. 'I don't want to offend your grandma, but I can't have Dada upset like this.'

Feeling guilty for having stayed so long, Rosie hurried down the road; Mam would be worrying. But Ernie will be there, she reassured herself, so she's not on her own.

After the bright sunshine of the day the evening was hazy. Pulling the shabby coat about her and buttoning it, she began to run and by the time she'd reached Broadway she was out of breath and had to stop.

Looking into Pritchard's window, resting against the sill, she was lost for a moment in a child's world of wonder, for the window was filled with Christmas toys. On a green and red banner pasted across the window the message read: 'Christmas Club. Any Item Put Away Until Paid For'.

Promising herself a proper look on the way to school tomorrow, she turned away and saw Ernie coming out of Wesley Street followed by Bobby and Willie.

'Where've you been, our Rosie?' Ernie yelled as she waited to cross the road. When she reached the pavement she answered, 'Grandma's. Is Mam all right? Are you going to the magic-lantern show at the chapel?'

Ernie nodded. He had a scrubbed look and the fringe of his otherwise very short hair was plastered to his forehead by a generous application of water.

'Have you seen the toys in Pritchard's, Rosie? There's a real telescope . . .'

'Can we go and see?' Willie begged, and Bobby began to dance about in anticipation.

'I'll watch you across the road,' Rosie said. 'Then I'll have to run.'

The two younger boys were smaller editions of Ernie. The same brown eyes fringed with pale gold lashes, the same neat features in smooth round faces, the same fair heads with the very same haircut, which wasn't surprising because Dada put the same pudding basin on each to trim their hair.

When the boys reached the opposite pavement she began to run again and didn't stop until she reached home.

Realising in time that it was Wednesday and Dada's half-day from the gent's outfitters, Rosie turned the key quietly and tiptoed along the passage and past the kitchen door. She could hear her father singing:

> 'Ride a cock horse to Banbury Cross
> To see a fine lady ride on a white horse,'

and little Teddy's excited cry, 'Again, Dada! Again.'

Rosie lifted the latch to the yard and entering the wash-house was about to hide the basket under the old grey blanket that covered the mangle when the door leading from the kitchen opened and a shaft of light blinded her.

'Rosie, what are you doing?'

When Arthur Edwards caught sight of the basket his usually pleasant face grew red with anger. Tearing it from her grasp he marched in and dumped it on the kitchen table crying, 'That woman seems set on humiliating me. Does she think I can't look after you, Laura? I've always had a job, haven't I? Always managed to pay the bills and keep you and the children?'

'She means well, Arthur,' Laura said, her face white and drawn, putting a comforting arm about Teddy who was hiding in her skirts.

Albert, awakened by the unaccustomed noise, began to scream and as Rosie went to him Arthur emptied his pockets and flung a handful of silver and copper on to the table. 'There is my beer and baccy money. Yes! Take it and buy what you need. I won't have her handouts, do you hear me, Laura? I've had enough.'

He turned to Rosie, his dark eyes filled with hurt. 'That was very deceitful of you, Rosie, hiding the basket from me like that.'

Before she could think of an answer he'd grabbed his coat from the peg and slammed the kitchen door behind him with such force that the glass panels rattled. When they heard the front door slam Laura collapsed on to the sofa and buried her face in her hands.

As Rosie's arms went about her she raised her head, tears glistening on her lashes. 'I'll have to ask Mabel to tell Grandma not to send me things. I'd have done it before only she'll hold it against him, and I didn't want her to know that he minded. They both behave this way because they care, love. Your dada's a good man.'

Rosie nodded; it was only Grandma's gifts that could upset her usually easy-going father like this.

'Anyway, take those things into Ada's before he comes back – he mustn't find them here.'

'Aw! Do I have to, Mama? Mrs Jenkins will know there's been a row.'

'She probably heard it for herself,' her mother remarked with a wan smile.

Her steps dragging, Rosie took the basket and went next door, looking about her cautiously in case Dada should return.

The door was opened by Ada who smilingly drew her in and closed it behind her. Rosie stood in the passage on the flowered oil cloth gazing at the pink cabbage roses on the wallpaper, then turned her attention to the shiny aspidistra in its brass pot but still couldn't think of anything to say. When the basket was gently prised from her grasp she looked up into the friendly brown eyes in the plump, rosy face, and listening to the lilting voice, for Ada was born and brought up in the valleys, she felt all her embarrassment fade away.

'Your mam wants me to mind these things is it, Rosie luv? I've done it before you know.'

'It isn't Dada's fault Mrs Jenkins . . .'

'I know, cariad,' Ada cut in. 'He's got his pride and quite right too, you wouldn't 'ave him any other way. My Bert's just the same. And it's only natural that your Nana Hughes should worry about your mam, they've both got her interests at heart.'

On her return, Rosie let herself in quietly and opened the kitchen door. Laura looked up hopefully then, seeing that it was Rosie, her lips quivered.

As Rosie hung her coat and woolly tam on the peg behind the door Laura asked, 'Was it all right with Ada?'

Rosie nodded. 'She'll see you have the things when you go in there.'

'You must be hungry, Rose. There's some stew still warm on the hob. Then will you take Albert up, he's all ready, and I'll get Teddy undressed. Ernest can make toast in front of the fire when the boys come in.'

'I've got homework to do, Mam.'

'Well, Ernest can wash the dishes and see Willie and Bobby to bed.' Once more her mother glanced anxiously at the clock and Rosie knew that she wasn't expecting the boys to return just yet.

'Shall I go and look for Dada when I've put Albert to bed?'

'No, Rose, he'll be back in his own good time. Perhaps he's met a friend and gone for a drink and a chat.'

But looking at the little pile of silver and copper on the table, Rosie knew that he hadn't. Dada would never go into The Bertram unless he could pay his round.

After tucking Albert into his cot in her tiny back bedroom she took Teddy to the room he shared with the other boys. Mama had been telling him his favourite story, 'Goldilocks and the Three Bears', and he seemed to have forgotten the events of the evening. Almost as soon as his head touched the pillow the lids drooped over sleepy blue eyes and the tawny gold lashes fanned out over his plump cheeks.

She heard Ernie and the boys come in and went downstairs. Ernie was sitting on the rag mat holding a piece of bread to the fire on the long toasting fork and Willie and Bobby were spreading margarine liberally on the toast he'd already made.

'You can do your homework now, Rose,' her mother said, looking at the clock once more. 'Ernest can wash the dishes and go to bed with the boys.'

'Aw, Mam! Can't I stay up? When's Dada coming home?'

'He should be here soon,' his mother told him, and Rosie remembered just in time that Ernie knew nothing about the row.

She took her books to the front parlour and pulling back the lace cloth arranged them on the table and sat down. When she'd finished her homework she went to the window and lifted the paper blind.

The street was dark except for pools of light shed by the gas lamps. Around the lamp on the opposite pavement a group of older children were taking turns to swing round the lamp post on a rope thrown over the iron arms. The babel of excited voices drifted across. A lump came into her throat and Rosie blinked back the tears which stung at the back of her eyes. She longed to pull the front door open and run across to join them, but Mama wasn't yet strong enough to go upstairs if Albert or Teddy cried out. And she'd just heard Ernie go to bed with the other two.

Rosie dropped the blind and gathered her books together. Where was Dada? She went to the kitchen, made a pot of tea and cut some thin bread and butter for them both but her mother pushed her plate aside.

'Dada will be home soon, Mam. Shall I put the rest of the stew on for him?'

'No, love. Slice some cheese on the enamel plate and put that last rasher of bacon on top – he likes that and it won't take long.'

But what if he doesn't come home soon? Rosie thought, picturing the cheese brittle and ruined and the bacon burnt to a crisp.

'You have school tomorrow, you'd better go up, Rose.'

'I'd rather wait, Mam.'

'You go to bed. He's probably met a friend like I said – men have no sense of time.'

Reluctantly Rosie took the candle dish from the shelf, lit the candle and kissed her mother goodnight.

As she closed the door behind her gaunt shadows leaped ahead of her and danced on the ceiling. At the foot of the stairs, for a brief moment she let herself imagine that they were covered in thick red carpet with burnished stair-rods twinkling in the candlelight, the illusion rudely shattered as her bare feet touched the chilly oilcloth.

She'd reached the landing when she heard her father close the front door quietly behind him. When the kitchen door opened and there were no raised voices she sighed with relief.

Chapter 2

It was the worst winter that anyone could remember. January began with bitter east winds and when Laura caught a bad cold Dr Thomas confined her to bed. Once again Rosie had to stay at home to look after the children.

On Monday morning as the two big brass bells on the alarm clock began their clanmour Rosie dashed from her bed to silence them before they woke Albert. Shivering into her clothes she crept downstairs to rake the ashes from the kitchen range and lay the fire, putting a match to the crumpled paper and coaxing the still damp sticks to light. When it had taken she filled the big iron kettle and put it on to boil.

Going through to the wash-house she pushed with all her might to trundle the big iron mangle into the yard. It took her ages to get the fire going under the copper ready for washday to begin. She splashed her face and hands in the ice-cold water at the shallow brown earthenware sink and went into the kitchen to prepare breakfast.

Arthur came down earlier than usual, surprised to find her up. 'Thought you'd still be in bed, love,' he told her apologetically. 'I was going to do the fires.' Taking the cup of tea she'd poured in both hands he drank it gratefully, then took Laura's tray up and called the boys while Rosie sorted the dirty clothes into piles ready to start. But first Albert must be bathed and taken back to Mama to be fed.

When the house was quiet at last she put the tin bath on the narrow wooden bench in the wash-house and filled it with pans of hot water from the copper. The strong brown soap stung her hands as she soaped the clothes and rubbed them on the washboard, while steam billowed through the doorway to rise slowly on the chilly morning air.

The worst part was the mangling when she stood, teeth chattering, her back aching with the cold, struggling to turn the heavy handle, until water cascaded from the wooden roller to freeze solid on the flagstones within the hour.

The white calicos and linens were boiled and starched and blued ready for the line, where they quickly became as stiff as boards, and tears came to her eyes as she fumbled painfully with the dolly pegs with her frozen fingers.

It was the middle of the afternoon before at last she came to the socks and finally to the dusters. Ladling the water from the bath she gave a big sigh of relief and went into the comfortable warmth of the kitchen for a brief rest and a soothing cup of tea.

The days seemed to be an endless round of jobs. The fires had to be kept going, in Mama's room as well as the kitchen. There was the cleaning, cooking and shopping, with Albert fretful because he was cutting another tooth. Dada helped when he came home from work, and Ernie when he wasn't at school. Rosie lived in constant fear that she would open the door to the boardie come to find out why she wasn't at school herself.

Teddy spent a lot of time with Mrs Jenkins and she was grateful for this. Dada was usually home in time to put Bobby and Willie to bed, see to the fires and take Mama her supper tray, afterwards filling the coal scuttles and bringing in firewood ready for the next day.

Then on the tenth of February, just when everyone thought the worst of the weather was over, a flurry of snow in the late evening turned overnight into a blizzard.

Rosie woke early on that Monday morning; for once the two big brass bells on the alarm clock hadn't startled her into wakefulness, it wanting another ten minutes to six thirty.

Swinging her legs out of bed, she quickly swung them back – the oilcloth was freezing! Putting on her socks she went to the window and drew back the curtain, amazed to find soft flakes of snow swirling endlessly past driven by a strong wind; already it was piled high in one corner of the window.

From somewhere below came a dragging, scraping sound; she pressed her face against the cold wet glass and looked down, but couldn't see a thing.

Slipping on the old coat of Mam's that did for a dressing gown she hurried downstairs, delighted to find the fire in the kitchen range well alight with hungry orange flames licking the black coals into glowing life.

There was the noise again. Going through to the wash-house and opening the door to the yard she peered out, the snow swirling past her into the house.

'Dada!'

Her father stopped his shovelling and turned towards her.

'Go in, Rosie, you'll get soaked. Put the kettle on the gas stove, luv, and make us a cup of tea, it'll take ages on the fire.'

A few minutes later he came into the kitchen, beating his hands about his body to bring back the circulation.

'Duw! It's parky out there, Rosie.' He stood with his back to the fire, the front of his dark curly hair glistening with rapidly melting snow. His boots stood by the door in a puddle of water, though the caps were still white. She went to the stove to make the tea, hot and strong in the big brown pot. Putting his hands around the breakfast cup she handed him, grateful for the warmth, he took a long drink.

'Don't send the boys to school if it keeps on like this, Rosie.'

Her heart sank. It was bad enough with the two babies, for Teddy was little more, and all the cleaning and cooking; she didn't want the boys under her feet all day. She knew that as soon as they saw the snow they'd want to play in the back yard; they'd get soaking wet, and she'd have to dry all their clothes.

She went to her room and dressed quickly, taking care not to wake Albert, then downstairs again to wash in the ice-cold water at the sink in the wash-house. Gasping with the shock of it she grabbed at the roller towel and dried her face quickly, promising herself a decent wash with a bowl of warm soapy water later in her room.

She took Laura a cup of tea, then called the boys, all of them unwilling to move until she mentioned the word snow when they tumbled from bed and rushed to the window shouting excitedly, pushing it up and letting the snow swirl into the bedroom. Then, scooping it from the sill and rolling it into balls, they began pelting each other.

'I'll call Dada I will,' Rosie shrieked, slamming the window down and gathering a frightened Teddy into her arms, knowing that part of her anger was because she would have loved to do the same.

The blizzard got gradually worse as the day wore on. Dada struggled to work but the shop closed after only a few hours; there were no customers. Some people had braved the blinding snow to buy food but shirts and socks could wait until another day.

'Can I go to Pritchard's for an *Echo*, Dada?' Ernie asked hopefully. It was about three o'clock in the afternoon and he'd been trying one excuse or another all day to get out of the house. He was always restless and wanting action. Willie and Bobby had played quietly all day, even taking Albert in his pram up and down the passage until they'd lulled him to sleep. Now they were lying flat on their stomachs in front of the fire, chins cupped in their hands, playing Ludo.

'How bad is it now?' Arthur asked. 'I'd like to read the news and we'd know what was on the wireless tonight though I expect the snow will ruin the reception.'

In a moment Ernie had his coat and boots on and his hand out for the money.

When he came back nearly an hour later, his face glowing and his coat as wet as his feet, the round white patches where the snowballs had been told Rosie why he had been so long.

'You should see it, our Rosie, it's up to your waist round the corner,' he said excitedly, handing her the soggy newspaper.

She took the wet *Echo* and spreading it on the table scanned the headlines: 'Severe Blizzard Sweeps Over South Wales. High winds cause drifts many feet deep'. Then lower down, 'Epidemic of Influenza'.

Thank goodness Mama's nearly better, she thought. Mama was coming downstairs tomorrow for the first time in nearly a month.

Next morning the snow had frozen solid and the wireless told them there was twelve degrees of frost. By Thursday it was nineteen degrees and still snowing off and on, the surface freezing as it fell.

No horse and cart could venture out and Rosie was thankful for the tins of skimmed condensed milk she'd bought as reserve.

Ernie had gone with her the day before to Mr Llewellyn, the grocers on the corner. The snow had been so high that only the tips of the railings could be seen. With nothing to hold on to they'd slithered along spending more time on their bottoms than standing up. But they'd managed to get enough food to tide them over, including a couple of hocks to make pea soup, some onions and potatoes, and flour for soda bread in case they ran out of loaves.

Arthur had scraped a path as far as the Jenkins's front where Bert Jenkins's path met his. During the morning Ada came in to see how her mother was.

'Can you stay for a cup of tea, Ada?' Laura sat with a blanket about her shoulders in the armchair by the fire.

'Why not? I been givin' the place a lick, it'll 'ave to do till the weather's better. There's glad I am to see you up again, cariad. W'at can I do for you now I'm 'ere?'

'Oh, Ada! You've done far too much already. Rose, put the kettle over the fire, will you, love?'

'I'll take the boys in with me if you like, Laura, our Frank's gettin' bored all on 'is own.'

Frank, Ada's youngest, was a little older than Rosie and they'd always been good friends, playing rounders and other street games before Albert was born, and board games in one another's houses on wet days. Frank was tall and thin, with fair hair that seemed to get perpetually into his eyes, which were warm and brown like his mother's.

Ada's face broke into a wide smile as Ernie brought Teddy into the kitchen.

'Aw! There 'e is,' she cried, sitting down and putting out her arms. 'Come on, boyo! Give Ada a nice cwtch.'

Next moment Teddy was on her lap, his chubby arm about her, and she was hugging him tightly. No wonder he likes going in there, Rosie thought.

'I've dapped my ambarg down somewhere,' Ada said, releasing her hold on Teddy and looking around. 'Ar, there it is! I've got some losins in there.'

Snapping open the capacious black bag she brought out two twists of sweets. The pear drops she put on the table for them to help themselves, then she poured a mound of Dolly mixtures from the other twist into a saucer and put them in front of Teddy, watching him lovingly as he chose each one with care and popped it into his mouth, his round eyes wearing an expression of utter bliss.

'The ashmen won't come in this weather, Laura. We'll 'ave to keep the rubbish out the back.'

Laura nodded. 'Arthur says the snow's like glass in the street and the traffic's almost at a standstill, and I read somewhere that Roath Park lake has frozen.'

'That boating lake at Cold Knap in Barry is frozen solid,' Ada told her, 'an' lots of people are skating on it.'

Rosie tried to picture the scene, lots and lots of people all skating around on the ice. There would probably be a hot chestnut stall. Oh, yes, there was sure to be a stall!

Tomorrow while Teddy is next door, she promised herself, I'll go with the boys to the yard and we'll build a snowman, and she was happy at the thought. But when tomorrow came it was still snowing and freezing hard and Laura forbade them to go.

On the Monday it began to thaw at last. The hushed world outside suddenly became a hive of activity as families dug to reach the lifeline of the corner shops at each end of the street. First they shovelled a path from each house to the middle of the road, then they dug a passageway through waist-high snow the whole length of the street, the mission accompanied by much banter and good humour.

Digging by her father's side Rosie caught snatches of conversation:

'Daro! It's been an 'ell of a week, mun. Glad I am to get from under 'er feet at last . . .'

'We 'ad Betty's ol' pram las' Monday an' there's a job we 'ad gettin' coal from the yard . . .'

'She 'ad to ask our Dai to get 'er some things. She couldn't send 'er kids, they only 'ad daps, pooer dabs!'

Looking around at the people she knew and had been brought up with Rosie felt a keen sense of belonging. Today, especially, Wesley

Street was 'our' street, a feeling always strong in times of celebration or crisis.

A lot of the neighbours were the second generation of migrant families from rural Somerset and Devon and even further afield who had come to Cardiff towards the end of the last century in search of work at the booming docks, the Great Western Railway, or the big Dcwlais steelworks on East Moors. With names like Yeoman, Protheroe and Rapsey they were as Welsh now as any Thomas, Morgan or Evans, butties one and all, throwing jokes at each other, laughing loudly, though few had anything to joke about, for since the General Strike of 1926 many had not worked at all.

When the path had been completed Rosie took the spade and shovel through to the yard then set off with her father, who was hoping to reach the shop where he worked. At the corner they said goodbye and Rosie joined the queue outside Llewellyn's the grocer. The warm glow from digging began to leave her and she pulled the scarf over her nose and mouth and jammed her tam down, covering her ears.

A voice in the queue somewhere behind her said, 'That's the Edwards girl, innit?' And another voice answered, 'Yes, proper little mother she is an' all.'

When the first woman asked, 'Is 'er pooer mam still bard?' curiosity got the better of her and she pushed up her tam and turned to stare. They weren't looking in her direction now as the one with the lank brown hair and thick glasses said, 'Well I 'eard she mustn't 'ave any more kids.'

Rosie's mouth dropped open in surprise and the colour rose in her cheeks at the way they were discussing Mama. She turned around to face the shop, her mind seething with questions. Who had said Mama mustn't have any more children? Just then the other woman answered, 'They say he's only got to look at 'er an' she's 'aving another.' Rosie turned again to find it was Mrs Clark, a short fat woman, carrying a baby of about Albert's age, Welsh fashion, who had spoken. They didn't look towards her but the woman with the straight brown hair replied, 'Arthur's good as gold, I know, but 'e's only 'uman, an' a man's appetite's gorrw be satisfied, 'asn't it?'

19

Rosie's eye's were round with surprise. Dada's appetite? Well, that was something she could take care of, she thought, as the queue bore her towards the door of the shop. The butcher was on the next corner; she'd buy some scrag end and tonight they'd have a big pot of stew and dough-boys.

What had the lady said about him only having to look at her mother? That couldn't be true anyway; Uncle Ted looked at Aunty Mabel, didn't he, and they'd only ever had Vi.

When she got home she watched her mother anxiously, remembering the conversation she had overheard. Laura looked so pale and her blue dress hung about her thin body in folds. It must have fitted once, Rosie thought, remembering them going to the dressmaker's for Mama to be measured.

'Shall I make some stew tonight, Mam?' she asked. 'Dada will be cold when he gets in.'

'I'm feeling better now, Rose, you haven't got to do all the cooking.'

'I like doing it, Mam. What time will Dada be home?'

'Well, I shouldn't think they'll do much business, but he'll probably stay to help clear the pavements round the shop.'

By six o'clock the kitchen was filled with an appetising smell as Rosie lifted the lid of the big stewpot and watched plump dumplings simmer in the rich brown liquid.

She heard her father open the front door and saw how tired he looked when he came into the kitchen, his dark eyes red-rimmed from the biting cold. Supporting his back with his hand he eased himself wearily to the comfort of the sofa.

Poor Dada, Rosie thought. Well before dawn he'd been digging yet another path to the coal-house and the lavatory, then the long hours shovelling snow in the street, and most likely doing the same when he'd got to work.

Arthur's face brightened momentarily with relief at seeing his wife downstairs. He'd been really worried when she'd taken to her bed; having Albert seemed to have sapped all her strength. He was glad he'd had that little talk with Dr Thomas – the doctor had promised to explain to Laura the wisdom of taking precautions against having any more babies until her health was fully restored.

A tender smile played about his lips as his thoughts went back to the day he'd met her; it had been in 1915, at Bethesda chapel's Whitsun treat.

He'd been staying in Cardiff for a couple of nights with a friend – both of them on leave from the army. Bill and his wife Maisie had two little girls, and on Whit Monday afternoon they'd gone to the Whitsun treat, held in a field at Llanedeyrn. They'd been playing bat and ball, fielding for the youngsters, when the ball had gone much further than usual and he'd run to retrieve it. It had landed about five or six yards from a young woman surrounded by toddlers. She was making daisy chains and the little ones were gathering the daisies from the grass around them.

The sunlight filtering through the leaves of an ancient oak dappled the grass and shone fitfully on the long golden hair which fell about her shoulders. She was wearing a white muslin dress embroidered with forget-me-nots, and on the grass beside her was a wide-brimmed straw hat encircled with the same blue flowers. When she'd looked up, her lovely violet eyes had disturbed him strangely, and as he'd stumbled towards her, his heart beating fast, and stood awkwardly looking down, she'd held out her hand in a friendly gesture.

'Laura Hughes,' she'd told him with a warm smile, and he'd felt absurd relief that there'd been no ring on the third finger of her left hand as she'd waved it towards the children saying, 'This is my Sunday school class.'

Unable to leave this beautiful creature, he'd thrown the ball to Bill for them to get on with the game.

Her mother had been against their courtship from the start; she'd wanted security and an easy life for the daughter who'd been delicate ever since a bout of rheumatic fever at the age of eleven. But with the arrogance of youth and their deep need of each other they'd laughingly ignored her concern, Laura continually assuring him, 'I'm not an invalid, Arthur, I feel fine, honestly I do.'

The letters had flown back and forth between them, for after his next leave, when he'd spent every precious day in Cardiff with Laura, only getting the train home to Llandarron to sleep, he'd been sent to France.

In the mud and carnage of the trenches he'd thought only of coming home to her, of marrying and having a family. Surrounded by senseless horror that hope had kept him sane.

His mam had welcomed Laura warmly when he'd so proudly taken her home, and it had been comforting to know that she spent the occasional weekend with his family in the Rhondda valley in the little cottage at the foot of the mountain where he'd been born and brought up.

Then in January 1917 he'd got a Blighty – shrapnel in his foot brought him back to England. By the time he was discharged from hospital on crutches they were engaged, and plans for the wedding in a couple of months' time were well ahead.

He remembered their wedding day: Laura lovely in a white crepe-de-Chine dress she'd made herself. His hand on hers, they'd cut the cake, after removing the fancy white cardboard cover decorated with satin ribbons and silver horseshoes that by this stage of the war had replaced the traditional marzipan and icing. He'd guided her delicate hand on the knife with both of his, glad that he'd managed to discard the crutches in time to walk down the aisle.

When he was fully recovered and the war had finally ended he hadn't gone back to the pit, but looked instead for a job in Cardiff. He had been grateful to Mr Spackman when, despite his inexperience in the retail trade, he'd taken him on.

But the conditions of work at Spackman's Gent's Outfitters was positively Victorian and the hours of work long. Mr Spackman had opened his shop at the turn of the century and some of the stock looked as though it had been there since then. There was little room to spare within its cluttered interior – clothes were displayed even in the shallow doorway. The pitted oilcloth that greeted the customers didn't extend beyond the dark wood counter behind which Arthur stood. He'd given up trying to persuade his employer of the advantages of modernising his shop, and indeed its very appearance seemed to encourage trade, for here people could handle and try on the garments and read the price tags for themselves, whereas in classier shops some of the assistants looked down their noses at the shabbier customers, mentally assessing their ability to pay before fetching the clothes for them to see.

*   *   *

'You'd better get washed, Arthur, Rose says the stew is almost ready.' Laura's voice brought him back to the scene in the kitchen. And, as he looked across at her, he felt a pang of conscience. She was so thin, the skin on her face pale as alabaster, the shadows beneath the wide violet eyes making them look huge. He smiled at her gently, secretly determined to take Dr Thomas's sensible advice. He couldn't bear it if anything happened to her.

Rosie was smoothing the white damask cloth over the table while Ernie brought the condiments from the pantry and went to the safe in the yard for the milk. Cutting thick slices of bread Laura piled them on to a plate.

Albert, who had been fed and washed, lay gurgling in his pram in the corner. Bobby and Willie, tired of being good, began to argue about who would sit next to Dada, which he solved with his usual good humour by moving them apart and putting his chair between them. His pleasant, good-looking face had regained its colour, and his brown eyes watched indulgently his sons' satisfaction as they both got their own way.

For Arthur's portion Rosie took the largest pudding basin, for the others the shallow soup dishes.

'Thought you'd be hungry, Dada,' she murmured, putting the steaming bowl before him. Her father's appetite would certainly be satisfied tonight.

'If I get through this lot, Rosie, I'll be all right,' he answered. And Mama will be all right, too, Rosie told herself with relief. The stew was followed by treacle pudding with Arthur again having the largest portion.

After the table was cleared and the dishes washed, Ernie drying and stacking them away, it was time to bring the bath in for the boys. This was usually done on Wednesdays and at weekends when her father was home to drag the tub out and empty it, but with the snow in the yard being so deep they'd had to make do with a bowl of water in the kitchen.

Now the rag mat was rolled up and the bath brought from its nail on the whitewashed wall. Rosie put in a couple of bowls of cold water, then her father added hot, drawing it from the boiler at the

HILDA McKENZIE

side of the range. The boys' night things hung over one end of the guard and a large towel was warming at the other.

Little Teddy was first; Rosie soaped and washed him with the flannel, then, protesting loudly, he was lifted from the bath by her father and enveloped in the warm towel.

While Teddy was being dried it was four-year-old Bobby's turn, and when he was wrapped in the towel Arthur brought fresh water and draped the clothes-horse with an old sheet as a screen before Willie stepped in. Willie was six and he and Ernie bathed themselves, so Rosie went to help dress the other two for bed.

The nightgown she slipped over Teddy's fair curls had been her own until outgrown. 'Not a brack in it,' Laura had said as she'd threaded the needle to shorten the hem.

When Ernie came from behind the clothes-horse he looked very smart in his new pyjamas with a dark blue stripe. They would eventually find their way through to Willie, to Bobby and would, doubtless, then be worn by Teddy if they lasted that long.

The three older boys sat on the sofa, their faces glowing from the rough towel, damp hair combed flat against their heads. When they'd drunk their cocoa and were ready for bed, Laura drew each one to her in turn, putting her arms about them lovingly and kissing them goodnight.

After Ernie had taken Willie and Bobby up, Rosie lifted Teddy and rested him on her hip but he leaned sideways towards Laura crying, 'Story, Mama, Teddy wants story.' She smiled indulgently and put her arms out for him.

Suddenly Arthur gave a little moan. 'Oh, Rosie!' he said, pressing his hand to his stomach. 'I shouldn't have been bending after all that food. I think I'd better have a small glass of bicarb.'

As she prepared it, Rosie thought, Better him have bellyache than her have another baby.

She had no mercy: the following day his plate was piled high with vegetables. On Wednesday she brought the pudding basin out again, this time for peasoup.

'No, Rosie!' Arthur said firmly, pushing the basin aside. 'What are you trying to do to me?' He insisted on using a soup dish and even then didn't finish his share. Afterwards he took another dose of bicarb.

When her father had gone out Rosie made a cup of tea and prepared a light supper. Laura looked at her thoughtfully.

'Rose, I want to have a word with you before you go to bed. Why are you giving your father such big helpings? You can see that you're upsetting his digestion.'

'I'm sorry, Mama, I was doing it for the best.'

'But why, Rose? Why?'

Rosie sucked in her lips and looked about the kitchen, avoiding her mother's eyes.

'You insisted, even though he said he didn't want it. Why, Rose?'

She thought quickly, knowing her mother would be upset if she repeated the conversation she'd overheard. Blushing fiercely she burst out with, 'I heard some ladies talking about 'aving babies, and they said a man's appetite's got to be satisfied . . .' She trailed off as her mother, struggling unsuccessfully to keep a straight face, burst into laughter, stopping immediately when Rosie, looking upset and miserable, told her in a hurt voice, 'I was only trying to stop you 'aving any more.'

'Having any more, Rose,' Laura corrected automatically. Then taking her daughter's hand she pulled her to her feet saying, 'We'd better go into the parlour where we won't be disturbed. I think it's time I told you a few facts, my love.'

A quarter of an hour later Rosie ran up the stairs to bed, forgetting in her embarrassment to take off her clattering shoes – she longed to reach the privacy of her tiny bedroom.

As she lay in the dark listening to Albert's soft breathing, her tears quickly soaked the pillow – Mama had laughed at her. Sitting up, she folded her arms across her chest, hugging herself for comfort, rocking herself to and fro. The lady had said Mama mustn't have any more and now she knew there was nothing she could do to stop her.

It was icy cold in the bedroom so she snuggled back under the bedclothes gratefully, pressing her burning cheeks into the cold damp pillow.

She heard her father return and go through to the kitchen. There was a low murmur of voices, then suddenly his laughter rang out and went on and on as though he couldn't control it. When her mother joined in, the tears that had been a trickle became a flood and Rosie sobbed until her throat ached.

Presently self-pity gave way to a new feeling and she was consumed with anger. She'd show them, they wouldn't laugh at her for long, and if Mama had any more she could look after them herself, she thought. Soon she would be sitting the scholarship, she'd pass and go to grammar school, then when she left school she'd get a good job and have all the things she wanted.

Mama had had everything when she was young. She'd been a delicate child and had gone to a little private school run by two old ladies. Rosie pictured her going home to the comfort of Grandma's house, perhaps to do her piano practice, sitting on the red velvet stool at the big rosewood piano, the music lit by two brass candleholders.

Rosie wondered if the room had looked as it did now, with its beautiful cream Indian carpet embossed in delicate colours; the marble fireplace flanked either side by deep buttoned leather armchairs, and in the wide bay of the window a matching sofa; on one wall an elegant bookcase with leaded light glass doors and a whatnot filled with dainty china ornaments, and on the other, the rosewood piano.

The sound of her parents' footsteps on the stairs broke into her thoughts, and as they bent over Albert's cot she pretended to be asleep. Then Laura tucked the bedclothes around her and bent down to kiss her cheek. 'Poor child,' she whispered, 'she must have cried herself to sleep.'

Arthur chuckled quietly. 'Talk about shutting the stable door when the horse has bolted,' he whispered. 'Did you tell her, Laura?'

'No, Arthur, I didn't have the heart,' her mother replied. 'She'll know soon enough that there's another baby on the way.'

Chapter 3

'Mam! Mam!' Rosie shouted excitedly as she closed the front door. 'Vi's getting me an invitation to Ceridwen's party. Ceridwen's her best friend now.'

'That's wonderful for you, Rose. Isn't that the girl whose father's a solicitor?'

Rosie nodded. 'Vi says that last year they had a magic show and presents from the bran tub for everyone, and they danced to the gramophone, Vi's going to teach me to dance 'cos she's been taking lessons.'

'When is this party?'

'In a few weeks' time. The invitations will be given out soon.'

'Well, now that the scholarship exam is over it will give you something to look forward to, love.'

Whenever Rosie remembered that day in the spring when with the rest of the scholarship pupils she'd sat in a strange classroom with an unfamiliar teacher watching their every movement, the feeling of apprehension came back to her. Supposing she didn't pass? She wanted so much to go to the grammar school. Mama wanted it for her, too, they'd talked about it a lot.

'I know you'll do your best, Rose,' Laura had said. 'A good education can open so many doors for you, my love, and this will be your only chance. It's such a pity that you've lost so much schooling because of me. It will be my fault if you fail.'

'Of course it won't, Mama,' Rosie assured her, but she'd felt sick at the thought. She wanted so much to do well, to show that her poor school attendance had made no difference. She'd worked so hard in class, and at the homework for which Mama always made sure she had time. Sometimes she felt elated with her performance on the day of the exam; at other times despondent. At a given signal all heads had bent to their task; there'd been no sound but the dipping of pens in inkwells, the scratching of nibs on paper, and the turning of pages. The spring sunshine had streamed unheeded through the tall windows and the hands of the clock seemed to be running a race of their own.

Mama had said over and over how important getting to grammar school was for her future. Without it Rosie might possibly get work in a local shop or factory; with it she could apply for a job as an assistant in the big fashion shops in town, or in an office, or in the library, maybe even go on to college and become a teacher.

It was a fortnight later that Ceridwen brought the invitations to school. For a sickening moment Rosie thought there wasn't one for her as Ceridwen passed her by, but then she turned and with a friendly smile put a pink envelope on her desk. In it was a deckle-edged card and on that in gold lettering:

Miss Rose Edwards is invited to attend the birthday party of Miss Ceridwen Bowen Jones at 'Cartref' on 15 June at five thirty.

At playtime Vi asked, 'What are you going to wear, Rosie?'

'Well, I had a new cotton dress for Whitsun.'

'Everyone wears a party dress,' Vi told her, 'but don't worry, Rosie, my mother's going to give you my last year's pink – it's getting short for me anyway. I've only worn it twice and no one from school has seen it.'

Rosie couldn't believe her luck: the lovely pink dress that she'd admired so much with its embroidered bodice and full skirt. She was still in a state of euphoria when she reached home.

Laura was sitting at the table sewing the hem of a tiny flannelette baby gown. Rosie took the invitation from its envelope and laid it proudly in front of her.

'Oh, Rose! I'm so pleased for you. I went to a lot of parties when I was young. Sometimes in those days they sent a carriage for you and you felt so grand—' Then she put her hand to her mouth and gave a little gasp. 'But what will you wear, my love?'

'Aunty Mabel's giving me Vi's pink dress, the one she had last year,' Rosie told her excitedly.

Taking her daughter's hand in hers Laura looked at her sadly. 'Supposing Dada won't let you have it? You know how he is about presents from my family?'

Then, seeing the stunned look on Rosie's face, she said quickly, 'I'll speak to him tonight, Rose. I'm going to tell him how much the dress means to you and that it's about time you had some enjoyment. Cheer up, love. If you really can't have the pink dress, perhaps I can do something with the one you had for Whitsun.'

Laura, now more than eight months pregnant, lifted herself with difficulty from the chair and, folding the sewing, put it away in a drawer. Then seeing the tearful disappointment on Rosie's face she put an arm about her shoulders and stroked the springy curls. 'I'll do my best for you, love. He hasn't said no yet, has he? And he loves you very much.'

After tea Ernie went off to Band of Hope. Until Mama became ill Rosie had gone with him; it was there that they'd both signed the pledge to be teetotal.

Miss Williams who took the meetings was a bubbly little woman with enough enthusiasm to keep the children interested. Everyone enjoyed watching the slides on the magic-lantern, with the harrowing pictures showing the effects of the demon drink, and Miss Williams telling them the accompanying pitiful stories. Rosie's favourite had been the one about the drunken husband stumbling home to his starving wife and children who cowered in a corner while he smashed up the furniture. It was always a wonderful moment when he saw the light at the end and fell to his knees, begging his family's forgiveness.

Perhaps it was too near the truth for some children: more than one would be in tears before the end. They always began and finished the evening by singing 'My drink is water bright, water bright, water bright', at the tops of their young voices.

Later, when the other boys were in bed, Rosie took her homework into the parlour and spent a nail-biting hour waiting anxiously for her father to come home. It was a Friday evening and the shop didn't close until eight o'clock. She couldn't concentrate, the words on the page were just a blur.

At last the gate clicked and she heard the letterbox rattle as Arthur fumbled for the key on the end of its string.

She listened anxiously to the murmur of voices from the kitchen, then she heard Dada shouting in anger. Gripping the edge of the table she listened white-faced as the shouting grew louder.

He wouldn't let her have the dress. She'd known he wouldn't. She bit hard on her bottom lip and closed her eyes to ease the pain of unshed tears. She knew one thing anyway: she wouldn't go – she couldn't go in the cotton dress, whatever Mama did to it.

Suddenly she became aware that the shouting had stopped. The kitchen door must have opened because she heard her mother saying, 'I'm so glad you've changed your mind, Arthur. Rose will be very happy. There are times when you have to swallow your pride for the sake of those you love.'

A minute later Arthur came into the parlour and seeing her white, strained face he came across and laid his cheek against hers, saying, 'Aw, Rosie, there's sorry I am for upsetting you. It's just that I'd like to have been able to buy you a dress myself, see?'

His expression was shamefaced, and knowing what it had cost him to give in she put her arms about his neck and hugged him.

She saw that Mama was smiling, there was colour in her usually pale cheeks and her eyes were bright with satisfaction. As she went back to her homework Rosie saw the loving look that passed between her parents before they left the room. They were all right, her mam and dad.

The waiting seemed endless but at last it was the fifteenth of June. Hurrying home after school Rosie filled the big china jug on the washstand with hot water and hung a clean towel on the brass rail, but before she washed and dressed for the party she went downstairs.

'Anything you want me to do, Mama, 'fore I get ready?'

'No, Rose. I think I'll lie down for a while. Ada's coming in as soon as you've gone.'

Rosie watched her mother anxiously as with a great effort she rose from the chair and walked slowly to the door. The baby was due any time now.

Rosie ran back upstairs and got dressed. She gave a little twirl in front of the cheval mirror on the low chest of drawers but she couldn't see much of herself. Looking down at the dainty silver shoes Rosie thought how lucky she was to be smaller than Vi.

Then she heard a strange noise. Had it come from the front bedroom? She went out into the passageway.

'Mama,' she called. 'Mama, are you all right?' There was no answer. She was just turning away when she heard a little moan. Pushing the door open she found her mother doubled up on the bed. Rosie was shocked to see her face beaded with perspiration and contorted with pain.

'What's wrong, Mama? What's wrong?'

'I didn't want you to know, Rose,' she gasped, breathing heavily. 'I didn't want to spoil the party for you. I've had the pains on and off for about half an hour, I think you'd better call Ada – she'll know what to do.'

'But Dr Thomas said you had to send for him.'

'Yes, well, we'll see.' Another spasm of pain racked her body and sent Rosie rushing downstairs and round to their neighbour.

'Mrs Jenkins! Mrs Jenkins!' she cried through the letterbox, banging the knocker at the same time.

Ada opened the door and with one look at the distraught child took in the situation.

'Your mam, is it, Rosie?'

Rosie was gripping her hand, trying to pull her over the step, crying, 'Quick, Mrs Jenkins, quick!'

'Loose go of my hand, there's a good girl, the baby won't come yet, cariad. Now you go in an' put some saucepans on to boil an' I'll be there now jest. I've got to swill my hands and put a clean pinny on.'

Rosie had just filled the first saucepan when she heard Ada push open the door and go upstairs.

Rosie stood at the bottom of the stairs looking up. Within minutes Ada was back on the landing calling down, 'Fetch Dr Thomas, Rosie, and on the way ask the midwife to come quickly. 'Ave you put them saucepans on?'

Rosie nodded, then ran to the door. She tore along the street, the sash of her pink dress floating behind her. As she rushed round a corner the dress caught on some chicken wire stretched along a front garden. In her haste to be free a piece of the satin tore away, and a little sob rose in her throat.

Pounding on the midwife's door she almost fell inside when it was opened and the startled woman cried, 'What is it, child?'

'Mama – Mrs Edwards – the baby's coming.'

One look at Rosie's distraught face and the midwife jammed on her hat, threw a bag into the basket of her ancient bicycle and rode off so quickly that when Rosie sped round the corner, now on her way to fetch the doctor, she was nowhere in sight.

Breathlessly she ran on to Dr Thomas's surgery. The little waiting room was full, all the chairs occupied, and people were standing round the walls. A baby wailed pitifully, and a young woman rocked it to and fro. As Rosie made her way to the brown shutter in the wall and rapped it urgently a man shouted, ' 'Ere, you, miss, you'll afto wait youer turn. We been waitin' f'rages.'

A woman yelled at him, 'Shut up, Ianto, you don't take a blind bit of notice of w'at I do say. I told you she was fetching the doctor.' At that moment the shutter flew up, making her jump, and Dr Thomas was looking at her inquiringly.

'It's Mama, Doctor,' she cried, 'Mrs Jenkins says could you come right away?'

His kindly red face filled with concern and calling back into the surgery, 'Tell Dr Brown I have to go out on an urgent case,' he lifted his coat from a peg and jamming an ancient trilby on his thick greying hair, picked up his bag and opened the surgery door. Taking Rosie the side way through the empty private patients' waiting room, he led her out to the car.

Dr Thomas helped Rosie into the back of the black Austin Seven, then hurriedly cranked the handle and slipped into the driver's seat. Rosie had never been in a car before; gripping the leather seat she stared through the window as the car gathered speed.

'Is the midwife with your mother, Rose?'

'Yes, Doctor, Mrs Jenkins sent me for her.'

'Oh, well, she's in good hands with the two of them. We'll soon be there,' he added comfortingly as they turned into Wesley Street.

As the car drew into the kerb the door of the house flew open and Ernie dashed out and up the street without a backward glance.

'Gone to fetch youer father,' Ada explained as the doctor took the stairs two at a time, and followed breathlessly behind him.

Rosie felt numb with anxiety. Why had Mrs Jenkin's sent for Dada? What was happening?

Fifteen minutes later Arthur rushed into the kitchen, his face white as chalk as his anxious eyes met Rosie's.

'What's wrong, love? Why have they sent for me?'

They heard footsteps on the stairs and dashed together into the passage, but Mrs Jenkins shook her head. 'No news yet, Arthur, I'm afraid.'

'But what's wrong, Ada, you sent for me—?'

'Maggie, she's the midwife, thought I should. Laura's pretty weak, but she's got Dr Thomas with her now, thank goodness.'

Arthur rushed upstairs. When he came down about five minutes later, he sat in the armchair gripping the arms so tightly that his knuckles showed white.

When Mrs Jenkins came downstairs again he looked up at her anxiously, but she'd only come to take the boys next door.

'Our Frank will keep an eye on them,' she said, ' 'an I can call Ernie if we want 'im for anything.'

Teddy, quite at home in the Jenkins's house, couldn't get in there quick enough, but Ernie, Willie and Bobby were very quiet as they followed Ada out of the kitchen.

The minutes ticked by. Suddenly Arthur jumped to his feet and began pacing up and down. It had all happened before, why was he so worried this time? Rosie wondered. When he sat down again he gripped and ungripped his hands, his eyes on the open door, the cup of tea she'd made him ages before cold by his side.

Presently they heard the bedroom door open and the thin cry of the new baby and they both jumped up, listening for footsteps on the stairs, but there were none.

A quarter of an hour later they heard someone on the landing, then heavy footsteps coming down. When Rosie and her father reached the banisters and looked up, the doctor's usually jovial face was grey with exhaustion. Wiping the beads of perspiration from his upper lip he said, 'You've got another boy, Arthur,' and there was something wrong with his voice.

'And the wife, Doctor?'

There were tears now in Dr Thomas's eyes and Rosie felt cold with fear as he answered: 'Her heart wasn't strong. She had rhuematic fever when she was a child, you know.'

'But – but she'll be all right, won't she?'

'I'm sorry, Arthur, there was nothing I could do. If she'd only taken my advice. Poor little Laura, I've looked after her since she was a baby.' He took out his handkerchief and blew his nose.

With a cry of anguish Arthur bounded up the stairs. Rosie hung on tightly to the banister until Dr Thomas guided her gently to the kitchen and settled her on the sofa. She felt a sickness rising in her stomach, but when Dr Thomas said 'Will you be all right, Rosie? I'd better see to your father,' she nodded.

The hard lump that had begun in her chest seemed to swell until it filled her whole body. She shivered and the sickness came again, rising to her throat, and putting her hands to her mouth she dashed through the wash-house to the yard. Unable to reach the lavatory she stood over the outside sink, heaving uncontrollably. When at last she could raise her head she leaned it against the cold drainpipe and she was still there when Ada came in search of her.

Putting her arms about Rosie she led the girl indoors and, sitting her down, got a bowl of soapy water and bathed her face and hands as she would a little child. And that's all she is, Ada thought worriedly, just a child, poor little dab.

'Lie there until you feel better, cariad,' Ada said, settling Rosie on the sofa and pulling off her shoes.

A little while later Ada brought the Moses basket into the kitchen and put it on the table. Rosie got up shakily and went across, and as she looked at the tiny baby the cold feeling inside her began to melt.

There was a sheen of gold in the soft fuzz that covered his head. He yawned and opened his eyes; they were blue, not yet the violet blue of Mama's eyes but Rosie felt sure they would be. Her heart went out to him – poor little soul, to come into the world without a mother. The pity she felt brought the tears to her eyes, and Mrs

Jenkins, watching her, put comforting arms about her and cwtched her, smoothing the wet curls from her forehead.

Arthur, who'd been upstairs all this time, came into the kitchen, and looking neither at the Moses basket nor at Rosie he sat in the wooden armchair and sank his chin on his chest.

'We'll make a cup tea for youer dada and you'd better have one yourself, luv, an' put plenty of sugar in.' Ada went to the stove and put the kettle on. She'd sent Ernie a little while ago to fetch his Grandma Hughes and Aunty Mabel – they should be here soon. She'd written a note and it hadn't been easy; there was no way of breaking the news gently.

As Ada poured the tea there was the sound of a taxi drawing up and when the knock came Rosie was already halfway to the door. Some of the pins had fallen from Grandma's hair and her face was ashen as she rushed past Rosie, Mabel anxiously trying to catch up, and made straight for the kitchen. Then Mabel grabbed hold of her skirt and tried to drag her back but there was no holding her. She rushed towards Arthur, her finger outstretched. 'Murderer!' she cried. 'Murderer! Murderer!'

Rosie felt cold and sick again as Ada quickly took charge and bundled Grandma out of the kitchen. Arthur hadn't moved but tears were now streaming down his face.

Mabel put an arm about him saying, 'I'm so sorry, Arthur, she knows it wasn't your fault. Laura told us that she'd forgotten to take the precautions she promised the doctor.'

'She's gone, Mabel. What am I to do without her?' He gave a long shuddering sigh.

'Drink this, Arthur,' she said, putting the cup Ada had given her into his hands. 'I'll take Mother home. She's in an awful state or she'd never have spoken to you like that. I'll come back when Vi gets home.'

Rosie hadn't understood the conversation but she was glad that Dada wasn't to blame – Aunty Mabel had seemed to be sure of that.

In the parlour Grandma was sitting bolt upright in an armchair staring in front of her. She looked up when Rosie and Mabel came in and asked pitifully, 'Can I see Laura now, Mabel?'

'Of course, Mother. Come on.'

Something had been troubling Rosie; it had started when she'd looked at the new baby and the worry wouldn't go away.

'I want to see Mama, too,' Rosie called after them and Aunty Mabel turned on the stairs with a look of surprise.

'Wouldn't you rather remember her as she was, love?'

Rosie shook her head, trying to blot out the memory of her mother's face contorted with pain. There was something she must do but she would wait until Grandma and Aunty Mabel had left.

When they had gone into the bedroom she went to her own room and waited. She could hear muffled sobs and Aunty Mabel entreating Grandma to go home; then, at last they were back on the landing and going down to the stairs. She stayed where she was until at last the front door closed behind them, and the taxi started up. Then she went to Mam's room and approached the bed.

Ada Jenkins had laid Mama out in her best embroidered nightgown. Her eyes were closed and she looked very peaceful, her lovely hair fanned out on the pillow like a halo.

Rosie swallowed hard then dropped on to her knees.

'Oh, Mama!' she whispered. 'I didn't mean it when I said I wouldn't look after any more babies. I'll always look after Dada and the children, all of them. The new baby, he's beautiful, Mama, I hope you saw how beautiful he was before you . . . I haven't asked Dada yet but I'd like to call him David 'cos you told me once you liked that name.'

Hearing footsteps on the stairs she got up quickly and with a last backward glance at the bed wiped her eyes with the edge of her pinafore and went out, closing the door behind her.

'Awright, cariad?'

'Yes, Mrs Jenkins, I feel better now.'

'I'm just going to put the boys to bed in my house. I've come up for their things.'

'I'll come with you and kiss them goodnight like Mama always did. And Teddy will want a story.'

Ada gave her a tender smile. 'Awright, luv, I'll get my Bert to come in with your dad for a bit.'

Next door, the boys were playing snakes and ladders at the table, and a sleepy Teddy lay in Frank's arms sucking his thumb.

The three older boys were very quiet but Teddy asked, 'Where's my mama, Rosie?'

She looked at Ada, then at Teddy. He ran into her outstretched arms and she cwtched him to her, telling him gently, 'Mama's gone to stay with Jesus, Teddy.'

He rubbed his eyes with a chubby fist, saying plaintively, 'I wanted Mama to tell me a story, Rosie.'

'I'll tell you a story, love. Which one do you want?'

'Goldilocks.'

'All right.' She took him in her arms and settled on the sofa. 'Well, there were three bears . . .'

'Mama always says "Once upon a time". '

'Well then, once upon a time there were three bears, a Mama Bear, a Dada Bear, and a Baby Bear . . .'

Ada brushed the tears from her eyes with the back of her hand. That Rosie was a real little trouper. A real little trouper, that's what she was.

Chapter 4

The house was filled with sadness. Rosie was glad to be kept busy with David's three-hourly feeds, the cooking, the cleaning, the mounds of washing, though it didn't ease the pain. But the moment she picked up the baby and held him in her arms she felt a strong bond of love and compassion that she could never remember having with Teddy or Albert.

Her heart went out to David as she looked into the wide blue eyes, and sometimes his lips seemed to curve into a smile especially for her, though Mrs Jenkins assured her it was only wind. When Ernie or Ada Jenkins offered to give him his bottle she'd hurriedly refuse, for these moments with David were precious interludes in the long day.

Rosie was dreading the funeral, when Dada and Grandma Hughes would meet. What would happen? She still shuddered at the memory of Grandma dashing into the kitchen, her finger outstretched accusingly.

The service was arranged for Monday morning and on the Saturday before, Nana Edwards arrived from Llandarron. She wasn't much taller than her granddaughter but what she lacked in size she made up for in energy. She was a bustling little woman, neat in appearance, with kindly dark brown eyes and a gentleness of expression that endeared her to everyone.

Carefully unpinning her hat, a pleated silk affair the shape of a pork pie that sat neatly on top of her bun, she said to Rosie, 'Don't worry, cariad, Nana will find a way of helping you. Youer dada and me will have a talk after tea. Youer Uncle Dai will be down for the funeral. Duw! There's a job he had getting a day off from the pit.'

That evening, as soon as the boys were in bed, Nana put the

chenille cloth on the kitchen table and said to her, 'Go and fetch youer dada, Rosie, you know where he'll be.'

When she opened the parlour door Arthur was sitting on a chair by the coffin, his head in his hands.

'Nana wants to talk to you, Dada.'

He followed her meekly from the room, closing the door gently behind him.

'You, too, Rosie, come by here,' Nana Edwards said as Arthur took his place at the table.

'Now! Something will have to be done to help Rosie, Arthur,' she began as soon as they were seated. 'I'm quite willing to take one or two of the children—'

'No, Nana, no!' Rosie broke in. 'They've never been parted. I – I can manage.'

'Well, supposing they come for a holiday to give you a break, cariad? Then if they settle—'

'But who would you take, Mam? I don't want the family broken up, Laura wouldn't have wanted that.'

'Well, the babba's better off with Rosie, I've been watching her, and I think the younger ones need her, too, and Ernie, he could be a big help in the house and doing the shopping.'

'But that only leaves Willie and Bobby, Nana. They're always together, you can't part them.'

'Of course not, Rosie, and if they don't settle I'll bring them back. That's a promise, girl, so don't you worry.'

It was Monday, the day of the funeral, and the moment Rosie had been dreading was drawing near.

Since nine o'clock Ada Jenkins and Nana Edwards had been preparing food for the mourners when they came back from the cemetery. Ham boiled the night before, fresh salad from the garden, plates of thinly cut bread and butter, and a cake stand piled with Welsh cakes.

In the front room with its drawn blinds and closed door the scent of flowers was overpowering as the wreaths were piled around the coffin. There was one from Grandma and one from Aunty Mabel, Uncle Ted and Vi, one from Nana Edwards and Uncle Dai, and a few from relatives Rosie only knew from birthday and Christmas cards. There was a wreath of pale and deep pink carnations from the neighbours of Wesley Street and one in the shape of a cross from Ada and her family. The wreath Dada had ordered was of dewy roses and had all their names on it, including little David's.

When she heard Grandma Hughes's voice Rosie bit her nails hard and looked anxiously towards her father. As Grandma came into the kitchen Arthur pretended not to see her, and Rosie noticed that her eyes looked sunk with grief as she made a beeline for him. Rosie held her breath then let it out again in a long sigh of relief as Grandma said, 'I want to apologise, Arthur. I'm sorry from the bottom of my heart for what I said, I know it wasn't your fault. Can you ever forgive me? We both loved Laura and miss her so terribly. We should be comforting each other, Arthur, not quarrelling.'

She held out her hand towards him and for an awful moment Rosie thought Dada wasn't going to take it, but he had to wipe his eyes in the snowy handkerchief she'd put in his breast pocket before he took Grandma's hand in both of his then leaned over and kissed her cheek.

The day after the funeral, Nana Edwards went home to the valleys taking Willie and Bobby with her. At the railway station, as they climbed the steps to the platform, the boys hung back looking thoroughly miserable, and guilt weighed heavily on Rosie as she waited for them to catch up. When they passed the Fry's chocolate machine Nana fumbled in her purse for some coppers, but even this didn't cheer them up.

Bobby clung to Rosie's skirt, sobbing into it, while Willie stood at her side, his lips quivering. When Nana went to put an arm about his shoulders he shrugged it off and followed Rosie to a wooden bench where she sat down and lifted Bobby on to her lap. Holding him tightly, her free arm about Willie, she wanted desperately to run back home with them – little Bobby was only five. Nana, her gentle face concerned, was coming back from the newspaper stall with comics for the journey.

'They'll be all right, Rosie, just wait until their Uncle Dai comes home from work.' She sat down and cwtched Willie to her, and although he'd manfully tried to hold back the tears, they suddenly streamed down his face.

At the mention of Uncle Dai Rosie felt a little comforted. All the boys worshipped him; he was a keen rugby player, a formidable forward for his local team, but off the field, despite his broad shoulders and rugged strength, he was as kind and gentle as Nana. From the moment he'd arrived on the day of the funeral the boys had followed him around from room to room as though he was the pied piper himself, disappointed when he couldn't stay the night because he was on the early shift the next day.

With a hissing of steam and a grinding of brakes the train drew into the station. There was a bustle and commotion and slamming of doors as people got off and on. Still the boys clung to Rosie as she whispered words of comfort. Through a mist of tears she saw the guard standing ready with his flag and whistle, and wiping her eyes with a hanky before they saw she was upset, she guided them unwillingly towards the train.

Nana Edwards kissed and hugged her, saying comfortingly, 'Don't you worry, cariad, they'll be as right as rain with me and Uncle Dai.'

Still protesting, but half-heartedly now, the boys got into the carriage with Nana who slammed the door and, letting the window down, leaned towards Rosie saying, 'I'll bring them down whenever I can manage it.'

Standing on tiptoe Rosie kissed each of the boys in turn. 'I'll come to see you as often as I can – we'll write to you every week . . .'

The last glimpse Rosie had as the train drew slowly out of the station was of two tearful little boys waving goodbye. Swallowing the lump that came to her throat she returned the wave. She'd promised Mama she'd look after all of them and now Willie and Bobby were gone. Her father had been deeply upset this morning when he'd kissed them goodbye; she knew that he'd only agreed to them going to help her cope.

Staring after the fast disappearing train, reflecting on her promise, she thought, Well! There are still two babies and Teddy and Dada and Ernie to look after, and I expect Willie and Bobby will love having fields to play in and green mountains to climb, and she pictured them, their faces rosy from the fresh air, perhaps after kicking a rugby ball about with Uncle Dai, going home to an enormous tea in Nana's little terraced cottage on the steep mountainside.

Chapter 5

It was a fortnight since the funeral. Whenever Arthur Edwards was at home he'd sit in the armchair, head bowed, often with tears coursing down his cheeks. Teddy, too young to understand, would pull at his hand crying, 'Cock horse for Teddy, Dada! Cock horse for Teddy.' Then he'd take the child on his knee and jig him, his voice breaking as he sang the jingle. Lifting Teddy down Rosie would try to interest him in something else but the child would break free and with a bewildered expression stand and watch his father's tears.

'When will Mama come back from Jesus?' Teddy had asked on one of these occasions and she'd realised with a shock that he didn't know she was gone for ever.

As though to compensate a little for the tragedy at his birth David was a contented baby. Ada Jenkins called him 'little angel'. He'd lie for hours gurgling and kicking or looking about him with those violet-blue eyes so like Laura's.

But Albert, now toddling, grew more boisterous every day, demanding constant attention; Ernie showed a patience with him Rosie wouldn't have thought possible a short while ago.

Ada looked after the children in the mornings while Rosie was at school. Only her husband and Frank were still at home; the older children were all married and living away. Bert Jenkins was a docker in fairly regular employment and Rosie knew that some people in the street envied him and her father for having a steady wage. She liked Mr Jenkins – he was kind and jolly just like his wife.

Rosie's headmistress had obtained special permission for her to attend school only in the mornings, bringing the rest of her work home, but at the end of a long day she often fell asleep over her books.

There were never enough hours in the day, or in the night either, for she'd get up to prepare David's feed, her head nodding forward with tiredness as she gave him his bottle. It seemed she'd hardly fallen asleep again before the alarm proclaimed it was six o'clock and she'd silence it hurriedly before it woke the babies.

One summer's morning she rushed downstairs to put the big kettle on the gas stove in the wash-house and light the kitchen range. Glancing through the window she saw the sky promised another warm day, but the fire was needed to bathe the babies and air the pile of napkins she'd washed yesterday. That was the only thing against going to school in the mornings: by the time she'd got the midday meal, cleared up and finished the washing the best of the drying weather was gone.

After a quick cup of tea, Rosie brought the small bath from the yard and when it was half filled tested it with her elbow. Then she brought David from his cot, tiptoeing for fear of waking Albert. When the baby was bathed and dressed in fresh day gowns, the embroidered cotton one on top of the flannelette, she laid him in his pram while she made his bottle, lingering as long as she could with the baby in her arms taking his feed.

When David was settled it was time for Albert's bath, a much more boisterous affair, but now she stood the bath on an old towel on the mat in front of the guard, for Albert's chubby fists sent water flying in all directions as he gurgled with glee.

Ernie got up in time to feed Albert in his high-chair – a messy business with Albert determined to bang his spoon down on the dish of porridge, sending it flying everywhere.

Dada and Ernie had taken over the washing-up while Rosie got the children ready for Ada Jenkins. She was glad when her father was busy filling coal scuttles or wiping dishes, for once he sat down in the armchair he would have time to remember, the expression on his face mirroring his despair.

Ada was always ready waiting for the three little ones, and Frank would also wait to walk with Rosie to school. On Mondays he'd tell her about the film he'd seen in the twopenny seats at Splott Cinema on the previous Saturday afternoon, and if it was a funny one like those with the Keystone Cops he'd make her laugh despite her unhappiness.

One sunny Monday morning Frank was telling her about the film he'd seen the previous Saturday when his face became serious and very red as, flicking back the lock of hair that fell over his eyes, he said, 'You ought to go to the pictures sometimes, Rosie. Me and Ernie could mind Teddy and Albert, and my mam will have the baby, I know she will—'

'Your mam does too much for me already,' Rosie broke in, and with a surge of gratitude she thought, Frank's nice, he's the best friend I've got.

But Frank was persuasive. 'She'd be glad to, honestly, Rosie, I heard her saying yesterday that you needed a break sometimes.'

'Well, I would like a break, Frank, but I wouldn't need anyone to mind David 'cos I'd take him with me.' Then, seeing Frank's look of astonishment, she said quickly, clicking her tongue at him, 'Not to the pictures, silly! I'd like to take David out in his pram. I can't manage the three of them, and even if I just took Albert at the other end of the pram he grabs at everything and screams if you take things off him. But there's no need for you to miss the pictures, Frank, Sunday afternoon would do lovely.'

On the following Sunday afternoon, with Arthur gone to the cemetery and Frank and Ernie minding Teddy and Albert, Rosie took David in his pram to Waterloo Gardens. Proudly wheeling him along the street she was stopped every few yards by neighbours exclaiming, 'Ooh! Isn't he lovely, Rosie?' or, 'Can I see the babba, luv? Aw! Isn't 'e bewtiful?' and she was glad she'd dressed him in one of the lovely matinée jackets Grandma had crocheted for him.

She walked along Broadway and through a couple of side roads until she reached Newport Road, turning off at Waterloo Road, past St Margaret's Church and through the iron gates of the gardens. The flowerbeds were riot of colour: there were massed displays of bright red geraniums, sweet-scented pinks, red and white pelargoniums and petunias in shades of mauve and pink and red.

There were lots of people in the park parading in their Sunday clothes. A girl a little younger than herself was skipping along in front of her; a short while ago Rosie would have been envious of her freedom, but now, smiling indulgently at David, she passed her by. The baby was asleep, one tiny hand, fingers curled, resting on the pillow.

Rosie sat down on a bench, rocking the pram with one hand. She wished that someone she knew would come along and see David in his pretty new jacket. Some people smiled down at him briefly as they passed, but she soon got tired of looking at the flowerbeds and at birds pecking worms from the lush grass.

She thought ruefully of all the jobs waiting for her at home, but the fresh air was doing David good and she didn't want to go back yet. It had taken ages getting the baby ready, polishing the shabby leather hood of the pram and putting on the frilly pillow case and cover that Mama had embroidered. It isn't far to Grandma's, she thought, they'd love to see David. She got up quickly and pushed the pram along Newport Road until she reached Oakfield Street.

'Rosie! It's lovely to see you and little David, bless him. Mother! Look who's here.' Mabel, still smiling, eased the pram over the polished step and into the hall.

Grandma hurried from the kitchen to bend over David and make baby noises. He was awake now, his wide violet eyes looking up at her, and Grandma picked him up and held him tight to her, closing her eyes against the tears that threatened to spill over.

When at last she could speak she said, 'The jacket looks nice on him, Rose. Shall I crochet some more?'

'You'd better make them larger, Mother, I swear he's grown since we last saw him.'

'Have you said anything to Rose, Mabel?'

'No, Mother, I should leave it for now, things are all right as they are.'

But Grandma motioned Rosie to sit down. Puzzled and a little apprehensive she went to the armchair by the fireplace.

'Rose, we were wondering if Dada would let us take David – Why, what's wrong, child?'

Rosie, her face blanched of colour, looked pleadingly at her grandmother.

'No, Grandma! No! Nana Edwards has already taken Willie and

Bobby. I'm managing fine, really I am. I could have managed them an' all.'

'But I thought it would help you, Rose.'

'We're all right, Grandma. Please don't ask Dada for David. Anyway, he didn't want the boys to go with Nana – he said Mama would have wanted us all kept together.'

Seeing how upset Rosie was, Mabel gave her mother a warning look. As she went to put the kettle on Grandma Hughes reflected that she'd only wanted to help. Rose was missing her schooling, wasn't she? And that Mrs Jenkins was doing more than her share, and her not even family.

To Rosie's delight, about a month after the boys had gone to live with Nana Edwards they were able at last to go to visit them at Llandarron. Her father was still consumed with grief and took little interest in what went on around him, but he was feeling as anxious about Willie and Bobby as she was. So on a Sunday morning in July they all left the house and took a tram to the station.

Rosie carried David in the cream embroidered cashmere shawl that had been new when she was born. Arthur Edwards wheeled Albert in the wooden-framed, carpet-seated pushchair, the bag containing the baby's napkins, bibs, bottle and feed slung over the back, and Ernie held firmly to little Teddy's hand.

As they waited for the train on the same platform where she'd stood with the boys a month before, she kept seeing Willie's and Bobby's tearful faces as she'd waved them goodbye.

When they'd got into the carriage and the train began to move Teddy knelt by the window, his eyes round with wonder as he watched the countryside speed past. Soon the green fields and neat hedges gave way to a strange, tortured landscape of pit-wheel and slag-heap, softened only by the distant mountains.

Leaving the station platform at Llandarron they walked along the steep main road of the village, its small, grey stone houses seeming to fold into each other as they marched ever higher up the street. At the top the houses gave way to rough grassland, and a path led to the foot of the mountain where Nana and Uncle Dai lived in No.8 Top Row.

Out of breath from the climb, the baby getting heavier by the minute, Rosie was thankful to see the door suddenly burst open and Willie and Bobby rush towards them, their faces pink with excitement.

Two steps inside the cottage and a door opened into the kitchen where the table was laid ready for their meal. Smiling her welcome Nana rose from bending over the range, her face red from the heat; there was a delicious smell of roast lamb pervading the room.

Nana flung her arms about them and kissed each one in turn before saying, 'The dinner won't be long. Would you like a cup of tea, Rosie? Arthur? The boys can have herb beer. Oh! and you can put the baby in that new clothes basket, Rosie. Padded it I have with blankets, cariad.'

'I'll feed him first, Nana. After he's changed he'll probably go back to sleep.'

As she gave David his bottle Rosie looked appreciatively around the kitchen. The Welsh dresser was filled with colourful china, with a pattern of yellow tulips and a deep blue border edged with gold. There was a vase of pink, red and yellow roses on the deep white sill of the window and the sunlight shone on a pair of prancing brass horses that stood at each end of the high mantelshelf, flanking the big black marble clock. Most of the flagstoned floor was covered in brick-red and beige striped coconut matting. They hadn't been to Llandarron since before Albert was born. Mama had always said they'd visit when she was feeling better.

Arthur Edwards was sitting in the plush-seated rocking chair, staring vacantly before him. Rosie felt the sadness welling up inside her. They all missed Mama so much.

Willie and Bobby burst in on her thoughts, talking excitedly about their new school and all the things they'd done since they'd arrived.

'We've got a bedroom of our own with a table and chairs and everything to do our homework,' Willie told her, 'and our teacher plays rugby with Uncle Dai.'

'Do you like school, Bobby?'

He nodded. 'I've got a new friend, Rosie.'

She got up to change David and put him in the wicker basket in the parlour. As she closed the door softly behind her Willie and Bobby were waiting to show her their room, which faced the field at the foot of the mountain. The pretty flowered curtains stirred in a light breeze as she looked around her at the ornate dark oak wardrobe with its mirrored doors, and the matching chest of drawers. The big double bed was draped in a dazzlingly white huckaback bedspread, and there were soft floral rugs on the oilclothed floor. The boys dragged her over to the window where there were two chairs and an oblong table. Willie opened the long drawer in the front of it to show off proudly their school books, pens, pencils, a rubber, and a bottle of ink.

'Will Mama ever come back, Rosie?' Bobby asked suddenly.

Rosie's eyes filled with tears. She sat down and patted the bed beside her.

'Mama's gone to heaven – we'll meet her again one day when we go there ourselves.'

'She's dead, isn't she, Rosie, she won't never come back?' Willie asked.

Rosie put her arms about them and pulled them close to her. They stayed this way for some minutes, then Rosie said, 'We've got Dada and we've got each other, always remember that, and if you ever want to come back home Nana will understand.'

At this they shook their hands emphatically and Willie said, 'It's nice here, Rosie, and Nana and Uncle Dai are real kind. It's just when you remember about Mama – you know.'

Downstairs again Rosie chopped up mint for the sauce, and, bringing plates from the dresser, put them to warm.

When Uncle Dai came home the boys all rushed towards him; even little Albert toddled over and lifted up his arms.

'If you want to come with me and knock a ball about after dinner you'd better get washed and sit at the table,' Dai told them, lifting Albert up and giving him a hug.

Nana was spooning golden roast potatoes on to plates already half full with tender slices of lamb and runner beans from the garden. Rosie filled the deep gravy boats and handed the plates round and even the boys were quiet while they ate the delicious meal. No one really had room for the sugar-topped rhubarb tart that followed, but no one refused it.

A quarter of an hour later, Dai said they were all too full to run after the rugby ball and took the boys for a short walk partway up the mountain. Rosie insisted on washing the dishes and Arthur roused himself to dry them while Nana took a rest. They returned just in time for Willie and Bobby to go to Sunday school. Arthur decided to stay until their return, thinking the boys would like to come to see them off at the station.

But when the two boys dashed in they were accompanied by two friends who waited in the doorway.

'Nana, can we go to Gwilym's house for tea?' Willie asked breathlessly.

Nana stopped rocking David to lean forward and say, 'I don't think you need to worry about them, cariad, they're settling down fine. Gwilym's mam's a good friend of mine.'

'I think we'd better get the next train, Mam,' Arthur told her.

The boys rushed back to hug them all goodbye and then, with Willie crying, 'Come on, mun, we'll be late,' they tumbled out of the door with their friends.

Watching them leaping over the tufted grass Rosie thought ruefully of the sleepless nights she'd spent after they'd gone when she'd tossed and turned until the small hours imagining them tearful and homesick.

Chapter 6

When the letter came telling Rosie that she'd won the scholarship to the High School, she couldn't help feeling a surge of excitement, wondering if there was some way that she could go. Perhaps Grandma and Aunty Mabel could help after all? Perhaps she could come home in the lunch break and take the children straight from Mrs Jenkins to Grandma's for the afternoon – but she knew she was clutching at straws. Anyway, the High School wouldn't be as indulgent with her circumstances as the headmistress of Stanley Road had been.

She couldn't help thinking how different it would be if Mama were here. How excited she would have been, sending her first to tell Ada the news, then all the way to Grandma's. And after school, if Mama had been well enough, they might have gone into town to look at the High School uniform in Robert's shop window.

Suddenly she remembered her mother putting small amounts of money away for when she needed to buy a new school outfit; it was kept in a tin cash box on the top shelf of the cupboard. Rosie reached up and fumbled for the box until her fingers touched the cold metal. When she opened it there were two ten-shilling notes, three half-crowns and some coppers. A lump came to her throat and tears to her eyes, melting the bitterness away.

When she showed the letter to her father he gave her a sympathetic look and said, 'It's such a pity for you, Rosie, your mother would have been thrilled. I'll try and make it up to you one day, love'. He blew his nose hard and she knew, as she'd really known all along, that there was no hope of her going at all. He hugged her tight and there were tears in his eyes as he left the kitchen for work.

As soon as she arrived at school Vi came across to tell her she was going to the High School, asking, 'Did you pass, Rosie?'

'Yes. I won a scholarship.'

Before she could say any more Miss Evans, the head mistress, entered the class and stood talking to their teacher. Then she said, 'All those who have heard they have passed the scholarship exam raise their hands.'

Rosie raised hers and kept it up when the others had dropped theirs.

'What is it, Rose?'

'Please can I see you, Miss Evans?'

'Of course, child, come to the desk. What is it you want to say?'

All eyes upon her she walked to the front of the class, blushing furiously, wishing she'd waited to see the headmistress in her room later.

'I – I can't go to the High School, Miss Evans,' she told her quietly. The headmistress looked at her compassionately. Poor child! She was a bright, intelligent girl and would have done well at grammar school but she was having a very hard time looking after her family and she always looked so tired. It was such a waste.

'Haven't you anyone who could take over, Rose? Your education is very important.'

'No, Miss Evans. Mrs Jenkins, our neighbour, helps me a lot as it is.'

'Does your father know about this?'

Rosie nodded miserably, suddenly unable to speak. It was for the best, wasn't it? She could go on attending school in the mornings at Stanley Road. Grandma would suggest taking David again when she heard about the scholarship, perhaps even offer to have Albert while she was at school. But if giving up David was the price she had to pay, she didn't want to. She knew that each time she saw those wide blue eyes looking trustingly at her; and Albert and Teddy needed her; and Dada, too. The decision was out of her hands.

As soon as she got back to her seat Vi leaned forward and said, 'I'm really sorry, Rosie. It would have been nice to have been together at High School. But it won't make any difference to our friendship, we'll still see lots of each other.'

But Vi spent playtime in a huddle with those girls she'd be with next term. Rosie watched them with envy, longing to be one of them.

That evening Ada Jenkins said to her husband, 'It's too much for that child, Bert, with all she's d'do. Missing 'er mam something awful she is. Bless 'er, she's younger than our Frank.'

'Well you can't do no more, cariad.' He shook his sandy head, the grey eyes in his round face full of loving concern. Ada was minding the babbas in the mornings, wasn't she? And she wasn't getting any younger either. That Albert played her up dreadfully. Still – she was doing it for young Rosie, and she was a nice kid. Ada would do what she wanted anyway, he wouldn't be able to stop her.

'W'at she needs is something to look forward to, like, something to take 'er mind off things. She was so disappointed 'cos she couldn't go to that grammar school, pooer luv.' Ada said staring into the fireplace. Then, as though sudden inspiration had come to her, she jumped up and began to rummage in a drawer.

'W'at you looking for?' Bert asked.

'That street outin' I run to Barry Island last year, Bert. I 'ad six free places for filling the two charas. I'll write an' see if I can arrange one for August an' take Rosie and Ernie and the little ones. What d'you think?' She beamed.

A few weeks later Ada Jenkins sat down opposite Rosie and laid her plump, mottled arms on the kitchen table, then, as a cup of tea was pushed across to her, she leaned forward, her ample bosom resting on her arms, and said, ''Ow'd you like to go to Barry Island, cariad?'

'Oh I couldn't, Mrs Jenkins – not so soon after Mama . . .' Rosie's voice trailed away, avoiding the dreadful word.

'Not yet, luv, not until the end of August, but it would be somethin' to look forward to, wouldn't it? An' it won't cost you a penny 'cos I've got some free places.'

Rosie shook her head but she couldn't help feeling a flutter of excitement. 'But they're your free places, Mrs Jenkins. I couldn't take them, and how about the baby?'

'Well now, if we was to ask your grandma and Aunty Mabel to mind David, and I know they'd just love to, there'd be a place each for you and Ernie and Teddy – 'e's no trouble, and I'd manage young Albert on my knee.'

Rosie jumped up and hugged Mrs Jenkins. 'Do you think it will be all right with Dada?'

'Awright? Of course it will. 'E won't mind David going to your grandma's now that she's said she's sorry and they've made friends. I'll make it awright with 'im, Rosie, we've known each other a long time.' Anyway, Ada thought, Arthur doesn't 'ave a spark in 'im to object with these days, pooer dab.

On a warm day in late August the two open-topped charabancs were filling up in the street. Rosie, dressed in the flowery cotton she'd had for Whitsun and wearing a black armband, was in the kitchen buttoning Teddy into his suit while Ernie hung on to Albert.

'You ready, Rosie?' Frank Jenkins yelled through the letterbox. 'Our dad's waiting to take youer picture.'

Frank helped Teddy up the steps of the charabanc and held on to him until he'd found them two seats together. His fair hair shone like burnished gold in the bright sunlight as he bent to lift Teddy on to the seat beside her.

Rosie saw Mr Jenkins moving backwards and forwards on the pavement trying to get them all into the view-finder of his box Brownie.

'Sit down by here, Frank,' she said, 'and I'll take Teddy on my lap. 'Ernie, go in with Mrs Jenkins quickly.' They huddled together, grinning like Cheshire cats.

At last Rosie could relax the smile she'd held for the past few minutes. Frank and Ernie had gone to be with their friends at the back. Just then, with a series of minor explosions and several jerks forward, the charabanc got under way and they waved goodbye to those left behind.

Teddy bounced excitedly on the leather seat. Soon they were passing through Grangetown and Rosie tried to look into the shop windows – she'd never been in this part of Cardiff before – but the charabanc was moving too quickly. Within ten minutes they were going through country lanes and Teddy stopped bouncing and gazed in wonder at the cows, lambs and horses in the fields. They had caught a glimpse of the Bristol Channel and busy Penarth docks full of ships, then when they'd passed through Dinas Powys with its large detached houses facing the road Mrs Jenkins said, 'It won't be long now, Rosie.' But it seemed a long time to Rosie before they turned at last into the Island Road and saw the harbour. Then to cries of delight, the charabanc swept round a corner and before them was the wide curve of Whitmore Bay, guarded at each end by Nell's Point and Friar's Point, and in the distance the tide licking the edge of the sands.

The sun beat down and the sea shimmered in the heat. Mrs Jenkins shepherded her party halfway towards the sea and the adults settled themselves in a wide half-circle. The younger children, including Teddy, his face almost covered by Mrs Jenkins's floppy straw hat, dug frenziedly in the sand, begrudging the time even for sandwiches and ginger beer. Some of the older children went to paddle in the sea.

'You run along and enjoy yourself, Rosie, I'll see to 'im.' Ada nodded in Teddy's direction.

She had just caught up with Frank when Ada yelled to her, 'Tuck youer dress into youer knickers, Rosie,' and she blushed to the roots of her hair.

Seeing her embarrassment Frank cried, 'Race you to the water, Rosie.' They arrived laughing and gasping as the icy cold waves slapped against their legs. Frank rolled up his trousers as far as they'd go, saying, 'Better do as she says or you'll get soaked.' And he ran off to find his friends. Looking round her she saw that most of the girls not wearing bathers had their dresses tucked in.

It was wonderful, everything was wonderful: the shrill cries of the children, the rhythmic sound of the waves breaking on the shore then hissing as they receded to rise again and race up the beach, leaving a frothy tideline until the next wave washed it away.

There was a golden glow about everything; the bright summer dresses, the colourful bathing suits, the children running in and out of the sea shrieking with delight. Looking towards the beach Rosie saw Ernie and Frank running towards her, and Teddy dangling between them. As they swung him over the frothy waves near the shore, his eyes bright with excitement, he cried, 'Again! Again!'

If only Mama could see us now, Rosie thought, she would surely be content to see the boys so happy.

All too soon Ada called them to gather their things together, and they trudged up the beach to the row of shops set in the wall at one end of the promenade. Rosie bought a thank-you present for Ada, a vase with violets painted on it and Barry Island scripted in curly gold lettering. She also bought a stick of bright pink peppermint rock for Dada and one each for Bobby and Willie, who were coming home for the weekend.

'Think your mam'll like the vase, Frank?' she asked, noticing him behind her. He took it in his hands, turning it round carefully.

'It's really swanky, Rosie. I'll bet she'll put that on the sideboard in the parlour.'

There was still time for the fairground, and gazing about them in wonder they strolled amongst the happy, jostling crowds. Rosie climbed on to a gaily painted horse on the roundabout and Ernie lifted Teddy to sit in front of her. Up and down they went, up and down, slowly at first then with gathering speed, faster and faster to the swelling music until her head spun and Teddy screamed delightedly.

Then it was back to the seafront for a last look at the beach, now almost deserted except for the seagulls, whose plaintive cries filled the air as they circled round, swooping suddenly on some titbit left by the trippers.

With many backward regretful glances, they made for the charabancs and when everyone was counted in they started for home through shady, leafy lanes dappled by the setting sun, a ball of fire that washed the sky with colour. With Albert asleep in Ada's arms, and Teddy lying happy and content against her, Rosie gave Ada the vase.

'Ooh! You shouldn't 'ave done it, Rosie, but there's luvly it is.' She beamed her pleasure.

At last they turned into Wesley Street and a now subdued little group slipped down from the charabancs.

As Ada placed the vase proudly on the sideboard in her parlour she said, 'Fancy her giving me a present, Bert, bless 'er heart. She looked sad sometimes as though she was thinking of her mam, but I think she 'ad a day to remember. There's glad I am I thought of the trip.'

If she could have peeped next door Ada would have been agreeably surprised; Rosie certainly was. Arthur had put a crisp white cloth on the table and prepared lettuce, tomatoes and cucumber fresh from the garden in the big cut-glass bowl that had been a wedding present. Next to it stood the flowered cheese dish; there was a plate of thinly cut bread and butter and another plate piled with slices of slab cake that he must have bought at Lewellyn's shop.

'The kettle's boiling, Rosie,' he said.' I thought the sea air would make you all hungry.'

She buried her face against his chest and hugged him gratefully. 'Oh, Dada! Thank you! Thank you! Oh, it's lovely to see you like this. Mama will be glad, too, I know – she wouldn't want you to be so unhappy all the time.'

'I know, Rosie, I know, but I miss your mother so much.' His eyes were moist and he swallowed hard before saying, 'You've been wonderful, love, and I know how much you miss her, too.' He shook his head sadly, adding, 'And I've been no help to you at all.'

'We need you, Dada. The boys need you.' She stood on tiptoe and kissed his cheek and hugged him warmly.

Teddy had been watching them solemnly, and as soon as Rosie went to the stove to make the tea he put his arms out to his father and asked hopefully, 'Cock horse for Teddy, Dada?'

Smiling for the first time in months his father lifted him on to his knee.

Chapter 7

On a foggy Saturday evening in November 1932 Rosie joined the shoppers in Clifton Street. The gas lamps cast an eerie glow over the glistening pavements as she hurried to join the throng pressed around the butcher's doorway.

The butcher, a stocky, good-humoured man in straw boater and blue-and-white-striped apron, stood on a wooden butter box auctioning the left-over meat. In half an hour it would be closing time and there was no means of keeping joints fresh until the next week.

The crowd was quiet – he'd have to liven things up. When he'd dropped the price twice and still no one bought the piece of beef he was holding, he cried, 'Come on! Come on! This isn't a blutty Punch and Judy show.' He was rewarded with a few chuckles.

A few minutes later, wrapping up half a pig's head that someone had bought, he joked, 'Shall I leave the eye in missis, to see you through the week?'

Waves of laughter went through the crowd now as he kept up his cheerful banter.

Rosie was hoping for a piece of lamb but none had yet been auctioned at the price she wanted to pay. When a shoulder was offered at half-a-crown her hand shot up. The kind-hearted butcher said, quick as a flash, 'Two bob then, gone to the little lady in the front.' That Rosie Edwards had had a hard time since her mother died, poor little dab, he thought. Her mother had been a regular every Friday morning, coming for her weekend joint.

Tucking the meat into her shopping bag, Rosie moved on to the greengrocer's, for here, too, there were bargains to be had. Next to the Penny Bazaar for darning wool and elastic, then to the sweet shop for a twist of liquorice laces for the boys.

61

As she made her way to Goldberg's Drapery Emporium she wondered if the smart outfit she had noticed last week would still be on display. It was! Gazing enraptured at the fashionable navy blue coat and little felt cloche hat, she didn't see Aunty Mabel and Vi coming towards her.

Her aunt looked at her pityingly, recognising the coat Rosie was wearing as one that had belonged to her sister Laura, but now it hung shapelessly from Rosie's thin shoulders, and with the drastic alterations the well-meaning Ada Jenkins had performed the pockets were far too near the hem.

Since her mother's death the child had refused to let her aunt or grandmother help with clothes for herself or the boys in case it upset her father, but he seemed far more tolerant than he used to be about such things. Only last week Vi had told her mother he'd seemed quite pleased when she'd taken him one of Grandma's Christmas cakes.

As Rosie turned and recognised them her face registered surprise and delight, and somehow the badly fitting coat didn't seem to matter. At fourteen her rich curly hair had grown long and was now tied back from the pretty heart-shaped face with a wide ribbon. Her cheeks were bright with colour.

Nodding towards the window Aunty Mabel asked, 'Do you like it, Rosie?'

'It's lovely, real grown up,' sighed Rosie, her brown eyes gazing wistfully at the model. 'It would look nice on Vi, wouldn't it?'

'We have to go into Goldberg's and they'll soon be closing,' Aunty Mabel said. 'Why don't you come to tea on Sunday? You know how Grandma loves to see you all, that's if you're not going to visit Willie and Bobby.'

'We won't be going this week,' Rosie told her. Life had settled into a pattern at weekends: most Sundays Dada went to the cemetery; sometimes she went with him and on those occasions Ernie would take the children to Sunday school on his own. Once a month they all went to the little village in the valleys where Willie and Bobby had settled quite happily with Nana Edwards and Uncle Dai.

For a few minutes after Aunty Mabel and Vi had gone into the shop Rosie continued to look at the window, then to her dismay an assistant came and lifted the coat and hat from the model, which she then draped in a calico sheet. Watching the girl leave the window with the outfit Rosie felt sad, for although she knew she couldn't have it, it had still been there for her to look at and enjoy.

The thought came to her that perhaps Aunty Mabel had bought it for Vi; she felt a sharp stab of envy, tears stung her eyes and a lump came to her throat, and she hurriedly left before they came out of the shop.

Standing in another doorway further along the street she saw Aunty Mabel and Vi leave the shop carrying several parcels. When they'd gone she went back to Goldberg's window but the model was still draped in calico. Hoping the outfit hadn't been sold and would soon be back in the window, she waited in the doorway for her father to pass on his way home from work.

That morning she had come as usual to Clifton Street to do the main grocery shopping at the Candle King Stores where bacon was only ninepence a pound and margarine fourpence halfpenny a roll. Rosie bought the butter at the Maypole – she loved to watch the assistant making the butter pats, finishing up with a thistle pattern impressed on the surface.

She still bought some of their groceries at Mr Llewellyn's shop on the corner of Wesley Street, but keeping the boys in boots and other clothes meant watching every penny. She always made sure they had tidy boots and Dada mended them himself, for if a child stayed away from school for lack of boots or shoes a message went round the classes asking pupils to bring any they had outgrown. Rosie thought she'd die if her brothers had to receive any of these handouts in front of everyone.

Sometimes she felt bad about not buying all the groceries from Mr Llewellyn, for he was a friend as well as a shopkeeper. One of her earliest memories of his shop was as a small child sitting on one of the bentwood chairs swinging her legs while Mama sat on the other with baby Ernie on her lap ordering the groceries. The first thing Mama would ask for was, 'A bar of chocolate for Rose, please, Joe, and would you wrap some paper round it, please?'

Placing the cardboard box on the dark polished counter Mr Llewellyn would turn back the crinkly white paper and take out a bar of chocolate. Rosie would suck the chocolate to a point while the groceries piled up on the counter.

Mr Llewellyn's shop never seemed to change with the years. The corn bin still stood just inside the doorway, sides of bacon still hung from hooks in the ceiling, the mingling smells of bacon, cheese, spices, salt-fish, hot bread from the bakery next door, even the freshly dampened sawdust on the knotted wooden floor, all contributed to the special aroma of the grocery store.

Seeing her father pass Goldberg's Rosie came out of her reverie and ran after him, linking her arm in his, noticing how thin and shabby his coat was for the chill, damp November evening.

They walked companionably for a few minutes before her father said, 'You know that letter I took from the postman this morning as I was leaving for work? It was from my Cousin Bronwen.'

'Is she the one in the Whitsun treat pictures Nana Edwards showed us, the one who lives in the valleys?'

'Yes, that's her. Anyway, Rosie, Bronwen is parted from her husband. She wrote to ask if she could come and stay with us and help look after the children.'

'We don't need any help,' Rosie protested hotly. 'David will be four next June and there aren't any babies to look after.'

'You've managed very well, love' – he looked down at her tenderly – 'but you never have any time to yourself. Both your grandmothers have been telling me that you need company of your own age. Perhaps if she came you could get a job in a draper's, you'd enjoy working with all the young ladies.'

'Are you going to let her come then, Dada?'

She looked up into his tired face and he shrugged his shoulders.

'I don't know what to do, we're quite all right as we are, but if you'd like to go to work like the other girls you left school with, this would be your chance.'

All night Rosie tossed and turned, trying to make up her mind. Supposing Cousin Bronwen came and the children didn't get on with her? There was no room for her anyway – Dada couldn't have thought of that. She wondered what it would be like to work in a drapery store; it would be nice, surrounded by all the smart clothes and helping people to choose from the many fashions.

In the morning she told her father that she didn't think they had room for Cousin Bronwen.

'Well,' he said, 'she could have the parlour as a bed-sitting room if she comes.'

Rosie didn't answer. For a long time she'd been planning the way she'd decorate the parlour if she ever had enough money for wallpaper and paint and some new rugs. It was one of her favourite dreams, along with the one where they had red stair-carpet and brass stair-rods like Grandma Hughes.

Arthur didn't press her any further, but he wrote to his cousin suggesting she came to stay for a week to see how they all got on. He was sure Rosie would come round to the idea in time.

As soon as Ernie and Teddy came home from school on Monday afternoon Rosie left for Clifton Street. She had decided to look around Goldberg's Emporium to see what it would be like to work there.

She had just entered the shop when a gentleman came towards her and asked with a smile, 'Can I help you, madam? What department do you require?' She told him she was just going upstairs because she couldn't think of anything else to say.

She climbed the dark polished stairs and walked through an archway over which a notice proclaimed 'Mantle Department' in wrought iron and gilt, but here, too, someone approached her, and in a panic, before she could look round properly, she turned and fled down the stairs and out into the street.

One thing she had noticed: all the shop assistants had looked smart. But they'd been nice, too; several of them had smiled at her in a friendly way as she'd passed them. She'd been impressed, also by the displays of silky petticoats and nightdresses trimmed with lace, and upstairs she had just caught a glimpse of a long rail of expensive-looking winter coats, some of them with deep fur collars and cuffs.

She sighed; it would be lovely to work there amongst the beautiful things.

Cousin Bronwen wrote to say she would be very pleased to come to visit them.

Several times in the following week Rosie made an excuse to go to

Clifton Street. Each time she took her school leaving report, which was a surprisingly good one, particularly in English and Arithmetic, considering that she'd only attended classes part-time.

She hung about outside the shop but couldn't pluck up enough courage to go in again, especially after she'd glanced into one of the spotted mirror panels which divided the windows and seen herself in the shapeless coat and shabby tam.

She turned and flew down Clifton Street and into Broadway and bumped into Aunty Mabel. Hiding her tears, she told her about cousin Bronwen.

'Well,' her aunt said, 'it may be a good thing for you, Rosie. Will you be trying to get a job if she comes to stay for good?'

Rosie nodded. 'I would really like to work in Goldberg's, but,' she swallowed, 'well, I haven't been in yet and asked.'

Mabel understood instantly. Poor Rosie. If Laura had lived she would never have looked like this. Ada Jenkins meant well, and she was very kind – but that coat! Rosie had been so stubborn about them buying anything for her, and she wouldn't accept anything of Vi's either, so Mabel'd given up offering. Rosie was growing up; perhaps she was getting sensitive about Vi's left-offs, though she always said her refusal was to avoid upsetting her father. The money they'd managed to get her to take from time to time must always be spent on the house or the boys – they often seemed to appear in something new just after.

Mabel had decided that this Christmas she was going to risk it and buy Rosie something really nice to wear, and Mother had felt the same. She was pretty certain Arthur had changed in that respect, and there wouldn't be any fuss – she'd soon know, wouldn't she?

'Look, Rosie I can't stop now, but I'll be coming to see you when Vi gets home from school,' she said hurriedly. 'Sorry I'm in a rush, love.'

Just over an hour later Rosie opened the door to Vi and her aunt, both laden with parcels.

'You're really going to love it,' Vi told her excitedly as Mabel held out the largest parcel saying, 'We were going to give you these on Christmas morning, Rosie, but I really think you need them right now.'

Rosie held her breath, hardly daring to hope, then the colour drained from her face and, white with excitement, she drew out the beautiful coat she'd admired in Goldberg's window. Breathlessly she held it against herself.

'Oh, Aunty Mabel!' she gasped. 'I can't believe it. Oh thank you, thank you!' And putting the coat down she hugged her aunt with such force that they both nearly fell over.

'Try it on, Rosie.'

She trembled so much that at first her hands couldn't find the sleeves. After buttoning the coat she lovingly caressed the smooth face-cloth. Vi was hovering with another bag and, as though unable to wait, pulled out the little felt cloche hat.

Rosie had to wipe away tears in case they marked the coat. The colour had returned to her cheeks and she could see the top half of herself in the overmantel mirror. She looked down at the graceful lines of the coat and caught sight of her heavy winter shoes and thick socks, but Vi was handing her another box and from it she took a smart pair of bar shoes, two pairs of fine lisle stockings and some pink garters.

'They'll change the shoes if they don't fit,' Mabel assured her, but they did fit, they all fitted beautifully. She kissed her aunt, hugged Vi, and told them that she'd be coming to thank Grandma and Uncle Ted as soon as Dada came home from work, suddenly growing pale as she remembered how he used to react to gifts from Grandma and Aunty Mabel.

But when he came home there wasn't any fuss at all; he seemed genuinely pleased for her, asking her to put everything on for him to see.

'You look very smart, Rosie, real grown up,' he said with pride in his voice, when she'd turned around once more to show him the box pleat in the back of the coat. 'I was wondering how we could get you some clothes if you got a job – I know you couldn't have gone to work in what you've got. It wouldn't have run to a coat though – that must have cost a pretty penny.'

'Your tea's in the oven, Dada. I must go and thank Grandma and Aunty Mabel and Uncle Ted.'

'Of course, Rosie, and thank them very much from me too, I'm very grateful. I know it means a lot to you.'

She could hardly believe her ears. Sighing with relief she left the house, luxuriating in the lovely new clothes.

The next morning she put them on as soon as the little ones were gone next door, and went to Clifton Street. This time she didn't hesitate outside the shop but walked straight in and up to a man standing at one of the counters signing a bill, and asked if she could make an appointment to see Mr Goldberg.

'I'm Mr Goldberg,' he told her. 'What can I do for you?'

When she told him why she'd come he asked her to accompany him to his office behind the cash desk and following him she felt full of confidence.

Mr Goldberg brought a chair for her and put it in front of a small mahogany desk. She'd noticed that he was very tall; now, as he sat facing her, his pale blue eyes magnified by the lenses of heavy tortoiseshell spectacles, she saw he had a long face and a long straight nose, and greying hair receding from a high forehead.

As soon as they were both seated he looked into the eager young face and took in the smart clothes. This was the sort of girl they needed, he thought, not the ones who came in holding mama's hand. Then he looked at the school report she had handed him.

'It's a very good report, my dear,' he said, 'but why have you been absent from school so much?'

Rosie explained about Mama dying, and her having to look after the children, and about Cousin Bronwen coming to look after them in a few days' time. He nodded, pondering a moment; they'd need staff for the Christmas trade and the January sales soon after.

'All right,' he said. 'Can you start a week on Monday? You'll be apprenticed for two years, the first at half-a-crown a week, the second at four shillings and sixpence, and you'll receive a small commission on everything you sell. Oh, and you'll need a dark green dress, young lady.' Shouldn't be any difficulty there, he thought; if he wasn't mistaken that coat and hat had come from one of their better ranges.

When Arthur Edwards brought Cousin Bronwen from the station Rosie had a hot meal all ready to serve. She was surprised how young his cousin looked until she remembered that in the snaps taken at the Whitsun treat Bronwen had been a little girl while Dada had already been a young man.

Bronwen was plump and pretty with light brown bobbed hair. Hugging Rosie she said, 'You're still the boss, young lady, you'll have to show me what to do. And you can't call me Cousin Bronwen all the time,' she added with a smile. 'Besides I'm only a cousin to your dad.'

So Bron she became to one and all, even Ada Jenkins.

When Rosie told her father about the green dress that she'd need, Bron said, 'I've got the very thing, lovely it is. I can soon alter it to fit you, cariad.'

Rosie remembered the coat that had been altered, and her heart sank. But she needn't have worried, for although Ada's skill at sewing didn't match her well-meaning enthusiasm, Bron had learnt her trade as a dressmaker and using Ada's machine she took in the little green dress in all the right places.

When Bron gave Rosie the dress to try on she said, 'You're going to take the job then, Rosie? Do you want me to stay on to look after the boys?'

Rosie's heart gave a little skip at the thought of young David depending on someone else, but she was looking forward to working at Goldberg's and Bron *was* wonderful with the boys – she knew her father would be pleased at her decision.

Bron was a bundle of energy, often tackling several jobs at once; it was as though she couldn't bear to be still. If she wasn't up to her dimpled elbows in soapsuds she would be mixing bread or cakes, or bathing and dressing the little ones.

At first David had clung to Rosie's skirt, peeping out at Bron then hiding his face, but even he was won over after a few hours. Rosie couldn't help feeling a little pang of jealousy when she saw Teddy's chubby arms creep round Bron's neck, his face close to hers as he begged for another story. And when David also went over to listen and put his arms out for a cwtch, she wished for a moment that Bron hadn't come, and instantly regretted the thought. You wouldn't be going to work at Goldberg's on Monday if Bron wasn't here, she reminded herself, and she was looking forward to starting her new job.

Bron was always cheerful when anyone was around, though sometimes coming upon her unexpectedly Rosie would see a sadness in her eyes. One night on her way downstairs to get a drink for David Rosie thought she heard the sound of crying from behind the parlour door, but in the morning Bron seemed her usual cheerful self.

On Sunday afternoon Dada went to the cemetery, and Rosie and Ernie dressed the children in their best for Sunday school. Afterwards they all went to see Grandma Hughes. Rosie was glad of the excuse to keep on her new clothes.

Vi was getting ready to go to a friend's for tea. 'Why don't you come up to my bedroom, Rosie, we can talk while I get dressed.'

Rosie watched Vi as she eased fine stockings gently over her feet and legs and fastened them to a frilly satin suspender belt. The petticoat she slipped over her head was like the ones Rosie had seen on the display stands at Goldberg's, the top embroidered with dainty flowers and both top and bottom trimmed with deep, creamy lace.

'Are you looking forward to starting work tomorrow, Rosie?'

She nodded. 'I hope you'll make sure I serve you when you come to Goldberg's, Vi, so's I'll get the commission.'

They both laughed but Rosie knew, as she had done for a long time, that despite Vi's kindness and thoughtfulness they had been gradually growing apart. Vi had been at grammar school for three years now; she had her own set of friends and many interests that Rosie, tied down with the children, couldn't possibly have followed.

Rosie watched Vi as she finished dressing and slipped her feet into dainty black patent shoes. She had put on a turquoise-blue suit and a frilly blouse, and her long fair hair fell about her shoulders. She looked almost grown up, a striking contrast to the weekday Vi of the gymslip, blazer and round felt hat with its striped band and school badge.

'I've made a cup of tea, Rosie,' Mabel called up.

'Mam made some cherry cakes this morning,' Vi said. 'I think I'll have some before I go.'

When they entered the kitchen the boys were all sitting at the table eating their cakes, and Mabel was pouring the tea.

'Can you stay to tea, Rosie?' her aunt looked at her inquiringly. 'It's all ready, I could have it on the table in five minutes.'

Rosie shook her head. 'Thank you, Aunty Mabel, but I'll just have a cup of tea and a cake. Dada will be home from the cemetery by half past five.'

Half an hour later, when Rosie opened the front door the house was very quiet. Bron wasn't bustling about in the kitchen, the parlour door was shut, and she wasn't in the yard.

Perhaps she's with Ada, Rosie thought, going to the garden wall to call over, but at that moment David came running towards her, his eyes enormous.

'Rosie! Rosie! I saw Bron. There was a noise and I reached up and opened the door. I didn't like the smell.' He wrinkled his little nose and buried his face in her skirt.

The parlour door was shut again now. Feeling apprehensive, Rosie tapped lightly at first, then harder. When there was no reply she opened the door quietly. The curtains were drawn and it was dark in the room. Bron was lying on the bed. When she saw Rosie she attempted to sit up but immediately fell back again, groaning and holding her head. There was a peculiar smell but Rosie couldn't place it.

'Sorry, love, I've had one of my turns,' Bronwen said, and the words were slurred. 'Just leave me in the dark, there's a good girl. I don't want anything.' And she closed her eyes.

'But hadn't I better get someone, Bron? Mrs Jenkins or perhaps Dr Thomas.'

'No! I'll be all right, really I will. I'm used to these turns.'

Still worried, Rosie went to the kitchen to prepare the tea. She had left Ernie and Teddy and Albert in the street talking to Frank and they'd probably gone in next door. Should she call Ada? What was wrong with Bron? If she wasn't strong, how was she going to cope with the boys?

When her father came home she told him her worries. 'Leave her for a little while,' Arthur said, 'then if she's no better we'll get Mrs Jenkins to have a look at her and see what she thinks.'

What was she going to do if Bron didn't get better by tomorrow?

Rosie's heart sank at the thought of losing the job before she'd even started. What was making Bron so ill and what was the funny smell? Was it perhaps some kind of medicine? She'd give Dada and the boys their tea and later on she'd take Bron a cup.

She lifted David into the seat beside Albert who was only eighteen months older than him but much bigger built. Albert had been a chubby baby; now, although tall for his age, he was still plump, with dark eyes and dark curly hair that had up to now escaped the pudding basin when the others had their hair cut. But David was a small, pale child.

Rosie was making fresh tea to take into Bron when the kitchen door opened and she came in and sat down shakily on the sofa. Taking the cup in her hand and trying to steady it, she assured them that she was feeling better. 'Just a bit of a headache, that's all,' she added.

A little while later some of the colour had returned to her cheeks and Rosie breathed a sigh of relief. Questions kept coming to her mind, but something stopped her from probing: she wanted so much to start work tomorrow and Bron was looking a lot better now.

See what happens, she told herself, no sense making mountains out of molehills. When she'd got the children to bed she'd wash her hair and put her things ready for the morning. Rosie felt a surge of excitement when she thought of tomorrow morning, of putting on the little green dress and her new hat and coat and going to work at Goldberg's Emporium.

Chapter 8

Next morning, as she approached Goldberg's, Rosie's eagerness had quite evaporated. Her mouth was dry and despite the warmth of her new coat she began to shiver as she struggled against the biting wind.

She was early and there was only one young lady waiting in the shelter of the deep doorway between the two long windows. The girl was about seventeen, smartly dressed in a grey coat with an astrakhan collar, her short dark hair almost covered by a grey cloche hat.

'Hello!' she said, smiling at Rosie. 'New here, are you, love?'

Rosie nodded, and just then a group of girls and a man arrived, almost blown into the doorway by a strong gust of wind.

'There's a morning, Dilys, isn't it?' a plump young woman said to the girl who'd spoken to Rosie.

'Yes, and there's a night we had, blew some slates off our roof it did.'

More staff arrived and Rosie was pushed nearer and nearer to the door. Suddenly there was a commotion and the staff parted to allow Mr Goldberg through, and as he turned the key they all surged forward and Rosie nearly fell inside.

Watching everyone scurrying about Rosie waited shyly for someone to tell her where to go. Presently Mr Goldberg left his office and approached her.

'Ah! Miss Edwards, I'd like you to start on the lingerie counter,' he said. 'Miss Williams is in charge, she will tell you what to do.'

Rosie followed the rest of the staff up the three flights of stairs to a cloakroom where she took off her hat and coat.

At the lingerie counter Miss Williams and her four assistants bustled about removing dust covers from the displays and putting bill books at strategic points along the counter.

Miss Williams was short, with fair hair, and her grey eyes darted from counter to fixtures making sure that everything was in order. The assistant who seemed to be next in charge was Dilys, the girl who had spoken to Rosie in the doorway and now she gave her an encouraging smile as she passed her with a pile of boxes.

There was one girl a little older than herself with short bobbed hair; the other two could have been sisters: both were short and plump with dark eyes and warm colouring.

While she waited Rosie looked around her, first at the long, glass-fronted counter with its display drawers filled with silky underwear, then at the tall cabinets with neatly labelled compartments which ran the whole length behind the counter, leaving just a narrow space for the assistants to work in. She went closer to read some of the labels. Combinations OS cream cotton. Twill corsets 28 to 30 inch. Directoire knickers, fleecy lined, medium and outsize. Fluffy bed socks, pink and blue. Interlock vests took up two drawers in various sizes.

Then her attention was taken by the overhead cash railway which fanned out in all directions over the partitions dividing the departments and ended directly above each counter with a wooden cup to receive the bill and money when a sale was made. When she'd been little, shopping with Mama, Rosie'd been fascinated by the busy little cups whirring back and forth whenever someone gave a sharp tug on the dangling wooden handle.

'Miss Edwards?'

'Yes, Miss Williams.'

'You'll be sixth sales on my counter, that means that you will serve whenever there are six customers. I shall call "Forward, Miss Edwards", and you'll leave whatever you're doing and greet the customer with "Can I help you, madam?" '

'Yes, Miss Williams.'

'Now, the best thing is to get familiar with the stock, so take one drawer at a time and examine the contents, at the same time noting the prices. You will always show customers the most expensive item first. That is Mr Goldberg's policy.'

Rosie loved the silky feel of the celanese French knicker sets, all in delicate pastel shades, with deep lace on their flared hems and matching petticoats, the fluffy pink bed-jackets and dainty embroidered camisoles. When at last she came to the interlock combinations and thick directoire knickers she tidied them hurriedly, and was just as quick dealing with whaleboned corsets held together with crisscrossed lace.

There were nightdresses, too, in all sizes and materials, from voluminous flowered winceyette to flimsy silk with matching negligées, brassieres trimmed with lace, vests – I'll never remember where they're all kept, she thought.

Rosie watched some of the assistants serving but there were never more than four people at the counter at one time, so she went on endlessly tidying drawers or polishing fixtures, starting all over again as soon as she'd finished, for as Miss Williams explained, 'You must never be seen to be idle or I shall be asked why.'

Mr Goldberg patrolled the departments ready to swoop on the bill whenever an assistant called 'Sign, please!'

As a change from polishing, Rosie cut sheets of brown paper into convenient sizes for wrapping and strung them together to hang on a hook at the side of the counter. Miss Williams complained that she was much too quick and Rosie was sent back to tidying the drawers.

Break times were spent in the cloakroom and the apprentices were always the last to go. Rosie felt a little nervous as she made her way upstairs in the first break, but when she pushed open the door she saw an apprentice who'd smiled at her earlier from Haberdashery was sitting at the table on her own.

'Hello! I'm Dorothy,' the girl said, pulling a chair out for her.

Rosie smiled warmly, glad to have company.

'I'm Rosie, I'm on the lingerie counter.'

'I know, you started this morning, didn't you?'

Dorothy went to the gas stove. She was a tall pale girl with lank fair hair that fell about her shoulders. Lifting the big brown enamel teapot she poured Rosie some tea.

'Take sugar?'

'Yes please!'

Two girls sitting at another table got up, swilled their cups under the tap at the sink and put them upside down on the tray that did as a draining board, smiling pleasantly at Rosie and Dorothy as they passed to go back to their counters.

'Ugh! This tea's cold.' Dorothy put her cup down. 'It usually is by the time we come up, and there's never time to boil the kettle again.'

Rosie took a sip and swallowed with a grimace. Then she looked around the room. It was long and narrow; rows of pegs were fixed along two of the walls, coats hanging from them. She checked to make sure that her lovely new coat wasn't crushed under somebody else's. The gas stove stood in the far corner, and a deep white china sink was set under a long narrow window which was open at the bottom, making the faded blue gingham curtains billow out over the sink.

There were three identical square wooden tables, all of them covered in worn American oilcloth, set at intervals down the room, and six dark bentwood chairs at each. On a battered tin tray resting on top of a cupboard near the sink was an assortment of odd cups, a jam jar of sugar, and a tall white enamel jug of milk.

Hurriedly she brought her thoughts back to Dorothy who was telling her that she'd started work at Goldberg's as soon as she'd left school in July.

Later, during the lunch break, they found themselves once more together. Having eaten their sandwiches they decided to go for a walk along Clifton Street.

'I wish I had lovely pink cheeks like you,' Dorothy confided. 'I look awful in this weather I do. I saw some stuff in Woolworth's, blush cream it was. I was wondering whether to try it, but they don't like the apprentices using make-up.'

'They won't know if you put it on carefully,' Rosie assured her as they turned into Woolworth's doorway.

Dorothy's green dress was far too wide for her thin figure and Rosie wondered whether to suggest a belt to pull it in. She looked down at her own neat dress proudly.

Woolworth's had open counters so that anyone could handle the things on display; you helped yourself and handed your purchase to the cashier. Miss Williams would have been horrified – at Goldberg's only the assistants were allowed to touch the stock, carefully displaying things one at a time, but then everything at Woolworth's was either threepence or sixpence and Goldberg's had some very expensive items.

After much deliberation as to the shade, Dorothy paid for the blush cream and they hurried back to the shop where Dorothy applied it liberally whilst standing at the cracked mirror in the dark little cloakroom.

The colour was too deep – Rosie had said so before she'd bought it – but Dorothy seemed pleased at the transformation. Giggling, they hurried downstairs to their respective counters. Before Dorothy reached Haberdashery Miss Peacock, who was head of the counter, strode towards her, horror etched all over her face. She held the same position as Miss Williams but there the similarity ended. Miss Peacock was a heavily built woman, her straight, greying hair pulled back at one side with a brown slide. Now, her lips set in a hard, thin line of disapproval, she pushed Dorothy before her towards the stairs. Dorothy's face was now a ghastly white with two garish red patches standing out on it, like a painted wooden doll. From the foot of the stairs came Miss Peacock's loud voice, clear to everyone: 'Wash that disgusting stuff off your face, young lady, or I'll come and do it for you.'

Rosie gave a sigh of relief when five minutes later she saw her new friend being escorted to her counter looking pale, shiny, scrubbed, and very subdued. Miss Peacock gave Dorothy a venomous look as she thrust a tray of ribbons at her to be sorted.

With little to do besides tidying and dusting the time had dragged terribly and Rosie could hardly believe that it was still only half past two. Her legs ached from standing for so long in one position and she was just suppressing a yawn when Miss Williams called her name.

'Mr Goldberg wants you to take some corsets out on approval, Miss Edwards. Get your hat and coat and I'll have the parcel ready for you.'

Rosie, pleased to be going out, hurried upstairs to get ready. Carrying the parcel carefully, she made her way to the address on the approval note and knocked on the door. It was a small terraced house not far from the abattoir, and the wind blowing from that direction wafted an unpleasant smell towards her, making her wrinkle her nose.

After she had knocked several times a loud voice shouted, 'Come in, push the door.'

The voice seemed to have come from the front room, so, finding herself in a tiny passage, she tapped on the door, pushed it open and was surprised to see a very stout old lady lying on a high bed. The room was full of heavy dark furniture, the flowered oilcloth on the floor barely visible. She saw herself reflected in the cracked mirrored door of the wardrobe, at the same time seeing the woman's face as she gawped at her in disbelief.

'Duw!' the woman cried. 'They've never sent a little one like you to try me corsets on me, 'ave they?'

Rosie gulped hard and nodded, rising panic making her mouth suddenly dry. She didn't know anything about corsets, and had supposed they would be taken from her and tried on in a bedroom.

'Well, come on, miss, get 'em out of the parcel and put 'em round me.'

With shaking fingers Rosie undid the string and attempted to get the corsets under the old lady.

'You'll 'ave to lace 'em different to that, don't you blutty know anything?' the woman bawled.

Rosie fumbled desperately with the knotted laces and tried to adjust the corsets. The customer was getting more angry by the minute.

'There's not 'an 'ope in 'ell of you getting them on me. Just wait till I sees that Mr Goldberg. I'll get our Blodwen to take me in the chair an' 'e'll get a piece of my mind, an' no mistake.'

Rosie tried once more, but her hands trembled so much it was no use.

The woman tore them from her grasp shouting, 'Give me the blutty things, they do go like this.' She fumbled with the knotted laces then threw the corsets on to the bed in disgust.

' 'E'll get the length of my tongue when I see 'im, sendin' a ninny like you.'

Rosie was near to weeping as the old lady dismissed her, yelling, 'Go on! Take 'em away, youer wastin' youer time. Next time tell 'im to send someone who knows 'er job.'

Leaving the house, blinking back the tears, she wondered uneasily what Miss Williams would say. She'd been told that if you lost a sale Mr Goldberg would always want to know the reason why.

When she got back, her face almost as pale as Dorothy's had been, Mr Goldberg was signing a bill at the lingerie counter. As she walked towards him he asked, 'Did you sell a corset, Miss Edwards?'

'No, Mr Goldberg,' she murmured, not daring to look at him.

'Why!' The question was more of an accusation.

Miss Williams joined them looking very anxious.

'I – I couldn't get them round her, sir,' faltered Rosie. 'She was a big lady and she was in bed – I – I couldn't lift her.'

'Good heavens!' He looked at Rosie in amazement. 'You were just meant to deliver them, Miss Edwards, and wait while she tried them on. I'd have sent someone with experience if I'd known she required help.'

With a sigh of relief Rosie went back to tidying the fixtures and heard him say, 'Send someone around there tomorrow, Miss Williams. Oh, and that young lady had better be instructed in the art of lacing corsets.'

At a quarter to seven she was sent to the front door to bring in the display roundabout of floral wrap-over overalls and was upset to find it raining heavily, wishing that she hadn't worn her new outfit.

At seven o'clock the dust sheets were put on and the bill books added up and put away. When the lights were dimmed in the department she followed the others up the stairs to the cloakroom.

A few minutes later, sheltering in the doorway hoping the rain would ease, she was surprised to see Frank Jenkins approaching under a big black umbrella. Frank had grown tall, his brown eyes were still kind and gentle, but his face was thinner and firmer. The fair hair still flopped over his forehead as it had when he was a little boy. Frank had been apprenticed to a carpenter since he'd left school over a year before.

'Mama was worrying about you getting wet, Rosie,' he said with a friendly grin. And gratefully she sheltered beneath the umbrella.

As they walked along, close together to stop the rain from running down their necks, Frank said, 'Our Mary's home from

Somerset for a few days and we're going to have a singsong around the piano tonight. Mama said she'd love you to come in, Rosie. And your dad, too, if he feels like it.'

Rosie had been looking forward to sitting in the armchair after her meal and putting her aching feet into a bowl of hot soapy water, but the Jenkins family were so good to her, and she'd intended to see Frank's sister Mary while she was here; Ada had told her she was coming.

'All right, I'll come in later on, Frank, and thank your mam, will you? I think Dada will want to keep Bron company.'

As they parted at Rosie's front gate she said, 'There's good of you to meet me with an umbrella, Frank, I'm ever so grateful.' And she glanced down at her new coat, thankful that it hadn't got spoiled.

'You look nice in that outfit,' Frank said shyly, and to hide her pleasure at his words she said, 'See you later on then.' And ran inside.

Bron, and her father who had just got in, were waiting to hear all about her day, and when she came to the part about the corsets and the old lady her father became angry.

'They expect a lot for half-a-crown a week.' His voice was concerned. 'You must refuse to go next time, my girl, you could strain yourself lifting people about.'

'But Dada, it was all a mistake,' she hurried to explain. 'Mr Goldberg only meant me to deliver them and wait.'

'David won't go to sleep until you've said goodnight, Rosie,' Bron said apologetically. 'Ernie has taken some old comics to his friend's house across the street, Teddy and Albert are in bed – they wore themselves out running around.'

There was an appetising smell as Bron opened the oven door, but Rosie said, 'Leave my dinner in there, Bron, I'll go up to David first.'

David, hearing her footsteps on the stairs had run on to the landing and was looking over the banister. Flinging his arms about her he said, 'Tell me about the big shop, Rosie, do they sell toys?'

She took him into her bedroom where he slept behind a partition Arthur had put up; the other boys were all in the big front bedroom now.

'David, love,' she said gently, sitting in the basket chair and cwtching him to her. 'I'll be very late on Thursdays, Fridays and

Saturdays, so you'll have to go to sleep before I come home then. But I will come up and see you, I promise, and I'll kiss you good-night and tuck you in even if you're asleep.'

She yawned wearily and David yawned, too.

'I'll tell you a little story then I've got to go downstairs.'

She put David into bed and tucked the blankets round him, then brought a book from the shelf. When she sat on the edge of the bed and had found the right page she saw that his eyes were closed. 'Once upon a time,' she began, looking down at him tenderly, then put away the book for he was already fast asleep.

Just over an hour later Rosie knocked on the Jenkinses' door; there were shadows moving about on the paper blind at the parlour window and she could hear the piano but didn't recognise the tune.

The music stopped, and Frank opened the door. She followed him into the front room and was surprised to see the table almost collapsing with party fare. It was a large round pedestal table covered with a crocheted lace cloth, but there was hardly an inch of the cloth showing except where it draped over the edge. There were plates of sandwiches with various fillings, buttered drop scones, Welsh cakes, fairy cakes, apple turnovers, – oh, she wished she hadn't eaten so much tea! – and on a little table in the corner were glasses and several bottles of home-made wine glowing red and gold in the gaslight.

Rosie sank down thankfully in one of the chintz-covered arm-chairs, and as she started to tell the assembled group about her day, leaving out the bit about the old lady and the corsets, her eyes roamed approvingly around the comfortable and homely room. The settee that matched the chairs was under the window, the chairs on either side of the blazing fire. The piano was old-fashioned, with lots of floral inlay along its front, and big brass candle-holders that Ada had polished until they glittered. The sideboard was of dark oak and most of its shining top was covered in family photographs, but in the middle and right in front was the vase that Rosie had bought for Ada at Barry Island.

She was handed a glass of beetroot wine when she had finished her tale and she turned to greet Mary and her eldest daughter Ceinwen, who had accompanied her on the visit. Meanwhile Frank sat on the red plush piano stool and began to accompany his mother as she sang 'I Hear You Calling Me', but Ada didn't really need a piano as her full rich voice reached the top notes effortlessly. Rosie marvelled at Ada's singing, for her voice held a quality that was totally lacking in her everyday speech.

When they'd all sung 'Bless This House' Bert Jenkins broke away to open a bottle of parsnip wine and Ceinwen passed the sandwiches round. Looking at the happy, guileless faces, Rosie sensed the strong affection this family had for each other: Ada, stout and placid, the focal point, Bert beaming as he poured the golden liquid carefully. 'Best year yet for my wines, Rosie,' he told her, handing her a full glass.

'Oh! I shouldn't, Mr Jenkins. I've never had wine before tonight.'

'It'll warm the cockles of your heart, cariad,' he replied, and that it did, and when she'd emptied the glass it had gone to her head, and even reached her toes, for as Frank began playing a medley of Strauss waltzes she whirled round and round with Bert, his ruddy face beaming from ear to ear.

Later they rested round the fire eating more sandwiches and cakes and Bert plied them with more wine. Frank went to the gramophone and winding the handle energetically put on a record he'd bought for the approaching festivities called 'Gracie Field's Christmas Party' and they rolled about laughing as only 'our Gracie' could make them. The leaping flames in the shining black grate, the warmth of the parsnip wine, and above all the affection and good humour of the Jenkins family seemed to cocoon Rosie in contentment and happiness.

Ada, dressed up for the occasion in a frock of peacock-blue marocain, her large bosom for once confined by a brassiere, began to sing 'Bless This House' once more, and Rosie, remembering the many sacrifices Ada had made for her, found the tears streaming down her face.

Ada was immediately all concern. 'I'll make you a cup of Camp coffee, luv. It's all that wine Bert gave you.' And she tut-tutted at Bert for having given her a second glass, as she went into the kitchen.

Rosie sipped the coffee gratefully, relishing the strong, sweet taste. Ada drew the chenille curtains over the window and lit the second gas jet in its frosted-glass shade. As it plopped into life Frank put on a record called, 'I'll Sing Thee Songs of Araby' and the talk turned to Christmas and the events around it.

'How about us all going to the pantomime at the New Theatre?' Frank suggested. 'It starts on Boxing Day.' But Ada and Bert didn't want to see *Robinson Crusoe* so it was decided that Frank, Rosie and the boys would go; he'd book the sevenpenny seats in the upper circle, and they would go on a Wednesday, Rosie's half-day.

Later, she crept into the house in case they'd all gone to bed but her father was waiting in the kitchen.

'You should have come in for an hour, Dada.'

'You've got to get up early for work, Rosie,' he said reproachfully.

'I was enjoying myself so much that I didn't notice the time,' she said, kissing him goodnight, then humming 'Bless This House' softly to herself she lit the candle and went to bed.

The next afternoon she heard the magic words 'Forward, Miss Edwards'. Two of the assistants were at tea-break, so nervously she went forward, remembering with a sinking heart Miss Williams's instructions about showing the most expensive items first, for the customer even in this cold weather wore only a shawl.

'I want a corset, miss, a cheap one, size twenty-six waist.' The woman's long face looked pinched with the cold and below the fringe of her grey woollen shawl Rosie could see that her black skirt was thin and faded.

Mr Goldberg was coming from the direction of the cash desk, his eyes darting towards the counters on either side, so she brought out the best Twilfit corsets and showed them to the customer.

'There's nice. 'Ow much, luv?'

'These are eight and eleven but we have other ranges.'

'You gorrw be jokin'? There's a price for you! My sisters do say you 'ave corsets at one and eleven.' And she opened her purse and showed Rosie the single half-crown it contained.

Wasting no more time Rosie brought out a corset at one and

elevenpence three farthings and made a sale. When he signed the bill Mr Goldberg gave her a sharp look, and as soon as the customer had left he came across and asked, 'Why didn't you show madam the whole range?'

Rosie explained about the single half-crown in the woman's purse and saw his lips twitch as he turned away.

Bron had arranged with Rosie to have time off on Sunday and Wednesday afternoons to visit a friend in hospital. On her first half-day Rosie hurried home to find her packing a basket with a cake and fruit, dressed ready to go out.

'Had a busy morning, Rosie?' Bron inquired.

Rosie started to tell her about the fat woman Dilys had served who'd insisted on buying three pairs of pink celanese bloomers at least two sizes too small, but she could tell that Bron was barely listening to her.

'Well, I'd best be off,' Bron said finally, frowning into the mirror as she smoothed her neat brown bob for the third time.

'Going to see your friend, are you?'

'What?' Bron looked startled 'Oh – oh yes! Be seeing you, Rosie.'

When the children came home from school Rosie sent Ernie to the coalyard with the old pram to get a hundredweight of coal. By the time Bron returned in the evening, a large saucepan of stew was simmering on top of the range. As Bron sat down wearily, the empty basket at her feet, Rosie asked, putting a cup of tea before her, 'Was your friend pleased with the cake you made, Bron?'

Bron stared at her blankly. 'My friend?' Her voice sounded puzzled. There was a long pause, then as though suddenly remembering their earlier conversation she said quickly, 'Oh yes! Rosie, my friend was very grateful.'

Chapter 9

Rosie had been at Goldberg's almost two years when something happened that brought her feelings, or rather lack of feelings, about boys to a head. She'd gone to the cellar to fetch some sheets of brown paper to cut into manageable pieces for wrapping and was followed down the steps by Tommy Morgan, the young general help from the manchester department. He came over and stood in front of her, wearing a stained khaki warehouse coat that was obviously meant for a fully grown man, and a tall one at that; the sleeves were, of necessity, rolled up several times and the hem almost reached his ankles. His face red with embarrassment he said, 'Can I walk you home tonight, Rosie?'

'I thought you lived in Grangetown?'

'I do. It doesn't matter if I'm late though.' Then, looking down at his dusty boots, he asked shyly, 'Would you come to the pictures with me, Rosie?'

At that moment they heard footsteps on the cellar steps and Tommy quickly pushed her before him into the broom cupboard and pulled the door behind them. With a sickly feeling in her stomach Rosie remembered Miss Williams warning that the penalty for being caught fraternising during working hours with members of the opposite sex was instant and shameful dismissal.

It was very dark in the cupboard and they were afraid to move, surrounded as they were by a miscellany of brooms, snow shovels, buckets and boxes, and Rosie soon became aware of the pungent odour coming from Tommy's warehouse coat. It reeked of a mixture of unbleached calico, flannel, and all the other things he carried to and from the assistants, including carpet and oilcloth.

85

Just in time she managed to free her arm and prevent the sneeze that threatened to betray them.

The footsteps were coming towards the cupboard. They stopped, and for an awful moment Rosie expected her worst fears to be realised. When at last they moved away again and were heard ascending the steps Rosie gave a deep sigh of relief.

'Open the door, Tommy.' Even her voice was shaking.

Instead, his arms fumbled in the darkness and went round her, and his breath was hot on her face as he tried to kiss her. Jerking her head backwards to avoid him, she fell against a shovel and sent it clattering to the floor.

Tommy tore the door open and bolted up the steps, and there was no sign of him when, holding her sore head and feeling weak at the knees, she reached the top herself and lowered the trap door.

When at break time she told Dorothy what had happened she was surprised at her friend's reaction.

'Why didn't you let him, Rosie? Kiss you I mean.'

'What! Tommy Morgan?'

'Well, he's a nice boy really.'

'He nearly got us both the sack, Dorothy!'

'Will you let him walk you home?'

'I hope he won't want to now.'

'Honestly, Rosie. Don't you like boys?'

'Of course I do. Come on, Dorothy, it's time we went down.'

Back on the counter Dorothy's remarks still rankled. Boyfriends and having crushes on film stars were the main topics of conversation amongst the apprentices, and of the film stars, Leslie Howard, Joel McCrea and Clark Gable were the favourites. Whenever an assistant became engaged and wore the ring there'd be cries of 'Ooh! Isn't it lovely? Ooh! It's gorgeous', and they'd talk about it for hours. Of course Rosie would be pleased for the girl who'd got engaged, and she too had a bit of a crush on Clark Gable, but she didn't go all soppy like some of them did.

She'd gone out with several young men over the past year, but as the country walks or trips to Roath Lake had to be on a Sunday afternoon and Bron was still visiting the hospital - wasn't her friend ever going to get better? - Rosie had to take David with her, and each of her prospective boyfriends had made it clear that they didn't approve of the extra company. But she knew that it was really her own attitude towards them that was to blame for their hasty departure. While other girls blushed and stammered and got excited about going out with a boy, she found their company less exciting than going out with Frank who had always taken David and often Teddy and Albert, too, on their little jaunts together.

Frank had seemed upset when she'd gone out with someone else, though he had tried to hide it. But he was just a friend, he didn't own her, did he? Then she'd felt ashamed of her thoughts after all Frank and his family had done for her.

Rosie felt a little puzzled at her own attitude to boys, which seemed so different from most of the other girls'. She was sixteen, and far from ignorant of the facts of life. But as yet she'd felt no special thrill in any boy's company.

'It's probably because you brought up a family of boys,' Bron had said wisely when she'd wormed out of Rosie the reason why she's stopped seeing her latest 'friend'. 'They're no mystery to you, cariad, that's the trouble. But believe me, Rosie, you'll meet someone some day, and when you do you'll fall hard. Warm-hearted, sensible girls like you always do, and when you give your heart to someone it will be for keeps, you'll see.'

If only it could be young Frank, Bron had thought wistfully. Couldn't Rosie see how it was with him? He was such a fine young man in every way. Tall and broad-shouldered, too. But if she had any hopes in that direction they were dashed by Rosie's next words.

'It's time Frank found himself a girl, Bron. I introduced him to Dorothy but he didn't show any interest at all. I felt really embarrassed.'

When Rosie had completed her apprenticeship she was summoned to Mr Goldberg's office.

'Well, Miss Edwards,' he said as soon as they were both seated. 'You have been with us for two years now and Miss Williams tells me that your work has been most satisfactory in every way.'

Rosie blushed with pleasure and looked down at her hands. 'You are a fully fledged assistant now,' he continued, 'and there is a vacancy for second sales with Miss Thomas in the mantle department. I think you should do very well there, you seem to be a very fashion-conscious young lady.'

Rosie thought gratefully of all the lovely clothes Bron had made for her, especially the green shop dress she was wearing which was a copy of one worn by Joan Crawford in a film magazine photograph.

Overcome by this wonderful piece of good fortune, she managed to say quite calmly, 'Thank you, Mr Goldberg, I'd like that very much.' She might have sounded calm but her heart was doing a somersault with joy. From the day she'd started it had been her ambition to be one day an assistant in the mantle department, and Miss Thomas, who was in charge, was a silver-haired darling, her gentle smile and friendly blue eyes putting customers and staff alike quickly at ease.

Leaving Mr Goldberg's office, making her way back to the lingerie counter, Rosie felt as if she was walking on air. Then she saw Dorothy tidying some ribbons and instantly felt a twinge of sadness. Poor Dorothy! With Miss Peacock as her superior she didn't stand a chance of promotion. They'd seemed to be at loggerheads ever since that business of the blush cream from Woolworth's on the day Rosie had started work. Dorothy had come out of her apprenticeship in August but fourth sales would be all she'd ever be if Miss Peacock had her way. It just wasn't fair.

Chapter 10

By the end of April 1935 the whole frontage of Goldberg's Emporium, except for the display windows, was adorned with flags and bunting ready to celebrate the Royal Jubilee. The windows themselves were decorated with smaller Union Jacks and gilt-framed pictures of King George V and Queen Mary. The lamp posts in Clifton Street were already resplendent in red, white and blue streamers.

Rosie, now seventeen and working in the mantle department, her own wardrobe reflecting her position as second sales, had developed a keen flair for fashion. With little money to spare she was lucky that she only had to show Bron an illustration or draw a picture of what she wanted and it would be made up for just the cost of the material.

They were a little better off these days, too, with Ernie working in the Co-op grocery store since he'd left school last year and bringing in another wage. Rosie's contentment was spoilt only by the increasing frequency of Bron's nasty turns.

As Frank walked her home on the Friday night before Jubilee week it was dark at the end of Clifton Street except for a few lights where shops hadn't yet locked up. Tucking her arm in his, he said, 'Shall we go to see *Twenty-five Years a King*, Rosie? It's on at the New Imperial Cinema all next week.'

'Oh! I'd love that, Frank. Could we go on my half-day? Bron's always back from her visit by half past five.'

They'd almost reached the end of the street when Frank stopped suddenly and drew her into the doorway of an empty shop. Putting his arms about her he began to kiss her gently. Not wanting to upset him Rosie remained passive, amazed to find that she wasn't really

89

surprised, but she soon realised that this was taken for encouragement as Frank's arms tightened about her and the pressure of his
lips became more urgent.

'Frank!' She pulled away from him.

'I'm sorry if I upset you, Rosie,' Frank said bitterly. 'I've tried to
be patient. Don't you feel anything for me at all? You must know
that I love you.'

'Of course I feel something for you, Frank. I'm very fond of you,
but that's not love, is it? I've never been in love with anyone.'

As they walked home neither spoke, and Rosie's thoughts were in
turmoil. She hadn't been surprised at Frank's behaviour, so had she
been deceiving herself? Had she known all along how Frank felt
about her while she was pretending it was just friendship? She was
very fond of Frank, and she suddenly realised that she liked to be
seen with him and enjoyed his company, and that a lot of her
workmates envied her when he came to meet her. But he was more
like a brother than a boyfriend.

Seeing he was upset, she linked her arm in his companionably,
saying, 'I may not be in love with you, Frank, but I'm very fond of
you. Let's just go on being good friends like we've always been,
shall we?'

Frank smiled at her then. She was such a child for all she'd
brought up a family. He'd have to be more patient with her;
fondness wasn't love but it was a start, wasn't it? And she didn't
love anyone else.

Towards the weekend the *Echo* published a programme of forth-
coming events and celebrations. On the evening of Jubilee day
beacons would be lit on the hills of South Wales and there was to be
a big firework display. All the important buildings would be flood-
lit and bands would play outside the City Hall and in the parks.

For months a weekly collection had been made to pay for the
street's Jubilee party. When May the sixth dawned bright and clear
patriotic fervour soon reached its height.

Long trestle tables joined the bunting and flags soon to be covered with red and white and blue paper cloths. China, glass, cutlery
and chairs were brought out from the houses.

By noon they were sweltering in a heat wave: bowls of jelly made the night before stood in cold water until they were needed; the sandwiches, made early that morning and now piled high in huge mounds, began to curl; the butter began to melt. But nothing could daunt the mounting anticipation.

Mr Llewellyn from the corner shop had given two whole slab cakes to supplement the plates of Welsh cakes, jam tarts and iced sponges that were set at intervals along the tables.

At last everything was ready. Paper hats were donned and the laughing, giggling, shouting children were seated, only to rise again, noisily, as Frank, who with his father had dragged the piano into the street on protesting castors, struck the first chords of 'God Save the King'.

The food disappeared rapidly and was just as rapidly replaced. Rosie, filling endless glasses with lemonade, which Ernie was helping to hand round, glanced at Teddy's, Albert's and David's happy faces, and wished that Mama could see them.

Later, when the tables were dismantled, Rosie and Bron took the Jubilee mugs the children had received from school and their other china and cutlery back into the house. Then the chairs were lined up on the pavements facing the road ready for the games and races to begin. At the height of the fun, as previously arranged, an ice-cream tricycle arrived and twopenny tubs were distributed to the children. Eventually people began to drift back indoors, though some remained to chat, unwilling to face their stuffy rooms on this hot sunny day.

The King was to speak on the wireless in the evening and a little group of friends gathered in Rosie's kitchen and waited in hushed expectancy. His voice came to them firm and clear yet filled with emotion, as he said:

'At the close of this memorable day I must speak to my people everywhere. How can I express what is in my heart? I can only say to you, my very, very dear people, that the Queen and I thank you from the depths of our hearts for all the loyalty – and may I say so? – the love with which this day and always you have surrounded us. I dedicate myself anew to your service for all the years that may still be given me . . .'

As Arthur rose to switch off the set Rosie hastily wiped her eyes. It had been a wonderful day, and for the boys the celebrations weren't yet over. Frank had promised to take them on Saturday to see the procession when the Prince of Wales visited Cardiff, and to the docks to see HMS *Neptune* when it arrived.

Soon though it was back to work as usual and the week of celebration reached its end.

On Sunday afternoon Arthur took flowers to the cemetery, Ernie was out with friends, the three younger boys at Sunday school, and Bron, in the throes of one of her nasty turns, was shut in her darkened room. Everything was quiet.

Rosie dressed herself carefully in her light grey costume and a frilly white blouse, and took a knitting pattern to Grandma Hughes. When she got back, the front-room blind was still drawn, but on entering the house she found the door of Bron's room wide open and the bedclothes flung back.

'Bron!' Rosie called softly, but she wasn't in the room or in the kitchen. She hurried down the dark little passage to the yard, and cried out in alarm, almost falling over Bron, who lay huddled at the bottom of the three steps, her body twisted awkwardly. Rosie, feeling sick with apprehension, bent over her and saw blood oozing slowly from a gash in her forehead. Kneeling closer and wrinkling her nose at the smell of Bron's breath, she sighed with relief that she was breathing.

Afraid to move her, she climbed over the wall to her neighbour's and within minutes Ada Jenkins was breathlessly bending over Bron and shocked Rosie by saying bluntly, 'She's been drinking 'eavy, luv, gin by the smell of 'er.'

'Oh no, Ada! Bron is very respectable,' Rosie protested, remembering old Meg who used to shelter in the doorway of an empty shop in Broadway. She was a meths drinker, always dressed in dirty rags, her face bloated and mottled purple. Dada had said she was more to be pitied than blamed. Old Meg always yelled the same thing at the children who taunted her, '*Cer i'r Diawl*', and Rosie remembered a man shouting at Meg one day, 'The way youer going, old woman, it's you who will be going to the Devil, maybe sooner than you think'. Bron wasn't like that, she was so neat and clean, there was no comparison.

'Look, Ada,' she said. 'Whatever Bron takes is for medicinal reasons.'

'That's all my eye for a yarn an' Betty Martin. I thought you knew, Rosie, that when Bron 'ad those nasty turns she'd been drinking. Anyway, go and ask our Frank to run to the phone by the post office an' ring for an ambulance, 'e can tell them Bron's 'urt bad, had an accident, like.'

When Rosie returned Ada was coming from the front room with a blanket from Bron's bed to put over her. Without a word she held up an empty gin bottle and Rosie's heart sank.

Glancing through the window ten minutes later, Rosie was thankful to see the ambulance drawing up in front of the house, the solid boxy lines of its white exterior, the big wheels under the heavy black mudguards, somehow calming some of her fears.

The boys arrived home just as it drew up and watched, their faces solemn and a little frightened, as the attendants gently slid the stretcher beneath Bron and carried her carefully through the house.

Seeing the ambulance arrive, a little crowd had gathered curiously around the gate; they parted in silence for the stretcher-bearers to pass with Rosie following behind. As she stepped off the pavement she heard someone saying, 'Has she been bard in bed under the doctor, then, our Lizzie?' and Lizzie James from the end of the street reply in a loud whisper, 'Bard in bed with a bottle would be more like it.' They giggled, and the colour flooded Rosie's cheeks as she bent her head to get into the ambulance. Everyone had known about Bron and her drinking except for her.

At the infirmary she sat on a wooden bench in a long corridor while a porter wheeled Bron into a room at the far end. There was a rustle of starched uniforms as two nurses hurried past her and went in after him. Then a door opened and two doctors in white coats, their stethoscopes swinging, walked briskly along the corridor talking earnestly and turned into the same room. Rosie stared at the white tiles which were halfway up the walls; above was painted a sickly shade of green. The smell of disinfectant made her feel queasy and she wished someone would come and tell her what was happening.

She felt a deep sense of shame that the doctors and nurses would know what had caused Bron's fall, and even worse, that Lizzie James, who was an awful gossip, would probably have informed half the street by now.

Just as Arthur arrived, out of breath from hurrying, one of the doctors came from the room where Bron had been taken and walked quickly towards them, his white coat flapping and his long thin face wearing a sympathetic smile. He was very tall and, fascinated, Rosie watched his Adam's apple bobbing up and down as he informed them that Bron was concussed and had to have stitches in the wound on her forehead, and that her left leg was broken and she was being prepared for it to be set.

'Is she married?' the doctor asked and Rosie nodded, explaining that Bron's husband lived away.

'I think you'd better get in touch with him as soon as possible,' he said. 'We would like a word with him about her condition.'

Arthur looked as though he wanted to say something but the doctor was already hurrying back down the corridor.

'There's awkward it's going to be, Rosie. That's really put the cat amongst the pigeons,' her father remarked as they walked towards the exit.

'How d'you mean, Dada?' Rosie was puzzled.

'I suppose I'll have to tell you, love, though I promised Bron that I wouldn't say a word to anyone. She isn't parted from her husband, well, not in the way she made out anyway. You see, love, he's in the asylum.'

Rosie stared at him, her brown eyes wide with surprise. 'Poor Bron – I wish she'd told me. Won't he be coming out, Dada?'

'Oh, yes, love! Just before Bron came to us he'd had a bad mental breakdown and tried to take his own life, but he's been having treatment and these last few months he's been very much better. It's her husband that Bron's been going to see every Sunday and Wednesday.'

'Poor Bron,' Rosie said again, remembering little incidents with a new understanding. 'Oh, if only I'd known.'

When she visited her, Bron had come out of the concussion, her head was still bandaged and she looked very pale. Propped against

94

pillows, a cage protecting her leg from the weight of the bedclothes, her eyes were sad as she gripped Rosie's wrist anxiously.

'What is it, Bron?'

Bron licked her dry lips. 'Your father has told you about Sid, my husband?'

Rosie nodded.

'I don't like to ask this, Rosie love, but would you go to visit him and explain? You see, cariad, I should have gone to see him that afternoon I fell down the steps – there's a daft thing to do wasn't it, girl? I'd drunk too much but I was trying to shake it off and get ready when I fell going to the wash-house. I'm all he's got, Rosie, I don't know what he's thinking.'

'Couldn't the hospital phone his ward and explain?'

'They've done that, love, but he'll be worried, I know he will. If you could just tell him that I've broken my leg but I'm fine otherwise . . .'

Asking Bron what trams she would have to take to reach Whitchurch Hospital, Rosie promised to go on Wednesday.

Ada had offered to see to the boys so on Wednesday afternoon, feeling a little apprehensive, she picked up the basket she'd packed with fruit, cakes and biscuits and went to the tram stop.

Entering the hospital grounds after two tram journeys that had taken nearly an hour, she took a deep, steadying breath. The air was filled with the scent of spring flowers and newly mown grass and the sun was pleasantly warm. It's like being in a big park, she thought, wishing she could dawdle and wander around the extensive grounds, but the visiting hour had already begun and people were hurrying past her towards the entrance. The main building, of red brick, had a tall water tower which dominated the skyline which Bron had told her to look out for.

Reluctantly she stepped inside the main building, surprised to find her surroundings light and airy and not at all depressing as she'd imagined they would be. There was a strong smell of disinfectant and gradually the feeling of apprehension returned as she tried to follow the instructions Bron had given her, losing her way several times before eventually finding Sid's ward.

Inquiring at the Sister's room she was told that he had gone with a nurse to the visitors' lounge, so she walked back along the corridor, the basket getting heavier every minute, until she reached the door of the lounge. As she pushed it open a buzz of conversation met her and she found herself in a large, pleasant room, light and airy like the other parts of the hospital she'd seen, and here too, only fainter, the smell of disinfectant lingered.

The room was nicely furnished with comfortable chairs set against the walls and two long dark wood tables in the middle on which vases of flowers were placed at regular intervals, their bright colours reflected in the highly polished surface.

The lounge was full of little groups gathered round the patients they were visiting. Some people turned and looked towards her as she closed the door but lost interest when they found it wasn't anyone they knew. She gazed around her, searching for Sid. An orderly with his back to her was in earnest conversation with a thin, middle-aged woman who was looking distressed.

Most of the patients were wearing their own clothes and at first glance could only be distinguished from the visitors because they wore slippers. A little group of people beside her were obviously trying to cheer up a patient, a girl of about eighteen in a frilly pink blouse and grey flannel skirt. The laughter seemed forced and the girl stared in front of her with a look of abject misery on her face.

Rosie turned away quickly and staring out of the wide windows, their cretonne drapes looped back, saw newly mown lawns and carefully tended flowerbeds already bright with colour; she found herself wishing fervently that her business here was finished and that she was out there, on her way home, taking deep breaths of the sweet-scented air.

She became aware that a man sitting with a young nurse over by the window was staring at her. He was tall and thin and wore a navy blue dressing gown over pale blue striped pyjamas and was looking at her so intently that she began to blush. I wonder if that's Sid, she thought, as he got up and walked towards her, plucking nervously at the braid on his dressing gown.

'You're Rosie, aren't you?' he asked when he reached her. 'I recognised you from a photo Bron showed me.'

Rosie nodded. 'How is she?' he continued. 'How is Bron? I've been terribly worried about her.' He looked so anxious that she felt a deep need to reassure him.

'She's quite well in herself, Sid,' she told him. 'She's broken her leg and is really upset that she can't visit you, but don't worry, she'll soon get better.'

Looking up at him she noticed the deep dark shadows beneath his grey eyes and the look of sadness in their depths. His light brown wavy hair was already lightly streaked with grey at the temples, and Rosie was embarrassed to see tears rolling down his thin cheeks. Fumbling in his dressing-gown pocket he pulled out a handkerchief and dabbed his eyes.

'Poor Bron,' he said, 'I've spoilt her life, I know I have. She never touched a drop before my breakdown. Oh, yes!' he said, seeing her surprise. 'I knew, Rosie, I could often smell it on her breath and it's all my fault.'

Suddenly he became very agitated, crying out, 'What have I done to Bron?' the tears falling unheeded down his hollow cheeks.

A nurse hurried across and, giving Rosie a sympathetic smile and telling her to wait, led Sid gently from the room.

As Rosie stood clutching the basket tightly, feeling very uncertain, the girl wearing the frilly pink blouse, perhaps disturbed by Sid's outburst, began to scream. An older woman, dressed in a tight brown tweed costume, put her arm about her begging her to listen. 'Of course I want you home, love,' she said soothingly. 'Of course Mama wants you home, but they do say you've got to finish youer treatment first. Hurt youer Mama deep you have, saying I don't want you—'

The girl began to scream again until she, too, was led away and the mother sat with her head in her hands being comforted by her daughter's other visitors.

Rosie wished passionately that she could walk down the corridor and out through the door. She'd been dreading this visit, and, she reflected ruefully, nothing that had happened so far had done anything to calm her fears.

A young nurse in a long, starched white apron over a light grey ankle-length dress came to take her to Sid's ward. As they walked side by side she smiled into Rosie's perturbed face and told her,

'Don't let what happened worry you, love. Coming on fine he was, going home soon I was told, but he's been very upset over his wife these last few days. Blaming himself he is, poor man, though goodness knows why.'

Rosie was pleased she could tell Bron that Sid was coming on well and might soon be leaving hospital. She would do what she could to set his worries over his wife at rest.

Sid was sitting up in bed. Apologising for upsetting her, he pointed to a stool.

'The nurse was saying that you could be going home soon,' Rosie told him. 'Bron will be pleased to know that.'

'She won't.' Sid's eyes were filled with sadness. 'Bron can't bear the thought of going back to that house. They know what I tried to do, you see.'

'Perhaps you could find somewhere else to live?'

'If only we could – a fresh start – but I haven't even got a job to go to, Rosie. It was losing my job that started it all.' When she didn't answer he said, 'Perhaps Bron's told you all about it?'

'She hasn't told me anything, Sid.'

'Well, I lost my job in the furniture shop when some money went missing. Everything pointed to me but I didn't take it, Rosie. Sharing a small house we were with two other families, awful it was, no privacy at all, Bron hated it there. When I got the sack I felt it was all my fault, even though I'd been wrongly accused. We'd never get a place of our own now and I'd never get a job without a reference.'

'Didn't anyone own up about taking the money?'

'Yes, but it was too late then – the doctor had given me medicine for the depression but it didn't help me. Bron was upset because the people in the house found out why I'd lost my job. It came to me one day that Bron would be better off on her own. Everything seemed so hopeless the day I took the overdose, then Bron came back unexpectedly and I was rushed to hospital. When it got round, about what I'd done, a young man at the shop owned up. He'd taken the money because he was in debt. My name was cleared and I was offered my job back, but it was too late – the black depression I felt wouldn't lift, melancholia they called it. Watched me all the time they did when I first came into the hospital, but I'd never do anything like that again, not when I've seen what it did to Bron.'

'What treatment did they give you, Sid?'

'Sedation mainly – bromide – force-fed me they did at first. It was awful, but it's a long time since I was sedated, and since I've been working on the gardens I haven't looked back.'

Visiting time was up and Rosie hurriedly put the contents of the basket into Sid's locker. When she stood up he caught her arm urgently. 'Don't tell Bron that I was upset, will you, Rosie?'

'Of course not, and don't worry – she'll be all right.'

Walking down the long ward she passed an old man muttering to himself. He stared at her and suddenly his face became animated; he shuffled across and before she could stop him he'd put his arms about her, crying, 'Mary, you've come back to me.' Next moment a nurse was gently pulling him away and as she led him back to his bed she said gently, 'It's not Mary. Your granddaughter will come as soon as they find out where she's living.'

Rosie gave a deep sigh; if only there was something she could do. Her heart was filled with sadness: so many unhappy people, so many problems, so much pain.

Thankfully she stepped out into the grounds. It all looked so normal here; patients were walking with their visitors or sitting on benches in the sunshine.

The sadness was still with her when an hour later she let herself into the house. They were all having tea and as Arthur poured her a cup he said, 'I went to see Bron and she may be out of bed tomorrow, trying her crutches. She was very upset, Rosie, she cried all the time I was there.'

'Does she want anything, Dada?'

'I expect she'd like some fruit. She begged me to bring her in a bottle but of course it isn't allowed.'

'What are we going to do, I mean about me going to work?'

'Well, Ada has offered to help out for a while but it couldn't go on, could it, love? She isn't getting any younger, it's too much to expect.' Sensing her keen disappointment Arthur gave her a sympathetic smile.

Rosie loved her job and the many friends she'd made. Miss Thomas, manageress of the mantle department, was to retire in the autumn and Rosie had cherished hopes of a promotion. She gave a deep sigh, foreseeing a bleak future filled with hospital visiting and household chores with very little money coming in.

She'd always be grateful to Bron for making the job possible and opening up a new world to her these past few years, grateful, too, for all the smart clothes she'd made her at so little cost. And she'd visit her tomorrow and cheer her up by repeating what the nurse had said about Sid. But that part of her life was over now.

Dada was right – it would be too much for Ada, and she'd done so much for them over the years. The boys needed Rosie now, particularly David. Remembering her promise the day Mama died, Rosie knew she loved her family, and whatever it cost her she could never be happy unless she kept it together.

Chapter 11

Next morning Rosie handed in her written notice to Miss Thomas, and during the morning Mr Goldberg sent for her. When she tapped on the door and he called 'Come in', she entered the little office remembering the day of her interview, her excitement at getting the job, and the time when she'd been told of her promotion.

Mr Goldberg was speaking on the telephone but he waved vaguely in the direction of the bentwood chair against the wall. She sat down and for the first time really looked around her. The office was very small but not an inch of space had been wasted. There was a filing cabinet and a bookcase against one wall, and Mr Goldberg's desk took up another. Against the wall facing her was a small leather settee and laid out on this were samples of merchandise.

Smiling at her Mr Goldberg put down the receiver and hung up the earpiece, motioning her to bring her chair to the desk.

'Ah, Miss Edwards! What is this I hear about you leaving us? I'd be very sorry to lose you indeed. Are you sure you can't make domestic arrangements so that you can continue to work?'

'No, sir, I only wish I could.'

He gazed at her thoughtfully, stroking his long thin face between his finger and thumb, his blue eyes kind. 'I may as well tell you that I have had something quite exciting planned for the near future. I've been observing you very carefully, and although of course you're far too young to take over from Miss Thomas, I had other plans for you.'

Rosie looked up with interest as he continued. 'I'm planning a new department catering solely for the younger person, and I felt that you would be just the young lady to put in charge: It is to be within the Mantle Department, or Fashion Department as I intend it to be known in future.'

'Oh, if only I could, Mr Goldberg! I'm very grateful, really I am, but I just can't leave the children.'

'Well, my dear, I am very disappointed. If ever you wish to come back there'll be a job here for you. When the time comes, of course, I shall have to fill the position I've just been telling you about.' He shook his head and added quietly, 'Such a pity.'

Rosie couldn't trust herself to speak. Nodding her thanks she escaped before the threatening tears could brim over.

Reaching the stockroom behind the Mantle Department she sat on the rickety chair trying to compose herself. Biting hard on her bottom lip, her eyes stinging with pain, the tears finally spilled over and she dabbed at them hastily, for at any moment she could be called to serve a customer.

As the full meaning of what she'd just turned down dawned on her her heart swelled with bitterness. To be in charge of this wonderful new department—. The ache in her throat was almost unbearable and she could hardly swallow, but when she heard Miss Thomas calling her she managed from long practice to smile, and hurried towards the customer asking pleasantly, 'Can I help you, madam?'

At home, as the months went by, Rosie's bitterness grew. She found herself feeling resentful because Ernie could stay at his job; often reminding herself that at Teddy's age she'd helped look after a baby as well as doing the family wash and going to school. Boys got away with it, didn't they? Girls were expected to make all the sacrifices, it just wasn't fair!

'A job is more important to a boy,' Arthur had explained patiently. 'Look, Rosie, one day Ernie will probably be the bread-winner of a family.'

She'd swallowed the bitter retort that rose to her lips, turning to the stove and stirring the stew so vigorously that some had spilled over and hissed on the freshly blackleaded hob.

In early September, because of her increasing depression and severe loss of weight, Bron was transferred to the same hospital as her husband and began treatment. Though segregated in different parts of the hospital they were able to meet in the recreation rooms and soon progressed to walking in the grounds together. By November the effect on both of them was remarkable and there was talk of them going home in the near future.

Bron was anxious for them to make a fresh start somewhere other than the cramped house in the valleys where their furniture still waited. 'It's so crowded, Rosie, three families sharing, and all the neighbours know what Sid tried to do. Ever since I've known that we can be discharged I've been sick with worry. Pleased I should be, girl, instead of which I can't sleep for wondering what to do.'

Rosie was suddenly ashamed of the feeling of resentment she sometimes felt about Bron's illness and the way it had affected her life. Poor Bron, she was the one who was suffering and now, with Sid well again, all they needed was somewhere to live. She made up her mind to try to find something for them. She'd go and see Nana Edwards; there was more likelihood of finding a place in the valleys. She hadn't seen Bobby and Willie for ages – they were both at grammar school now and played rugby at the weekend, and with all the work at home and the hospital visiting there hadn't been time to go.

She and Bron had been talking in the hospital canteen and now Sid came towards them. The hollows in his cheeks had filled out and his face had a healthy colour from all the time he spent out of doors. There was little he could do in November except tidy up but he loved to be out there. If only Sid could have a small garden of his own. Rosie was just picturing him growing all his own vegetables when he pushed the cup of tea he'd brought her a little nearer, saying, 'No sense in letting it get cold, cariad.'

On Sunday afternoon, while Dada went to see Bron and Sid, Rosie took David with her and they caught the tram to the station. As they waited for the train, David asked wistfully, 'D'you think Willie and Bobby will take me up the mountain, Rosie?'

'Well, it's a nice day but it gets dark early this time of year, you won't have to be too long.'

David was tall for his six years, but he was still thinner than she liked. Willie and Bobby were his heroes ever since Ernie had taken him to see them playing rugby at their school at the beginning of the season. When Bobby scored a try and Willie converted it from a particularly difficult angle to win the match there were loud cheers from their schoolmates and other onlookers and David had glowed with pride.

Looking through the train window at the misty November afternoon, Rosie watched the green fields and neat hedges gradually giving way to the now familiar landscape of pit-wheel and slagheap, the tops of the mountain lost in low cloud.

Leaving the station they came out on to the steep main road of the village and climbed to where at the top the path led to the foot of the mountain, and on to where Nana and Uncle Dai lived.

Rosie was still breathless from the climb when Willie opened the door, and his cry of welcome brought Nana and Bobby hurrying to them. After hugging her warmly, Nana cried, 'There is wonderful to see you, cariad, and you David bach. Our Dai will have a lovely surprise when he do come home. Duw! It's a tidy way up here from the station, isn't it, girl? Sit down, love, while I make a pot of tea.'

Rosie looked up at her two brothers, sure they'd grown since she'd seen them only a month ago, not only taller but broader too. It must be all that sport they have at the grammar school, she thought. They could almost be taken for twins with their big brown eyes and golden lashes, their cheeks the colour of wild roses from the fresh air.

It was too late now for them to climb the mountain but David seemed quite happy to kick a ball about with his brothers on the grassland.

As soon as they'd gone Rosie wasted no time in telling Nana about the problems confronting Bron and Sid.

Nana sipped her tea thoughtfully. 'Well, Rosie, thinking I am about what you just said, that Sid is keen on gardening and doing carpentry too at the hospital. Sounds exactly what old Mrs Bowen needs – lives the other side of the mountain she does, supplies a couple of market stalls with flowers and veg, crippled with the rheumatism she is now, pooer soul.'

'Do you think Sid could do the job, Nana? Where would they live though?'

'Well, her son and his wife had the cottage next to hers, this was before she got so bad. The wife was a town girl who couldn't stick the country, so they went off to Cardiff to live with her family. The cottage is vacant but it would need a bit of decorating.'

Rosie jumped up and threw her arms about her grandmother, crying, 'Oh Nana! It would be wonderful and Bron could take in dressmaking to help out.'

'Hang on, cariad, I'd better see how the land lies first. When will they be coming out of hospital?'

'Very soon. I think it depends on them having somewhere suitable to live.'

'Well, I'll go over and see Mrs Bowen now. She was talking about giving it up because she can't cope on her own. You stay here, Rosie, and give Dai and the boys their tea when they come in.'

Ten minutes later they trooped in dirty and hungry, and while they washed noisily at the sink Rosie set the meal. Afterwards they went into the parlour, Dai to listen to the wireless, the others to look at comics. David's eyes were bright, his cheeks flushed as he followed his big brothers through the door.

She'd washed the dishes and was putting them away when Nana lifted the latch of the back door and Rosie could see by her face that the news was good.

'She'd be very glad to have them,' Nana said, sinking into one of the armchairs and taking off her shoes. 'I saw the cottage. It isn't very big – just two up and two down – but at least it's a place of their own. I told her it may be a few weeks because they live in Cardiff and have got arrangements to make.'

'No one will know—?' Rosie began.

'Never!' Nana promised. 'They're a friendly lot round here, but Bron needn't worry – no one will ever know about Sid.'

'Will they have enough to live on, do you think?'

'Well, there's a wage, and the cottage is rent-free and they can take all the veg they want. I think Bron should do well with her dressmaking, too, it seems no one takes in sewing in the village.'

'How about their furniture, Nana?'

'Now don't you worry about anything, cariad, our Dai's friend has got a van. Bron's my own sister's girl, Rosie, Dai and me and the boys will keep an eye on them and see they're all right.'

When Rosie told them the news Bron was soon brimming over with plans, and Sid could hardly believe his luck that he would be working with a market gardener. 'I was dreading going back to shop work even if I could have got a job,' he confided. 'Oh Rosie! How will we ever be able to thank you and Aunty Edwards?'

It was a squally day and they went into the canteen. When they found a table and Sid had joined the long queue for cups of tea, Rosie asked, 'Do you think you'll manage all right, Bron? The cottage will be free but the wages aren't very much.'

'I can take in dressmaking like you said, Rosie. My machine is with all our other things.'

'Dai's friend is going to bring them over for you.'

Bron nodded. 'We're really lucky to have a family like ours. You've all been so good to us, love.' Her eyes were bright with happiness.

Half an hour later Rosie said goodbye at the end of the corridor, keeping the smile on her face until she'd left the building. She'd asked Bron if she'd be able to manage but the truth was she'd hardly been able to manage herself over the past few months. With neither Bron's contribution or her own, and only Dada's money and Ernie's small wages things were pretty tight. She was tired of scouring the shops for cheap food every weekend, fed up with the endless struggle to make ends meet.

The main groceries were now brought at the Co-op grocery store where Ernie worked. Co-op brand names were a little cheaper and the family had soon got used to Lutona cocoa, Wheatsheaf flour, Territorial sauce, and other items. Besides there was the dividend on purchases to be considered.

Rosie still had the lovely clothes Bron had made her, but they were too fancy for the house, and she had to make do with some of her mother's old clothes, which now fitted her. Arthur repaired the boots and shoes, and Rosie patched the boys' things.

Now at last the front room was empty and her longing to decorate was as strong as ever. It was a dream she had cherished all these years, but she knew it must remain just a dream. There was no hope at all of having enough money for even the cheapest wallpaper or paint.

Towards Christmas she was coming out of the Co-op, having given her order, when, looking across the road, she saw Mrs Todd, a neighbour from the top end of the street, about to enter the pawnshop opposite with a full pram. By the look of her the woman had nearly reached her time: she was huge and carrying the baby low. She looked weary and unhappy as she turned round and faced the street in an effort to pull the pram wheels over the high cracked step. Rosie's heart went out to her, and she wanted to run across the road to help, but knew that it would only embarrass the poor soul; she had watched her carefully looking round before attempting to enter the pawnbroker's shop. Her thin shoulders were covered by a grey woollen shawl; Rosie had never seen her in a coat even in the depths of winter.

Rosie had been standing in the doorway of the Co-op, but now, before Mrs Todd could see her, she stepped back into the shop.

'What you forgotten, Rosie?' Ernie was by her side.

'I just saw Mrs Todd going into the pawnshop,' Rosie whispered. 'I'm going now, I didn't want her to know I'd seen her.'

'Ma Todd!' Ernie laughed. 'She'll be coming for her order then. It's a regular thing, Rosie – she takes the stuff over the road, gets the money, then over here to fill her pram with groceries. The manager stopped her credit ages ago. When she has her money she gets the stuff back.'

Poor Mrs Todd, Rosie thought, she had eight children, like little steps and stairs they were. She remembered Ada's annoyance when Lizzie James, who lived next door to the Todds and was the street's biggest gossip, had gone round telling everyone that her neighbour didn't want this baby and was really upset about it. And no wonder, poor woman, Rosie thought sadly. No sooner had she weaned the last baby than there was another one on the way. It wouldn't have been so bad if she'd had a good husband – her own mother had had seven children. But Mr Todd suffered from chronic bronchitis and hadn't worked for years, but Arthur once remarked that he still managed to bend his elbow regularly at the Bertram pub.

Suddenly she remembered a while ago when Mrs Todd's face had been black and blue, and the neighbours said it was because her husband couldn't find his tidy jacket to go to the pub. She'd thought it funny at the time. Jackets didn't just disappear. Now she knew better.

She was deep in thought when Frank caught up with her on his way home from work.

'Penny for them, Rosie,' he said, but she had no intention of telling him her thoughts about Mrs Todd, and merely shrugged her shoulders.

He glanced down at her, his brown eyes full of concern. She looked so tired, all in she was. He wished there was something he could do for her besides their weekly trip to the cinema which, when the film was suitable, included David and Teddy. Knowing there was something troubling her, his voice was warm with sympathy as he asked, 'Are you still thinking about that job?'

'If only I could have stayed, Frank.' Looking up into his face, warmed by his concern, she marvelled at how tall he had become. His shoulders had broadened and his face had filled out, and it suited him. 'A gentle giant' Bron had called him once; it was a good description.

Pushing the fair hair from his forehead, he said, 'I've got some new records, Rosie, would you like to come in and listen to them tonight? Mam and Dad are going to the pictures.'

Later, when Albert and David were in bed, Teddy doing his homework and Arthur hidden behind the *Echo*, Ernie came into the kitchen dressed to go out. Another clean shirt, Rosie thought resentfully, that's the third this week, never a thought for all the washing. Then, looking at his light brown hair flattened with brilliantine, she thought with interest, I wonder if he's trying to impress a girl?

Rosie went upstairs and put on the emerald-green dress, with its wrap-over bodice pleated into a wide basque, that Bron had given her one Christmas. Despite her annoyance with Ernie, Rosie had thought how nice he'd looked in his best clothes. Perhaps she should make the effort herself, even if she was only going next door. She looked in the wardrobe mirror, pleased at what she saw and the way the emerald-green dress brought out the colour of her hair. Powdering her nose she remembered the little bottle of Evening in Paris Ernie had bought her last Christmas and dabbed some liberally behind her ears.

Frank had been busy; there was a bright fire in the parlour grate, and the lamp with its red shade cast a warm glow over the room. He'd put a lace-trimmed cloth over the chenille one; on it were a plate of sandwiches, a box of chocolates, two wine glasses and a bottle of his father's home-made wine.

There were four new records: 'You Are My Lucky Star', 'Lovely Lady', 'Red Sails in the Sunset', and 'I'm Putting on My Top Hat'. He put them on the table while he poured two glasses of wine.

'Shall we have this one first, Frank?'

As the plaintive lyrics of 'Red Sails in the Sunset' filled the room she sipped her wine, noticing that Frank seemed nervous, licking his lips as though about to say something, lifting his glass, then putting it down again without drinking.

As the last notes died away he picked up 'Lovely Lady' and put it on the gramophone saying, 'I've made your Christmas present myself, Rosie. I've been working on it since the summer.'

'What is it, Frank?' Since he was learning to be a carpenter she knew it must be something in wood.

'Wait and see,' he said teasingly, but his next words made her mouth dry with apprehension. 'It's something to put your jewellery in. I'll buy you that an' all one day, Rosie, you'll see.'

As the record began to play he put his arm about her and pulled her gently towards him. Resting his chin lightly on her head, he began kissing her hair, her cheeks, murmuring that she smelt lovely. Suddenly his lips were pressed hard on hers and an excitement rose in her and her lips clung to his. Frank's fingers caressed her face, her neck. She became frightened of her own reaction: this was all wrong, he was her friend. When his hand touched her breasts, modestly covered by the bodice of her dress, and he began fondling them, she pushed him away violently but he caught her in his arms, gently again now, and cradled her to him, whispering endearments into her hair. Then his arms tightened about her and she felt his passion rising again as his lips came down hard once more on hers.

Rosie pushed at him with all her strength and with a strangled sob ran from the room. Frank caught up with her as she struggled to open the front door. His face red with embarrassment he said, 'I'm sorry, Rosie, I was sure you had begun to feel the same way. I've tried to be patient, you looked so lovely tonight – you know that I love you. I'm fond of the boys . . .' But she was through the door, banging the gate and up the path, and her heart beating like a sledgehammer she fumbled through the letterbox for the key.

Frank, bewildered and upset, stood for a moment watching her. When she disappeared into the house he sighed deeply and went back to the parlour. How had he made a mistake like that? He could have sworn that she'd responded, that she felt the same way. What a clumsy fool he'd been to upset her; he'd been so patient waiting for just the right moment, and now he'd spoilt everything.

Rosie closed the door and rested her back against it, taking deep, painful breaths. Hearing a movement from the kitchen she crept upstairs and lay on the bed, staring up at the sloping ceiling, listening to David's gentle breathing, trying to calm herself. The memory of that moment when her intensity of feeling had matched Frank's brought a hot blush to her cheeks.

For a few days she managed to avoid him, hurrying indoors if she caught sight of him in the street or the garden. Then one morning, turning the street corner, she bumped into him. Frank looked down at her with the old tender look.

'I'm really sorry about the other night, Rosie,' he said. 'I've been wanting to see you to apologise. I thought you knew how I felt.'

'I like you a lot, Frank,' she began, but seeing his eyes light up, she mumbled quickly, 'I'm sorry, Frank, really I am,' and made an excuse to hurry on her way.

She saw him often in the next few weeks, but the old easy comradeship had changed – she was unsure how to react and felt embarrassed when they met. Frank, too, seemed ill at ease, not daring to express the feeling that his eyes couldn't hide.

Towards Christmas the weather got worse. Headlines in the *Echo* on the twenty-third of December read 'Traffic Stands Still on Coldest day', and the paper reported how frost, fog and ice had caused havoc, disorganising road and rail traffic throughout Great

Britain. There was one amusing story of how several conductors on Cardiff trams had found their ticket punches frozen.

Rosie did her shopping early on Christmas Eve, thankful the errand boy would be delivering the heavy order. The cake and puddings had been made weeks ago, and now it was pleasant in the warm kitchen rolling out pastry for mince pies and sausage rolls.

The boys had helped her to decorate the tree in the parlour with home-made novelties and silver glitter, and after tea she went in there to put the presents under it. Teddy, Albert and David were sulking on the sofa in the kitchen because she wouldn't let them go carol-singing, but it was freezing cold and the foghorns in the Bristol Channel bellyached constantly. Later, however, when she went back in they were playing snakes and ladders on the rug in front of the fire.

Ernie came home and filled the coal scuttles and got firewood in ready for the morning, and when the boys were in bed she filled their stockings, wishing there was something more exciting than the nuts, fruit, sweets and new penny she had put in each. The annuals she'd bought could go at the foot of the beds, together with a jigsaw for Teddy, and a colouring book and small box of paints each for Albert and David. Rosie had taken the money from the cash box for these and for the ties she'd bought Dada and Ernie.

The kitchen looked festive with brightly coloured paper-chains the boys had made and Christmas cards all along the mantelshelf. Faintly she could hear children carol-singing and on opening the kitchen door the strains of 'Away in a Manger' became louder, accompanied by a rat-a-tat on the knocker. Taking her purse she hurried to open the front door.

Huddled on the step were six of the Todd children, their steaming breath mingling in the bitterly cold air.

'Merry Christmas,' they chorused, as surprised at herself, she put three pennies instead of the usual one into Billy Todd's outstretched hand.

'Cor! Threepence!' he cried excitedly. 'We gorr enough for a bag of oranges now. Will the shop round the corner be open, missis?'

Rosie nodded. A girl of about three years, wearing a coat many sizes too big and with a floppy woollen tam almost hiding her face, was swinging on the gate whining, 'I wanna go 'ome, our Billy.'

'Shurrup, Peggy,' he said not unkindly, and with a hand either side the two older boys swung her along until her small feet of necessity began to run to keep up with their rush to reach the shop.

Rosie had bought a bag of oranges there only that morning at twenty for a shilling; she was glad now that she'd given them three pence. Mrs Todd, she knew, was still in bed after the birth of another boy only a few days ago. Mr Todd would likely be celebrating Christmas in the 'spit and sawdust' at the pub.

Poor little kids, she thought, but they'd seemed happy enough and the neighbours were good – she'd seen Ada taking them a tray covered with a teatowel this morning, and had rushed in to add a few things herself, wishing she'd known them well enough to help in other ways.

Early on Christmas morning Frank came in with her present. She murmured her thanks and brought his gift from under the tree. Unwrapping the parcel he'd given her she gasped, 'Oh Frank!' as she gazed in wonder at the beautiful jewellery box in the shape of a miniature chest, the front of each drawer and the top intricately inlaid with floral marquetry. Opening a drawer she found it lined with rich, dark blue velvet.

'Oh it's beautiful, Frank, it must have taken you a long time to make it.' Rosie's fingers caressed the satin-smooth wood. Forgetting for a moment the strained atmosphere that had been between them, she was about to fling her arms about him and plant a kiss on his cheek by way of thanks when David walked in to show off the model car that had been Grandma's present.

Frank admired the car, then opened his own present and held the fawn knitted pullover Rosie'd made him against his chest.

'There must have been a lot of work put into this, too,' he said. 'It's lovely, Rosie, it will look really nice with my brown suit.'

He didn't suggest their usual visit to the pantomime with the boys, and left soon afterwards.

At three o'clock, glad to sit down after all the cooking and washing up – the boys had wiped and put away – Rosie settled herself in the armchair to listen to the King's Christmas broadcast. She thought his voice weaker than she remembered from his Jubilee speech and recalled the rumours she'd heard about his health. She discussed this with Ada when she came in to try her cake and have a glass of wine; she didn't stay long and wasn't her usual chatty self. Rosie suspected what was troubling her, but tried to tell herself that Ada couldn't know what had passed between her and Frank, he would never have spoken to anyone about it, and anyway their relationship had seemed almost back to normal when they'd exchanged presents. But in her heart she knew this was wishful thinking.

It was just over three weeks later that Ada brought her the news that King George V had passed away. It was no surprise – earlier a bulletin had announced: 'The King's life is moving peacefully to its close.'

Ada unashamedly wept as she said, 'There'll never be another like 'im, Rosie. The people loved 'im. Remember Jubilee day?'

Recalling parts of the King's speech on that happy day only seven months ago – when he'd concluded with 'I dedicate myself anew to your service for all the years that may still be given me' – Rosie felt a lump rise in her throat and busied herself making tea. 'The Prince of Wales will be King now, Ada,' she said, sitting down and handing her a cup.

Ada helped herself to two sugars and stirred vigorously. 'They say he's courting an American woman. It's in all the American papers. My cousin Cissy 'eard it from friends who 'ave relatives there. Duw! There's bound to be a fuss about that.'

'I've heard that rumour, Ada, but surely it would be in our papers if it were true. Did you see the pictures in the *Echo* of the Duke and Duchess of York and the little princesses?'

Ada nodded, there was a short silence, then, as though she expected Rosie to be aware of her thoughts, she said, 'I 'ope you know what you're doin', Rosie. Our Frank's taken a real shine to you – mopes about something awful 'e does.'

Her cheeks flushed with embarrassment, Rosie looked across the table and said, 'I'm, sorry, Ada, really I am. I'm very fond of Frank, but . . .'

'There's good 'e is with the boys,' Ada cut in. 'You'll 'ave a job to find anyone else who'll take care of them like 'e would.'

Rosie knew this to be true but in all the love stories she'd ever read
no one chose their life's partner for sensible reasons like that. She
felt upset that Ada should think she should. She'd made sacrifices
all her life and the way Ada put it she should make this one, too.

'Encouraged 'im you 'ave, Rosie,' Ada said.

'I haven't,' Rosie cried indignantly. She felt sorry for Frank and
missed his company but really! . . . What was Ada saying now?

'Taken you to the pictures 'e 'as, regular every week, and out for
walks. Treated you tidy he did, an' never looked at another girl.'

'But Ada, we've been going round together since we were children, we've always been good friends.'

Ada snorted. 'Wants something more than a good friend 'e
does,' she remarked tartly, rising to go. 'Well, ta-ra, Rosie.' Her
tone was distinctly cool.

Remembering all the sacrifices Ada had made for her over the
years, and Frank's kindness and thoughtfulness ever since they'd
been children, Rosie felt miserable and confused. She wanted to
fling her arms about Ada but she'd hesitated too long and her
neighbour was through the doorway and going along the passage.
When she heard the front door shut none too gently she sat down at
the table, put her head in her hands and let the tears flow.

Encouraged Frank, had she? Well, she'd just have to make sure
that she didn't encourage him again.

Arthur Edwards had gone straight from work to a political meeting
at the Cory Hall. Lately he'd become very interested in the Labour
Party and he'd started dressing up to go out, a thing he hadn't
bothered much about since Mama had died.

Rosie was sitting alone in the kitchen when she heard him let
himself into the house. There were voices in the passage, then the
kitchen door opened and he ushered in a woman of about his own
age.

Rosie looked up at her. She was thin and fairish and wore a
fashionable velour coat in dark blue with a wide fur collar. But it
was the eyes that held her attention: they were light blue and slightly
prominent and had an almost defiant expression as they surveyed
the daughter of the house, though her words were friendly enough

as she said after Arthur had introduced them, 'I've heard such a lot about you, Rosie, and how well you've looked after all the family.'

'Make a pot of tea, love, Miriam's frozen.' Her father was warming his hands at the fire.

Lifting the big iron kettle which had been singing on the hob Rosie was filled with misgiving. When she turned with the full teapot Miriam was looking round the kitchen with interest. She was sitting in Dada's armchair and her coat lay over the head of the sofa.

'It's sad the King dying, isn't it?' Rosie said, making conversation. 'It's bound to make a difference when the Prince of Wales is King, they say he's courting an American lady.'

Miriam nodded. 'Yes, I've heard that – a customer who has a daughter living in New York says her name is Wallis Simpson, a funny name for a lady, isn't it? She says there are pictures of them in all the newspapers over there.'

Arthur watched Rosie anxiously; he'd been feeling nervous about this meeting, wanting so much for Rosie and Miriam to be good friends.

When Miriam had finished her tea she glanced at her watch and then at Arthur who immediately put his coat back on to take her to the tramstop.

'Well, goodbye, Rosie,' she said, 'I expect we'll be seeing quite a lot of each other.'

Rosie nodded cautiously. It seemed to her that Miriam was the sort who usually got what she wanted. She followed them to the door, and as the gate clicked behind them, watched as they linked arms and laughed over some remark her father made. Suddenly Rosie shivered, and it wasn't from the cold night air.

Chapter 12

Early November sunshine lit up the little parlour with its bright new wallpaper and gleaming white paint. It fell on the rose-patterned rug in front of the fireplace and twinkled amongst the brass ornaments on the mantelshelf. Rosie gave a deep sigh of contentment.

She drew down the lace-edged paper blind to keep out the sunlight, but even in the darkened room saw it all as before, the picture lovingly imprinted on her mind. The savings tin was empty and she'd persuaded her father to let her have a small club from the tally-man, but it was well worth it all.

In October when she'd shown Arthur the wallpaper she'd bought, he'd said, 'I wouldn't bother with decorating just yet, Rosie, I've promised the party that they can use the parlour as a local committee room for the council elections in November.'

Rosie had just stared at him. Committee room, what did he mean?

'But Dada—' she began to protest.

'I'm sorry, love, I've promised now. A few weeks and it will all be over.'

The next day he'd brought home two big posters with pictures of Mr Joseph Rogers, the socialist candidate. Pushing back the curtains at the parlour window, he'd said, 'Nip outside, love, and see if I'm putting them straight, there's a good girl.' He'd brushed aside her protests, and when the pamphlets began to arrive and the table and floor were littered with election material, Rosie, Ernie and the other boys were kept busy folding leaflets and addressing envelopes, and then delivering them all over the Roath ward. In the evenings she was expected to sew endless green and white rosettes and to wear one herself.

117

One day Arthur persuaded her to go canvassing. As she closed the gate behind her, her arms full of election leaflets, a huge green and white rosette pinned to the lapel of her coat, Frank was leaving his house.

'Where are you going with that lot, Rosie?' he asked, looking at her quizzically.

'I'm canvassing for Mr Rogers,' she told him. 'Would you like a leaflet, Frank?'

He took it from her and looking down at the bundle of leaflets she was carrying she didn't see that Frank's eyes were twinkling with amusement as he said, 'I'd never have thought of you as a socialist agitator, Rosie.'

The colour flooding her cheeks she replied huffily, 'I'm disappointed at you thinking like that, Frank. At least I'm trying to help the working people.' Frank's mouth opened in surprise as she left him and hurried up the street. He looked after her in despair. All these months patiently waiting for the right moment to settle things between them and he'd only managed to make things worse. Why hadn't he kept his big mouth shut?

Rosie was fuming. Things had been cool between her and Frank for a long time and she knew it was her own attitude that was the real cause of the rift, for, ever since Ada had accused her of encouraging him, she'd deliberately kept her distance, at the same time wishing with all her heart for the days of their warm and uncomplicated friendship.

She had been canvassing for half an hour when she turned into a narrow street of tiny houses and saw a different world even from her own. It was a warm, golden October day and outside many of the doors which opened straight on to the pavement old ladies sat on kitchen chairs. They were dressed in voluminous skirts with shawls about their shoulders and some wore men's flat caps and smoked clay pipes. Their purpose seemed to be to keep an eye on the numerous babies and children that crawled or played on the pavement.

Timidly she approached the first house. The old lady outside gave her a toothless grin and pointing to a poster of Joseph Rogers covering most of the tiny window said, 'For 'im we'll be voting, luv.

You needn't bother to knock round 'ere, solid Labour we are.'
Bending down she picked up a squirming baby and Rosie watched
her enter the little flagstoned passage before she continued her walk
down the street.

The day of the election Dada was angry – an editorial in the
morning paper had urged the electorate to vote anti-socialist; that
was the only way, it told its readers, to prevent the ratepayers'
money from being squandered.

At the start of the day there was much toing and froing at the
committee room and Rosie was kept busy making endless cups of
tea, then the activity faded away like a damp squib. Arthur came
back from canvassing looking dejected.

'It makes me sick,' he said bitterly. 'The apathy of people. They
don't seem to realise that it's in their own interests to vote.'

The next day the newspapers proved him right: less than half the
electorate had voted. Mr W. R. Wills, the Liberal candidate, had
polled 2,130 and Joseph Rogers, Labour, only 874. But there was
brighter news in one part of Cardiff: the three new wards at Ely,
which was quickly becoming a massive council estate, had all been
won for Labour.

Rosie had sighed with relief that the election was over. And the
parlour had been decorated at last.

'Who's dead, our Rosie?' Ernie grinned. 'That blind hasn't been up
for a week.'

'Well, the sun's not really strong but it might fade the new curtains. Are you going out tonight, Ernie?'

'Yes, I'm going to meet a boy who started at our shop yesterday,
but I wish Jan would come home.'

Since the spring Ernie had been going out with a girl from the
next street. Rosie liked Jan, who was shy and pretty. Ernie towered
over her; when she looked up at him the expression in her grey eyes,
fringed with long dark lashes, left no one in any doubt of her love.
Rosie had noticed the glances that passed between them and the
way they held hands. Then a few weeks ago Jan's grandmother had
fallen ill and she'd been sent to London to look after her.

When Ernie left the house Rosie felt a pang of jealousy – he'd taken ages getting ready and looked very smart in his navy blue suit. Now she no longer went out with Frank there was little reason for her to dress up at all.

She was alone in the house; Arthur was at a meeting with Miriam, and Teddy, now ten years old, had taken Albert and David to Band of Hope. She listened to music on the wireless while doing the ironing then sat by the fire and picked up the jersey she was knitting for David. Presently the boys came home and after they'd had supper she went upstairs with David. Although he was now seven, she still read him a story every night and he loved her to sit on the bed, ready as soon as the story was finished to keep her there a little longer by telling her about his day at school.

As she tucked him in he asked wistfully, 'Why doesn't Frank take us out any more, Rosie?'

Knowing how fond he was of Frank she answered carefully, 'I think he has a lot of things to do just now.' Her voice was wistful, too.

The boys in bed, she made herself a cup of tea and picked up the paper. At half past ten she glanced at the clock. Ernie should have been home by now; she knew that Dada would be on the last tram. She'd made another pot of tea and had poured herself a cup when she heard the front door open and took another cup and saucer from the dresser, but no one came through to the kitchen.

Going to the foot of the stairs she called softly, 'Don't you want a cup of tea, Ernie?' There was no reply so she poured one anyway and took it. When she got no answer to her knock she opened the door quietly, afraid of waking Teddy and Albert, asleep behind the flimsy partition Dada had put up.

Ernie, still fully dressed, was sitting on the edge of the bed, his head resting in his hands. He looked up at her, his face ashen in the light from the lamp.

'What's the matter, Ernie?' she whispered, putting the cup of tea on the marble-topped washstand. When he didn't answer she leaned towards him and asked, 'Have you been drinking, Ernie?'

'Leave me alone, Rosie, I've got a bad head, it'll be better in the morning.'

She was about to close the door when he gave a little groan and his head drooped forward again. A sudden fear gripped her – it must be more than a headache to make Ernie behave like this. Supposing he was in trouble with the police? But hastily she rejected this thought; he wouldn't get into trouble, not Ernie. She was letting her imagination run away with her. She'd have a word with him tomorrow.

Next morning Arthur and the boys were up before Ernie and there was no chance to question him. His face was still very pale and he hardly touched his breakfast; mumbling that he was late he took his coat and hurried to the door. When he came home in the evening Ada was there. The tiff they'd had over Frank at the beginning of the year had lasted only a few days but Ada still made cryptic remarks which, for the sake of their friendship, Rosie chose to ignore.

For a while Ernie seemed to be restless and on edge, but as the days passed he was more like himself, spending a lot of time in his room writing to Jan.

Arthur still brought Miriam home occasionally; their relationship seemed to be founded on their mutual interest in politics, and Dada had confided to Rosie that although he enjoyed Miriam's company very much no one could ever take Mama's place in his heart.

One evening at the beginning of December Rosie opened the door to two women, one stout and middle-aged, the other an equally stout and slovenly-looking young girl. The older woman was carrying a suitcase. Rosie looked distastefully at the grubby fawn coat, and at the mottled face and fuzzy faded hair which stuck out from beneath a shapeless velour hat.

'Let us in, miss. We want a word with Ernie Edwards,' the woman demanded rudely.

The girl hung her head. Long greasy hair hid her face, the stained pink coat she wore was faded, almost grey.

Feeling apprehensive, Rosie led the way to the parlour and left them while she went upstairs.

'There's a woman and a girl in the front room, Ernie. They want to talk to you.'

His face paled and he put down the pen and jumped to his feet,

asking anxiously, 'What's she like, Rosie? The girl downstairs?'
When Rosie described her he gripped the doorknob, crying, 'Oh,
my God! Let's get rid of her before Dada comes home.' And he ran
down the stairs and into the front room.

Feeling increasingly perturbed, Rosie returned to the kitchen but
hearing the older woman's voice raised in anger and the younger
one sobbing loudly, she hurried into the parlour.

The girl was sitting in an armchair crying noisily into a grubby
hanky. Ernie's face was very red and his eyes held the expression of
a cornered animal.

The woman turned to Rosie belligerently. 'Telling 'im I was 'e's
got to marry 'er,' she said. 'Going to 'ave a baby she is, our Bella,
an 'er just turned seventeen. It's 'is doin', 'e can't deny it.'

A sick feeling in her stomach and her heart beating fast, Rosie
glanced at Ernie who was shuffling from one foot to the other, his
eyes on the floor.

'Dada will kill you, our Ernie,' she said, instantly regretting her
words as he raised his head and she saw his fear.

'Anyway my father isn't at home,' she told the woman. 'We'll
come round tomorrow and talk about it.'

'You can do that, miss, but I'm not taking 'er with me.'

Rosie suddenly realised the full implication of the suitcase as the
woman left the room and a moment later slammed the door.

There was a stunned silence, then Bella began to cry noisily again.
Rosie looked distastefully at the flabby face now blotched with
tears. Ernie made no movement to comfort her. Rosie couldn't
understand the situation at all – she'd been so sure that he loved
little Jan.

'Can we talk in the kitchen, Rosie?' Ernie held the door open for
her.

'We won't be long, Bella,' she said as Ernie followed her out.

Red with embarrassment she closed the kitchen door behind her,
determined to have this out with him.

Looking at her piteously Ernie asked, 'What am I going to say to
Dada?' When she didn't answer he continued, 'It was that evening I
came in late and you brought me up the tea. Oh, God! I don't know
how I let it happen. I love Jan, Rosie, and I wouldn't let it happen

with her. It must have been the drink. She's Eddie's sister, you know, the boy I went out with that night.'

'You must have known what you were doing,' Rosie said, trying to harden her heart.

'I'd only met him when he'd started work at the shop that morning. He insisted on taking me to his house, then he left me with Bella and went out. I didn't know he was gone until she told me. She kept giving me wine and then she put her arms about me. I felt really embarrassed, but when I got up to leave, the room was going round and I had to sit down. Oh, God! If only I hadn't touched that wine. I don't even like her – she's a slut.'

'Ernie!' Rosie was shocked. 'If she's carrying your child you shouldn't speak of her like that.'

She made tea and took a cup in to Bella, wondering what to do about her. If she had to stay the night Rosie didn't want the parlour all messed up and they hadn't a spare bed. Glancing at the clock she thought, Dada will be home soon.

Ernie came back to the parlour and paced about the room; Rosie'd never seen him like this. When they heard Arthur's footsteps Ernie stood very still, his face grey, and Rosie dug her fingernails into the palms of her hands and braced herself.

Arthur came into the room and seeing the huddled figure in the armchair, asked anxiously, 'What's up, Rosie? What's wrong?'

'Bella's going to have a baby.' Then, as Ernie didn't seem capable of opening his mouth, she added, 'Ernie's baby.'

She saw Arthur's look of surprise, then his anger rose as he lunged towards Ernie, but suddenly he let his arms drop as he looked at his son.

'True is this, boy?' he bellowed.

His eyes still on the floor Ernie answered, 'Yes.'

'You'll have to marry her, then, won't you? How you'll keep a wife God knows, but I'll have no bastards in my family.'

'Where can we live, mister?' Bella had visibly perked up at his words.

'Ernie only earns a pittance.' Dada spat the words. 'He's still an apprentice. You'd better be off home, miss. We can discuss it tomorrow.'

'My mother won't have me home, she brought me here.' Bella lowered her eyes and pointed to the suitcase, but not before Rosie had seen the triumphant expression on her round face.

'She'll have to sleep with you then Rosie.' Dada turned on Ernie, his eyes blazing. 'There's a stupid little fool you are, boy. Not yet seventeen. My God! I feel sick to my stomach.'

Reluctantly Rosie took Bella up to the bedroom and Ernie followed with the suitcase. Later, when she'd made Arthur a light supper, she went up to bed herself, her nostrils twitching at the stale smell pervading the room. Suddenly she knew she couldn't sleep in the same bed as this girl and crept back downstairs to the parlour, taking only a blanket, waking shivering as dawn broke to the sickening realisation of what had happened.

On Ernie's half-day she opened the door to a smiling Jan, hugging a present for him.

'He's – he's not in, Jan,' she faltered, praying she wouldn't have to be the one to explain.

'I couldn't let him know I was coming home. I only made up my mind this morning. Much better my gran is now.'

'Jan,' Rosie broke in, ushering her through to the kitchen, 'I – I'd better tell you something.'

When they were seated side by side on the sofa she began to explain the situation, watching the colour drain from Jan's cheeks and her eyes fill with tears of disbelief.

'Not Ernie,' Jan said, almost to herself. 'Ernie wouldn't go out with another girl—'

'He didn't go out with her,' Rosie cut in. 'Look, Jan, the brother took him home. Oh if only he'd stayed sober, the little fool!'

Suddenly Jan's face crumpled and her shoulders began to heave as she sobbed aloud.

'Oh, don't, don't, Jan,' Rosie cried, putting her arms about her. She wanted to shake Ernie hard for putting her in this position.

When Jan rose to leave, her eyes swollen and red, she said, 'Going back to Gran's I am now. I only came home because of Ernie. Oh, Rosie, how could he?'

Squeezing her hand gently, Rosie thought, if only it was Jan that he had to marry, their problems could soon be overcome. As it was, Ernie's would be a loveless marriage – worse than that even, he positively disliked Bella. The whole business was awful.

When she heard about Ernie's troubles the sympathetic Ada forgot all about her little differences with Rosie. 'Poor boy,' she said. 'You wanta watch that family, girl, artful as a cartload of monkeys they are. I'd be askin' to see a doctor's sustificate if I was 'im.'

Much to Rosie's dismay Dada had said the young couple were to have the parlour as a bed-sitting room when they were married. Despite her distress Rosie could see that there was no other way. But when Ada asked, 'Where they going to live then, Rosie?' there was bitterness in her voice as she replied, 'They'll have to have the parlour – there's no alternative.'

'Oh, Rosie! An' after all you've done.'

Rosie hated having Bella under her feet all the time, and, as the day of the registry-office wedding approached, a new problem had to be overcome: they had no spare bed to put in the parlour.

In the end, Bella's own bed was sent round.

Ada came in to help move the piece of furniture, bringing with her a bar of brown Windsor soap and a saucer of water.

'What's that for, Ada?'

'Well, I 'ope I'm wrong, cariad, but I'm takin' no chances.'

They stood on either side of the bed, the snowy twill sheet hovering over the stained feather mattress. Suddenly Ada grabbed the soap from the water and pounced on the bed, coming up triumphantly with a small creature stuck to the wet tablet.

'Fleas!' she said, giving a little snort. 'I feared as much.' And she pounced again and again, with Rosie looking on in horror.

'Oh no!' she cried in despair. 'Oh Ada, let's get it out of here quickly.'

'I've got a spare bed you can 'ave, Rosie. Let's get this out the back, our Frank can set fire to it.'

Half an hour later Frank and his father brought in a brass bedstead and went back for the mattress. Ada pulled a pretty floral cover over the ticking.

'It'll 'elp keep the mattress clean,' she said, pummelling the feathers forcefully into shape.

'Thank you, Ada, I'm very grateful.' Rosie still hadn't got over the shock of the infested mattress.

'Alive this room would 'ave been if we'd left that bed in 'ere. You'd better persuade that Bella to get in the tub, 'an wash 'er hair in something strong. I'll help you get the bath an' things ready if she'll 'ave one now.'

'Thanks, Ada, but she'll probably make a fuss. How am I going to get her to take a bath if she doesn't want to?'

'She'll 'ave to get in the tub, Rosie, otherwise puttin' the bed clean is a waste of time.'

Ada took up the rag mat and brought the bath from the yard, while Rosie collected the towels and a sheet to drape over the clothes-horse. Then, feeling distinctly apprehensive, she went with Ada to the front room.

Rosie knocked, expecting Bella to open the door. When she called 'Come in' in a surly voice they found her lying on the sofa with the cushions piled behind her head, reading.

'Would you like to have a bath now, Bella, before the boys come back? It's nice and warm in the kitchen and no one will disturb you.'

'I don't want no bath,' Bella answered without raising her eyes from the magazine.

'But you're getting married tomorrow—'

This time she didn't bother to reply and her eyes never left the page.

'You won't have a chance to bath tomorrow before you go to the registry office. If you give me your change of clothes I'll put them on the guard to warm, and your nightdress, too, ready for tonight.'

'I don't wear no nightdress, I sleeps in my vest. And I don't want no bath.' This time she glared at Rosie belligerently.

Ada's temper had been visibly rising throughout this conversation. Suddenly she could contain it no longer. Her face red with anger, she stood over Bella, her finger pointing to the open door.

'Out!' she cried at the astonished girl. 'Out, and get into that kitchen before I drag you there!'

Bella opened her mouth and shut it again before herself pointing to the door and yelling, 'You get out, both of you, this is my room, innit?'

'You goin' to bath yourself?' Ada asked, ignoring this outburst. 'If you are, we'll leave you to it, the towels are warm and everything's ready.'

As Bella turned back to her magazine and picked it up, she was grabbed by a pair of capable hands and propelled towards the kitchen, Rosie following behind.

As soon as Ada let go of her to test if the water was still warm enough Bella dashed for the door, but Ada was too quick of her. Grabbing her by the arm she said, 'Come on, Rosie, get 'er clothes off.'

Between them they managed to strip her of an assortment of grubby under-garments, right down to an even grubbier vest. Lowering Bella's grossly overweight body into the bath wasn't easy – she struggled fiercely, sending water flying in all directions, hissing and spitting on the hot range and splashing the fender and floor. She continued to thrash about until the coconut matting was soaked through, but Ada, apparently unperturbed, soaped the flannel generously with carbolic soap and rubbed it hard over every part of Bella's anatomy she could reach.

'You bugger! I'll 'ave you for this,' Bella screamed, but Ada just went on applying more soap, then rinsed her thoroughly.

When at last the girl stood upright in front of the glowing fire, the big bath towel about her, Rosie remembered the change of clothes.

'Where are your things, Bella? Shall I fetch them?'

'You'll blutty well afto, I can't go in there like this.'

On opening the case Rosie was relieved to see the things she needed were at the top; the clothes had a greyish tinge but had obviously had some contact at some time with soap and water.

Bella had stopped struggling now and seemed to be enjoying the warmth of the fire as she dressed. Ada emptied the bath and brought fresh water ready to wash her hair.

'You make us a cup of tea, Rosie,' she said. 'I think Bella deserves one now, don't you?' Mollified by the unexpected praise, Bella bent her head obligingly. There was a hint of colour in the pudgy cheeks as Rosie towelled her hair. While it was drying she sat by the fire drinking two cups of tea and eating half a dozen biscuits, then she got up without a word and, leaving the dirty washing where it was in a heap on the floor, went back to the parlour and slammed the door.

Ada had gone home to fetch Bella a nightdress; she brought one in blue winceyette patterned with faded roses, and as she shook out its folds the room was filled with the sweet scent of lavender.

'You won't make yourself short, will you, Ada?' Rosie asked worriedly. Ada had found so much that they needed for Bella, including the bed.

'No, cariad. I treated myself to some new ones. I can spare another if she needs it.'

Rosie put her arms about Ada and kissed her warmly, saying, 'Thank you! Thank you for everything. I'd never have got Bella to bath on my own. I think she enjoyed it in the end.'

'She's a lazy article, Rosie. God 'elp Ernie if she don't pull 'er finger out. She's real flabby, isn't she? She wants to lose some of that 'cos it's not the baby yet with 'er only two or three months gone.'

The next day, while Bella and Ernie were at the registry office with their witnesses, Rosie prepared a small wedding reception. She'd made a cake and iced it, and Ada had lent the decorations from her youngest daughter's wedding cake. Rosie cut dainty sandwiches and brought Mama's lace doylies from their tissue paper – but there was no joy in her efforts.

The papers had been full of the story of the new King and Mrs Wallis Warfield Simpson, the American woman he was in love with. Then on December the tenth King Edward VIII abdicated. The following evening he made a farewell speech on the wireless. He'd got no further than, 'I have found it impossible to carry the heavy burden of responsibility without the help and support of the woman I love—' when Arthur switched the set off in disgust.

But the nation's troubles hardly touched Rosie – she had more than enough problems of her own. Money was very short, the boys always seemed to need something and Ernie's money being insufficient to keep him and his wife, Arthur had decided they should live rent-free – and that went for coal and light as well. Now Rosie had to find more and more money for the meter, for as the days grew darker Bella kept the light on all day.

Rosie was glad when Christmas and New Year were over for although she'd tried to make festive preparations she'd found little pleasure in the celebrations.

As the months went by she grew more and more frustrated. Bella insisted on doing what little cooking she did on her own fire instead of sharing the range or using the gas cooker in the wash-house. The smell of cabbage water from the parlour pervaded the house for days. Most of the time Ernie was at work Bella spent lying on the bed reading love stories. She was putting on weight rapidly, her arms and legs wobbling with fat when she walked.

The boys didn't like Bella, especially as she was forever sending them on errands to the Co-op stores during their school lunch break. By the time they were served and got home there was hardly time for their meal. Inwardly fuming, Rosie didn't want to encourage them to be rude, but the problem solved itself for they soon became adept at disappearing whenever Bella called from her doorway.

David and Teddy wouldn't go near her since the day they'd dashed into the parlour to retrieve a balloon. She'd lumbered towards them, her hands outstretched menacingly. Teddy had run out, but she'd caught David, shaken him violently and pushed him through the doorway, crying, 'Bugger off, you little sod, an' give me some peace for a change.' Slamming the parlour door, she'd turned the key.

Rosie hadn't witnessed her shaking David but she'd heard her outburst, and seeing his frightened face she felt hot with anger. Putting her arms around him and cwtching him to her, she said, 'Tell me what happened, David.' She had to know the truth if she was to tackle Bella when they'd gone back to school.

Sitting up, he wiped his eyes with the back of his hand. 'Me and

Teddy went into the front room to get our balloon. She – she told me to bugger off, she shook me hard, Rosie.'

Deeply shocked by Bella's action and his repeating the swearword, she said sharply, 'You're never to repeat that word again and you're not to go into the parlour unless you've been invited.'

'I don't want to go in there, Rosie, the room smells, an' she smells.' He held his small nose then wrinkled it in disgust.

It was late afternoon by the time she was able to confront Bella. 'Look here,' she began, 'you'd better mind your language,' but the parlour door was slammed in her face. She wouldn't complain about the girl to Ernie, though – poor Ernie had more than his share to put up with as it was.

It was March the first, St David's Day, a blustery morning of bright sunshine and sudden showers. At breakfast the boys were excited because after the celebrations at school there would be a half-day holiday. Pinning leeks on to their jerseys Rosie remembered how Mama used to tint one of her cotton dresses yellow with a Dolly dye for St David's Day and Dada had cut daffodils from the garden to pin on the bodice.

When she went to the door to see the boys off, a little girl was passing, wearing a tall Welsh hat trimmed with lace beneath the brim, a black and white triangular shawl draped over her white blouse. Rosie had always loved the celebrations, the little plays enacted by every class, and the rafters in the school assembly hall ringing to the Welsh National Anthem, *'Mae Hen Wlad Fy Nhad-au'* – 'The Land of My Fathers'.

Waving the green paper flags emblazoned with the red dragons, flags they'd made at school, and filled with patriotic pride that would last the rest of the day, their voices would swell as one:

> *'Mae hen wlad fy nhad-au yn an nwyl i-mi,*
> *Gwlad beirdd a chan-tor-ion en wogian o fri*
> *Ei gwr-ol ry fel wyr, gwlad gar-wyr tra-mad*
> *Tros rydd-id coll-as-ant eu gwaed.*
> *Gwlad! Gwlad! . . .'*

On and on it went, its rich cadences fervent and strong.

She hummed the anthem softly, thinking the words in the English she was more used to.

> The land of my fathers is dear unto me,
> Old land where the minstrels are honoured and free.
> It's war-ring de-fen-ders so gallant and brave,
> For freedom their life's blood they gave.
> Home! Home! . . .

Oh, and the year she'd been in Miss Davies's class! – she remembered that well, for the teacher had brought in a tall Welsh wicker basket, the handle tied with yellow ribbon bows, and when she'd removed the snowy white cloth the basket had been filled with generous pieces of Teison-lap, one for each child. Rosie's mouth watered when she recalled how delicious that cake had tasted.

A glance at the clock brought her out of her reverie – the boys would be home from school earlier today and she had to wash dishes and go for groceries.

When she arrived at the Co-op Ernie was serving a customer and she thought how miserable he looked. He saw her and smiled, but the smile didn't reach his eyes and pity welled up in her.

Back home she opened the front door and was passing the parlour when Bella called her. Surprised at this apparent courtesy, she went in and found Bella doubled up on the bed, her face twisted with pain. Frightened now, Rosie hurried to her side, telling herself it couldn't be the baby, not yet.

'I fell over the mat in the passage,' Bella gasped.

'But you're only six months – I'd better send for the midwife.' Rosie was worried.

'I 'aven't bothered to see 'er yet.'

Thankfully Rosie heard the boys arrive and hurried out to meet them. As Albert and David waved their flags at her she saw that their leeks were definitely the worse for wear. Sending Teddy for the midwife she took the other two next door to Ada's.

'When will we have the new baby, Rosie?' Albert asked, and David said, 'We'll be its uncles but she won't let us mind it, you'll see.'

Ada came to the door and Rosie was glad to hand them over without answering Albert's question.

'Frank's passing the Co-op on his way back to work. Shall he give Ernie a message, Rosie?'

'Thanks. I'd better get back.'

As she turned in at the gate she saw the plump figure of the midwife approaching on her bicycle and gave a sigh of relief.

Waiting anxiously while the midwife examined Bella, she couldn't help feeling ashamed at the state of the room and the stale smell. If Bella loses the baby, Ernie's tied to her for nothing, and then berated herself for her bad thoughts.

By the time he arrived Bella was in hospital, for the midwife, murmuring something about the position of the baby and Bella's blood pressure, had sent for the doctor and he'd quickly called an ambulance.

After Ernie had hurried off to the hospital the hours passed slowly. Rosie got out the baby clothes David had worn last, and the new garments she and Grandma Hughes had knitted, and put them on the end of the fireguard, but six-month babies didn't usually live, did they?

Teddy had taken the other two boys to the shops in Clifton Street. After the ambulance left with Bella they'd come back from Ada's full of questions about the baby that she couldn't yet answer. She went into the parlour to tidy up but the mess was too much for her, a thick layer of dust over everything. Rosie promised herself that she'd clean it up when she knew what was happening. She was longing for, yet dreading, Ernie's return.

When he did come home it was very late. She rushed to the door crying, 'How is she, Ernie? What about the baby – will it be all right?'

She wasn't prepared for the bitterness of his tone as he answered, his voice loud with anger, 'The baby's fine, Rosie. An eight-and-a-half-pound boy, a full-term child they said – and I only met the scheming bitch six months ago!'

'Oh Ernie!'

'It must have been all arranged,' he went on bitterly. 'Her brother took me there that night and cleared off, leaving us alone. My God, Rosie, I swear she'll not come back here.'

His eyes blazing he went into the parlour, and Rosie stood in the doorway with a thumping heart as she watched him drag Bella's suitcase from behind the sofa and cram her things into it. He rushed past her with the case.

'Where are you going?' she cried.

He looked back over his shoulder, saying. 'Her mother dumped this and her on us, Rosie. I'm going to dump them back.'

Long after he'd gone she stood in the parlour trying to take it all in. What a mess! Poor Ernie was married to Bella now, and even if they didn't live together he wouldn't find it easy to get out of that.

Chapter 13

A week it was since Ernie had taken Bella's belongings back to her mother, a week Rosie would never forget. Neighbours turned their backs as she approached, little David came home from school with a black eye and a bloody nose, and Bella's mother knocked on the door at all hours, yelling her grievances to anyone who would listen.

'Expected I am is it to blutty well keep 'er an' the babba,' she'd yelled only that morning for everyone in the street to hear.

'Daro, woman! Go home,' Arthur had replied angrily. 'And just be thankful your grandson's got a name. Wasn't that what your daughter wanted when she played that dirty trick on my son?'

'I didn't know at the time, mister, 'onest I didn't.'

'Well, you know now! I don't blame my son – why should he father another man's child? What she did was despicable. Despicable!' Arthur spat the last word in his fury.

Bella's mother, retreating as far as the gate, asked, ' 'Ow about 'er bed? I 'eard you burnt it.'

Slamming the door, Arthur went into the kitchen, and Rosie watched sadly as he lowered himself into the wooden armchair and cupped his head in his hands.

'I'm so glad your mother hasn't had the shame of all this.' He sighed deeply.

Later, on her way to the shops, Rosie had to pass some gossiping neighbours. They eyed her coldly as she approached.

'Just look at Miss Hoity-Toity there, thinks 'erself better'n the likes of us, she does.' Lizzie James, known in the street as a trouble-maker, leaned over her gate, her skinny arms wound tightly in a rough sacking apron.

Blushing scarlet, her heart pounding, Rosie walked past. The other two women lowered their gaze, but she could feel Lizzie's spiteful eyes boring into her, and although there were only two more houses and the side window of the shop to pass, the corner seemed a long way away.

Suddenly she was a child again back in the school yard and Rhona James, Lizzie's eldest, was yelling, 'My mam says your mam's a toffee-nosed bitch', and poking out her tongue. Searching vainly for a hurtful retort the young Rosie had cried, 'And your mam must be lazy 'cos she never scrubs her patch.'

She managed to smile now at the memory. Her words must have had about as much effect as a damp squib, but the respectable women of Wesley Street were still judged by the arms-reach patch of scrubbed pavement outside their front gate. Some would rather leave the kitchen floor unscrubbed than that sacred patch whose degree of whiteness proclaimed their virtue as a housewife, and soda-reddened hands were a small price to pay for the measure of respectability a clean doorstep conferred on a household. Lizzie James had never even tried to be respectable and now even she looked down on the Edwards family.

Soon after Rosie returned home, Ada came in. Seeing the girl was upset she said, 'Somebody been bothering you again, luv?'

'I used to think the neighbours were my friends, Ada.'

'So they are, most of them, but it's only 'uman nature, Rosie. Youer family's always been too respectable for Lizzie James, green with envy she is. There's never any debt collectors at youer door. When youer mam was alive, bless 'er, youer dad never gave 'er a black eye, did 'e *chwara teg*? Now when Lizzie's old man's 'ad a few drinks, she's lucky if she can see out of one of hers.'

Rosie poured the tea as Ada went on, 'Bella's mother's stirring things up she is, an' that Lizzie's fanning the flames. They're tellin' everyone how you burnt the bed an' she 'as to sleep on the floor.'

'But, Ada, you know it was full of fleas,' Rosie protested indignantly.

When Ernie came home from work and heard they'd had another visit from his mother-in-law, he looked grim.

'I'm going round to have it out with them, Rosie, they're not going to upset you and Dada.'

'It won't do any good, Ernie. She wants money and you won't earn enough until you're eighteen.'

'Well, I can't live with her, Rosie. It makes me feel sick just to think of it,' he said, putting on his jacket.

When he returned, his face white and strained, the younger boys were at the table doing their homework. Without telling her what had happened Ernie went straight to bed.

'What's wrong, Rosie? When is Bella coming home with the baby?' David looked up at her expectantly, and the other two stopped writing and waited for her reply. She looked at David tenderly – he'd have to be a lot older before he could understand the situation.

'Bella won't be very strong yet. She's going to stay with her mother for a while.' She hated telling him a lie, but David seemed satisfied and went back to his books.

Later, when she went to her room, sleep wouldn't come. She tossed and turned, her mind going over the events of the day.

Presently she heard a door open, then the creak of the stairs as someone crept down. Pulling on her dressing gown she lit the candle and went downstairs, but reaching the kitchen door the sound she heard made her shiver. Pushing it open, she saw Ernie at the table, his head buried in his arms, great sobs shaking his body.

Watching his heaving shoulders she realised the full extent of his suffering. Her first instinct was to creep away – he wouldn't want her to see him like this – but she couldn't: he was her brother and she loved him. When she touched him on the shoulder gently, he raised his head and stared at her, and although his eyes were almost dry they looked drowned in sorrow.

Rosie sat beside him and cradled him to her, stroking his hair as though he was still a child, and presently he grew calmer. Pulling himself away he sat up and took her hand.

'I'm sorry, Rosie, I didn't think anyone was awake. It's just that I saw Jan tonight on my way home. I've never stopped loving her, you know. I've made her so unhappy and there's nothing I can do about it.'

Seeing Ernie's distress, Rosie was shocked to find herself wishing with all her heart that Bella was dead. To shake off her unwelcome thoughts she went to the range. Raking the glowing coals into life she said,' I'll make you a cup of tea, Ernie. You didn't have any supper.'

The task of putting out the cups and saucers and fetching the milk and sugar was comforting, and when she'd poured the tea and cut Ernie some bread and butter he took the cup in his hands and drank gratefully. Then putting down the cup he looked at her, saying, 'Rosie, I want you to know how grateful I am. I know all you've had to put up with from her, and never once have you complained to me about anything.'

'Oh Ernie! You're my brother. Why did this have to happen to someone like you? What will you do now?'

He gave a deep sigh and shook his head.

When he'd finished the tea she persuaded him to go to bed. Unready for sleep herself, Rosie washed the dishes and put them on the dresser.

Back in the bedroom she tossed and turned once more, watching as the darkness lightened and a pink and grey dawn streaked the sky. She must have dozed, for the alarm startled her into sudden wakefulness, and, with a feeling of foreboding, she recalled the events of the night.

Pulling back the curtains in the kitchen Rosie saw the note propped against the tin tea-caddy.

Very sorry for all the trouble I've caused. I'm going away to look for a better job, then I can send money to Bella, for although she tricked me she is my wife and I should keep her. Hope you'll be left in peace now. Will let you know when I have an address.

Love,
Ernie

Dada was very distressed. When another letter came, still without an address, the envelope had a Swansea postmark. In his note Ernie assured them that he was all right, and that he hoped to find a job very soon.

Arthur went to Swansea and made inquiries at the Labour
Exchange and some of the small boarding houses. He tramped the
streets for hours but found nothing to tell him of his son's where-
abouts. A few days later a letter came telling them that Ernie was
going to sea – he would have sailed by the time they read the note.

Once more the neighbours got hold of the wrong end of the stick.
Now they said that Ernie had run away from his responsibilities.

To take her mind off things, Rosie tackled the parlour. Bella had
burnt a hole right through the pretty rug in front of the fireplace,
and the wallpaper was covered with greasy finger marks. Rosie
sponged the walls and furniture with a cloth wrung out in hot soapy
water but it only made the stains worse.

Papering once more, this time with a cheap wallpaper which she
soon found creased and bubbled, and replacing the rug with one
from her own bedroom which once had been her pride and joy, she
viewed the room in despair. She sighed deeply. When would things
look up for the Edwards family? Surely they'd had more than their
share of sadness and it was their turn for some luck and laughter –
and love.

Towards the end of April David rushed into the house crying
eagerly, 'Rosie, we're all going to have sixpence, a present and a bag
of losins on Coronation Day.'

Looking down at his glowing face she hated to shatter his
happiness.

David,' she said gently, 'you know there's been a lot of trouble in
the street over Ernie? Well, no one has called to collect our money,
so you won't be going to the party.'

'But it can't be too late yet, Rosie. I'll take the money to Mrs
Roberts, she's doing the collecting—'

'I'm sorry, love. Look, we'll go somewhere nice instead.'

Dejectedly David trailed upstairs to his bedroom and Rosie's
heart went with him. Over the last month she'd become increasingly
aware of all the toing and froing in the street as collections were
made and raffle tickets sold, dreading the day when she'd have to
tell the boys they wouldn't be going to the Coronation party.

Suddenly she remembered a day about five weeks ago when, still

139

smarting from some remark of Lizzie James's, she hadn't opened the door to Mrs Roberts and her friends. They'd knocked several times, then, twitching the lace curtains in the front room for a better view, she'd seen them close the gate. Mattie Roberts had held a notebook in her hand, Rosie remembered now. They must have called for the collection.

Albert and Teddy weren't so easily put off as David. They pleaded incessantly. 'Rosie, just go and see Mrs Roberts. She's all right, honest she is. She always gives us biscuits when we call for their Dennis.'

She knew for the boys' sakes she would have to swallow her pride but first she would have a word with Ada.

They were decorating the streets now as they had for King George V's Jubilee less than two years ago. Everyone had been so friendly then, so concerned for Bron when she'd fallen down the steps; it was hard to believe that it was the same street and the very same neighbours. With the bad feeling towards her family over Ernie's affairs she found herself dreading the celebrations.

When Rosie mentioned the boys' disappointment to her neighbour, Ada turned puce. 'You'll probably be annoyed, cariad, it was done on the spur of the moment when Mattie Roberts said she didn't like to knock your door again because of the trouble.'

'What was done, Ada?'

'Well, it was Frank really. 'E was there, an' 'e said it was a shame to disappoint the boys, an' – well, 'e paid for them to go.'

'You mean that without asking me—?'

'Don't take on, Rosie, 'e meant well,' Ada said worriedly.

'I'll see that they thank him properly when he comes home,' she said, feeling mean and ashamed of her own treatment of Frank when he was always so generous.

'You seen Bella's babba, Rosie?' Ada asked, eager to change the subject.

Rosie nodded. She had seen them several times. He was a podgy child, a miniature Bella, and noticing the state of him and of the pram, she'd been thankful they weren't living at her house. She'd last seen them only a few days ago when she'd almost walked into the pram as she came out of the Penny Bazaar. She'd been consumed with anger as she came face to face with the cause of all their misfortunes, but the abhorrence of scenes in the street which Mama had taught her kept her silent as Bella said, her voice filled with self-pity, 'You tell your Ernie when you write to 'im that I gorrw 'ave some money.' And Rosie had replied icily, 'He'll send you some as soon as he can. That's why he's gone away.'

' 'E 'asn't given me anything towards keepin' 'im.' Bella glanced down at the baby. ' 'E's still my 'usband, you know.'

Rosie had been about to let her temper fly and tell Bella exactly what she thought of her when Lizzie James bore down on the pram, showing her long teeth in a grimace as she cried, 'Who's a luvly boy then?' at which the baby, obviously frightened by the apparition, began to scream. Lizzie straightened up and shouted to Bella, 'A crying shame it is that 'is dada don't want 'im, poor little babba.'

'You both know perfectly well that it isn't our Ernie's baby,' Rosie cried, but they'd completely ignored her angry retort and moved away, both pushing the pram, their heads close together, their voices raised in mutual grievance.

When the boys came home and she'd told them about Frank paying for them to go to the party, they rushed next door, excited and happy, to thank him, and Rosie consulted the tin savings box where she still put away spare coppers for a rainy day. When they returned in boisterous mood, she said, smiling at them, 'Go and get yourselves washed. We're going to Clifton Street.'

'Aw, Rosie!' they cried. 'Have we got to?'

'No,' she said, 'you haven't got to, that's if you can run races in those boots. I was going to buy you black daps.'

She laughed as they stampeded to the wash-house, falling over each other in their eagerness to be on their way. When they returned from the shops they hardly raised their eyes for the rest of the evening as they admired the shiny toecaps of the new black plimsolls.

On a Wednesday afternoon in June, Rosie was about to bring the washing in from the back garden when Dada went to answer a knock at the front door. Fearing it might be trouble again, in the shape of Bella's mother, she hung about in the wash-house with the door slightly ajar.

A minute later she heard Grandma Hughes. 'I'm glad I've caught you alone, Arthur. I want to talk to you about Rose.'

'Well, don't take too long because she's only getting the washing in.'

Why, oh why, hadn't they got on like this when Mama was alive?

'Look, Arthur, I've only got Rose's welfare at heart. We don't want her to end up an old maid, do we? Not that she's likely to, of course, our Rose is a real beauty, but – well, she doesn't seem to have any social life at all since she stopped going out with the Jenkins boy.'

'Funny that,' Dada mused. 'Always together they were—'

Poor Frank, Rosie thought, if only she could have fallen in love with him, but being fond of him just wasn't enough. Besides, she was in love with someone else now. Someone, she had to admit sadly, who didn't seem to know that she existed . . . Feeling guilty about eavesdropping, she was about to enter the kitchen when Grandma spoke again.

'What I'm trying to tell you, Arthur, is that while other girls her age are playing tennis or going to the cinema, Rose is at home getting the evening meal and seeing to the boys.'

'What can I do?' Dada asked. 'You know I'd do anything for Rosie.'

Making a big to-do of closing the wash-house door as though coming in from the garden, Rosie stepped into the kitchen. Hugging Grandma, she kissed her affectionately on the cheek, then moved the kettle to the hottest part of the range and set out cups and saucers and a plate of freshly made scones.

'Is there anyone you'd like to bring to Vi's party next month, Rosie? All her student friends will be there.'

'No, Grandma,' she replied, knowing full well that there was, the thought of him making her heart beat fast and hot colour stain her cheeks.

Quickly turning to the fire and pouring boiling water into the pot, her thoughts were with the new librarian she'd seen for the first time only three weeks before. He'd looked up at her after stamping her books and the moment she'd gazed into those warm brown eyes – like dark, soft velvet, she'd thought afterwards – she'd experienced a wonderful heady feeling.

He'd handed her the books and as their fingers touched she'd felt a thrill of pleasure. Then, with a brief smile, he'd turned to attend to someone else.

She'd turned at the door to look towards him, her emotions still in turmoil. She'd stood there irresolutely, unable to leave, but he didn't look up. Disappointed, she pulled herself together, opened the door and left.

The following week Arthur had wanted a book by George Bernard Shaw, and she'd approached the desk with a fluttering heart, glad of the excuse that she couldn't find the volume she wanted on the shelves. He'd gone with her and glanced along them, saying after a few minutes, 'I'm sorry, it must be out. Shall I keep it for you when it's returned? I'll just take your name.'

Rosie had thanked him, vainly trying to think of something to say to keep him talking. Her mouth was dry and her heart beating so loudly she was sure he could hear . . .

'How about the young man next door, Rose?' Grandma's question brought her thoughts abruptly back to the present. What had they been talking about? Of course, Vi's party.

'I don't think Frank would want to come, Grandma,' she replied, and not wishing to discuss it further she changed the subject.

As they talked over the tea and scones an overwhelming desire to see the young man at the library came over Rosie. When Grandma got up and put on her coat, she picked up a book to return, even though she hadn't finished it, and they walked up the street together.

He wasn't at the desk in the library, and she was filled with disappointment, but a few minutes later he appeared from the back room with the book Arthur had wanted and she felt the dreaded blush suffuse her cheeks once more.

'Have you read any of Arnold Bennett's novels, Miss Edwards?'

She shook her head, wishing that she had as he went on, 'He's my favourite author, I think I've read nearly everything he's written.'

Suddenly, more than anything, she wanted to read them too. He

143

went to the shelves and came back with *Clayhanger*. She took it gratefully, hanging on his every word as he told her, 'I was hoping to find you *The Old Wives' Tale* but it isn't there. This book is the first of a trilogy: *Clayhanger, Hilda Lessways* and *These Twain*.'

Just then the other librarian called, 'Roy, could you come here a minute?' With an apologetic smile he hurried back to the counter and disappeared into the little back room.

Rosie hung around, staring blindly at the shelves. When after ten minutes he hadn't returned, she swallowed her disappointment and took her books to the counter to be stamped. At least she knew his name now, she comforted herself, and hurried home to *Clayhanger* and thoughts of Roy.

She returned the book and was halfway through *Hilda Lessways* and still did not see him to tell him how much she was enjoying the novels.

Soon Vi's party was less than a fortnight away and she wasn't really looking forward to going. Since her cousin had been at college she had a new, sophisticated set of friends and Rosie felt that she'd be like a fish out of water among them.

The weather was very unseasonable for, although the sun shone, there was a stiff breeze more reminiscent of March than early July. Rosie hurried to finish reading *Hilda Lessways* so that she'd have an excuse to visit the library during the afternoon. To her intense disappointment Roy was once more nowhere to be seen. She had been going to ask if he'd kept *These Twain* for her as he'd promised to do when it was returned, but decided not to ask the other librarian but to keep the inquiry as an excuse to speak to Roy when she saw him.

She hung about the library, but after half an hour there was still no sign of him. Perhaps it was his day off – she hoped he wasn't ill. Anyway she was glad he didn't know how she felt about him. He obviously didn't return her feelings, and if he guessed, she would never be able to show her face in the library again.

She had reached the corner of Clifton Street and was turning into Broadway, her hair blowing across her face in the breeze, when she heard footsteps pounding behind her. Turning quickly she saw Roy running towards her, his jacket billowing out behind him, holding a book in his hand. Glancing down quickly to make sure the books she had borrowed were in her shopping bag and finding they were, she looked up into the dark brown eyes laughing into hers, noting with approval the dark, silky brows, the straight, neat nose and firm chin. Her heart beat fast and new hope kindled as he said breathlessly, 'I was cataloguing the books, I just saw you leaving – you forgot to ask Trevor for *These Twain*.'

So that was why he'd run after her. Feeling sick to her stomach, all hope gone, she followed him back to the library to get the book stamped. They were almost there when he suddenly stopped and turned to her. 'Look – Miss Edwards – Rose' – he smiled at her, then licked his lips— 'Would you come out with me on Saturday? It's my half-day.'

Overjoyed, her heart thumping, her mind already working on how she'd manage about the children, she said quickly, before he misinterpreted her silence, 'Yes, I'd like to but it would have to be in the afternoon.' Teddy could take the other two to Splott Cinema. Teddy was eleven now, they'd be all right.

'Is there someone else?' Roy asked dejectedly.

'It isn't that,' she said, pushing back the hair that would blow across her face. He drew her into the library entrance out of the wind as she told him, 'I look after my young brothers. I have to be at home in the evenings when my father's not there. He's going to a meeting Saturday evening.'

They continued into the library and Roy stamped her book before saying, 'Shall I call for you at your house? Will two o'clock be all right?'

She would have much preferred for them to meet somewhere else this first time, but they were attracting curious eyes as a queue formed with books to be stamped. 'Yes,' she said, 'that will be fine. You know the address?'

'Yes. See you then.' He smiled at her as he picked up a book to be stamped.

On Saturday at one thirty Arthur was finishing his lunch before going back to work and the boys had left for the cinema clutching their threepences. Rosie took a jug of hot water to her room and poured it into the flowered bowl on the washstand and proceeded to wash herself carefully.

Slipping a pretty pink frock over her head, she was standing in front of the swing mirror to comb her hair when there was a knock on the front door. As she heard her father go through to open it panic gripped her.

Please God, don't let him take Roy into that awful front room! she prayed silently, clutching her hands until the knuckles showed white. With a sigh of relief she heard them go down the passageway to the kitchen.

When a few minutes later she opened the door they were talking easily together while Arthur made preparations to leave.

They decided as they walked up the street to take a tram to Rumney Hill. As they approached Lizzie James's house Rosie looked anxiously towards it, but there wasn't even a twitch of the curtains.

'Slow down, Rose, we're not running a race,' Roy said, laughing at her, and sighing with relief she fell into step beside him.

Leaving the tram they strolled down Ball Lane and over the bridge to Morgan's tea-gardens, then after tea and cakes they walked on to St Edeyrn's Church and back through the leafy lanes to Llanrumney. The hedgerows were bright with wild flowers, the fields full of ripening corn.

Climbing over a stile he took her hand to steady her, then slipping his arm around her waist pulled her close, and they walked like this until they reached the main road once more and approached the tram stop.

Half an hour later they were turning into Wesley Street. When she saw Lizzie James at her gate, Rosie, filled with misgiving, looked anxiously at Roy, but it was too late to go back.

'Well!' said Lizzie to no one in particular as they passed her. 'If it isn't Lady Muck 'erself, an' it's 'er own brother what lets 'is poor wife starve and sleep on the floor, isn't it?'

'It isn't true, Roy,' Rosie told him, her heart hammering, 'I can explain – she's always making remarks.'

'Is this lady annoying you, Rose?' he asked, striding up to Lizzie. 'Would you care to repeat what you've just said to a police officer, madam? I'm sure it could be arranged – I believe the charge would be harassment. In fact I'll ask my brother. He's a superintendent.'

Lizzie's long face fell. She gazed open-mouthed first at Roy then at Rosie.

'I didn't mean no 'arm, mister—'

'One more word and they'll be round to see you.'

Lizzie retreated into the house and shut the door.

Rosie looked at Roy in wonder. 'Is your brother really a police superintendent?'

'No. He's an accountant and lives in London.'

They both laughed, then Rosie became serious.

'I'd like to explain everything, Roy.'

'There's no need, really.'

'But I want to very much, only we're nearly home.'

'Let's go to the library then. We can go into the staff room and I'll make a cup of tea.'

At the library Roy told his colleague that he wanted to show Rosie some books. Taking several from the shelves they went into the little room and closed the door.

As he put the kettle on the gas ring and set out the cups, Rosie began to tell him about Ernie and Bella, and why her brother had gone away. When at last she looked up Roy's brown eyes were warm with sympathy and understanding, and she read something else there that made her heart leap with joy.

When once more they turned into the street, Lizzie James glared at them balefully from her doorway.

'Please, Roy, don't say anything if she calls after us.'

'She'd better not, Rose,' he replied with a smile. 'If she does I shall have to invent an uncle who's Chief Constable at least.'

They began to laugh and were still laughing when they reached the house.

Chapter 14

Half an hour later Roy was leaving to go home. As he kissed her goodbye at the door he said, 'How about tomorrow, Rose? It's Sunday, so I've got the whole day.'

'I'm sorry, Roy, but tomorrow we're going to visit my brothers at Llandarron, the two I told you about who are living with my grandmother in the valleys.'

'Well how about Monday evening? I could meet you straight from work.'

'Yes, that would be fine.' Dada wouldn't be home until gone seven, but Teddy was quite capable of looking after David for an hour. 'I was thinking, Roy, if the weather is like today we could go to the lake.'

On the Monday evening, dressed in a frock of lupin-blue crepe-de-Chine, a cardigan of matching colour over her arm, she met Roy outside the library and they walked to City Road to get a tram to Roath Park. When it came clanging to a stop, they climbed the twisting stairs to the open deck on top and sitting side by side on the slatted wooden seat enjoyed the slight but welcome breeze.

At the lake the promenade was crowded with people strolling in the evening sunshine. The musicians in the bandstand on the green were playing a medley of waltzes, and it was all she could do to stop her feet tapping out the tune. As they stood watching the rowing boats passing to and fro children on the bank shouted happily to the already overfed ducks who gobbled the bread the youngsters threw them.

Just then a pleasure boat passed on its way to the little landing stage, the bright colours worn by the women and children heightened by the evening sun. All the boats would soon be called in for the day so they decided to join the small queue waiting for the last trip.

'I'll take you rowing next time Rose,' Roy promised. 'Pity it's too late this evening.'

When the boat had come in and it was their turn to board Roy got on and held her hand as she stepped on to the wooden seat that ran all around the inside, then jumped down to the boards below. When they were all seated and the boat was nosing its way out into the lake, she leaned over to watch the green water slip-slapping against its side. Roy's arm was about her protectively and she felt an almost overwhelming desire to bury her face in the rough tweed of his jacket.

It was dark as he walked her home from the tram stop and there was no one about as, just before they reached Wesley Street, he stopped and kissed her gently. Then, as she answered his kisses, he drew her into the shadow of a shop doorway and his lips came down hard on hers and his body strained against her, but almost at once he pulled away, and taking her face in both his hands he kissed her gently once more.

'I'm sorry, Rose – I had no right. It's too soon, I know, I just meant to kiss you goodnight.'

Her heart beat fast with happiness. He loved her! This wonderful young man she was head over heels in love with, loved her, too!

'When can I see you again, Rose?'

It was then she remembered Vi's party and Grandma asking if there was anyone she'd like to bring. But when she told Roy about it he said doubtfully, 'But I wouldn't know anyone—'

'Neither will I except for my cousin Vi. Most of the guests will be her friends from the university. I don't know any of them.'

'All right then,' he said, 'we'll be company for each other. But can't I see you before then?'

They decided on Thursday evening but as it was one of her father's late nights at the shop she couldn't meet him until eight thirty at the earliest, for she'd never left the boys alone for long in the evenings. Roy had intended to take her for a spin in his car but it was hardly worth it for so short a time, so they decided they'd just walk round for an hour.

150

'Until Thursday, love,' he said. 'I'd better go now, my mother will be on her own.'

Her eyes bright with happiness, she listened to his firm footsteps retreating down the street. He'd called her love! Lots of people in Cardiff used the word as a pleasantry, even to strangers, but she was certain Roy would use it only as an endearment.

He'd told her about his family, that his mother was a widow, and his only brother was married and living in London, and that his mother often went to stay with him and his wife. From what Roy had told her she gathered that his mother led quite a busy social life.

They didn't have long together on Thursday evening because Roy had to fetch his mother from a friend's house where she was playing bridge. Rosie had felt uncomfortable about her evening off, for Miriam had accompanied her father home from work and from the way she was dressed had obviously been expecting to go out, too. But Miriam hadn't seemed to mind; she was a generous soul and thought the world of the boys. Rosie knew now that her first impression of her had been wrong. When she said that she hadn't realised they'd intended to go out, Miriam had replied quickly, 'You run along, cariad. It's time Rosie had some fun, isn't it, Arthur? I'm quite happy to stay here with your dad.'

Now she was looking forward to Vi's party and to introducing Roy to her grandmother, Aunty Mabel, Uncle Ted and Vi. She'd already decided to wear the emerald-green dress with the wrap-over bodice. She'd had it for a long time, but she was still as slim as when Bron had made it for her, and Frank had once remarked that the colour brought out the red-gold tints in her dark chestnut hair.

Thinking of Frank made her sad, for she knew Ada was deeply troubled about him; he rarely went anywhere now except to work, preferring to spend the evenings with the gramophone and his pile of records. Rosie couldn't help feeling guilty whenever Ada mourned to her about it, knowing that however innocently it had come about, she was to blame.

'Rosie! Roy! Come in and meet everyone.' Vi greeted them at the front door. Behind her, party guests spilled out into the hall. Snatches of conversation and giggles floated out to them, vying with a rendering by a male singer of 'Lovely Lady' on the gramophone, which no one seemed to be listening to.

Rosie introduced Roy to her relatives, though Uncle Ted had decided to be out for the evening, and was satisfied at their obvious approval. Then Vi called, 'Come on, you two, and meet everyone!'

'This is my cousin Rose,' Vi began as soon as they reached the first group. 'And this is Roy, her young man.' Rosie blushed scarlet at this introduction, but Roy looked pleased as Vi went on, 'These are my friends. This is Vera, Dulcie, Joan, Gloria—' She went on from group to group, and Rosie soon felt exhausted with the effort of fitting names to faces. Then Vi introduced her latest boyfriend, a tall, thin young man with a shock of fair hair and a serious expression in the light blue eyes behind heavy tortoiseshell spectacles. His name was Lennard and she remembered Vi telling her that he was a very brainy student, a leader in the Communist movement in college, and that he hoped one day to get into Parliament.

A long trestle table along one wall of the dining room groaned under the weight of a delicious-looking buffet. Filling their plates, Rosie and Roy went over to some chairs against the other long wall to eat the chicken and mushroom vol-au-vents and little sausages. Grandma and Mabel were kept busy in the kitchen filling cups with coffee and tea, and there were bowls of punch and trays of glasses laid out in the dining room.

'He seems a nice boy, Rose's friend,' Grandma said to her daughter. 'Why couldn't Vi have picked up with a smart, well-mannered boy like that?'

Mabel, used to her mother's directness, refused to be upset. 'Now, Mother, Lennard's quite a nice boy really, just a bit of a rough diamond, that's all, and you know how Vi gets wrapped up in causes, but they never last.'

In the dining room a few people were beginning to dance in the middle of the room. Vi came across.

'Come on, you two.' She dragged Rosie to her feet. Mabel was at the piano now playing a slow waltz and Rosie's nervousness soon disappeared as Roy guided her through the steps. There were only about half a dozen young men, obviously boyfriends of some of the girls; all the other girls were dancing together. As more and more people joined the dancers it became something of a bumps-a-daisy and, laughing, Roy and Rosie left the floor and sat down.

When the party had thinned out and they had chatted a while with Grandma, they got their coats from the hall, gave their thanks for the party, said their goodbyes, and went out to Roy's car.

Seated beside him in the little Morris Rosie felt like pinching herself to see if it wasn't all a dream, but when he asked, 'Can I see you tomorrow, Rose?' and put his arm about her and kissed her, she knew that it wasn't.

'I could meet you in the afternoon,' she told him happily, knowing that Dada and Miriam were planning to go to a meeting on Sunday after tea.

Chapter 15

'Mother wants to meet you, Rose. She wondered if you'd come to supper tomorrow evening?'

It was a warm September afternoon and they were rowing on the lake at Roath Park. Despite the sunny day, Rosie shivered. She'd been longing for, yet dreading, this invitation. Would Mrs Cunningham approve of her?

Roy's mother had recently been on a visit to London. Just before they'd met this afternoon, Roy had picked her up at the station and taken her home.

'Mother loves London,' he was saying now. 'My brother and his wife take her to a lot of plays and concerts there. I think I must be a big disappointment to her. She says I have no ambition.'

Rosie smiled. She couldn't imagine him being a disappointment to anyone.

Everyone at home had cooperated these past months, making sure she had free time in which to enjoy herself. Sometimes she felt guilty that Miriam and her father stayed at home with the boys instead of going to the Labour Hall. When Rosie had voiced her misgivings Miriam had hugged her warmly, saying, 'It's no hardship, love. I'm very fond of the boys. We just want you to be happy.'

Rosie still felt ashamed when she remembered how wrong her first impression of Miriam had been.

The following evening, as they approached Roy's home in a smart modern suburb off the busy Newport Road, Rosie marvelled at the wide, tree-lined avenue, and the large colourful gardens in front of the semi-detached houses.

As he fumbled for his key in the tiled porch of the Laurels, she was admiring the colourful sunrise depicted in the stained-glass door when it opened suddenly and Mrs Cunningham stood there.

Elegance! That was Rosie's first impression of Roy's mother. Her beautifully waved hair was softened by tiny pin-curls, and the pale blue twin-set in fine lamb's wool was enhanced by a double row of glowing pearls. There was an air of expensive simplicity about her.

'I've heard such a lot about you. I thought we'd better get acquainted, Rose,' Mrs Cunningham said, taking the girl's coat. But there was no welcoming smile on her face. Rosie's lips trembled nervously and she bit them.

The wide hall was decorated in restful shades; blue-grey for the thick carpet, and gleaming white walls. In contrast the lounge was a warm beige with frilled chair covers and curtains in dainty floral linen. Two table lamps, their shades held aloft by slim green goddesses standing on tiptoe, cast a soft apricot glow through pleated satin shades.

As Rosie sat awkwardly on the edge of an easy chair and accepted a small sherry, the talk was of London.

'One is never bored there,' Mrs Cunningham was saying. 'Alun and his wife certainly know how to entertain. If only Roy was more like his brother, but he's such an old stick-in-the-mud.' She sighed deeply.

For a while the talk was of the films and plays she'd seen on her visits, then, putting some glossy magazines on a low table, and refusing Rosie's shy offer of help, she went to the kitchen.

'Better see if I can do anything,' Roy said, dropping a kiss on to Rosie's head and giving her an encouraging hug.

Alone in the room Rosie looked about her in admiration: at the wide tiled fireplace displaying dainty porcelain figures on either side of a handsome gilt clock, and at the beautiful walnut china cabinet with its pretty, fine china tea service decorated with pink rosebuds and edged with gold.

Suddenly she heard raised voices coming from the kitchen. 'You're very ungrateful, Roy.'

'But, Mother, you promised it would be something simple. Just a family supper.'

'I've worked very hard to please you. I do think you could show a little appreciation.' Mrs Cunningham's hard-done-by voice was full of self-pity.

'I'm sorry, Mother.' Roy's tone was conciliatory now.

A few minutes later, entering the dining room, Rosie thought she understood why Roy's mother had gone to such trouble. The table was laid as if for a small banquet. An astonishing array of shining silver cutlery and cut-crystal glass glittered on the snowy damask cloth. It looked ostentatious, and she didn't think for one minute that Roy and his mother usually ate in such style. Had this display been put on in the hope of embarrassing her?

As Roy pulled back her chair Rosie smiled to herself, thankful that all those years ago Mama had insisted she learn how to set a table.

As the meal progressed she picked up the appropriate cutlery for each course with assurance. And once, glancing up quickly, she caught the look of surprise on Mrs Cunningham's face.

Coffee was served in the sitting room as they turned the pages of an old photo album. Roy's mother smiled reminiscently as she pointed proudly to various snaps of her sons. Roy in his pram, Roy in a sailor suit. Alun in his school uniform: saying, 'There's Alun holding the cup his team won. Have I told you that Alun and his wife entertain a lot? They have help, of course, but she's a wonderful cook. Alun has just had a big promotion – he's always made the most of his opportunities.'

At last it was time for Roy to take Rosie home. There was no repeat of the invitation and she sensed the lack of warmth in Mrs Cunningham's goodbye. Surely their mutual love for Roy should have brought them together? She had hoped for so much.

The cold feeling of disappointment persisted as she sat in the car, closing her eyes tightly and swallowing a painful lump in her throat. Roy got in beside her, and suddenly his arms were about her, his warm lips gentle on hers.

'It wasn't so bad, was it, love?' he asked, grinning at her, and she realised that he hadn't even noticed his mother's coolness.

When she didn't answer, he pulled her to him again, his arms gradually tightening about her, his lips gently forcing hers apart.

At first she didn't respond, but soon her lips were answering his, the upset forgotten. They clung together, his mouth hard on hers until with a shuddering sigh he released her, and taking her face in his hands, he said, 'Oh Rose! You know how I feel about you. I know we've only known each other a few months, but I wish we could be married soon.'

'I love you very much, Roy. I wish we could be married, too, but I can't leave Dada and the boys, not yet.'

The noise he made sounded like a groan, but before she could put her arms about him to comfort him he'd got out to crank the car.

As Roy drove through the wide gates and along the road they were silent, and she felt alarmed because she couldn't think of anything to say to make him happy again. If only she could have told him, truthfully, 'I'm sure we won't have to wait very long.'

As they turned into Wesley Street, Roy said cheerily as though there hadn't been that painful silence, 'We'll have to think of something, Rose. I don't expect to be married right away but it will be years before your brothers can manage without you.'

That night she dreamed that, dressed in her wedding gown, she sat beside Dada in a taxi bedecked with white ribbons, and the scent of pink carnations from her bouquet filled the cab. As they approached the church she was surprised to see Roy standing on the steps. Why wasn't he inside waiting for her?

Gathering speed the taxi flew past him. Faster and faster it went, swerving and swaying, throwing her about the cab – and Dada wasn't there any more! Terrified she began to scream, 'Roy! Roy!'

Someone was holding her tightly. Trembling with fear she opened her eyes and looked up into her father's concerned face.

'Rosie love, you've been shouting in your sleep. Are you all right?'

Clinging to him she looked round the familiar bedroom, then pulling herself up in the bed she managed a wobbly smile.

'I must have had a nightmare, Dada.'

'You used to sleep like a baby. Do you feel all right?'

'It was just a bad dream,' she told him, smiling reassuringly.

*   *   *

Early in October Roy asked if they could get engaged at Christmas. Taking her in his arms, his brown eyes intent upon her, he said, 'I know we can't get married for a while, Rose, but we'd be promised to each other, and that's something.'

'Oh, Roy, I'd love that. The boys are growing up. Perhaps it won't be so long to wait.'

So just before Christmas an announcement appeared in the *South Wales Echo* under the heading ENGAGEMENTS. It said:

The engagement is announced between Rose, only daughter of Mr Arthur Edwards and the late Mrs Laura Edwards of Roath, Cardiff, and Roy, second son of Mrs Elizabeth Cunningham, and the late Mr Lionel Cunningham, also of Roath.

The same day Grandma Hughes was giving a party for the occasion and during the evening Roy would put the engagement ring on Rosie's finger. He'd measured her ring size weeks before, and ever since then she'd been rubbing her hands with a snowfire block to make sure her hands were soft, white and smooth, ready for the moment when he slipped it on.

She had bought a new dress for the occasion, a pale blue silk with a cross-over bodice, very like the style of the green one she had liked so much, and the assistant at David Morgan's had assured her that it was very flattering.

That evening as she dressed for the party all her problems were forgotten. She tied back her long curly chestnut hair with a matching blue chiffon scarf and made it into a wide bow, then slipped on the dainty, pale blue satin court shoes she'd bought to go with the dress. Her eyes were bright and her cheeks pink with excitement as she looked at herself in the cheval mirror, twisting round to see the skirt twirl about her. Suddenly the memory of another party day saddened her as she remembered herself as a rosy-cheeked child wearing the pink dress of Vi's that Aunty Mabel had given her. She'd twirled the skirt then in just the same way, in front of this very mirror, and only a few minutes later she'd been running for Dr Thomas and the midwife, and soon afterwards her mother had died giving birth to David. She took the lace-edged lawn hanky she'd put ready on top of the chest of drawers and wiped her eyes.

'Oh Mama!' she whispered. 'I know you must be happy for me tonight. I know you'd have loved Roy.'

There was the sound of knocking on the front door and she dabbed her eyes quickly once more. She mustn't be sad tonight. Mama would want her to be happy, she knew that. Hearing Roy's voice as he went through to the kitchen, she hurried downstairs, watching his eyes light up as she stepped into the room carrying an embroidered cashmere shawl that had been Mama's to put about her shoulders.

They left the house with Arthur and Miriam, who was staying with the boys, came to the door to see them off, but first Dada called at the Jenkinses, and collected Ada.

All the Jenkins family had been invited, but Bert had said he'd feel like a fish out of water, and no amount of persuasion could get him to change his mind. Frank had gone to spend the night with a friend who lived in Tonypandy. Rosie suspected that he'd arranged the visit purposely, but she understood how he must feel.

As Roy drew the car out from the kerb and they waved again to Miriam, Rosie said, 'It's good of Miriam to stay. She was invited but she suggested it herself rather than get one of the neighbours in. I know you offered, Ada, but I was determined you would come after all you've done for me.'

'I only did what anyone would do,' Ada said modestly, 'but that Miriam's got an 'eart of gold and no mistake.' Arthur beamed with pleasure.

When they arrived at Grandma's lights were blazing from every room. Electricity had been installed in most of the houses in Cardiff for years now, replacing the mellow gaslight, and, as they got out of the car, lights from the lounge and hall streamed down the path, welcoming them in.

The furniture in the dining room had been moved against three of the walls. The whole of the other wall was taken up by long trestle tables draped in white tablecloths, on which was laid a delicious-looking buffet, just as there had been at Vi's party.

Rosie looked around her appreciatively. How she loved this house – it held so many happy memories for her.

True to herself and despite their protests, Ada spent most of her time helping in the kitchen, or carrying trays of drinks. She and Bert had bought a damask tablecloth and napkin set for Rosie's bottom drawer, and Frank had sent a present he'd made himself, a rosewood tray inlaid, under glass, with roses in lighter woods. It was beautifully made, obviously with loving care, and like the jewel chest, must have taken Frank hours of detailed craftsmanship. They're the sort of presents a man would make for the woman he loves, Rosie thought uneasily, but shook off the thought. They'd long ago put all that boy-and-girl nonsense behind them. They were good loving friends now. Nothing more.

The pile of presents in the hall grew with every knock on the door. Grandma had given them a beautiful bone china tea set, and Aunty Mabel and Vi a set of thick towels, embossed with satin flowers, half a dozen of them, from bath towels to guest. She'd received money from Dada to buy sheets and pillow cases, Miriam had made her two dressing-table sets in hand-crocheted lace, and from Roy's mother came a dozen silver Apostle tea spoons in a leather case lined with dark blue velvet – she couldn't imagine disturbing the lovely things from their nest.

Rosie couldn't help being excited about the presents – she'd never had things showered on her like this before – but seeing them stacked on the long table in the hall brought home to her that it might be a very long time before they could be put to use.

The boys were expected from Llandarron at any minute, but Nana Edwards was unable to come because she was looking after Bron who, to everyone's delight, especially Sid's, had just given birth to a baby daughter.

Rosie hadn't seen Bobby and Willie for several months. When they came in, their arms full of presents, she felt proud of them. Willie was now fifteen and Bobby thirteen, and they looked so smart in their grammar-school blazers, worn with spotless white shirts and obviously new grey trousers. And they looked so like Ernie that she was immediately reminded of him. Poor Ernie, she hadn't seen him since that night in early March when he'd left home and gone to sea.

He was sending money regularly now to Bella, though in his letters to Dada and the family he said she never acknowledged receiving it. But as she'd stopped complaining to all and sundry she must have done.

When all the guests had arrived and everyone had had a glass of champagne, except of course the boys who had lemonade, Mabel went over to the piano and began playing 'Love Is the Sweetest Thing', and all eyes were on Roy and Rosie as he took her hand in his and with everyone raising their glasses in a toast slipped the ring from its velvet bed and on to her finger.

Rosie looked down at her hand in wonder. Under the chandelier the half-hoop of diamonds scintillated, and glowed with a myriad of colours. She looked up at Roy proudly; he looked so handsome in his new dark blue suit, and yet with his neat features and fresh colouring so boyish, too. The glasses were raised again and again. 'To Rosie and Roy, and their future happiness.'

Roy's mother came across to congratulate them, too, making all the right noises and kissing Rosie on the cheek, but the thin lips were cold against her skin and the expression in the pale blue eyes lacked any warmth, belying her fulsome words.

Mabel finished playing 'Love Is the Sweetest Thing' and began 'If You Were the Only Girl in the World', and Ada came and stood by her and began to sing. When she'd sung the lyrics through once with her rich voice, she asked everyone to join in, which they did with gusto.

Rosie saw her father with Grandma and Mrs Cunningham, all laughing together – Dada looked so happy, and younger than he'd looked for ages in his best grey suit, his still dark, curly hair smoothed down with brilliantine.

Roy's mother had stayed close to Grandma Hughes ever since she had arrived, and several times Rosie had overheard her making flattering remarks to Grandma about her house and furnishings. Mrs Cunningham was obviously impressed with part of her family at least.

*   *   *

Now on Sunday afternoons they went window-shopping round the closed stores, choosing dining-room furniture, a bedroom and a lounge suite, china, glass, pots and pans, laughing together as they frequently changed their minds about what they would select when the time came.

But as the months went by the laughter faded; the strain and frustration of being engaged but still having to wait indefinitely to marry began to tell.

Rosie tried hard not to show her resentment as she went about the daily chores, but when she and Roy were in each other's arms, desperately telling each other that it wouldn't be long now, nothing else seemed as important as Roy's happiness.

One Sunday in March they decided to walk to town. The cutting wind of the day before had gone, and it was a bright, early spring day, so when they reached City Road they walked along it until they came to the Roath Furnishing Company, where in the front of the window, set out on a beige carpet, was a dark brown three-piece suite in real hide with boxed velvet cushions. The price was nineteen guineas.

'We don't want to give as much as that, I know,' Rosie began, 'but it's beautiful, isn't it?'

'I suppose it would wear much better than Rexine,' Roy said thoughtfully. 'Perhaps it's worth the extra money.'

When they reached Queen Street, they stopped at Cavendishe's window where there was a Rexine suite at twelve and a half guineas.

'That doesn't look nearly as good, Rose, I think the hide suite would be better value, don't you?'

She agreed, then pointed to a heavy oak dining-room suite in the same window.

'That's good for seven and a half guineas, Roy. Oh, look at that bedroom set! It says figured walnut, isn't it lovely? I like the triple mirrors on the dressing table.'

They moved on to Campbell's where Rosie fell in love with a tapestry three-piece suite with walnut facings on the front of the chairs and settee.

'That looks really comfortable, doesn't it—?' she began.

'Oh, what's the use?' Roy cut in bitterly. 'I'm tired of this game,

163

Rose. How can you choose furniture if you don't know where you're going to put it. This stuff will all be old-fashioned by the time we're able to marry.'

When she insisted on saying goodbye at the corner of Clifton Street, Roy being worried about getting home in time to drive his mother to her friend, the Mayor's house, Rosie's spirits were low. Roy looked so unhappy.

He kissed her quickly and hurried away, his shoulders drooping dejectedly. She couldn't bear it, there seemed to be no solution to their problem. She remembered Dada saying that no one could ever take Mama's place, and that he and Miriam were just good friends. How relieved she'd been about that at the time.

Rosie walked aimlessly down Clifton Street. Not wanting to go home, she stared unseeing into the shop windows. Roy was right. What was the use of the silly game they played? The furniture would probably be out of date by the time they were able to marry. As she walked her resentment grew. Other girls could please themselves – Vi, it seemed, had no responsibilities at all.

Finding herself in Goldberg's doorway between the high plate-glass windows, memories of the happy years she'd spent there came flooding back. She thought of the day Mr Goldberg had offered her promotion to manageress of the Young Ladies' Department, the very day that she'd had to give in her notice to stay at home and look after the boys, and her resentment grew even stronger.

Arthur and Miriam were going to a meeting tonight, but still Rosie dawdled, lost in thought. Supposing Roy met someone else? Immediately she felt guilty for doubting him. How could she, even for a moment?

Suddenly, remembering how good Miriam had been about staying with the boys, she felt mean to be keeping them waiting and, with a heavy heart, Rosie made her way home.

Chapter 16

When she arrived home Miriam and Arthur were dressed ready to go out. If they noticed her mood they said nothing.

Teddy and Albert were outside, knocking a ball against the wash-house wall. Thump! Thump! Thump! It seemed to keep rhythm with the pain in her head. She screamed at them to get indoors and they stared at her open-mouthed, surprise making them do as they were told. Teddy was twelve now, his deep blue eyes and straight fair hair favouring Mama's side of the family. Albert, although the younger by eighteen months, towered over him. Big-boned, with dark eyes and dark curly hair, his cheeks were bright with colour.

David was sitting at the table reading and didn't even look up. Nothing could disturb David when he had his nose in a book. Tall for his nine years, his hair had remained almost silver fair. Rosie looked at him tenderly; if only the other two were as easy-going.

'Can we go out, Rosie?' Albert recovered enough to ask.

'No!'

'But why not?'

'You know Dada won't let you play in the street on a Sunday.'

'Other kids play on Sundays.'

'Well, you're not to.'

'Tisn't fair! Can we go out the back again?'

'Yes, if you don't thump a ball.'

'But there's nothing else to do!'

Grumbling, they opened the door to the yard and Rosie went back to her own thoughts. When next she looked they had chalked squares on the path and were kicking a stone into them in their Sunday boots, but she left them to it.

If only she could see Roy again tonight – their parting hadn't been very happy. She longed to be with him, but knew she mustn't begrudge his escorting his mother occasionally. Tonight was one of her bridge evenings.

Feeling restless, she went over and over in her mind the events of the afternoon. Was Roy getting tired of waiting?

To make up to the boys she cut them extra-large slices of sponge cake and poured them some herb beer. They seemed happy enough and soon went back to their game.

By ten o'clock all three of them were in bed; she'd tidy the kitchen and put the kettle to boil ready for Arthur's and Miriam's return.

She was very quiet when they came in. When Arthur went upstairs to put away his best suit, Miriam asked, 'What's wrong, Rosie?' She was sitting on the sofa, and patting the cushion beside her added, 'Come by here, cariad, and tell me what's troubling you.'

'Nothing's wrong.'

'Oh, come on, now, you've got a face like a fiddle. Is it anything I've done?'

'No, of course not.'

'Rosie, is it your engagement? I mean having to wait so long?'

A tear rolled down Rosie's cheek followed closely by another. Suddenly Miriam's arms were about her, cwtching her, her fingers gently smoothing back the springy curls.

'Tell me what's wrong, love. If it's what I think, then there's an easy solution.'

Sitting up and drying her eyes Rosie stared hopefully at Miriam. 'If it's the boy, love – well, your dad and me would like to get married, only we thought you'd be upset—. You see, Rosie, no one can ever take your mother's place, but, well, we're good for each other and we are in love.'

'You want to get married, Miriam?'

'Of course we do, Rosie, and settle down here and look after the boys. Don't you see, love, it's the solution to all our problems?'

Then they were hugging each other and laughing and Rosie could hardly believe she'd ever resented the very idea. When Arthur came into the room, his look of surprise turned to a happy smile when they explained.

The glasses came out, together with a bottle of Ada's parsnip wine, and when they'd toasted each other and the excitement had begun to die down Rosie wished fervently that she could run to Roy's house and tell him the wonderful news, but he wouldn't be there. It would have to wait for tomorrow.

When her father took Miriam to the tram stop, Rosie felt too excited to sit still. Putting the flat-irons on top of the range and the basket of ironing on the table, her thoughts raced ahead to the time when she could tell Roy the news.

Later, she folded away the ironing blanket and hung the clothes over the kitchen line to air, then picked up the paper and looked through the advertisements for bedroom furniture, three-piece suites and dining tables, seeing them with new eyes.

Turning a page, she read about the German army marching unopposed into Austria. In January when Hitler had appointed himself 'Commander of all the armed forces of the Reich', Arthur had commented that Hitler would never be satisfied with that, he wasn't amassing troops for nothing.

The way Miriam and her father talked there could be a war. Rosie's happiness clouded as she thought about Roy. Supposing he had to go away? She couldn't bear it. They had to have a little happiness together first – something to remember.

What was she thinking of? Why should Germany marching into Austria mean war for Britain? Yet, only this morning Arthur had said that Hitler had his eyes on a part of Czechoslovakia where three million German people lived.

Hearing her father close the front door she put away the paper. They had things to discuss; he and Miriam would have been making plans.

Next morning she went early to the library. There were no borrowers and as Roy came across to meet her she said, eyes dancing, 'Guess what? Dada and Miriam are getting married. They're going to live in our house.'

'Rose, does that mean—?'

She nodded. 'Yes, love, it means we can be married.'

Giving a shout of joy he hugged her tightly, lifting her off her feet.

That evening they began their search for somewhere to live. Two months later, after wandering miles around bedrooms, bathrooms, living rooms and sculleries they still hadn't found what they wanted.

The houses they saw were too big or too expensive, too small or too old. Both were determined that the house they eventually picked would be the perfect one. They sensed that the decision they made now was crucial to their future happiness.

Then in late August they were told about the bungalow. It was Roy's colleague who saw the 'For Sale' notice on his way to work.

They went to see it in Roy's lunch hour. As the car chugged along the quiet suburban road, Rosie's eyes widened in delight. The freshly painted white bungalow gleamed in the sunshine, its green lawns bordered with colourful flowers, edged with blue lobelia and frilly white alyssum.

'Oh Roy!'

Excitedly they walked up the flagged path and he raised the heavy brass knocker. In a dream they wandered with the owner around the small dining room, kitchen, lounge, the two bedrooms and bathroom. It was perfect down to the name: 'Shangri-la'.

Through the kitchen window the vegetable garden was green with crisp lettuce, runner beans and peas, and the feathery heads of carrots.

The asking price was three hundred and ninety-five pounds. Roy whispered that he thought they could manage it if they could get a long mortgage.

'We'll get a surveyor to look it over,' he said as they walked towards the car.

'When will they be moving out?'

'If all's well we should be able to move in in a couple of months, love.'

Back at the library they arranged to meet that evening. 'I'll call for you about eight thirty, Rose. Mother won't be there when I get home. We'll break the news to her later.'

'She does know we're looking for a house?'

'Yes, I told her ages ago.'

Why did she have misgivings over Mrs Cunningham's likely reaction? Roy was over twenty-one. He was a free agent, wasn't he? Rosie asked herself anxiously.

That evening they decided to walk towards town, and call back at Roy's home about ten o'clock by which time his mother would have returned.

When they reached the closed shops they played their old game of choosing furniture for their future home with renewed interest now they could picture it in the rooms of the bungalow. Wandering from shop to shop the time flew, until looking at his watch Roy exclaimed, 'We'd better take a tram, Rose, it's nearly half past nine.'

It began to rain; the big spots turned to a downpour before they reached the shelter of a doorway.

'Happy, Rose?'

'You know I am. It's wonderful, isn't it? Everything!'

'Supposing there's a war. How would you feel about being alone in the house?'

His mention of war disturbed her more than she would admit. But there may never be a war, she told herself.

'Let's be happy while we can,' she replied, laying her head against his shoulder.

His lips came down hard on hers as he pulled her to him. They clung together in the darkness of the doorway, the tram forgotten, then his arms slackened and his lips left hers to explore her eyes, her cheeks, her hair, as he murmured endearments.

'Oh, Rose, Rose! I can't believe it. We'll soon be married. We'll soon be living in the bungalow. We'll be so happy.'

She sealed his lips with hers once more and trembled with the ecstasy of being close.

Five minutes later as they walked along to the tram stop, she asked, 'Won't your mother be lonely without you?'

He laughed. 'I shouldn't think so, she's never at home anyway. Mother has lots of friends.'

Despite this reassurance, her misgivings grew. Roy seemed very casual about keeping his mother informed. How would Mrs Cunningham react to him leaving home?

His mother was surprised to see them, and even more surprised when Roy told her about the bungalow they'd decided on.

'How much are they asking?'

'Three hundred and ninety-five. It's grand, Mother, only ten years old.'

'You haven't paid a deposit, Roy?' Her voice seemed anxious.

'Not yet, we have to get a surveyor in. You must see it. It's got—'

'I'm glad you haven't paid a deposit,' she cut in quickly, 'because I've a proposal to make.'

Rosie watched her apprehensively, feeling a coldness in the pit of her stomach as Mrs Cunningham went on. 'Major Evans was saying tonight that it looks as though there will be a war, something to do with Hitler and Czechoslovakia. He says there's already talk of issuing gas-masks, and the provision of air-raid shelters.'

'But what was the proposal, Mother?'

'Well, if there is a war your Aunt Evelyn has asked me to stay with her in the country. She's very lonely now that she's on her own.'

'But, Mother, there may not be a war.'

'In which case I shall take up Alun's offer of converting part of his house into a flat for me. With you married there'll be nothing to tie me here.'

'That's fine. A good idea. You won't have to worry about me. I hope that Rose and I will be living in the bungalow—'

Quickly she cut in again. 'You don't understand, Roy. I'm making you both an offer to live in this house. There will only be the rates to pay, and it will save you a great deal of expense on furniture and things.'

There was a long pause, then Roy asked, 'What do you think, Rose?'

Rosie looked at him in horror. The fact that he was asking her, rather than simply saying no, meant he was seriously considering it.

'But we've committed ourselves. We've told them we'll have the bungalow.' She was clutching at straws.

'Nothing's definite, love, not until we've paid a deposit.'

Rosie couldn't believe her ears. 'But we won't find a lovely bungalow like that again,' she cried desperately.

'What Major Evans said has made me think, Rose. Perhaps it isn't wise to take on a mortgage if there's going to be a war. Mother's offer is worth considering. We could think of buying a house when she returned home.'

Trying hard to hide her terrible disappointment Rosie murmured her thanks to Mrs Cunningham, saying she'd talk it over with Roy when they were alone. He couldn't possibly have meant what he said. Why, he'd loved that bungalow!

As they walked to the car, she said hopefully, 'What do you really want to do? I know you had to seem grateful to your mother.'

His reply sent her spirits plummeting.

'We'd be alone, Rose, that's what matters. You'll come to love the house as I do, and more importantly, if I have to go away the money will still be in the bank. I wouldn't be leaving you with a mortgage to pay and no savings.'

'But, Roy—' she began desperately.

'Let's think about it and decide tomorrow, Rose.' But she knew in her heart that he'd already made up his mind.

Was it only this afternoon they'd walked round the bungalow, hardly able to believe their luck? She saw it now as clearly as she had walking up the path between the scented borders, and her lips trembled.

Full of the pain of bitter disappointment, she got into the front seat. Struggling to keep control of herself, she marvelled that Roy could act as though nothing of importance had happened.

Chapter 17

'How did it go, love? What did Roy's mother think of the bungalow?'

Laughter from the kitchen had greeted her as she'd opened the front door. Now as Arthur asked the question he and Miriam looked at her expectantly.

'We – we mightn't have it now, Dada.' She couldn't bring herself to say they definitely wouldn't be having it. 'Mrs Cunningham has offered us her house for a while.'

They looked at her in surprise. 'But why, Rosie? What's changed your minds?' Miriam asked.

When she explained Mrs Cunningham's fears, Arthur admitted, 'She's right. Hitler wants Bohemia, and if he gets it he won't stop there.' And Miriam nodded her agreement.

'She says she's going to stay with her sister in the country,' Rosie explained, 'and if there isn't a war she's been offered a flat in Alun's house in London.'

'Perhaps it won't be for long, love. You and Roy can buy a place when things settle down,' her father said soothingly.

'But we'll never find another bungalow like that one,' she wailed.

'What does Roy say about it?' Miriam was shrugging on her coat.

'He seems to think it's a good idea to live at The Laurels. He says if there is a war then he doesn't want to leave me with a mortgage to pay and no money in the bank.'

Arthur nodded approvingly. 'Sensible lad. How would you pay a mortgage on army pay?'

When they'd gone out Rosie went upstairs and flung herself on the bed, engulfed in self-pity. In one short day her hopes had been raised and happiness had soared. Now she just couldn't come to terms with the bitter and unexpected disappointment which followed.

Hugging the pillow and burying her face in its cool depths, she rocked to and fro in an agony of doubt. Had Roy really let her down, or had he only been thinking of her welfare, as Dada had said?

She slept badly and next morning was on tenterhooks wondering if Roy had told the owners of the bungalow that he'd changed his mind. She couldn't bring herself to go and find out; for a while, at least, she could still hope.

By midday the suspense could be borne no longer. That afternoon, she decided, when her father had gone back to work, she'd go to the library.

Upstairs, Rosie draped her prettiest frock over the end of the bed and took her favourite white buckskin court shoes from the wardrobe. As soon as they'd had their meal, she'd get ready.

When they'd finished the meal and her father was leaving for work, Rosie followed him to the door.

'There's some dung from the baker's horse in the road,' he called back to her as he reached the gate. 'Get one of the boys to shovel it up right away, will you, love?'

She nodded. The bucket kept for the purpose was behind the cucumber frame. She called to the boys to bring it and the shovel out to the street.

'Albert,' she said when they brought them. 'Dada says to pick up the manure from the street right away.'

'It's Teddy's turn, our Rosie!'

'One of you will have to do it.'

'It's Albert's turn. I did it Saturday.'

'I did it twice before, our Teddy.'

They argued back and forth. It was getting late. The dirty dishes were still on the table, and the pots in the sink. She must have time to wash and get ready to go to the library.

Pushing the boys aside and yelling, 'Go on to school, you'll both stay in for this tonight!' she grabbed the bucket and shovel and dashed out into the road herself.

Those boys really are the limit, she fumed. Bending, shovel

poised, she didn't see the car coming down the street until it drew into the kerb. Then, with sinking heart, she saw Roy get out and go round to open the other door, and watched with growing horror as Mrs Cunningham gracefully emerged, dressed in a pale grey costume. They hadn't seen her. Wildly she looked around for somewhere to hide as they took the few steps up the path to knock on the open front door.

Her thoughts raced ahead to the table full of dirty dishes, and she groaned. So many times she'd planned for the day Elizabeth Cunningham would finally pay them a visit, and pictured the kitchen with the grate blackleaded until you could see your face, brass ornaments twinkling on the mantelshelf, the snowy damask cloth laid with the best china and cutlery.

'Rose!' Roy had seen her. She saw his mother's lips come together in a thin line of disapproval. Then, noticing the look of amusement in Roy's eyes as he came towards her, her cheeks flamed with embarrassment.

'Why didn't you tell me you were bringing her?' she hissed under her breath.

'I didn't know, honestly. Mother came to meet me at the library and insisted I bring her here.'

Dumping the bucket and shovel in the gutter she took them in, and leading them through to the kitchen she hurried into the wash-house.

Drying herself on the rough roller towel, her thoughts were in turmoil. Roy's mother would be looking round now in disgust, at the cluttered table and the clothes airing on the line strung across the kitchen, staring at Dada's long-johns and the patched sheets.

Rosie took off her wrap-over pinny and smoothed down her faded cotton dress, thinking longingly of the frock laid ready on the bed upstairs.

Mrs Cunningham refused tea with the excuse that she was going to Cheltenham later in the afternoon to stay with a friend for a few days. She was in a hurry to go home but wanted Rosie's answer to her offer.

Rosie longed to express her misgivings, her bitter disappointment about the bungalow. She wanted to talk to Roy alone, to ask if he'd definitely turned it down.

His mother was getting impatient. 'Well, Rose?'

175

'We can't marry until the banns have been called. There are lots of arrangements to make.'

'Rose! I'm only asking what you intend to do about my offer.' Mrs Cunningham's voice was sharp.

Rosie looked at Roy's anxious face and suddenly her resistance crumbled. 'Have you definitely refused the bungalow, Roy?'

He nodded. 'It was only fair, love. Someone else was interested.'

As Rosie struggled to suppress her disappointment Mrs Cunningham said, 'You and Roy can live rent-free, you need only pay the rates.'

When Rosie still didn't answer Mrs Cunningham picked up her gloves and began pulling them on. 'Can I take it that you've made up your mind then?'

Rosie nodded, murmuring thanks she didn't feel, and they all moved towards the door.

When Roy and his mother had gone she felt angry with him and with herself. Why had she given in so easily? Hadn't she vowed to put up a fight? She'd been at such a disadvantage when they'd arrived, too embarrassed to say what she really felt. Anyway, all hopes of having the bungalow were gone now. With a deep sigh she set about washing the dishes.

The wedding was set for the twenty-eighth of September, nearly a week after Miriam and Arthur were to marry at the registry office.

'Look, Rosie, you don't have to rush your marriage,' Miriam assured her. 'This is your home, and the fact that I'm marrying your father need make no difference.' But they both knew that it would.

When Rosie told the boys that she was marrying Roy in September, David asked, 'Will he be coming to live with us?'

'We're going to live at his mother's house, David, Miriam and Dada will be married by then.' She felt a pang of conscience when she saw his face fall.

'How far away is that?'

'It's across the Newport Road, one of the turnings off Roath Court Road.'

The other two were giggling. 'Can we be pageboys and wear velvet suits with lace collars?'

The thought of Albert in a pageboy suit made her laugh, but David was silent and after a moment got up and went upstairs.

The laughter died on her lips, and she busied herself laying the table. She felt as though she'd been doused with cold water – she hadn't thought about David's reaction. She'd brought him up, been a mother to him, the only one he'd ever known; she should have predicted how upset he would be. If only they were buying the bungalow she would have asked Roy if David could live with them. Then she wondered if, perhaps even now, it would be possible, as they were to be on their own at The Laurels. She decided to ask Roy when they got back from their honeymoon, but she wouldn't say anything to David until it was settled.

Grandma Hughes had taken over the arrangements for the wedding reception and was sending invitations to family and friends. Despite herself, Rosie was excited. If Roy had never mentioned buying a place of their own she knew she'd have welcomed his mother's offer with open arms. In Wesley Street it was usual for the first one to marry to settle down in the front room like Ernie and Bella had done. Only those two would never have settled down anywhere, she thought. In some of the houses there were three generations living together. Even when a house went empty, a couple on their own often couldn't afford the nine shillings' rent.

Arthur gave her the money he'd saved for the wedding and there were exciting shopping trips to town, after which she and Mabel and Grandma would board the homeward-bound tram loaded down with parcels of all shapes and sizes. She had never been so spoilt. Everything must be new for her trousseau: crepe-de-Chine underwear edged with lace, nightdresses, pretty slippers, a going-away suit for their honeymoon in London, new frocks and dainty aprons for the afternoon.

On these shopping trips they'd lunch at the Carlton Restaurant near the Friary, and have afternoon tea at the Dutch Café in Queen Street.

Grandma insisted on paying for the lovely wedding dress of satin and lace, its shimmering train to be carried by two of Ada's little granddaughters in long pink dresses. At first Bron had been going to make her dress, but with the short time available and the distance

177

to travel for fittings, they'd had to find a dressmaker nearer home.

Rosie could hardly believe all the fuss was for her. Every day the papers were full of the rumbling threats of war, but in all the bustle and excitement she hardly gave them a thought.

Roy had booked a room for their honeymoon at the Cumberland Hotel at Marble Arch in London. Rosie was elated about visiting the sights of the big city and seeing for herself the wonderful stores that Roy's mother had boasted about: Selfridge's, Marshal and Snelgrove, Swan and Edgar.

Then on a day towards the middle of September, when the placards screamed 'War Crisis Deepening', they received a letter from Alun, advising them to cancel their honeymoon.

'They're digging trenches in Hyde Park,' he wrote, 'Anti-aircraft guns have been put in place. They've been testing the air-raid sirens . . .'

The honeymoon was cancelled.

On the fifteenth of September Mr Chamberlain had gone to Berchtesgaden to meet Hitler. Then on the twenty-second he went to Bad Godesberg for further talks. On the same day that Miriam and Arthur were married the Czechoslavakian government resigned, and Czech troops began to evacuate the Sudetenland.

Ada arranged a small reception in her front room. 'It'll be easier than bringing the piano into your place, Arthur,' she had said.

And once again the Jenkinses' front room echoed to happy chatter and laughter, and the chink of glasses being raised – even though Arthur popped next door to listen quietly to every news bulletin, and each time he returned to the party the jollity would give way to hushed expectancy while he told them about the latest events.

But the celebrations couldn't be dampened for long for this was a happy occasion, something to celebrate joyously.

And for Rosie and Roy, so soon to be married themselves, it was a time of happy anticipation.

As Rosie and Roy's wedding day drew near a new crisis loomed. Britain was preparing for war. On the twenty-seventh the British Fleet was mobilised and the Auxiliary Air Force mustered. Mrs Cunningham sent off a large trunk to her sister's cottage, and a letter telling her that she would be leaving to join her immediately after the wedding ceremony.

Two days before the wedding Alun sent a telegram to tell them that he couldn't be best man; the crisis meant he had to stay in London. The firm had decided to move to the outskirts and he was needed to take charge of the operation. Trevor, Roy's colleague at the library stepped in.

Early on the twenty-eighth, amidst the bustle of leaving for Grandma's, Rosie opened the door to Mattie Roberts who held out a parcel wrapped in tissue paper.

'A little wedding present from all the neighbours, Rosie, with our best wishes.'

As Mrs Roberts handed her the parcel the tissue paper slipped, revealing a large cut-glass salad bowl. Rosie's face was pink with pleasure, and her voice husky with emotion as she cried, 'There's lovely it is, Mattie, really beautiful, thank you all very much. We'll cherish it always.' She knew only too well the sacrifice it must have been for most of the neighbours to give even a small amount. Since Ada had made sure everyone knew that Ernie was sending money regularly to Bella, and especially since Bella herself had been carrying on with anyone who would take her out, leaving her mother to cope with the child, the neighbours' attitude had changed. But the present was still a welcome surprise.

Arthur had ordered two taxis to take them all to Grandma's; from there the boys were to go to the church with Miriam and Ada.

When they arrived long trestle tables draped in white damask tablecloths were laid ready for the wedding breakfast.

Rosie went upstairs to get ready. At last she stood in front of the mirror in Grandma's bedroom, gazing in wonder at her reflection. The lovely satin gown shimmered as she moved. Grandma adjusted the orange blossom and kissed her warmly before she lowered the veil, and the bouquet of pink carnations and gypsophila heavy with perfume was brought from the cool of the conservatory.

Presently she heard the front door close, and watched at the window as Grandma, Mabel and Vi got into the car.

She looked at Arthur. They were alone in the house. He took her hands in his. 'You look lovely, Rosie,' he said, his voice breaking with pride and emotion.

She lifted the veil and kissed his cheek warmly, 'Thank you for everything, Dada.'

'It's I who should be thanking you, Rosie love, looking after us all these years . . .'

She clung to him then, her cheek against his, her heart filled with love. It was a poignant moment, broken by the sound of the wedding car arriving. As she hastily smoothed her gown and adjusted the veil, Arthur said with a smile, 'Well, Rosie Edwards, you'll be Mrs Cunningham before you enter this house again.'

The door of the ribbon-bedecked car was held open. As she sank on to the cream leather upholstery she smiled tremulously, thinking of her father's last remark.

At the church door they were joined by the excited little bridesmaids, six-year-old Amy who was fair and plump, and tall, dark-haired Pansy who was nine, carrying their posies, a ring of flowers on their heads, and white buckskin shoes peeping from beneath the frills of their long pink satin dresses.

The organist began to play the Wedding March and on her father's arm Rosie walked slowly down the aisle. All eyes were turned towards them and when she joined Roy at the altar his expression told her all she wanted to know.

The reception went on all afternoon. After the wedding breakfast Rosie changed into a pale blue suit. Mrs Cunningham was to be escorted to the station by the bride and groom. Rosie thought the arrangement a novel one, but Roy didn't seem to mind. Soon they had to leave, going first to The Laurels to pick up Mrs Cunningham's two small cases.

It was early afternoon and the platform was crowded with travellers, and luggage was piled high everywhere. The train was half an hour late, but at last with a deafening hiss of steam the familiar chocolate and cream carriages of the GWR drew into the station. As people tumbled off and others struggled to get on Roy found his mother a corner seat and put the luggage on to the rack.

Mrs Cunningham shed a tear as she clung to Roy, then hugged

Rosie quickly, begging them to take care. The whistle blew, steam enveloped the platform once more and the train began to move, taking Roy's mother on the first lap of her journey to the West Country.

Back at Grandma's, after the happy atmosphere earlier, the mood became almost sombre as the guests crowded round the wireless in the lounge to listen to the six o'clock news. As Grandma tuned in to the National programme Bram Martin and his dance orchestra were just fading off the air. The newsreader's voice was sombre too, as he told how the House of Commons had sat that day to discuss the crisis, and to listen to Mr Chamberlain's account of his two visits to Germany. While the Prime Minister was still speaking, a letter had been handed to him, and after reading it he'd said, 'I have something else to tell the House now,' and went on to explain that the letter was a further invitation to meet Herr Hitler in Munich on the following day, when Mussolini would be present, and M. Daladier, the French prime minister, was also expected.

Cheered a little by the news, Mabel brought the *South Wales Echo* into the room and began to read the headlines aloud. Yesterday's headline, Rosie remembered, had been the King's message to his people: 'Be of good cheer despite the dark clouds'. But Mabel was reading: 'Today was another day of tension in the European crisis, and each succeeding hour brings new efforts to preserve the peace.'

'What else does it say, Mabel?' Grandma asked.

She read them two other items. The first was about four Cardiff buses that were to be first-aid posts manned with doctors and nurses. The two white-painted buses were for the use of patients who had not suffered gas poisoning. The two painted red would be used exclusively for gas casualties.

The second item was accompanied by a picture, and the caption read: 'Pedestrians at Cathay's Park today stand in the rain watching as men dig trenches as a protection from air-raids'.

Rosie was watching her father's anxious face, knowing that he was thinking of Ernie, as she was herself. Anyone at sea would be particularly vulnerable if war broke out.

The guests began to thin out, the news they'd heard making it difficult to recapture the festive mood of the wedding. Mr Chamberlain's invitation from Herr Hitler had brought fresh hope, but this would be his third visit in search of peace.

When Miriam, Arthur, Ada and the boys were ready to leave and all the goodbyes had been said, Rosie embraced them. With Teddy and Albert it was a quick kiss on the cheek and away, but David lingered, hugging her tightly, and she saw that his eyes were moist as she waved them all goodbye and there was an expression in them she wouldn't easily forget.

When they'd gone it was time for Rosie to put her arms about Grandma and thank her warmly for all she'd done, and Roy echoed her thanks as he kissed Mabel and Grandma goodbye.

Despite the gloomy news Rosie could hardly contain her happiness at being alone at last with Roy. With her heightened awareness she thought the sky looked like soft dark velvet, hung about with glittering stars. Her arm tucked into Roy's, her cheek resting on his shoulder, they wandered the short distance home. But could she ever come to think of The Laurels as home? Rosie wondered.

When they reached the house and he'd unlocked the door, he bent towards her and, smiling, scooped her into his arms and carried her over the doorstep, kissing away the laughter that rose to her lips. Rosie wanted to pinch herself. She could hardly believe it: they were together at last and she was Mrs Cunningham. She looked proudly down at the band of gold that nestled against her engagement ring. Yet something was troubling her even now. She could still see David's face as he'd left Grandma's to go home to Wesley Street. He'd looked so vulnerable, his eyes full of hurt, or had it been reproach?

If only they'd bought the bungalow, she thought: then they could have had David to live with them.

'Well, Mrs Cunningham! I must say you're not showing much enthusiasm. Have you found someone else already?' Roy had stopped kissing her and was looking at her quizzically.

'It's David, love. I was thinking of him.'

'Don't worry, Rose, youngsters soon get over things, and we're not a mile away. Get out of your glad-rags, love, and put a dressing gown on. We haven't finished celebrating yet.' He left the room and brought back a bottle of chilled champagne and two glasses, and he winked at Rosie. She hurried upstairs.

A few minutes later she came back, tying the belt of her new blue satin housecoat, and they sat side by side in silence, sipping their drinks, eyes warm upon each other.

Then Roy's arm came about her pulling her towards him until his chin was resting gently on her head. After a little while, he yawned widely. 'Why don't we have an early night, Mrs Cunningham?' he said as his hand cupped her chin and turned her face towards his.

They spent the next afternoon in town, and the evening at the cinema. Just to be together was enough. And last night, after she'd self-consciously switched off the bedside lamp, he'd been so gentle, so understanding with her. When she'd woken this morning with the sun streaming into the bedroom, she'd glanced tenderly down at his sleeping face and her heart had melted with love. She'd smoothed back the crisp, wavy hair and watched the strong black lashes stir and his eyes open wide, then he'd freed his arms from the bedclothes and thrown them about her, gathering her to him.

She'd woken early, but they'd been very late having breakfast, and this became the pattern of their first days together. As Roy pointed out, 'You don't have to go away to have a honeymoon.'

On Saturday, the first day of October, Arthur sent Teddy round with the *Daily Herald*. The headlines read: 'Mr Chamberlain declares, "It is peace for our time!" ' It was wonderful, wonderful news.

There were smaller headlines further down the page: '5,000 British troops will be sent to Sudetenland'. Then, 'Prague's day of sorrow', and in smaller print 'Czechs cry,"We want to fight!" ' and she knew her father had meant her to see these, too.

The *Daily Herald* lay on Mrs Cunningham's walnut occasional table. Rosie smiled as she thought that this must be the very first time a socialist newspaper had rested there.

Watching the Pathé news a few days later sitting hand in hand in the cinema, they saw Neville Chamberlain leaving from Heston on his third peace mission after passing through an avenue of cheering people. Later in the programme they saw his triumphant return, waving the piece of paper signed by Hitler. It was a deeply emotional moment. Despite the healthy scepticism Arthur had instilled into her, tears rolled down Rosie's face, and most of the audience too found a sudden need for handkerchiefs.

Finally, as they watched Chamberlain stepping into the car that was to take him to Buckingham Palace, a heartfelt cheer echoed round the auditorium.

On the last day before Roy returned to work they met Mrs Cunningham's friend, the Major.

'Is your mother still in Devon, Roy?'

'Yes, but I believe she's going to London soon, sir.'

'I hear that you and your wife are minding The Laurels. I'm glad she took my advice about not leaving it empty. I told her, "If there is a war, Elizabeth, they'll probably requisition empty houses" .'

So that's why she'd been so generous with her offer, Rosie thought bitterly. That's why we had to lose the bungalow. But the significance of the Major's remark didn't seem to have dawned on Roy.

On their return, they opened the front door and as Rosie fumbled for the light switch, she almost fell over the suitcases in the hall.

'Is that you, Roy?' Mrs Cunningham stepped out of the kitchen and stood waiting for them both to kiss her.

'But, Mother, why didn't you let us know you were coming?'

'Well, I've been in London for a few days and I'm very cross with Alun. He is not going ahead with my flat at the moment. He says they've all had a nasty shock and that London is no place for me to live permanently.' She paused, dabbed daintily at her eyes with a lace-edged hanky, then continued. ' "Better wait a while," he says. Well, I ask you, did Mr Chamberlain bring back a peace treaty or didn't he? Still, I won't go where I'm not wanted.'

'Mother, you know that's not fair. Alun's concerned for your welfare, that's all.'

'Well, I'm disappointed, Roy. I was relying on having that flat. We'll have to make the best of living together for the time being, I suppose. I was very bored in the country.'

Rosie felt sick with apprehension. This was just what she'd been afraid of. Tonight she had been going to ask Roy if David could come and live with them and now it seemed they would be stuck with his mother instead. She looked at Roy willing him to be strong. 'It's your house, Mother,' said Roy, 'we'll look around for a place if you like.'

'Well, there's enough room in this house for us all,' Mrs Cunningham said quickly. 'You have your own bedroom and we'll have to share the rest. I'm sure we'll get along famously.'

The smile she bestowed on Rosie didn't quite reach her carefully made-up, pale blue eyes.

Chapter 18

'Rose dear, I do wish you wouldn't take your morning break with Mrs Thomas.'

Rosie looked at her mother-in-law in surprise. Mrs Thomas came three times a week to do the 'rough'; she'd cleaned for Mrs Cunningham for years and their relationship was friendly but distant, each knowing their own place. To Rosie, living in the unfamiliar world of suburbia, Mrs Thomas was a welcome friend.

'It isn't that I mind you sharing her tea-break in the kitchen, Rose, but I pay her by the hour and those breaks seem to be getting longer.'

Rosie laughed. 'All right, Mother, I'll see that we don't run over the ten minutes next time.'

It was almost mid-December and by now she was really fed up with living at The Laurels with her mother-in-law. For one thing they had absolutely no privacy. If they discussed any small problem in their bedroom, Mrs Cunningham would await their return downstairs and ask pointedly if anything was wrong.

'I feel as though I'm being watched all the time,' Rosie had complained to Roy.

'Nonsense, Rose,' he'd laughed,' 'it's just that Mother has always made her presence felt. I suppose she's entitled to, it is her house we're living in.'

'And whose fault is that?' she'd whispered in exasperation under her breath.

Lately they'd taken to spending a lot of time at the cinema, for strangely, in the crowded darkness, they could really feel alone. Last night at the Olympia she'd seen Judy Garland and Mickey Rooney in *Love Finds Andy Hardy*, and two nights before, at the

Queens, Joe E Brown in *Funny Face*. What they really paid for was to sit close in the darkness, her head on his shoulder, conscious only of each other.

If only Roy's mother would go out like she used to, Rosie thought wistfully, for since the war scare last September she had altered her way of life completely. Alun was still in disfavour, because he hadn't yet begun converting the top of his house into a flat, and she no longer made those frequent trips to London. The Major and his wife were in Madeira until the spring so the bridge club had broken up. Mrs Cunningham was visibly bored.

Rosie found it strange that in the suburbs you never really got to know your neighbours. You nodded to each other over the garden fence and remarked on the weather, but whatever small dramas happened behind those neat lace curtains was kept strictly private.

She took over the washing, dusting and shopping, but it was all so easy compared to what she was used to. No copper to light with sticks and coke, no standing in bitter winds to mangle clothes: her mother-in-law's gas boiler was in white enamel, and she had a Ewbank wringer whose rubber rollers folded away to make a useful table.

Shopping was a pleasure, too, with tradesmen solicitous and anxious to please, and the heavy groceries delivered by an errand boy.

Rosie wished she had some preparations of her own to make for Christmas, for Mrs Cunningham had organised everything; she'd made the cakes and puddings weeks ago with Rosie allowed only to wash up and clear away. When she had suggested to her mother-in-law that she could put up some decorations to make the rooms look festive, Roy's mother had raised her hands in horror.

'Oh, no, Rose! Paper decorations are so tawdry and they are such dust gatherers. Besides, I am expecting some of my friends to call over Christmas, but you can decorate your bedroom if you like.'

A few days later when Rosie suggested that it would be nice to have a Christmas tree, and that she would buy the decorations and trim it herself, Mrs Cunningham gave her that special 'Don't be silly look' before replying, 'Trees make even more mess than paper decorations, dear. Just think of all those pine needles. I'm sure I don't want to go round picking them up all day.'

Rosie would gladly have picked them up but she knew when she was beaten.

After lunch on Christmas Day she was glad to escape with Roy to Wesley Street where they had all been invited to tea. Mrs Cunningham had made her excuses, saying she'd be glad of a rest after all the hard work.

All of a sudden Rosie felt happy and excited at the thought of spending the rest of the day at home. The presents for the boys had been delivered yesterday for Father Christmas to bring, though she knew that even David didn't really believe in him any more.

She could hear the familiar noise the boys were making even before they opened the door. Whistles blowing, voices high with excitement. When Roy knocked for the second time the door burst open at once and Albert, Teddy and David rushed out to pull them inside.

If Roy's mother thinks that paper-chains are tawdry I wonder what she'd make of this lot, Rosie thought with amusement. It wasn't just the kitchen and parlour that were festooned with brightly coloured paper. In their enthusiasm the boys had decorated the passage as well, and even draped paper-chains over the large print of 'The Boyhood of Raleigh' which hung on the wall by the door.

Tea was a riotous affair with crackers for everyone which meant more whistles to blow, paper hats to wear, and mottoes to read aloud. Then, when even Miriam couldn't persuade them to eat another thing, Roy knelt on the rug to play with the Hornby train set he'd insisted they buy David for Christmas. He's just a big kid at heart, Rosie thought fondly, as she watched Roy and David, their heads together.

Teddy had gone up to the bedroom to look through the telescope they had bought for him, and Albert to the yard to kick the leather football she'd known he'd been coveting in Pritchard's window, leaving the kitchen curtains open wide to let the light out because it was already dark outside.

Miriam handed round a dish of sweets and a bowl of nuts and the nutcrackers, and Rosie remembered this morning when Roy's mother had set out silver filigree bonbon dishes, two with wrapped sweets and two with shelled nuts. Shelled, Rosie knew, not to make them more convenient for people but to save the mess the nut-crackers would surely make. Each little silver dish had been carefully placed on a crocheted doyly on the four corners of the walnut occasional table. In the centre she'd placed a cut-glass bowl of fruit – oranges, apples and bananas piled carefully into a mound – and Rosie remembered thinking it looked too good to be disturbed.

Suddenly she became aware of the piano next door tunelessly pounding out 'While Shepherds Watched Their Flocks by Night', and Ada's voice rising strong and clear above the notes.

'Ada's in her element,' Miriam told her. 'They've got Mary and Ceinwen there. Let's go in for half an hour shall we? We're not needed here.' And she smiled as she looked towards the group on the floor where Arthur, Albert and Teddy had joined the train driver and guard. Now there was a little station with tiny tin porters, and a bridge and a tunnel across the railway track, and a set of signal lights, too.

'Frank found those for him,' Miriam told her, and Rosie remembered when she was quite small playing on the rug in the Jenkinses' parlour with Frank's train set and the very same little accessories.

Ada welcomed them warmly, and soon they were sampling her Christmas cake and Bert's rhubarb wine, and chatting to Frank's sister Mary and her daughter Ceinwen. After a while Frank went to the piano and began to play carols again and they all gathered round and sang. They were in the middle of 'Good King Wenceslas' when Rosie noticed that it was nearly nine o'clock by the big marble clock on the mantelpiece. Poor Mother-in-law. She had been on her own all evening.

'We'll have to go now,' she whispered to Miriam.

'But why, Rosie? You can sleep on in the morning, it's Boxing Day.'

'It's Roy's mother, she's all alone.'

'Well, she should have come with you!' Miriam retorted.

But Rosie was glad that she hadn't. It had been a lovely evening. She hadn't realised how much she'd missed them all. If Mrs

Cunningham had accompanied them there would have been a lot of polite conversation and no spontaneous fun, and certainly no carol-singing in Ada's house. But now her conscience was troubling her because they'd been away so long.

Back home, Roy and Arthur and the boys were still on the floor playing with the train set, but Roy got up right away when she mentioned the time. She was glad they'd come in the car – they could be home in less than ten minutes.

Mrs Cunningham was reading a book under the standard lamp when they got in. The bottle of wine on the side table was still unopened and the sweets and nuts looked undisturbed.

'Why didn't you have a drink, Mother?—' Roy began.

'It wouldn't have been much fun on my own, would it?' she told him cutting in. 'I thought you would never come home.'

She refused supper, saying she was tired, and went up to bed. Rosie, feeling worried now, went to the kitchen, but when she lifted the kettle from the gas stove it was still hot, and the teapot, although emptied, was warm, too.

Christmas was over, and with the long dark days of January Rosie spent more time in the house. The chores and essential shopping were finished early, and there was little to do. She missed David, and even Teddy's and Albert's endless arguing. If only Ada could pop in sometimes for a cup of tea, especially as very soon she hoped to have some wonderful news to tell.

Since the middle of December Rosie had woken to a feeling of nausea, but she didn't want to raise Roy's hopes, not until she was sure. Every morning as she left the bathroom, looking white and shaken, her mother-in-law seemed to be on the landing either entering or leaving her bedroom, and she'd give Rosie a speculative look.

The morning came when she asked kindly, 'Are you pregnant, Rose?'

'I think so, Mother.'

'Have you seen Dr Phillips? You must take care of yourself now.'

'I'll make an appointment today. I haven't said anything to Roy – I wanted to be certain.'

'I'll come with you, dear. Sit down and I'll make you a cup of tea.

191

Oh, I do hope it's a little girl! You'll be looking for a place of your own now, I suppose?'

Rosie looked up hopefully. Would Roy agree to look for a house again? If only they'd taken that bungalow.

As she left the doctor's surgery later she was walking on air. She couldn't wait to tell Roy. Surely he must have guessed. When he came home for lunch his mother busied herself in the kitchen and Rosie led him to the settee.

'Sit down, Roy, I've something to tell you.'

'What is it, love? I haven't got long—'

'We're going to have a baby.'

She almost laughed as she saw his expression change from surprise to joy. Taking her into his arms, his voice filled with emotion, he said, 'Oh, Rose, that's wonderful, really wonderful. Wait until Mother knows she's going to be a granny.'

'I'll not be called Granny.' His mother had come quietly into the room. 'It makes me think of someone with steel-rimmed spectacles and a bun. I shall be Grandma Cunningham.' She beamed at them as she set the table for lunch.

Mrs Cunningham's remark about them finding a place of their own stirred all the old longings.

That evening as soon as they were alone, Rosie brought up the subject that was closest to her heart.

'What's wrong with it here?' Roy was genuinely puzzled. 'Look, love, we've got the run of the house. We can even save money towards a bigger deposit when we do buy. What more could we want?'

'We need to be alone,' she said stubbornly, disappointment making her voice shrill. 'We haven't any privacy, not even a room of our own downstairs.'

'That's unfair, Rose. Mother's made us really welcome. She's over the moon about the baby. Besides there could still be a war, things are pretty unsettled.'

'We need a place of our own with the baby coming,' she persisted, her lips quivering as she struggled to hold back the tears.

'And another thing,' Roy continued as though she hadn't

spoken, 'you'll need someone with you now you're pregnant, especially when it gets nearer the time.'

'Aren't we ever going to get our own house?' she cried angrily, the tears suddenly brimming over. Roy rushed to her side and cradled her in his arms, but the body remained rigid.

'Of course we will, Rose,' he told her, 'but not yet. Best wait until the baby's born. We'll look around then. You go on up, love, I'll check the doors.'

And what excuse will you make then? Rosie thought bitterly, fuming with frustration as she went upstairs.

When Roy came in to the bedroom, Rosie was already in bed, her eyes closed. Roy crept into bed and put his arm about her, but she made no sign that she was awake. As he moved closer, her body remained stiff and unyielding, then she turned over, her back to him as she stared at the darkened window.

It's the first time we won't have fallen asleep in each other's arms, she thought miserably.

When a sob broke from her lips, Roy turned her towards him and he said, 'I feel awful about it, Rose. But it isn't the right time, believe me, love. You must see that.' And he gently kissed away her tears.

Despite her bitterness and disappointment, Roy's warm body was having its usual effect on Rosie. Her arms went around him and her lips sought his, and she could feel his heartbeat strong against her breast as his body hardened against her.

The baby was expected at the beginning of August, and Rosie would have been fairly happy and content except for a nagging worry over David. She couldn't help noticing the gradual change in him. With his naturally pale colouring David had never looked robust, but lately there were dark shadows under his eyes. He'd always been a quiet child but now he seemed withdrawn. Miriam had told her he ate very little. She'd taken him to see Dr Thomas a couple of times, but he could find nothing physically wrong.

'What do you think it is?' Rosie asked worriedly.

'I think he's missing you,' her stepmother said bluntly. 'After all, you're the only mother David has known, and he's such a sensitive child.'

When he came home from school Rosie made a fuss of him, but David was very quiet, nibbling the end of his pen as he sat at the table doing his homework.

When Miriam said, 'You'll soon be an uncle, David, Rosie's going to have a baby,' she thought he looked at her reproachfully, but he came and sat by her side, saying wistfully, 'I was your baby once, wasn't I, Rosie? 'Cos when Mama died you looked after me.'

'You were a lovely baby.' Rosie gently smoothed his fair hair. He seemed satisfied and returned to his books. She remembered the tragedy on the day he was born. Poor little soul, she thought, left to the care of a ten-year-old already overburdened with responsibilities. David had never suckled at his mother's breast, had never known the warm rapport that flowed between mother and child. She'd done her best, but with Albert not two years old and Teddy only three there'd never been much time to spare. Things would be very different for her own child, she vowed.

It was a bitterly cold January day. As she left her father's house and walked up the street it was deserted except for a group of children playing marbles in the gutter. She looked about her and for the first time saw the peeling paint and air of shabbiness of most of the houses.

Life at The Laurels had satisfied some longing she'd always had for tasteful surroundings, a longing that had begun with her admiration for Grandma's house when she was a child. But sometimes nowadays she thought wistfully of her old life with its intimacies and involvements, and Ada keeping her informed over a cup of tea.

The second week in February was unusually warm. On the Friday, as the temperature soared into the sixties, Rosie was on her way to visit Miriam and the boys when she decided to call at Ada's first.

Coat over her arm but still uncomfortably hot in a winter jumper and skirt, she knocked on the door. There was a roaring fire in the grate, and seating herself at the table as far as possible from its heat she took the cup Ada offered.

'Our Frank's makin' you a present for the baby, Rosie,' Ada told her. " 'E says I might just as well tell you in case you go and buy one. 'E's makin' you a cradle.'

'There's good of him. He's given me some lovely things. What's it like, Ada?'

'Making you a rocking cradle he is.' There was a sharpness in Ada's voice. 'Labour of love, I reckon it is. 'E 'ardly stops for 'is meals. An' the way 'e caresses that wood—'

Rosie blushed scarlet as Ada continued remorselessly, 'Besotted, 'e is. I wish 'e'd meet a nice girl and get married, instead of pining after you.'

'Ada, don't!' There were tears of guilt and pity in Rosie's eyes. If what Ada said was true, and Frank really was pining for her . . . But no, Ada had always had a bee in her bonnet about her son's feelings for Rosie. He'd backed off quickly enough once she'd made it plain that she saw him only as a brother, and that was how she would always see him, she told herself firmly.

Ada interrupted her thoughts. 'Youer David's looking poorly. Miriam says 'e don't eat enough. I think 'e's missing you too.'

'I'm going in to see him now. I've got a little present each for the boys.'

'If our Frank was youer 'usband, you'd probably 'ave 'ad the boys living with you, real fond of them 'e is.' Then seeing the tears which sprang to Rosie's eyes, she said quickly, 'Aw! Take no notice of me, cariad, I don't know what makes me rant on. It's just our Frank. I wish he'd find someone else and settle down.'

Shaken by Ada's words, Rosie went next door. Teddy and Albert had gone to the shops. She took a colourful yo-yo from her bag and David's eyes lit up.

'You going to stay to tea, Rosie?'

'Just for a cup.'

'Has Mrs Cunningham heard any more from Alun about the flat?' Miriam asked.

'Well, he'd got as far as consulting a builder when there were more of those bomb outrages. They think it's the IRA sympathisers. It said in the *Echo* last week that eleven people were injured when bombs went off at those two underground stations, at Leicester Square and Tottenham Court Road. I don't think she's so keen herself now with all this happening'.

'Has she made it up with Alun now?'

'Yes, I think she realises that he's only thinking of her.'

It was June and they hadn't yet found a place of their own. Despite Rosie's pleading Roy still thought it would be time enough when the baby arrived. He'd rather she wasn't alone when her time came. They'd looked at a few places but nothing seemed as good as the bungalow they'd turned down.

She felt big and cumbersome. Soon the maternity dresses she'd been so proud of would be let out to their limit.

The weather was warm and as Roy had a day due to him they decided on a trip to Barry Island in the car, for she wouldn't be able to go for much longer. When they left the house it was warm and sunny, but as they drove through the country lanes the sunshine became fitful, hiding behind grey clouds which had suddenly appeared, then peeping out in an increasing blaze of glory until another mass of cloud hid it once more from view.

As Roy unfolded the deck chairs on the fine dry sand just beneath the promenade the sun was bright and a slight breeze blew from the sea. Dropping the bag containing the sandwiches and thermos flask on to the sand he helped her to settle in the deck chair and poured the tea.

The beach wasn't crowded but there was a fair sprinkling of chairs around them, mostly occupied by family groups, the children digging in the sand.

'Why don't you go for a swim, Roy? I put your things in.'

'Better not, love.' He looked up at the sky which had clouded over again. 'If it rains I'll have to get you to shelter. Here, have my pullover behind your head – you don't look very comfortable.'

She accepted it gratefully, finding it difficult to feel comfortable anywhere these days. She lay back, her head against the pullover, her eyes scanning the beach and the receding waves in the distance. Two little boys, their chubby bodies bare except for tiny swimming trunks, were running around the groups of deck chairs with screams of delight. On the wet sand below the waterline sandcastles sprouted, most of their turrets topped by flags like some medieval encampment, their small builders scurrying to the sea's edge to fill colourful tin buckets to pour into the moats, the water slopping over their bare legs and feet.

The sight of the gulls swooping above the grey waves and soon to invade the beach reminded her of that hot August day just after Mama died when Ada had brought her here on a charabanc outing and she'd raced Frank down the beach, her face aflame with embarrassment after Ada had called to her, 'Tuck youer dress into youer knickers, Rosie,' and Frank, considerate for her even then, had tried to put her at ease.

Rosie must have dozed, for the next thing she knew Roy was shaking her gently, his voice urgent. 'Wake up, Rose, wake up. It's raining.'

Holding the towel over her head and shoulders she hurried with him across the beach as fast as the soft sand would let them, then, his arms about her shoulders, they crossed the road to the café opposite. Sitting at a table by the window, the tea tray in front of them, they watched the large spots turn to a downpour and a veil of rain sweep across the sands.

They arrived home about half past seven and Roy went to fetch his mother who was at the Major's house.

Half an hour later there was a knock. Surely they both couldn't have forgotten their keys? As Rosie opened the door, she was surprised to see her stepmother.

'Is David with you, Rosie?'

'No, Miriam, he isn't. We haven't been home long. Did he say he was coming here?'

'Took some books back to the library he did. Haunts that place he does because Roy sometimes brings him back here in the car. Complaining about his throat being sore he was, so I told him to come home as soon as he'd changed the books.'

'Roy wasn't at the library, he had a day off,' Rosie said worriedly.

'Where can he be? I was so sure I'd find him here. Oh, Rosie! He must be soaking wet. It's been raining since just after he left the house.'

When Roy came back they took Miriam home, then drove slowly round the streets. It was getting dark. Sitting in the back of the car Rosie could hardly see the pavements.

'Perhaps he's home by now,' she said hopefully, but one look at Miriam's face when she opened the door told them that he wasn't.

'Youer dad's gone to the police station, Rosie,' she whispered.

When her father returned he and Frank had organised a search party.

'I want you to go home, Rosie, you look tired,' he began. But she shook her head. 'I can't, Dada, not until he's found.'

But Roy said firmly, 'I'm going out with the men, Rose. I'll take you home first. Mother will be worrying.'

Unwillingly she got into the car. As she went up the path, Mrs Cunningham opened the door.

'Any news of your little brother?'

Rosie shook her head and her lips trembled. Putting a comforting arm about her shoulders, her mother-in-law said, 'They'll find him, you'll see.'

When Roy's mother went to the kitchen, Rosie dropped her head in her hands. Where would David go? He got on well with Miriam, so why would he run away? If only she could have had him to live with them as she'd planned, and she would have if only they'd had a place of their own. Ada had said he was pining for her. The old bitterness over the way they'd been prevented from buying the bungalow rose in her. Roy got on well with David; if he'd been living with them the police wouldn't be out searching for him now.

Rosie heard the key turn and rushed to the front door.

Reading the question in her eyes, Roy shook his head. 'I've only come back for the lantern, Rose, it's in the shed, but there's a torch I could loan someone in the hall cupboard.'

Seeing her look of disappointment, he pulled her to him. 'We'll find David, don't worry. The police are searching as well.'

At his words she burst into tears. Kissing her gently, he said, 'I'll have to go, love, I must catch up with the others.'

Regretfully he left her and she followed him to the door and stood there as he went round the side towards the garden shed. Suddenly he was running back to her, shouting excitedly, 'He's here, Rose, David's in the shed. He's fast asleep on my old gardening jacket.'

By the time she reached the shed Roy had lit the lantern, and

David, awakened by all the commotion, was rubbing his eyes in bewilderment. His hair clung damply to his head, and as she knelt down she saw that his clothes were soaking wet.

Roy carried him into the house, then went to call off the search.

David was soon warm and dry, dwarfed in a pair of Roy's pyjamas and his dressing gown. Rosie waited until he'd drunk the hot chocolate Roy's mother had brought before asking, 'How long had you been in the shed, David? We've been worried sick. Why didn't you go home as Miriam asked?'

'I wanted to see you, Rosie.' His voice was hoarse. 'The man at the library told me Roy had a day off. I thought you'd both be here.'

'If you'd sheltered in the porch we'd have seen you when we came home.'

'A lady kept coming to her gate and staring at me . . .' he tried to clear his throat – 'so I went to the shed and waited. You were an awful long time, Rosie. My throat's real bad.'

When Roy came back he said he'd promised to take David home. 'I'll get some blankets, Rose,' he said. 'Your father's gone to tell the police, and Miriam's putting hot-water bottles in his bed.'

Kissing David she hugged him close, then followed Roy out to the car.

Next afternoon when she turned into Wesley Street she almost collided with Teddy, rushing round the corner.

'Steady on! You should be more careful,' she began.

But Teddy said importantly, 'I'm going for the doctor, Rosie. Our David's bad.'

She hurried then, and Miriam who had seen her coming greeted her at the gate.

'David's got a fever, Rosie. He seemed all right yesterday except for that sore throat. He keeps asking for you.'

He was tossing and turning restlessly in the bed, his eyes bright and cheeks flushed. Rosie sat by his side and bathed his face with the flannel Miriam had wrung out in cold water.

When Dr Thomas arrived she went downstairs, leaving Miriam in the bedroom. Presently the doctor came into the kitchen and she looked up hopefully, but his words weren't comforting. 'He's got influenza,' he said, 'and it's a rather nasty strain that's going around.' He smiled at her concerned face. 'Don't worry, Rosie, we'll pull him through.'

When he'd gone she sat by the bed holding David's hand in hers. After a while he became restless and rambling, bursting into excited chatter she couldn't understand.

When Roy came for her, despite his pleas and those of Miriam, she refused to go home.

'I'll be all right, Roy, I can't leave him like this.'

'You've got to think of yourself, Rose. You mustn't take any risks.'

When she still refused he went home, returning again about nine o'clock.

'Just come home for the night,' he begged. 'Please, Rose.'

Already her back ached from sitting huddled over the bed. She closed her eyes as though to shut out the temptation, seeing their pretty pink bedroom and the comfortable bed with its covers turned back invitingly.

'Rosie!' David's voice was just a croak, but her eyes flew straight to him and she saw his fingers feebly searching for hers. When she took his hand it was hot and dry. Looking at Roy she shook her head. 'I'm sorry, love, I can't leave him now. We'll see how he is tomorrow.'

Miriam and Dada added their pleas to Roy's, but with David's hand still in hers she wouldn't budge.

When Roy had gone, Arthur brought her an armchair and piled it with cushions. Teddy and Albert wandered in and out on tiptoe, unnaturally quiet, bringing cups of tea and food she didn't want and speaking to her in whispers.

Next morning when Dr Thomas called she went downstairs, afraid he might insist she go home.

The fever lasted three days and she hardly moved from David's side. A tiredness had come over her whole body. Only her eyes were watchful for any small change in the boy's condition.

On the third night she fell into a deep sleep, waking panic-stricken that she'd neglected her watch. Miriam was sitting at the other side of the bed.

'Look, Rosie!' Her voice was filled with relief. 'Look at him.' and Rosie saw that the bright colour had gone and his face was glistening with perspiration.

'It's what we've been waiting for,' Miriam continued. 'He's over the crisis now. I've just persuaded your dad to get some rest.'

Thankful and relieved, Rosie eased herself from the chair. Her legs felt stiff and she ached all over. As she stood upright, hand pressed to her aching back, her head began to swim. Then, as blackness enveloped her, she felt herself falling.

Chapter 19

Rosie opened her eyes in bewilderment to find Dr Thomas bending over her and Miriam and her father gazing down anxiously.

'What – what happened?'

'Fainted you did, love, don't you remember? It was lucky you fell across the bed.' Miriam smiled at her in relief.

Dr Thomas shook his head from side to side. 'You're not my patient now, Rosie, and you should see your own doctor right away. Has your husband got a car? Good. Well, wrap up well and let him take you home.'

'I'm just tired,' she protested.

'Let's hope that's all it is. I'd no idea you were going to stay and nurse David. If you get influenza it could be serious.'

Dr Phillips called soon after she arrived home. 'Your husband tells me you've been helping to nurse a patient with influenza?'

'Yes, my little brother.'

'Well, that wasn't very wise when you're pregnant.'

The tears welled up. If anything happened to the baby she'd never forgive herself.

By evening she was in a fever, tossing and turning, waking to push back the bedclothes only to have Roy pull them gently about her shoulders again. Whenever she woke he was there, his mother hovering anxiously in the background.

When at last the fever passed, Roy's mother brought her tempting trays of beef tea and dainty triangles of thin bread and butter, but her disapproval of Rosie for taking such a risk was hard to disguise.

Examining her after the crisis had passed, Dr Phillips gave a sigh of relief. 'Well, you're very lucky, young lady. The baby seems to be all right. You'll have to rest for this last month, though you can sit out of bed in that basket chair for a while.'

'There's such a lot I must do, Doctor.'

'Then you'll have to let someone do it for you, my dear.'

She had been looking forward so much to making the last-minute preparations for the baby. There was still much of the layette to buy, and her knitting lay neglected in its cretonne bag.

Instead, Roy's mother went shopping for the little day gowns and petticoats, and a few more matinée coats that she'd meant to knit. Rosie waited eagerly for her return.

When the purchases were laid on the bed Rosie's heart sank. It was all so frilly and pretty, hardly suitable if she should have a little boy. But her mother-in-law looked so pleased that she didn't have the heart to show her disapproval.

'I warned you Mother wants a granddaughter, Rose,' Roy told her. 'Anyway, you'll soon be up and about. You can choose the things yourself for when the baby's tucked and out of long gowns.'

'Supposing it's a boy, will she carry on like Alun told you she did when you were born?'

'Of course not. My aunt said Alun was teasing me, and that she soon got over her disappointment. Poor Mother, she's always wanted a little girl to dress in pretty clothes.'

It was arranged that when the baby arrived Mrs Thomas would come every day instead of just three days a week. She would take on the shopping as well as the housework and the nappies, leaving Mrs Cunningham free to look after Rosie and the baby.

The pains started one hot night early in August. It was almost dawn as Roy went for the midwife. In the intervals between the pains, nausea took over. Rosie felt so ill, so sick. It was a dry sickness that knew no relief as her stomach heaved constantly.

Roy's mother fluttered anxiously about, visibly relieved when at last the midwife arrived.

'Much too early to send for the doctor yet, love,' she told Rosie. 'You did book him, Mrs Cunningham?'

Rosie nodded.

'Well, it will be some time yet, cariad. Call back I will in a couple of hours.'

As the contractions became more frequent she had to grit her teeth and grip the rail at the top of the bed tightly, as wave after wave of excruciating pain tore at her body.

'It will soon be over, Rose,' her mother-in-law comforted, bathing her perspiring face, then resuming her vigil at the window. 'Here she comes now,' she cried in relief, hurrying downstairs to open the door again to the midwife.

The child was born at a quarter past one, a little girl with a sheen of gold hair and big solemn brown eyes.

Roy's mother couldn't hide her delight at having a grand-daughter, and Rosie soon forgot the hours of pain as Roy beamed and fussed over the new arrival. Holding the baby close, she kissed the silky head gently, then laid her cheek against the child's, her heart filled with thankfulness.

With the baby in the cradle Frank had made, Rosie slept. Later, when she couldn't feed the child herself, it was hard to explain the deep emotional disturbance she felt. Reluctantly agreeing to them sending for a feeding bottle, she brushed the tears away.

'It's probably because you're still weak, my dear,' Dr Phillips told her. 'The worst thing you can do is to worry. Baby milk is a very good substitute if you can't feed her yourself.'

Watching the baby suck hungrily at the bottle Rosie felt strangely inadequate. Much later when the child woke and began to cry, she was bending towards the cradle when Roy's mother hurried into the room.

'You'll need plenty of rest, dear,' she told her, plumping the pillows and settling her into them. 'I'll take baby downstairs, it's nearly time for her next feed anyway. It's such a nuisance coming up and down for her. I'll get Roy to take the cradle downstairs.'

Tears filled Rosie's eyes as Roy took the rocking cradle and followed his mother downstairs, but she felt too weak to protest.

By the time that Roy came home each evening the baby was asleep. Once he brought her to Rosie after her late feed, but his mother complained that it was difficult to settle the child again. When occasionally she carried her to the bedroom herself, she'd sigh breathlessly, and say, 'Those stairs. Oh, dear! I never seemed to notice them before, Rose, but there's so much to do.'

During the long hours Rosie spent alone in the bedroom, she couldn't concentrate on reading anything more demanding than the newspapers, and they depressed her, filled once again with the threat of war.

Putting the paper down one morning towards lunchtime, she dropped her head wearily on to her hands. She didn't hear Roy enter the room. Suddenly his arms were about her, his voice filled with concern as he said, 'You're not to worry, Rose. Mother is coping very well with the baby. You'll soon feel yourself again. Have you definitely decided to have her christened Elizabeth?'

She nodded. 'We'll name her after your Mother, Roy, but shall we call her Beth? Elizabeth's such a mouthful.'

It was the last weekend of August when the tension finally erupted; war was now a very real threat.

The Channel packets making their journey to and fro between Britain and the Continent were suddenly making two journeys a day in an attempt to bring home all British visitors who might otherwise be stranded.

When Mrs Thomas brought Rose a cup of tea she told her that sandbags had been piled round the beautiful civic buildings, the law courts, City Hall, and the museum; she'd seen them early that morning.

On the first day of September the news was grave. At dawn on this Friday morning German troops massed on the frontier between Germany and Poland had opened fire. War now seemed inevitable.

Suddenly the papers were full of articles with practical advice: 'How to Hang Your Blackout Curtains', 'Get to Know Your Air-Raid Warden', and 'Always Carry Your Gas-Mask'.

On the morning of 3 September Roy helped her downstairs to hear Mr Chamberlain's broadcast to the nation. Despite the solemnity of the occasion she felt excited about coming downstairs again, and was looking forward to lifting Beth from the cradle and feeding her from her bottle.

Glancing over the banister she was surprised to see the empty cradle under the stairs.

'Sh!' Roy put a finger to his lips as he led her towards the sitting room, where his mother beamed as she pointed to a frilly, muslin-draped cot decorated with pink satin bows. Under the pink covers little Beth lay asleep, almost as beribboned as the cot.

Roy looked delighted, and his mother obviously expected her to be pleased, too. Rosie managed a painful smile. She would use Frank's rocking cradle in their bedroom.

She sat in the armchair by the wireless. When Beth opened her eyes she was lifted and put into her arms. The baby gazed up at Rosie, then slowly her lips trembled and puckered. Thrashing restlessly, she began to scream.

Before Rosie could try to pacify her Roy's mother took the child, and lifting the cot cover produced a dummy which quietened her at once. Soon she was staring contentedly at the ceiling, her tiny lips moving rhythmically.

'But I didn't want her to have a dummy, Mother,' Rosie protested.

'Well I had to do something, Rose. I only have one pair of hands, you know.'

'Mother's been marvellous,' Roy put in quickly. 'We should be very grateful for all she's done for us, love, and for all the money she's spent on things for Beth.'

Rosie felt too weak to argue. Things would be different when she was strong again.

It was almost a quarter past eleven. Roy went across to the wireless and switched it on. As the clock on the mantelpiece chimed the quarter, Mr Chamberlain was announced.

'I am speaking to you from the Cabinet Room at Ten Downing Street,' he said solemnly. 'This morning the British ambassador in Berlin handed the German government a final note, stating that unless we heard from them by eleven o'clock that they were prepared at once to withdraw their troops from Poland, a state of war would exist between us. I have to tell you now that no such reply has been received, and that consequently this country is at war with Germany.'

As the fateful words died away it was some minutes before anyone spoke. Each sat deep in their own thoughts, then Roy's mother broke the silence. 'My goodness!' she said briskly. 'I'd better go and hang those blackout curtains at once.'

Chapter 20

As they got on the tram and Roy put his cases on the luggage rack, Rosie looked round anxiously for a seat where they could be together. In just over half an hour he'd be on his way to the army training camp. Despite the warmth of the May morning she felt cold as they sat hand in hand, savouring these last precious minutes together.

At the second stop a woman loaded with parcels got on and Rosie's heart sank as Roy, smiling at her apologetically, gave up his seat.

The woman smiled back at them both as she settled her parcels. 'There's a nice day, isn't it?'

'Yes, lovely.' Rosie spoke without conviction, for how could it be nice with Roy going away and even these last minutes together denied them? She wished the woman would get off at the next stop.

The railway station was heaving with people and suddenly they couldn't find anything to say. Hearing the train in the distance Rosie flung her arms about Roy's neck and buried her face on his shoulder.

They clung together, pushed and buffeted by the crowds, then, as the train drew noisily into the station, Roy kissed her gently.

'Time to go, Rose. Cheer up, love, I should get leave in a couple of months. Take care of little Beth for me.'

If only your mother would give me the chance, Rosie thought bitterly, but she nodded and smiled as Roy boarded the train. The carriages were packed. When he couldn't get near the door they mouthed words of farewell over the heads of the crowd. As she stood memorising every line of his face Rosie was painfully aware that his smile wasn't reflected in his eyes, which looked miserable.

Then the train was moving, steam hissing about the platform. Blinded by tears, she waved until it gathered speed and disappeared around the bend.

Joining the surge of people descending the steps from the platform, she felt an aching emptiness.

Outside the station, as she stood blinking in the bright sunshine, there seemed to be people in uniform everywhere, some departing, some arriving, with relatives or girlfriends pressing forward to meet them.

Rosie walked slowly towards the tram stop. A hand touched her shoulder, and her face lit up with pleasure as she recognised the slim girl who had greeted her.

'Jan!'

'Got time for a cup of tea, Rosie?'

Beth was safe with Roy's mother, it wouldn't make any difference to her.

'Where shall we go?'

They decided to walk to Queen Street where Jan wanted to do some shopping, then go to the Dutch Café which Rosie remembered affectionately from her visits with Grandma and Aunty Mabel when they were buying her trousseau.

She sensed that Jan was bursting to tell her something, but it was not until Rosie was pouring the tea that she said 'Bella's having another baby. She's about six months gone.'

'Does Ernie know?'

'Yes, I wrote and told him. Oh, Rosie, do you think he could get a divorce now?' Jan's hopeful eyes were fixed on hers.

'Well, I should think so. Perhaps Bella will want to marry the chap?'

'Hardly likely, Rosie, she probably couldn't say which one it belonged to! She wouldn't even know if the uniform was khaki or blue. Oh, I know that's spiteful, but I'm so bitter about the way she tricked Ernie into marrying her.'

'He must do something, Jan, or this one will have his name, too. Perhaps he could get compassionate leave now that he's in the merchant navy.'

Jan's face lit up. 'Rosie, wouldn't it be wonderful if he could?'

In the tram going home Rosie sat deep in thought. It would be marvellous if Ernie could get a divorce and marry Jan. He shouldn't have any difficulty in proving this child wasn't his. He hadn't been in Cardiff since he'd left home.

When she opened the front door her mother-in-law came into the hall. Rosie suddenly felt remorse for not returning sooner as she saw that the older woman's eyes were red and swollen.

'Mother!' Rosie put her arms round her and they clung together. For the first time she felt close to Roy's mother.

After lunch David came to walk Beth's pram up and down the garden. It had to be the garden because her mother-in-law insisted on watching covertly from the boxroom window, but of this David remained blissfully unaware.

Rosie pushed the curtain aside in the kitchenette and gazed outside at her brother tenderly as he bent over the pram, smiling and talking to the baby. Since David's illness, when Rosie had risked her own life and the baby's to nurse him, he seemed to have come to terms with the fact that while she lived with Mrs Cunningham she couldn't be with her. They'd had a long talk and she'd promised that when she and Roy had a place of their own David could come with them. Now they were closer than ever and David treated little Beth like a baby sister.

Very little had happened on the home front since that day early last September when war was declared. People carried their gas-masks everywhere, slung over their shoulders in little cardboard boxes. The blackout was irksome, and dangerous, too. It was easy to fall over a kerb or walk smack into a wall as Miriam had done.

'They'll think your father's been knocking me about, they will,' she'd joked, hiding her shiner under a pink eye-shade.

On the tenth of May the King called Mr Winston Churchill to Buckingham Palace and asked him to form a government, and Rosie was surprised to find her father and Miriam approving.

'A coalition government is a very good thing in wartime,' Arthur said. 'The best brains from each party in the War Cabinet, that's what we need in times like these.'

A few weeks later the Germans had cut off the British Expeditionary Force in the countryside behind Dunkirk. Somehow the men had to be evacuated. When the government broadcast an appeal for seaworthy small boats to brave enemy mines and help to bring them home, the response was overwhelming.

'Frank's over there,' Miriam reminded her. 'Ada says he'd have missed this lot if he'd waited to be called up.'

Rosie knew that Ada blamed her for Frank volunteering in the early days. She was very thankful a few days later to hear that he was back in Britain at a military hospital, suffering only from exhaustion after his ordeal, especially when Ada told her that they'd been bombed continually as they lay on the beaches waiting to be rescued.

Now the Germans were within easy striking distance of Britain. Night after night as the sirens wailed Rosie'd lift Beth from her cot and carry her Welsh fashion, wrapped tightly against her body, to the shelter at the end of the garden. Here they'd sit on the blanket-covered benches listening to distant ack-ack fire. Sometimes the ominous throb of enemy planes would threaten them. They would sit silently, straining their ears to listen, relaxing only when at last the planes had passed over.

With her hair messed up from sleep and with no time for her customary careful grooming, even Roy's mother looked vulnerable in the sickly glow from the shelter lantern. Poor Mother, Rosie thought, her well-ordered world had been turned upside down.

As the all-clear sounded they'd climb stiffly from the shelter to a sky reddened by distant fires and thankfully drink a cup of tea before going back to bed.

It was September and Roy had gone back from leave only a week ago, promising to try to be home for Christmas. On the third, after a particularly bad night when bombs had dropped all round them, Roy's mother broached the topic of taking Beth to her sister's in Devon for safety.

'I don't really like it there, Rose, I was very bored last year, but I'd put up with anything for Beth, you know that.'

Rosie knew it only too well, and her heart contracted at the thought of parting with the baby. She was only just beginning to make headway with her since Roy's mother had taken sole charge during the aftermath of influenza and the birth.

'Well? What do you think, Rose?'

'Couldn't it wait a little while, Mother?' Rosie licked her dry lips anxiously.

'Really, Rose!' her mother-in-law cried angrily. 'I'm willing to make the sacrifice. Most mothers would be thankful just to know their baby was safe.'

With tears in her eyes Rosie took the little dresses she'd been ironing when the raid started upstairs to the nursery bedroom. Folding the tiny garments and putting them in the drawer, she went over and over their conversation. She knew that Roy's mother was right, Beth's safety must come first. She'd never forgive herself if anything happened to her. She could visit them, couldn't she?

Heavy-hearted she went downstairs. Her mother-in-law was cradling Beth in her arms, a tender expression on her face as she watched the sleeping child.

Rosie moistened dry lips. 'You can write to your sister, Mother. I'll come to visit as often as I can.'

'Why don't you come with us, Rose? I'm sure she'd put you up.'

'But we can't leave the house empty.' She could see her mother-in-law's face blanch at the thought of its being requisitioned. Her precious home taken over by careless inhabitants. Nowhere for Roy to come back to . . .

'Well, perhaps you could come to stay sometimes, Rose?' It was as though the invitation to accompany her had never been made. Seeing the look of dismay still on her face, Rosie said quickly, 'Don't worry, Mother, I'll stay here for a while. If you take Beth to Devon, I should look for a useful job.'

Rosie's heart swelled as she looked at the sleeping baby. Although she was relieved at the decision she'd made, her lips trembled at the thought of parting with her.

The letter was sent. A few days later the reply came. Mrs Cunningham's sister had four evacuees, and already had her hands full. If they came, they'd have to sleep in the kitchen. The parlour already had two beds. Roy's mother decided not to go for the time being.

*   *   *

On the day Rosie took the Christmas presents for her father, Miriam and the boys, she stayed longer than usual. She was loath to leave the warm kitchen, festive with home-made decorations and alive with memories of her childhood.

She had just shrugged unwillingly into her coat to leave when the siren wailed. As they hurried down the garden path to the shelter, Ada, Bert and other neighbours were making for theirs, shouting and joking with each other. When the shelter door was closed and the lantern lit, the boys began to sing, 'We're Gonna Hang Out the Washing on the Siegfried Line', and one by one they joined in as though they hadn't a care in the world.

As they finished singing 'Lilli Marlene' and began 'Shine on, Victory Moon', Miriam produced a flask and sandwiches from the shopping bag she'd brought with her and they began to talk about Christmas. Rosie couldn't help contrasting the scene with a typical night in the shelter at The Laurels where they often sat in silence, listening anxiously, the silence broke only by Beth's occasional whimpering.

At the thought of Roy's mother alone with Beth the happy mood left her. Feeling suddenly worried, she wished the all-clear would come quickly.

When half an hour later they climbed out and walked towards the house, David slipped his hand in hers. 'Couldn't you stay with us tonight, Rosie?' he pleaded. 'You can have my bed.' But now she was anxious to be gone, and Arthur was waiting to walk her home.

Roy didn't come home for Christmas. Filled with disappointment she wrapped the Fair-Isle pullover she'd knitted him in tissue paper and put it away, than posted the warm balaclava helmet and army socks, together with a Christmas cake.

The New Year came in freezing cold. On the second of January Beth had a slight chill and it was a long time before she got off to sleep. Rosie was just tiptoeing away from the cot when the siren wailed its warning.

For a moment she was tempted to leave her there. Poor little thing, she'd been snuffling all day.

'Rose! Come down quickly!' Her mother-in-law's anxious voice from the foot of the stairs galvanised her into action. Lifting the child she wrapped her warmly in two shawls.

As they banged the side door shut and hurried down the path, incendiaries began to fall. The menacing throb of planes, sounding very near, made them scuttle for the shelter. The sky was a greenish yellow, the afterglow of incendiaries and flares. As they closed the door, the terrifying whistle of falling bombs began overhead.

During a lull Rosie pushed the door open a fraction and glanced upwards. Sweeping searchlights crisscrossed the sky, now stained red from the reflections of many fires.

Suddenly the gun barrage seemed to be immediately overhead. The terrible noise frightened Beth awake and she began to scream. Above it all came the whistle of bombs and the steady rat-a-tat of ack-ack fire.

Roy's mother, her face white and taut, held out her arms for the baby. She rocked to and fro, cradling the child, whispering endearments, until the frightened screaming became little hiccuping sobs.

'Poor little love,' she said. 'It isn't fair, Rose, we'll have to do something.'

At four-fifty in the morning came the longed-for all-clear. Stiff and cold they climbed out to the smell of acrid smoke and a sky that seemed on fire.

Carrying the now sleeping Beth upstairs, Rosie switched on the bedroom light and blinked in the sudden brightness.

Moving towards the cot she stopped dead, staring in horror at a hole in the mattress. Above the cot festoons of plaster swayed in the breeze from a gaping ceiling. Her gaze travelled downwards past the cot, her mouth open in surprise. Embedded in the floorboards beneath it was the cap from an anti-aircraft shell. Realizing what could have happened had Beth been there, she began to shiver.

When Roy's mother had recovered from the shock, her mind was made up.

'I'm taking Beth to my sister's today, Rose,' she said. 'We can't take any more risks. What will you do?'

'I'll stay for a while, Mother, in case Roy gets leave.' Rosie wanted to protest, 'I want Beth with me,' but knew that in her heart she'd be grateful to have the baby safe.

Early that afternoon, when the train was drawing out of the station, she stood forlornly waving until it was out of sight. She felt empty, drained, reliving her last sight of Beth's plump pink cheeks and wide brown eyes, as her mother-in-law had carried her aboard. Telling herself over and over that it was for the baby's own good, a sob rose in her throat. She lowered her head to hide her tears and left the station.

Now she lived for the postman's visits, and for Roy's leave which should be only a few weeks away, already planning for them to spend a night at the village inn to be near Beth and Mrs Cunningham.

Preparations and plans kept her busy. He hadn't been home for Christmas and she was determined to try to make it up to him, scrimping and saving on her rations, having her main meal out sometimes; it all helped. The day before he was expected she'd just put a tray of mince pies in the cooker when there was a knock on the door. Still flushed from the heat of the oven she hurried to open it.

'Roy!' Suddenly they were locked in each other's arms, clinging to each other, her love for him swelling until it hurt. Their lips met in a long kiss, but presently he held her from him, gently dusting flour from her cheek. Flinging his gas-mask on to the hall-stand, he said, 'I've got something I must tell you, Rose, but don't let it spoil this time together.'

Her heart gave a little lurch as she guessed, even before he said, 'This is embarkation leave. I've only got seventy-two hours.'

'Oh Roy!' She flung her arms about him once more, her heart full of love and fear of the unknown, and of the great distance that would soon be between them.

'Rose,' he said gently, pulling her down to the sofa, 'we've got to plan. I have to be back at barracks on Thursday morning.'

'What shall we do about seeing Beth and your mother? Won't we be able to spend a night in Lynford?'

'We could go today, Rose. It's only twelve o'clock – we could be there this evening.'

'But we haven't booked a room, love. There's nowhere for us to sleep at the cottage.'

'Don't worry, we'll find somewhere.'

Roy's face and hands were still blue with the cold, his cheek had been icy against her own. She pulled him towards the kitchen and the glowing fire, and when he was seated in the armchair beside it she made a pot of tea with the already boiling kettle, using two spoonfuls, knowing she would be short before the next ration was due. He looked so tired she longed to spoil him with a decent meal and all the comforts she could give him but with a cup of tea and two mince pies before him he talked anxiously of seeing Beth and his mother as soon as possible, and she understood why when he explained, 'I'm on standby, Rose, they could send for me. I've given them the address in Devon as well as here. There's a train at about two o'clock, isn't there?'

Rosie nodded, her mind already on the few things she must pack. There was no way of letting them know they were coming, for the cottage, like The Laurels, was not on the phone.

'If only we had some petrol, Roy.'

'There may be a little in the car, but not enough to get us to Devon, never mind getting us back.'

There was certainly no way of getting any without the necessary coupons.

They spent the train journey as far as Bristol in the crowded corridor, pushed this way and that, as servicemen with kitbags and civilians with cases nudged past them in a fruitless search for a carriage with an empty seat.

At Bristol they dashed down one flight of steps and up another to the platform where the train to Devon should be leaving in about twenty minutes.

When they reached the platform a lady porter was coming towards them pushing a trolley stacked with boxes, baggy dark serge uniform trousers emphasising her wide hips, a peaked cap perched on top of a fuzz of dark hair.

'Train to Lynford?' She pushed her cap back, even further. 'Ah, yes! I'm afraid it's been cancelled, m'dears.'

'Cancelled!' they chorused, looking at her in dismay, the same thought in both their minds – seventy-two hours.

'What time is the next?' Roy asked as she turned to trundle the heavy load down the platform.

'Tomorrow morning, the milk train. Don't think there'll be one through before.'

'Oh Roy! What shall we do?' Rosie wailed.

'Well, first of all we'll see if we can get a cup of tea and something to eat, if they can manage anything with a war on.' He smiled down at her and she knew his bantering tone was just to cover his own dismay.

'I've got some sandwiches, Roy.'

'Better keep those for later on, Rose, I've got a feeling we'll be needing them.'

They returned to the platform after a luncheon-meat sandwich that curled at the edges and made Rosie think longingly of the ones she'd made with the whole two weeks' ration of corned beef. It was already dark and the blackouts were drawn over all the windows. They pushed open the door of the restroom and closed it quickly. The single light inside was dim, the ashes in the grate cold, and the coal scuttle empty. It was a few minutes before they even noticed the young sailor with his girlfriend on his knee, sitting on the bench in the far corner. He raised his head long enough to give them a cheeky grin, then went back to kissing his girl.

Hours later the sound of a train sent them rushing outside, but the blinds were drawn in every carriage as it went through the station at speed.

'A troop train?' Rosie asked. But Roy just shrugged his shoulders.

At about five in the morning they were woken shivering by the sound of a bell, and minutes later there was a grinding of brakes and a hissing of steam as a train drew in. They dashed out; there seemed to be nobody around, but then a carriage door opened and a man got off, answering their question. 'Yes, it's going to Exeter.'

The carriage they got into was cold and smelt of stale cigarette smoke but they were thankful to be on their way at last. It was a slow train, stopping at every halt it seemed, noisy with the clatter of milk churns being rolled into the goods van. Soon it was full daylight and when the dim blue light in the carriage went out they were able to put up the blind.

At last they were off the train and walking down Lynford's main street. They were stiff, cold and hungry, but both of them were excited at the thought of seeing little Beth again. Roy's mother opened the door, flinging her arms about him, her cheeks wet with joy, and then they were in the tiny kitchen, where Beth was playing with a rag doll in front of the guarded fire.

When Roy bent to pick her up she screamed with fright.

'She doesn't recognise you in that uniform,' Rosie comforted him, seeing the hurt and disappointment in his eyes. But fifteen minutes later, his jacket removed, he was bouncing her on his knee singing, 'Jack and Jill went up the hill to fetch a pail of water—' and Beth was chuckling happily.

When Roy's Aunt Evelyn returned from shopping she was surprised to see Rosie and Roy walking up and down the garden path with Beth toddling between them, her hands clasped tightly in theirs.

'Oh! it's lovely to see you both,' she said, putting her arms about them. Rosie got on well with Aunt Evelyn, who had put her quickly at ease on her very first visit. Rosie knew that the little evacuees, who had not yet returned from school, adored her, and that all her sweet ration, and probably Roy's mother's, too, was spent on them and little Beth.

They got home to The Laurels in the early hours of Wednesday morning, lucky to find a taxi waiting at the General Station. Roy had been quiet on the way home, which had been a much easier journey, with only an hour's wait at Bristol. She had put his silence down to lack of sleep, but also to an emotional parting from his baby daughter, his mother and his aunt. And their own parting was soon to come, Rosie thought sadly, the dreaded moment never far from her mind.

The house was cold when they got in and the first thing she did was switch on the two bars of the electric fire in the lounge before she went to the kitchen to make tea. Roy, his face now grey with fatigue, had flung himself on the settee. When Rosie returned with the tea tray he was slumped against the cushions, fast asleep.

'Roy,' she called softly, then a little louder, 'Roy!' But he didn't stir, and the tea in his cup became cold as, after trying unsuccessfully to wake him, she took off his boots and lifted his feet on to the cushions, then fetching the eiderdown from the bedroom tucked it round him.

She sat watching him tenderly, thankful to see the healthy colour return to his cheeks, gazing at his face as though she would memorise every feature; the straight nose, the firm chin, the strong, dark lashes. Rosie smoothed back the crisp, wavy hair, but still he didn't stir. Going to the bedroom once more she brought a warm blanket to put round her shoulders, and drawing a comfortable chair towards the couch, she sat down, her head against the cushions, the blanket about her, and took Roy's hand in hers. She couldn't bear to leave him, even to go to bed; she had to be with him. Their time together was now so short. Thursday morning would come all too soon.

Chapter 21

On a bitterly cold night in February Rosie boarded the Ordnance factory bus. She was glad to have a little time to herself before Mollie got on, for she knew her new friend would talk non-stop until they reached the factory.

The bus was almost as dark as the blackout outside and soon she was lulled into a reverie in which she, Roy and Beth were living in the lovely white bungalow they had so nearly bought. If only they had, she thought wistfully, then Beth would be with her now.

It was 1942, almost a year since Roy's embarkation leave and her longing for him was intense. At first she'd worked at Goldberg's Emporium again, taking the place of a young man from the manchester department who'd been called up. It had been hard work lugging the heavy bales of cloth and flannelette to the counter for measuring, and, although she'd enjoyed the company, it wasn't like the lingerie department she'd once worked in.

Suddenly she'd wanted to do something more useful for the war effort. For a while she toyed with the idea of joining the ATS or the WAAF, but that would have meant seeing Beth only when she was on leave. The Ordnance factory had seemed the obvious choice.

When at the end of 1941 it was announced that women were to be conscripted into the forces and munitions factories, she was glad she'd made her own choice.

It hadn't been easy visiting Devon even when weekend shifts allowed. A cancelled train last month had resulted in her missing a shift. There'd been such a fuss that she hadn't gone again until last weekend.

And after all her efforts to arrange the trip, it had ended in disappointment. Reaching the gate of the cottage, the door had opened and she'd run towards Beth, gathering her into her arms, hugging and kissing her. But there'd been no answering hug. Instead, Beth had twisted away from her and held out her arms, crying, 'Grandma! – Grandma-a.'

Roy's mother had taken the child, murmuring softly, 'Shush, darling, Grandma's here.'

It had been like a knife twisting in her heart to see her mother-in-law taking Rosie's rightful place with Beth – and knowing that until the war ended there was nothing she could do about it. Her eyes stinging with unshed tears, she'd followed them into the cottage.

The Ordnance factory bus had stopped for the third time when Mollie got on, her pale gold pageboy bob still swinging as she sat down beside Rosie. She was tall and slim, and Rosie reflected that only Mollie could look like a fashion model while wearing faded dungarees and wooden-soled clogs. Mollie turned towards her, her wide blue eyes dancing with good humour as she began telling Rosie about her weekend. Heart-whole as she intended to stay, Mollie was enjoying the war. She was only halfway through her story when the bus entered the factory gates.

As Rosie tied the snood about her hair and walked to her machine, the clatter and noise was deafening, and the now familiar smell of warm lubricating oil stung her nostrils. Smoothing Roselex into her hands, she switched on and started the gun barrel rotating, then, adjusting the cutting tool, brought it into contact, watching hot swarf twist and turn as it rose from the machine, rapidly changing colour through various shades of purple to indigo. Pulling away the swarf with a long-handled hook, she stopped the machine and reached for the callipers.

Mollie was working in the next bay; she could see her over the top of her machine laughing with a man who was pulling the swarf away for her. They had very little in common, Rosie thought, but there was something about Mollie's irrepressible good humour that attracted her; to be with her was a relief from her own worries about Roy, Beth, her mother-in-law, and her brothers, for at nineteen Willie, too, was in the army, and Bobby planned to follow him as soon as he was old enough.

At break time, as they walked in the darkness towards the canteen, Mollie continued her tale.

'Tom's taking me to the pictures tonight, Rosie. He's smashing to go out with.'

'I thought you said he was married?'

'So he is, but the poor bloke's got to have some fun, hasn't he?'

'What about his wife?' Rosie ventured.

'Lucky she is that it's me he's going round with. I've got no designs on him other than having a good time.' Mollie laughed.

Rosie thought how she would feel if it was Roy playing around.

'It's not right, Mollie,' she said. 'It'll all end in tears, you mark my words.'

On the stage at one end of the canteen the curtain was going up on a 'Workers' Playtime' variety show, and as Mollie replied she was shushed into silence.

One Thursday early in March as she sat beside Rosie in the bus, Mollie's blue eyes were awash with tears.

'Could I come to stay with you for a few nights, Rosie?'

'Oh, I don't know, Mollie. I'm going to Devon on Saturday.'

'Well, just till then?' Mollie begged.

'What's happened? Why can't you stay at home?'

'My mother's making an awful fuss. She's – she's found out that Tom's married. It's only a bit of fun, Rosie, but the way she's carrying on you'd think I was a scarlet woman.'

'Well, I did warn you. Why can't you go out with someone who's single?'

'That's just it, Rosie, I don't want to be serious. I don't want to be left like you, never having any real fun.'

'Thanks,' Rosie said drily, but Mollie was warming to her subject. 'You could have a good time too if only you weren't married. Some girls have plenty of fun anyway, even when they are.'

'I don't want fun, Mollie, I just want this war over and Roy and Beth back home.'

'But can I come and stay with you, please? I'm a bundle of nerves, jonick I am. We'll have a lark, you and me, Rosie. Come on, you look as though you could do with some brightening up.'

'Just for a couple of nights then. I hope you'll soon make it up at home – I don't think Roy's mother would like it.'

Mollie grimaced. 'Tonight can I come then, after work?'

When about eight that evening Rosie opened the door to Mollie, she was surprised to find her accompanied by a soldier carrying two enormous suitcases.

Introducing Tom, Mollie said, 'How about a cup of tea, Rosie, the poor boy's worn out lugging that lot.'

As she made sandwiches, noting ruefully that it took the last of her cheese ration, Rosie had a sinking feeling that Mollie had no intention of making it up with her mother.

It was nearly half past ten when Tom rose to go, and by that time the corned-beef part of Rosie's meat ration had gone, too.

'I hope this won't happen often—' she began when she and Mollie were alone.

'Well, I had to show him I was grateful for his help,' her friend broke in defensively.

The following night Tom brought a box of chocolates, and Mollie promised she'd get her rations for the week. It became obvious to Rosie that she wouldn't be able to go to Devon.

They were on the night shift the following week and Tom was still a constant visitor. Every evening he'd stay until they were ready to leave for work, and at the last minute Rosie had to rush round in a panic making sure their cigarette ends were out.

On the Wednesday evening as the darkened bus droned its way to the factory, Rosie decided to tell Mollie once more that she'd have to find somewhere else by the weekend.

'I been looking, Rosie, honest I have. Tom goes on leave on Friday. It'll be better without him, you'll see.'

'You'll have to find somewhere by Saturday.'

'I'll try, honest I will.'

But when the weekend came Rosie had to cancel her plans to visit Beth once again.

On the Saturday evening, her heart heavy with disappointment, she washed her hair and curled up on the settee with *Gone With the Wind*. Mollie had gone out with some friends, saying she would be home early.

At eleven o'clock Rosie tore herself away from the book to put the kettle on, telling herself that when the supper dishes were washed she'd go to bed, even though Mollie had no key. She was putting the dishes away when the knocker was banged repeatedly. Going into the hall, she heard giggling and scuffling outside the door.

In the porch, Mollie, accompanied by two young soldiers, was laughing as she prepared to usher them into the house.

'Oh no, Mollie,' Rosie said firmly. 'You'd better see your friends to the tram stop. I'm just going to lock up.'

The smile left Mollie's face. 'Don't get your hair off, Rosie, the poor boys have just lost the last tram.'

When Rosie didn't answer, she wheedled, 'Ructions there'll be if they're missed. If they could stay here until morning they might get in without anyone noticing.'

'No!' Rosie said determinedly. 'It isn't my house, and I've had enough anyway.'

But Mollie hadn't given up. 'Like your Roy to walk the streets all night, would you? They didn't miss the tram on purpose.'

Filled with misgivings Rosie let them in reluctantly and bolted the door.

'Thanks! We'll be gone first thing.' The soldier who spoke looked too young to be in uniform. The other echoed his agreement.

Rosie put the kettle on, and when the sandwiches and tea were finished, blankets brought and the soldiers directed to the bathroom, she and Mollie went up to bed.

Rosie had just dropped into an uneasy sleep when she woke suddenly to the sound of a car door slamming. Dragging on her dressing gown she hurried to the window in time to see a taxi draw away. Even in the darkness, with a sinking feeling in her stomach, she recognised her mother-in-law coming up the path.

Her mind leapt to the soldiers asleep in the lounge, and her eyes flew to Mollie curled up like a kitten in bed.

As she heard the key turn in the lock the flush was pulled in the bathroom and there was the sound of heavy footsteps descending the stairs. She froze as her mother-in-law's voice rose angrily above the soldier's.

'Get out, do you hear me? Get out! Where's my daughter-in-law? Well, I never thought to find this—'

Suddenly galvanised into action, Rosie flew down the stairs, crying, 'I can explain, Mother—'

'I think you'd better,' Roy's mother broke in angrily. 'It's going to take some explaining—'

The door slammed behind the two soldiers who had rapidly got dressed and run out when confronted by the livid Mrs Cunningham. Rosie was saying, 'The poor boys missed their last tram,' when Mollie appeared at the top of the stairs in her skimpy cotton nightie.

Mrs Cunningham's mouth opened in astonishment. Her face was beetroot red, her eyes accusing.

'Well! I can see it's high time that I did come home and see just what's going on. To think I felt sorry for you, Rose, all on your own, eating your heart out over Roy.'

'It's all my fault—' Mollie began.

'Who are you? And what are you doing in my house?'

Rosie closed her eyes and clung to the doorpost. It was like a nightmare, but painfully she knew she was awake. When she opened them her mother-in-law was staring at her with icy coldness. Again she tried to explain.

'It isn't like you think, Mother—' But Mrs Cunningham was in no mood to listen.

'I've noticed your visits aren't as frequent as they used to be, Rose, and now the reason seems obvious. I came because I had a letter from Lilla saying the Major has been very ill, but is recovering, thank goodness. I felt I must pay them a visit. Also I need to take back some summer clothes for Beth and myself. I'd have written and asked you to bring them but we can't rely on your visits these days, can we?'

'Please, Mother, let me try and explain. I'll make you a cup of tea—'

'No, thank you. I filled a thermos for the journey. If the train hadn't been cancelled I'd have been here hours ago. I was looking forward to staying for the night, Beth's fine with my sister, but really I'm so upset I don't know what I should do. I don't really believe you're a bad girl, Rose. I suspect that friend of yours has led you into this.'

Brushing all explanations aside, she picked up her case. With her chin high, and looking every inch the injured party, she went upstairs to her room.

Chapter 22

Waking from a restless sleep to a feeling of apprehension, Rosie looked at Mollie resentfully. No hint of conscience had kept her awake; she slept like a child, long lashes curling on her flushed cheeks, silky fair hair spread over the pillow.

When, washed and dressed, Rosie went downstairs, Roy's mother was sitting at the kitchen table, her face pale and her lips drawn into a thin line of disapproval.

Putting a cup of tea in front of Rosie, she said, 'I still can't believe that you could act so stupidly, Rose.'

'But they were Mollie's friends, Mother, and they had missed their last tram.'

'You didn't know them. You admitted that you'd never set eyes on them before, yet you left them alone and went to bed. Supposing they'd been dishonest? You realise they could have taken anything?'

'They wouldn't do that. It was my fault anyway, I persuaded Rosie to let them stay.' Mollie, still in her dressing gown, shut the door and sat down.

Roy's mother shot her a look of malevolent dislike. 'You seem to have taken a lot on yourself,' she said. 'I hope your stay here isn't for very long, young lady. I think you're a bad influence—'

Mollie jumped up, knocking over the tea Rosie had poured for her. As the stain spread on the white damask cloth, she yelled, 'I won't stay where I'm not wanted. Cor! I'd rather my mam any day, even though she makes a lot of fuss about nothing.'

'Look, Mother, Mollie's my friend. I may have acted without thinking but there was no harm in it. She'll be leaving here soon, there's no need for bad feeling.'

'I dare say there was no harm meant, Rose, but did you stop to think what the neighbours would make of it?'

Mollie had dashed upstairs. She came down a few minutes later, coat flapping, lugging one of the heavy suitcases.

'Goodbye, Rosie. See you at work,' she said, darting a venomous look at Mrs Cunningham.

'Hang on a minute—' Rosie began, but the door slammed behind Mollie, and Roy's mother continued in a pleasanter tone, 'I'm just going to see Mrs Thomas – she'll be at home on a Sunday morning. It's a pity she had to leave us for that job in the Ordnance factory canteen. I was wondering if she could recommend someone to work here for a few hours each day.'

'But I've managed fine since she left,' Rosie protested. Then it dawned on her that her mother-in-law might want someone to keep an eye on her. She blushed scarlet and her anger rose.

'I insist on telling you exactly what happened,' she said firmly, and Mrs Cunningham looked at her in surprise. Rosie explained about Mollie having nowhere to stay, leaving out the reason why, and about the soldiers missing the last tram and coming back with Mollie. 'Now I'm going to see if I can find Mollie,' she said, flinging on her coat and slamming the front door.

Hurrying along to the tram stop, her anger began to evaporate. After all, it must have been a shock for Roy's mother. How on earth had she got herself into this situation?

The cause of it all was leaning against the wall, grinning.

'Looks as if I'll have to finish with Tom after all – there's a pity, but I'll have to make it up with my old lady,' she said.

The arrival of the tram prevented Rosie from voicing the angry retort that rose to her lips. It was just a game to Mollie; she didn't seem to realise the havoc she caused by her thoughtlessness.

Returning to the house, her thoughts were with Roy. He was somewhere in North Africa. What if his mother wrote to him about last night? But she wouldn't upset Roy; whatever her mother-in-law's faults, Rosie knew she wouldn't do that. Anyway there was nothing really to tell, but it might seem very different to Roy all those thousands of miles from home.

Opening the door she remembered the Coty face powder she'd

bought at the factory concession shop. She'd managed to get her mother-in-law's favourite shade, and Rosie's occasional gifts of good-quality make-up were much appreciated even though they had the words 'Front Line Duty' stamped all over them.

There'd been a day before she'd worked at the factory when, queuing outside a shop in Queen Street, she'd bought a box of face powder to take to Devon. Accepting the gift eagerly, Roy's mother had opened the box and dabbed the powder puff over her face. Rosie had watched in amazement as the powder turned to cocoa-coloured streaks on her skin. They'd laughed about it, but the gift had been a disappointment to both of them.

Mrs Cunningham had already left on her visit and Rosie had lunch almost ready by the time she returned. Hanging up her coat, she said, 'Mrs Thomas has recommended a Mrs Griffiths, Rose – she'll be starting the week after next. You'll be on the day shift then, won't you? Once you've met her you can make your own arrangements.'

Rosie nodded miserably.

'I'm doing this to help you, Rose. You can't feel like doing housework when you come home from the factory. Oh! I've made a little present for you, you've been so good about the face powder and cream.'

'I've got another box of Coty for you, Mother, it's in the side board dresser.'

Thanking her warmly, Mrs Cunningham went upstairs, returning with a lacy, hand-knitted jumper in a pretty shade of turquoise.

Rosie held it against herself in front of the hall mirror.

'It's beautiful, Mother, really lovely. I could give you some clothing coupons for the wool.'

'No need, Rose. I don't have to buy many clothes myself, living in the country.'

On a sudden impulse she hugged her mother-in-law and kissed her cheek warmly. 'Oh, Mother! It is good of you to make it for me, such a lovely pattern too. It must have taken a lot of concentration.'

Poor Mrs Cunningham, she thought, she would have looked forward to coming home for a couple of days, and it had all been spoilt for her. She looked pale and heavy-eyed today; she must have had a worrying night because Rosie hadn't been allowed to explain the situation until this morning.

When, late in the afternoon, they parted at the station, Rosie felt a strong urge to jump on the train and go with her to Devon. Anyway, she thought, with Mollie gone there'll be nothing to stop me visiting Beth next weekend.

On the Monday that Mrs Griffiths was to start, Rosie breakfasted early. She knew Roy's mother wouldn't have approved of the way she'd spent yesterday, polishing and cleaning, determined to make a good impression on the new daily help.

When she heard feet crunching on the gravel path, she hurried to the door. Opening it wide, she stared dumbfounded at the shabby figure of Lizzie James, who stared back in equal astonishment.

'Rosie!' she spluttered. 'I – I wasn't expectin' you. I came to see a Mrs Cunningham.'

'I am Mrs Cunningham,' Rosie informed her. 'But why do you want to see me?'

'About the job it is, Rosie.' Lizzie shifted uneasily from one foot to the other.

'But it's already taken. I'm expecting a Mrs Griffiths.'

'That's my sister,' Lizzie told her. 'She can't leave 'er job for a few weeks. Going to do the two she was, but she's agreed to let me work 'ere until she's free. That's if you don't mind.'

Rosie hesitated, thinking how carefully her mother-in-law had vetted Mrs Griffiths. Lizzie, taking her silence for approval, stepped into the hall saying, 'Earn my money I will, Rosie, an' God knows I need it. I carn even get the kids a pair of daps to wear to school. Duw! I'd die, girl, if they gave them some other kid's cast-offs right there in front of the 'ole class.'

Remembering her own dread of this very thing when the boys were young, and how Dada had always managed to get a bit of leather to mend their boots, Rosie felt a pang of sympathy for Lizzie, despite her qualms.

' 'Opeless it is,' Lizzie went on. 'You don't owe me no favours, I know that, and sorry I am now that I upset you. 'E didn't pass the Army medical, and 'e can't pass a pub with 'is dole money, Rosie. I've 'ad a bellyful, I can tell you.' She stopped breathlessly.

Looking at the tired, lined face – and she must be still only in her early forties – Rosie thought how awful it must be to have a husband like hers, drinking away the money that was so desperately needed.

She took Lizzie through to the kitchen, thinking ruefully of what Dada had said when she'd told him about the trouble over Mollie.

'You're too much of a soft touch, Rosie love. You'll have to learn to harden your heart.'

Despite the fear of what her mother-in-law her might say if she found out about the deception, for the sake of Lizzie's children she couldn't harden her heart this time.

Chapter 23

'These posh 'ouses don't take much keepin' clean, do they?' Lizzie remarked, rolling up her overall and taking her threadbare coat from the hall-stand.

It was two weeks since she'd started working at The Laurels and Rosie, who was once more on the night shift, was waiting for Lizzie to finish so that she could go to bed. Thinking of her own cleaning spree each evening she smiled to herself, determined her old enemy would find nothing to criticise or discuss with her neighbours.

Lizzie was right, of course, about The Laurels; Rosie herself had almost forgotten what it was like to have the coalman carry dirty sacks right through the house to the coalshed in the back yard.

Rosie sighed with relief as the door closed behind Lizzie, but her dislike of the woman whose strident voice had yelled abuse at her when Ernie left Bella was now mixed with pity. This morning Lizzie's left eye had been puffed and discoloured, and she was thinner even than Rosie remembered. She was glad she'd given her those cakes and sweets for the children, and Lizzie had been so grateful. Whatever her faults she loved her kids.

A few weeks later Rosie broached the subject that had been worrying her.

'When is your sister going to take over the job, Lizzie?'

Lizzie looked flustered, then put on an injured expression. 'Don't I suit you then, Rosie? 'Aven't I done it proper like?'

Rosie shook her head. 'It isn't that at all. It was your sister my mother-in-law interviewed, and she's asking in her letters how Mrs Griffiths is getting on. I shall have to tell her if she isn't going to come.'

'Our Mary isn't goin' to leave her job now, Rosie. Offered 'er more money to stay the woman 'ave.' She fumbled in her coat pocket and brought out a crumpled envelope.

'But this was written a fortnight ago,' Rosie protested when she'd read the contents.

Lizzie gave a deep sigh, rubbing the duster slowly over the gleaming surface of the walnut occasional table.

' ²Oped I did you'd keep me on, Rosie. Wonderful it is workin' 'ere, and the kids 'ave a decent dinner every day now. I was 'oping to put some clothes on their backs before I left, and – and I love this place, Rosie, it's – it's like workin' in a palace.'

Comparing The Laurels to a palace made even Rosie smile, but she knew just what Lizzie meant. She ought to be angry about the deception, but she felt only pity and understanding.

'Don't worry about it, Lizzie,' she said kindly. 'I'll write to my mother-in-law and see if you can stay.'

The letter she wrote to Mrs Cunningham was factual. Mrs Griffiths had wanted her sister to stand in for her until she could come herself, but had now changed her mind. Rosie found her sister, Mrs James, very satisfactory. Could she stay on? She omitted to say that she'd known Lizzie James all her life.

The day Rosie told her she could stay Lizzie went round the house with the tin of Mansion polish and a duster, giving a good imitation of someone trying to rub holes in the furniture. Rosie could hardly believe the shining house was the work of the usually slovenly Lizzie. Why doesn't she put a little of this energy into her own house? Rosie thought, then remembered tales she'd heard of how her husband was always busting the place up.

The overall Lizzie wore to do her work was always clean, but the pattern had faded almost to non-existence, and the material had a greyish grain. Rolling the overall up one day, she said, 'Buy myself a new one I will as soon as I've got some clobber for the kids.'

A few days later, passing the gondola of overalls in Goldberg's doorway, Rosie remembered her words. There was a very attractive one with a pattern of cornflowers on a pale blue background, and an equally pretty one with sprays of pink roses on white. On an impulse Rosie bought the two.

When she gave them to Lizzie her gratitude was almost pathetic.

'Never 'ad nothin' new before, Rosie,' she told her. 'Glad I am, mind, of the things our Mary do pass on.' She put the cornflower-patterned overall on and preened herself in front of the hall mirror. 'Lovely, innit, Rosie?'

The next morning her hair was freshly washed, and she'd crimped a wave in it with curling tongs.

The days were getting warmer and Rosie's thoughts were as usual with Roy in the heat of the desert. The letters that had at first been fairly regular now arrived fitfully. Sometimes a month would pass and she'd be sick with worry, then two or three would arrive together.

On a morning early in July she was having breakfast and reading one that had just arrived when there was a loud rat-a-tat at the front door.

Going into the hall her heart missed a beat – through the glass she saw the outline of a small figure in a dark uniform and the unmistakable pillbox hat.

She opened the door and taking the buff envelope fearfully tore it open. The dreaded words leapt at her from the telegram:

'REGRET TO INFORM . . . CORPORAL ROYSTON CUNNINGHAM . . . KILLED IN ACTION . . .'

The colour drained from her face as she clung to the door for support.

The boy, his eyes filled with pity, asked, 'You all right, lady?'

'Yes. Yes thank you.' She just wanted him to be gone. He looked concerned, but turned and walked towards his bike, then glanced back uncertainly, but she was already closing the door.

Shaking uncontrollably Rosie put the telegram on the table and sat down. The letter still lay open before her but she knew the words by heart.

'. . . Can't wait for this war to be over, Rose, my love, to be with you and little Beth again. As soon as I get home we'll find a place of our own and . . .' A tear plopped on to the page, smudging some of the words. Dropping her head on her hands the tears spurted through her fingers and sobs shook her body.

Presently, hearing a key in the lock of the front door, she

fumbled for her handkerchief. When Lizzie entered the kitchen she stared at Rosie in astonishment.

'Rosie! I thought you'd have gone to work by now . . .' Then she saw the telegram, and Rosie pushed it towards her.

'Oh, no! Oh, you poor lamb! And you all alone too.' Rosie saw tears of sympathy trembling on her thin lashes, and as her arm came about Rosie's shoulders Lizzie exclaimed, 'You're shivering, cariad, come over by 'ere.' And she led her gently towards the armchair, and plumping the cushions, brought a blanket from the bedroom and put it about her.

'Make a cup of 'ot tea for you I will, luv. Then I'll fetch youer dad, shall I?' The tears were running down Lizzie's cheeks now; dabbing at them with the hem of her overall she went into the scullery.

Rosie, gulping back her own tears, couldn't answer. But when a steaming cup was put into her hands and she began to sip the scalding liquid the icy band across her stomach began to melt.

'I don't like leavin' you alone while I go to fetch someone, Rosie. You shouldn't be on your own just now and that's a fact.' Lizzie's troubled gaze rested on her. 'You sometimes share their shelter next door. Shall I ask one of them Miss Thomases to come in?'

Rosie shook her head. 'They're very kind, but I'd rather be on my own just now, really, Lizzie.'

When Lizzie reluctantly left, Rosie picked up the letter and turned the pages again. It was so alive, so vibrant with longing and love, so full of plans for their future '. . . I'm really looking forward to that holiday we've promised ourselves, Rose. I can just picture us running down the beach with Beth between us, and splashing into the water. She'll love it, won't she? Our very first holiday together. Have you decided yet where you'd like to go?'

Her lips quivered; the words which had warmed her less than an hour ago and sped her thoughts towards a happy future were now poignant with the knowledge that she would never see Roy again, never feel his arms about her, his lips sealing hers in ecstasy.

The wireless had been turned down and in the quiet kitchen Vera Lynn was singing, 'We'll meet again, don't know where, don't know when. But I know we'll meet again some sunny day.'

A sob rose in her throat; she put her head in her hands and the hot tears gushed once more.

She didn't hear Miriam come into the kitchen with Lizzie but suddenly warm arms were about her and Miriam was smoothing the damp curls from her forehead and cradling her in her arms.

Lizzie packed a small case for her and Miriam led her gently to the taxi she'd kept waiting.

'We should let Roy's mother know, Miriam.'

'We'll take care of all that, love.'

Picturing her mother-in-law reading the telegram they'd send Rosie's heart went out to her. If only there was a way of breaking the news gently, but in a telegram there was room only for stark facts – Roy was dead – he would never come home again – nothing could soften the blow.

Sitting on the sofa in the familiar kitchen, Miriam and Ada fussing over her, Arthur called from work, carefully wording the telegram they must send to Mrs Cunningham, she looked at Miriam's gentle, concerned face and wondered how she could ever have resented her. Yet once she'd met Roy she'd been only too glad for Miriam to take over. Roy had filled her world then and ever since.

The familiar longing to have Beth home came over her, but the memory of the near miss the child had had at home still made her shudder.

Teddy and Albert weren't expected home until evening. Teddy was apprenticed to a boot repairer, and Albert was an errand boy at the Co-op. When David returned from the grammar school Miriam rushed to the door to break the news to him. He sat down beside Rosie, putting his arm awkwardly about her shoulders, saying, 'Aw, Rosie! There's sorry I am.'

She watched his throat work convulsively, and his eyes moisten with unshed tears, and looking at the tall thirteen-year-old she felt again the strong bond she'd always had with this youngest brother.

Suddenly he pulled her close to him, saying, 'You can have my room if you come back home to live, Rosie, I'll go in with Teddy and Albert.'

Even in her distress she knew how generous this was. David's room was his haven from the noise and distraction of the other two; there he studied, and read, and dreamed his dreams.

'Thanks, David, I think I'll go up and lay down for a while,' she said, wanting to be alone.

David went with her to his room, turning back the patchwork quilt, then tucking it around her. As he was leaving, he said, 'When I finish school, Rosie, I'm going to look after you and Beth.' Despite her pain, she was moved by his love.

The little boxroom was crowded with furniture. She looked round her at the table and chair Miriam had put for his studying, the bookcase Frank had made now full of school books and annuals, the old-fashioned wardrobe, his striped blazer on a peg behind the door, the schoolbag hanging beneath it. Yes, she knew just how much this room meant to David, and even in her grief she was deeply touched that he'd offered it.

Tomorrow when she met her mother-in-law at the station she would go back to The Laurels with her, and when Mrs Cunningham returned to Devon she'd go too, to be with Beth, though soon she must return to work – Miriam had already written them about her loss. She wished with all her heart that she didn't have to go back to the munitions factory. God, how she hated this war. Picturing the fighting in the desert as she had seen it on a recent Pathé News reel at the cinema, she saw again the turmoil, and heard the noise of heavy gunfire, and bodies, some no more than boys, lying still on the sandy ground. With a cry of horror she sat bolt upright in the bed, closing her eyes at the thought that Roy might have lain just like that, his body still, blood oozing from his wound, staining the sand. And she herself was helping to make guns that would kill young German soldiers, men with families who would mourn them deeply too. Maybe a German girl, with a husband in the forces and a daughter just like Beth, had helped to make the gun that killed Roy. Pressing her hot face into the pillow she sobbed uncontrollably.

The next day Miriam offered to accompany her to the station, but Rosie refused, feeling that Roy's mother would prefer her to be alone. Miriam had sewn a black armband round the sleeve of her dark blue suit, and Ada had lent her a black headscarf, for she had felt unable as yet to face the ordeal of choosing mourning.

The train was nearly an hour late, and when it came in she hurried forward, watching the passengers alight through eyes puffy from prolonged weeping, failing to recognise her mother-in-law until she stood before her. Dressed in an ill-fitting black coat that she had obviously borrowed, her hair tucked into a black woollen turban, Mrs Cunningham looked smaller than she remembered, the sorrow in the sunken, pale blue eyes mirroring her own. The face, the expression usually so self-assured, the make-up perfect, was now ravaged by grief.

Feeling deep compassion Rosie put her arms about Roy's mother, and Mrs Cunningham's arms came about her, too, and as their cheeks pressed against each other their tears mingled.

The guard raised his flag. Carriage doors slammed, and people milled about them shouting farewells, but they clung together oblivious to everything but their own grief.

'Oh, Mother! I loved him so much.'

'Rose! My poor little Rose. Thank God we have Beth. We must carry on for her sake.'

Presently they made their way down the steps to the booking hall and out to the taxi rank to join the waiting queue. People turned to stare and seeing their distress turned away uncomfortably.

When a taxi came in a young airman who headed the queue with his friend asked where they were going.

'To Roath – off the Newport Road,' Rosie told him.

'Oh! We're going to Canton, we thought perhaps we could give you a lift. But you can take the cab, we'll wait for the next.'

When nobody demurred they accepted gratefully, and she helped her mother-in-law into the seat.

As the day wore on their mutual grief was comforting one to the other, and they talked as they'd never talked before.

'Do you know, Rose,' her mother-in-law confided. 'I was very upset when Alun failed his medical because of his eyesight. But I'm very glad he didn't go in the forces now, though I was worried about his eyes at the time.'

But when she brought out the photo albums, and began reminiscing about Roy's childhood, tears running down her cheeks, it was bitter-sweet for Rosie as each small remembrance stabbed at her grieving heart.

Chapter 24

'Oh, Rosie! Isn't it wonderful? Ernie's divorce has come through at last.'

'That's marvellous news, Jan. Ernie must be over the moon after waiting all these years.'

Looking at Jan's glowing face, Rosie remembered the awful day she'd broken the news that Ernie must marry Bella.

'He hasn't been home for ages,' Jan was saying. 'He thinks we could get married next time he has leave.' Then, glancing at her watch, she cried, 'I'll have to run now or I'll be late for work.'

Walking slowly home Rosie found herself behind a young couple, their arms about each other. As the boy drew the girl close and kissed her it seemed to emphasise her own loneliness, and she dragged her steps.

It was almost two years since the telegram had shattered her dreams. Outwardly she talked and laughed and tried desperately to appear interested in her family and workmates, but she'd never come to terms with her loss, and the tears still flowed at every poignant memory.

For some time she'd cherished the hope that there'd been a dreadful mistake. When Roy's things, the pitifully few possessions of a soldier on active service, were sent home, that hope vanished.

Back at The Laurels she took off her coat and turned on the wireless:

> . . . And Jimmy will go to sleep
> In his own little room again.
> There'll be bluebirds over . . .'

She tried another station and it was Vera Lynn, singing 'We'll Meet Again' – and the memory of listening to this very song on the day she'd received the telegram seemed to squeeze her heart dry.

Going up to the bedroom with her coat she sat on the bed. Roy's photo in its silver frame was turned towards her so that she saw it last thing at night and when she woke.

Roy was smiling, yet the brown eyes regarded her solemnly just as Beth's did. He looked so young. The tears brimmed over at the thought of their unfulfilled hopes and dreams. The years stretched ahead, years when Beth would grow to be a woman, and Rosie herself would grow old, living still on the memory of their few short years together. It dismayed her to think that Roy must always remain young in her memory, just as in the photograph.

Next day when she went to see the family, Ada had some very welcome news.

'They've gone and posted our Frank to North Wales. Glad I am 'e's back in this country, 'e should be able to get some forty-eight-hour passes from there.'

'He certainly deserves a break, Ada, after being overseas twice. He'll probably stay here now.'

'Wonderful that would be, Rosie. With Dunkirk an' all, our Frank's already done 'is bit.'

A few weeks later Rosie was washing up after her evening meal, when, teatowel in hand, she answered a knock at the door.

'Frank! Come in!' she cried in delight. He was leaner than she remembered, and sunburnt, and his fair hair, cut army style, no longer flopped untidily over his forehead.

When they were seated together in the lounge, he said, 'I've never been able to tell you how deeply sorry I was about Roy.'

'You wrote me a lovely letter, Frank.'

'I've thought a lot about you being all on your own, Rosie, with your mother-in-law and the baby away in Devon.'

'David wanted me to go home. He even offered me his room. I couldn't accept, they're crowded enough already. Anyway, I didn't want to leave the house empty. I must have somewhere for Mother and Beth to come home to.'

'She's been away a long time, you've had a raw deal.' His brown eyes were warm with sympathy. 'Look, Rosie, I was wondering if you'd like to see a film tomorrow night, there's a good one at The Pavilion, *For Whom the Bell Tolls* – you like Ingrid Bergman and Gary Cooper, don't you?'

Seeing her hesitation, he added, 'It'll be all right, Rosie – just good friends – no strings attached.'

'I'd love to come, Frank. It's ages since I went to the pictures.' She felt a stir of excitement at the thought.

It was typical of Frank, she thought, to invite her like this. Reminded her it did of the warm friendship they'd shared in the old days. Even when Frank was a boy he'd been sensitive to her needs.

The next evening she felt a twinge of excitement as she got ready to go out. It was nice to put on a pretty frock even if it was utility, as a change from the dungarees she wore at work, and the slacks she now wore at home.

As they sat in the stalls and the emotional story unfolded, she thought she'd never seen anyone more beautiful than Ingrid Bergman. When the lights went up at the end her lashes were glistening with tears.

'Brought you out to cheer you up I did,' Frank teased her with a smile.

On the tram going home they talked of old times and friends they both knew. When there was a lull in the conversation, he said, 'I should get a week's leave in about a month, Rosie. I was talking to my boss this morning—'

'The furniture makers where you used to work?'

'Yes, Mr Bradbeer. Anyway I was telling him about Beth and how you went all the way to Devon to see her, and it seems he makes stuff for a warehouse in Exeter, and delivers there with the van.'

Rosie was wondering where this conversation was leading, and seeing her puzzled expression Frank said quickly, 'He offered to let me drive a load up, so that I could take you to see Beth.'

'Oh, that would be lovely, Frank,' Rosie said gratefully. 'I heard you'd learnt to drive in the army. It's a long way though. I miss Beth very much.' She was thinking of the bleak journey she made by train every few weeks, with endless waiting on cheerless platforms for the connections.

They had reached The Laurels, and she was fumbling for her key. 'You'll come in for a cup of tea, Frank?'

'Better not, Rosie, I haven't seen much of Mam and Dad and I have to go back first thing tomorrow.' But he still seemed reluctant to leave. Suddenly he bent forward and kissed her cheek. 'Goodbye for now, Rose. Take care of yourself.'

She watched him walk down the street, stopping every few yards to look back and wave. He stood at the corner and waved once more, then he was gone.

Boarding the Ordnance factory bus next morning, Rosie put her handbag on the seat beside her, hoping to keep a place for Mollie. Apart from work they saw little of each other now, but they'd remained good friends.

Mollie got on and taking the seat by Rosie she said smugly, 'You're a dark horse!'

'What do you mean?' Rosie was puzzled.

'Last night at The Pav. You were three rows in front of us. Missed you I did in the crowd coming out. Who was the good-looking fellow? Told me, you did, that you wouldn't go out with anyone. Remember, I had to cancel that blind date I made for you?'

'Frank is a very old friend, Mollie—'

'And that's all my eye for a yarn.'

'I've known him all my life. He's the one who made Beth's cradle, and that lovely tray, and the jewel box. He lived next door to me at home.'

Rosie was spared further explanation as a girl who had just boarded the bus called, 'Come down by here Moll, I've got something to tell you.'

Mollie had been very good when she'd heard about Roy, coming round to The Laurels as soon as Rosie had returned from Devon, giving her sympathy and companionship, often staying the night. But after Rosie had mourned Roy for six months Mollie'd tried to persuade her to come out with her friends. Since Rosie had refused to meet the date Mollie had arranged for her she'd given up trying.

When Rosie visited Devon she wondered whether to tell her mother-in-law that Frank might be bringing her in a van the next time she came, but she wasn't sure when that would be. As soon as she received a letter from him she wrote to Mrs Cunningham and told her that Frank would be driving her down the following weekend, hoping that she, too, wouldn't jump to the wrong conclusion.

Frank came home on the Friday and called on her briefly to make arrangements for the following day. 'We'll have to make an early start, Rosie,' he told her.

'What time do you think? Six – half past?'

They decided to leave at six thirty. She was up at half past five, and as soon as she heard the van she picked up her coat and handbag, and the sandwiches she'd prepared, and went to the door.

The morning was misty, promising another fine day. Wallflowers in the borders were heavy with dew. She took a deep breath of the scented air then hurried down the path.

When she reached the van and Frank opened the double doors at the back to put her parcels inside, she saw a wicker basket covered by a white teatowel.

'Mam's doing.' Frank smiled at her. 'Must be a week's rations there. Afraid we're going to starve she is.'

Frank told her that he would drive to Lynford first, then, when he'd seen Beth and Mrs Cunningham, he'd go to Exeter and make the delivery. He'd be back in plenty of time to take her home.

As the haze lifted and the sun shone on the green fields and budding hedges, she thought how little the countryside seemed to be affected by the traumatic events of the last four years.

'Warm enough, Rosie? There's a blanket in the back.'

She nodded. 'Won't Beth be surprised?'

'I haven't seen her since she was a baby. A chubby little thing, I remember, with big solemn brown eyes.'

'That's Beth. She's nearly five now.'

When at last the van drew up in front of the cottage, Beth flew down the path to meet them. Pretending to gasp with astonishment Frank held the little girl at arm's length.

'Now who is this beautiful young lady?' he cried, sweeping the giggling child from her feet. When he put her down she tossed the long curls from her flushed cheeks and clung to his arm.

Beth wouldn't let him out of her sight; she danced round him excitedly until he took her to the swing in the garden, squealing with delight as he began to push her.

Roy's mother's greeting hadn't been nearly as enthusiastic. Her manner, if not actually chilly, was distinctly reserved.

Now she joined Rosie at the window, saying, 'Beth's been very lonely since the evacuee children left a few weeks ago.'

'Oh Mother! Surely they didn't go home. London isn't safe yet.'

'The two little boys have gone to join their sister at a farm a few miles away. It's a pity they ever had to be parted, but there wasn't room for them there when they arrived.'

Beth had got off the swing and was pretending to push Frank. Laughter came to them through the open window.

'He's good with children,' her mother-in-law remarked grudgingly. 'That young man is still in love with you.' Rosie's pleasure at the scene through the window turned to embarrassment.

'Roy was the only one for me, Mother,' she protested, her cheeks scarlet. 'Frank and I, we've always been friends. He's just doing me a good turn.'

'Look, Rose, I've sacrificed a lot for Beth, burying myself down here like this. You know I never could stand the country. I love that child like she was my own. Remember, I've been a widow since Roy was three. I was hoping we'd stay together when the war is over – bring her up between us – she's all I have of Roy now.'

Rosie's heart was filled with dismay. She saw her dream of finally taking her rightful place as Beth's mother fading before her eyes.

Glancing through the window again Rosie saw Beth dragging a laughing Frank up the path towards the cottage. They came into the kitchen and, remembering her mother-in-law's words about Frank, the hot colour burned in her cheeks. Turning to the stove she busied herself making the tea.

Chapter 25

On a Monday morning early in June Lizzie came hurrying up the path just as Rosie was leaving for work.

'Glad I am I caught you, Rosie,' she gasped, 'I wanted to warn you before you went. I wouldn't be surprised if we 'aven't been invaded.'

Rosie stared at her in surprise, then glanced anxiously at her watch.

'My niece Peggy lives in Penarth,' Lizzie went on. 'Well, this friend of 'ers saw a great big grey ship roundin' the pier, and she says the deck was packed with soldiers. She ran all the way 'ome in case they came ashore. She didn't stop to see which way they went.'

An invasion? Well, just after Dunkirk there'd been plenty of rumours, but it was hard to believe it had happened now, and without people being informed. She smiled reassuringly at Lizzie.

'Don't worry. I'm sure they'd have told us on the wireless if we had been invaded. Anyway I'll have to go now or I'll miss my bus.'

At break time as they took mugs of tea from the trolley and sat down by Rosie's machine, she was telling Mollie about the ship, when Ted, her machine setter, broke in. 'That's funny, Rosie. That's what my boy must have seen through his telescope. Got real excited he did, and yelled for me. He reckoned there were hundreds of American GIs on deck.'

'My friend's a GI and he's had his leave cancelled,' Mollie told them.

'Something's going on,' Ted said thoughtfully, 'and I don't think it's the Germans invading us.'

Rosie found herself staring at the poster on the wall beside her machine. She knew its message by heart:

CARELESS TALK COSTS LIVES
WALLS HAVE EARS!

Following her gaze, Ted nodded. 'Quite right, Rosie, we'll know soon enough.'

She was thinking of this as she walked towards The Laurels that evening, and saw Miriam waiting for her in the porch. As Miriam hurried to meet her, she could see her stepmother was upset.

'I'm afraid it's bad news, Rosie,' Miriam told her. 'We've just heard that Ernie's been taken prisoner-of-war by the Germans. Jan's breaking her heart at the house.'

Rosie went back with Miriam. In the kitchen, Ada was pouring tea at the table, and Arthur had his arm about Jan who was sobbing on his shoulder. Poor Jan! All her hopes had been dashed once again.

As Rosie sat down beside her and drew her close, Arthur said, 'Let's try and look on the bright side, Jan. At least he's safe from those U-boats now.'

'Perhaps you'll get some sleep at nights then,' Miriam said softly. 'I'm always waking to find your father at the window, Rosie, especially if there's a gale.'

Glancing quickly at Arthur, Rosie was shocked to see his face etched with weariness, and dark shadows beneath his eyes. Why hadn't she noticed this before? Had she been so wrapped up in her own grief that she'd given no thought to how the war was affecting others in her family? Poor Dada, worrying about Ernie at sea, a prey to German U-boats and planes. He'd have been worrying, too, about Willie and Bobby who were both in the Middle East, and Teddy, who would be the next to go.

'Our Frank's leave's been cancelled,' Ada told her, handing her a cup of tea. ''E'll write to you, I expect, Rosie. Wasn't 'e taking you to see Beth on Sunday?'

Frank as well! It all added up. But Ada was waiting for an answer. Trying to hide her own deep disappointment, she said, 'Beth will be terribly upset, she loves Frank.' Rosie remembered the previous weekend when she'd gone on her own.

'Mammy! Where's Uncle Frank? You promised to bring him.'

'I said he'd come if he could, Beth. Look, Mama's brought you some sweets.'

'But when's Uncle Frank coming again?'

'Uncle Frank, Uncle Frank! That's all I hear,' her mother-in-law had sighed.

Later, when Rosie had pushed her on the swing, Beth cried in disgust, 'Harder, Mammy! Harder! Uncle Frank pushes much better than you.'

Beth's disappointment only mirrored Rosie's own. Now Ada had told her about the cancelled leave she was filled with fear for him. If something was happening, it looked as though Frank might be a part of it.

She was missing him more than she thought possible. She'd tried to convince herself that it was the old fondness she'd always felt for him, but the way her heart thumped when she thought of him and the sickening dive it had taken at Ada's news belied this. Her feelings for Frank had grown and matured over the past months and had blossomed into love. She could no longer deny it, even to herself.

If only she'd told him she cared it might have been some comfort to him, Rosie thought regretfully. But it was still hard for her to admit that there was room for anyone in her heart but Roy.

The next day the news broke. The Allies were once more on French soil. It was the sixth of June.

On her way home from work she bought an *Echo*. The headlines leapt from the page: ALLIES LAND IN FRANCE. Germans Report Severe Fighting on Seventy-Mile Stretch of Normandy Coast.

She read all the small print but of course it told her nothing of what she was so anxious to know. Where was Frank? Was he in the landing force, as she'd suspected? Ada couldn't tell her, and the letter she'd sent to his camp hadn't been answered.

Each day brought good news of the progress of the Allied forces. Montgomery was in charge of the army group carrying out the assault. The war on the Italian front was also going well. But as the days passed and there was no news of Frank she grew sick with worry. If only she'd told him how she felt she could have shared her fears with Ada.

Gazing at Roy's photograph, she wondered if she was letting him down. Deep love still filled her memc ies, but she'd been wrong to think she couldn't love anyone else.

With every day the feeling of anxiety built up. If Ada thought it strange that she should call in most evenings on some pretext or other, she didn't say anything.

A fortnight later she was visiting home in the hope of hearing some news of Frank when Ada burst in waving a telegram.

'Been wounded our Frank has. It's 'is leg, it says in the telegram. 'E's in a military 'ospital.'

'Does it tell you where he is, Ada?' Rosie couldn't keep the anxiety from her voice.

'No, cariad, but there's a number to ring. Bert's gone to ask 'is boss if 'e'll do it – find out where Frank is and if we can visit 'im.'

The fresh colour had left Rosie's cheeks. Noticing this, Ada went on, 'Let you know I will as soon as Bert comes back.'

Miriam led Ada to the armchair. 'It must have been a nasty shock for you. Sit down there and I'll pour you a hot cup of tea.'

The cup rattled in the saucer as Ada took it. She gave a deep sigh, then said, 'Well, at least 'e's out of the fighting.'

Rosie stayed as long as she could, hoping Bert would return, but she was on the night shift, and half an hour later she had to leave to get the factory bus.

It was the middle of August; the first of the operations on Frank's damaged knee had been a success and he was recovering well. Ada had gone early that morning to Hampshire to see him. Now it was late evening and she was expected home at any time. Rosie had almost run out of excuses for hanging about until her return when, watching from the front-room window, she saw a taxi draw up next door. She rushed out just as it pulled away. Ada was beaming as she told Rosie, 'Our Frank's coming home for a rest before his next operation.'

'How will he manage?' Rosie asked with concern, though her heart had leapt with joy at the news of his home coming. 'Has he got used to the crutches yet?'

'Well, one of the nurses has a leave due. She only lives in Newport and she's offered to bring Frank right to the door.'

Rosie could hardly wait for Saturday to arrive. Frank was excepted in the early afternoon; she'd give him time to settle, then call at the house about four o'clock.

She changed her frock several times, settling at last for the flowered pink cotton, an old favourite he'd once said he liked. She tried to style her hair in the still fashionable roll, kept in place with clips, but the curls sprang away. Then she coaxed it under in a pageboy bob, but again it settled into its natural curl. Impatiently she brushed it back, tying it at the nape of her neck with a wide black velvet bow.

The only stockings Rosie had were thick lisle – these days you had to have a Yankee friend to wear silk stockings, but there were substitutes. Reaching for a bottle of suntan colour cream she smoothed some evenly over her legs; letting it dry she took a dark brown eyebrow pencil, kept for the purpose, and carefully drew a straight seam up the back of each leg as far as she could reach, then slipped her feet into smart white buckskin shoes.

Looking at herself critically in the long mirror she wondered again if she should change her dress for something smarter, but it was a hot day and the pink cotton looked crisp and fresh. Rosie was breathless with excitement. Why was she going to all this trouble and getting so het-up? Her eyes avoided the photograph on the bedside table. Turning again to the mirror she stared hard at her reflection, admitting to herself at last that she was deeply in love with Frank.

Her eyes were bright with excitement when Ada opened the door.

'Frank's resting after his journey. In the middle bedroom 'e is, Rosie. In for a big surprise you are,' Ada told her, and Rosie thought that she didn't look too pleased.

Taking the stairs two at a time she wondered what the surprise could be – but so long as Frank was getting better.

She tapped on the door, heard Frank call, 'Come in!' and her heart did a somersault at the sound of his voice.

She took a step into the room, her eyes automatically drawn

towards the bed. Frank was sitting up against the pillows, grinning, and in the basket chair beside him, holding his hand, sat a pretty fair-haired girl in VAD uniform. Frank proudly introduced her.

'Rosie, this is my young lady, Cynthia. We met at the hospital.'

Trying to cope with sudden and intense disappointment, Rosie could think of nothing to say. They were both looking at her expectantly and she managed a smile.

'Beth has been missing you, Frank,' was all she could think of.

He'd obviously told Cynthia about their visits to Devon, and as he inquired about the little girl Rosie was able to pull herself together and answer more calmly than she felt.

A quarter of an hour later Cynthia said she must go, and promised to come early the next day. Bending her slim body over the bed she kissed Frank warmly on the lips.

'Till tomorrow, Frankie love,' she said, reaching the door. 'Nice to have met you, Rosie. Any friend of Frank's is a friend of mine.'

Alone with Frank Rosie felt tongue-tied and uncomfortable. She was thankful when Ada rapped on the door with a laden tea tray.

'Coming back tomorrow she is, your young lady. I made her stop an' 'ave another cup of tea.' She was obviously taken aback by the turn of events. Rosie knew that Ada had always hoped that she and Frank would get together. Had Ada guessed at her own feelings before she even knew them herself?

'I'm very glad that your operation was so successful, Frank. Is it very painful?' She managed to sound quite natural.

'It will take time, Rosie. They say I'll only need one more operation.'

Later, when she went downstairs, Ada said, 'Invalided out our Frank should be now. They don't know yet how bad 'is limp will be.'

Rosie wanted to rush back upstairs and fling her arms round him, but it wasn't her place to comfort him now.

On the way home she tortured herself with thoughts of what might have been. Miriam had pretended to be pleased that Frank had a girlfriend. Had they all known her true feelings better than she did herself? She'd been so happy leaving The Laurels a few short hours ago, so sure of Frank. He hadn't found anyone else even when she'd married Roy. Remembering the kiss and the tender glances that had passed between him and Cynthia, Rosie knew all that had changed.

Back at the house, pulling blackout curtains over the windows ready for the darkness, she was conscious of its emptiness.

A sharp rap on the door made her jump. Switching off the light, she nervously opened it. The beam from a torch made her blink, then she recognised Mollie and pulled her into the house, closing the door behind them.

As Rosie switched the light back on, Mollie waved two tickets at her.

'I was wondering if you'd come to a dance, Rosie? My new boyfriend can't make it and it's a pity to waste them. We could dance together.'

'Oh, I don't think so—' Rosie began. Then she thought, Why not? Hadn't she been dreading being on her own tonight? Besides, she was more or less ready to go. But once on the way she had second thoughts. Tears weren't far away and her thoughts were constantly with Frank. If only she had realised the strength of her feelings for him sooner. What a fool she'd been to let her second chance of happiness slip through her fingers.

When they reached the church hall and deposited their coats, Mollie pulled her towards the crowded dance floor just as the Lambeth Walk started. As Rosie swung along to the rhythm she forced herself to smile and sing. Then came the Pally Glide and she found herself arm in arm with a young soldier who, when the dance had finished, insisted on finding her a seat and bringing refreshments.

Mollie had disappeared. Scanning the crowd, smart in their best utility dresses and uniforms of every service, Rosie saw her at the centre of a group of young airmen. A few minutes later when the soldier dragged her on to the dance floor for the hokey-cokey she knew it was no good looking to Mollie for help.

The ice broken with a few party dances, the band went into a foxtrot. The soldier gave Rosie an apologetic smile. 'Sorry, love, I can't do any real dancing.'

They went back to their seats to finish their refreshments. The tea was cold and when he went for more, Rosie looked round for a way of escape. But Mollie was nowhere to be seen and the serviceman was already returning with the tray. As they settled themselves at the little table he fumbled with the button on the breast pocket of his uniform and brought out a bunch of crumpled photographs.

'My wife and family,' he said.

Rosie gave a deep sigh of relief as she looked down at a creased sepia snapshot.

'That's my wife with our youngest.' He smiled proudly.

The picture was of a plump, fair young woman holding an even plumper baby, and as they went through the snaps Rosie found herself relaxing.

'You married?' he asked. 'Well, I suppose you must be, I can see you wear a ring.'

Rosie nodded, seeing no reason to tell him about Roy. She brought out a picture of Beth and explained that she was away in the country.

The time flew and after the last dance Mollie came over with a ginger-haired boy in air-force uniform.

'Coming again next week, Rosie? I've promised to meet Tim here.'

The boy took Mollie's arm possessively, saying, 'Come on, I'll see you girls home.'

The soldier turned to Rosie. 'Well, goodbye. Perhaps we'll meet again. I've enjoyed this evening. See you!'

Mollie and the young airman went with Rosie as far as the gate of The Laurels, or rather where the gate used to be, for both gate and railings had long ago been taken for the war effort. To Rosie's surprise Mollie went through the gateway before her.

'But I thought I was taking you home.' The young airman seemed annoyed.

'Oh! Didn't I tell you I was staying with my friend tonight? Thanks for seeing us home.' And Mollie walked on up the path without her usual lingering backward glance.

'What was all that about?' Rosie asked, turning the key and closing the door behind them.

Mollie laughed. 'Just self-preservation. I've a feeling that one would want more than just a goodnight kiss.' She glanced at her watch. 'Go and see if he's gone, Rosie, I've still got plenty of time to get the last tram.'

When Mollie had left, Rosie went to the bedroom and sat on the bed, too tired and dispirited even to undress. Her head was beginning to throb from the varied emotions of the day. Picking up the silver-framed photograph from her bedside table, she thought of the uncomplicated love and joy she and Roy had shared. But her feelings for Frank were still there – they wouldn't go away.

Her heart heavier than it had been for a very long time, she lay and stared into the darkness.

Chapter 26

As Beth picked herself up and ran screaming to her grandmother, Rosie swallowed her own hurt and went indoors for soap and water to bathe the grazed knee.

Ever since they'd returned home two months ago, Roy's mother had said in vain, 'Mammy's here now, darling, she will kiss it better.' Or, 'You'd better ask your mother first.' Beth still ran straight to her grandmother like a homing pigeon.

'It's only natural, Rosie,' Miriam had comforted her. 'After all, she was still only a baby when they went away.'

Rosie sighed. Poor little Beth. At five years old she had to get used to having a mother around.

With the Allies' successful landing in France in June, the air-raids over Wales had ceased, but it was October before Roy's mother had thought it safe to bring Beth home.

Now her mother-in-law was constantly worrying about Alun and his wife, for since June London had been plagued by doodlebug flying bombs and many thousands had been killed. With the autumn a new hazard, the V2s, had appeared, and against this forty-five-foot rocket there seemed to be no defence.

Preparations for Christmas were well advanced. That morning Beth, wearing a warm coat, pixie hood and scarf, had jumped about with excitement as Rosie dug up the small Christmas tree that she had planted in the garden last January. Rosie had expected objections from Mrs Cunningham about bringing it indoors, but she had given in right away to her granddaughter's pleading. She had even shown enthusiasm over the paper decorations Beth had made so laboriously.

They'd decorated it by sticking silver paper on both sides of pieces of cardboard, then cutting out stars and bells, and tiny Father Christmases. The result had fallen short of Rosie's expectations, but Beth had clapped her hands in delight. The tree dressed, she'd gone back to sticking the brightly coloured paper-chains with flour and water.

Rationing was tighter than ever. It had taken a month to save up the ingredients for a cake and pudding. This afternoon Rosie was to pick up the chicken from Ada's, and her heart contracted at the thought of meeting Frank. She'd avoided seeing him whenever possible, afraid of betraying her feelings. Beth, excited about the visit, was waiting impatiently long before her mother was ready.

When Frank opened the door it was obvious the old rapport was still there between him and the child.

'Come to tea with us Christmas Day, Uncle Frank,' Beth pleaded. Waiting for his answer, Rosie's heart beat fast, but smiling at the child he shook his head.

'Sorry, Beth, I've got a young lady coming to stay.'

Swallowing hard, Rosie asked, 'How is Cynthia, Frank?'

'She's fine. I haven't seen her for over a month.'

The crutches had been discarded and the leg was improving, but his face was drawn and pale. The impulse to put her arms about him was almost irresistible.

'You'll be looking forward to her visit,' she said to break the awkward silence.

'As a matter of fact, Rosie, Cynthia and I—' The door burst open and David stood there, saying breathlessly, 'Mrs Jenkins wants you, Rosie, she forgot to ask you something. She's in our kitchen—'

'I'll come now, David.' She had a feeling Frank'd been going to tell her something that she didn't want to hear. The sentence could easily have ended ' – are getting engaged at Christmas.' The thought was like a knife twisting in her heart.

Following David into the house she sat down at the table.

'Want another cup, Rosie?' Miriam lifted the pot from the range.

Accepting the tea Rosie looked expectantly at Ada.

'Would you like to come to us on Christmas evening, Rosie?' Ada asked. 'We're having a little do, Miriam and youer dad will be there.'

'I'm sorry, Ada,' she said, thankful for the excuse. 'Beth will be in

258

bed, and I can't leave my mother-in-law on her own at Christmas.'
The party would probably be to celebrate Frank's engagement –
the knife twisted deeper.

It had been a good Christmas. When Beth opened her eyes on
Christmas morning, and saw the baby doll with the rag body
dressed in a gown made from her own outgrown petticoats, and a
knitted coat and bonnet, she'd been overjoyed, playing with it all
day and rocking it to sleep at intervals in the cradle Frank had made
when she was born.

After breakfast the other presents were exchanged. For Rosie
another beautiful knitted jumper, this time in a deep pink. For
Beth a lovely lupin blue coat and hat to match, and all with Mrs
Cunningham's own coupons. In a second-hand jeweller's Rosie
had found a dainty fob watch, the porcelain back painted with
flowers, which hung on a pretty bow-shaped brooch. Her mother-
in-law was delighted, pinning the pretty thing on to the bodice of
her dress.

After the meal, when the dishes were washed and the remains of
the chicken put away in the larder, Rosie found the time begin to
drag. During the long afternoon no one called at The Laurels for a
chat and a cup of tea, or something stronger. She remembered how
at home in Wesley Street there was always someone dropping in.
The kitchen would be untidy with discarded wrapping paper.
Christmas cards would be everywhere, crowding out the ornaments
on the mantelpiece, strung on cord around the walls. Yesterday the
ceiling had been festooned with colourful paper-chains, and this
had been repeated throughout the house.

The decorations Beth had made had been allowed on one wall of
the kitchen only, and in the child's bedroom. And the Christmas
cards had been placed with such precision on top of the tiled fireplace and along the window ledge, they looked as though a measuring tape had been used to set them at equal distances. Any wrapping
paper must be consigned to the scrap paper collection as soon as
discarded. Even Beth's toys were kept in a box to be played with one
at a time. Beth had been very well trained.

*   *   *

259

It was New Year's Eve. In the evening Rosie went to wish Dada, Miriam and the boys a Happy New Year.

Ada and Bert were in the kitchen when she arrived, and Bert had brought in a couple of bottles of rhubarb wine. As Ada poured her a glass, Rosie asked, 'How is Frank?'

'There's miserable 'e is lately, Rosie. Worried about 'is leg, I suppose 'e is. How that Cynthia puts up with 'im I'll never know.'

'There's hard you are on the boy, Ada.' Bert shook his head. 'A bit down 'e is at the moment, but considering all 'e's been through that's only natural.'

'Frank's in there on 'is own, wouldn't come in with us,' Ada told her. 'Why don't you go in and see if you can cheer 'im up, Rosie? That Cynthia went back just after Christmas.'

'Go on, love,' Miriam urged. 'Take some of my Christmas cake, he hasn't tasted it yet. I'll just get a serviette.'

She saw the look that passed among them all, and knew what they were hoping for. But didn't they realise that Frank was probably unhappy because Cynthia had had to return to the hospital? She remembered just how bereft she had felt when Roy had gone back from leave.

She took the cake and moved towards the door.

'There's some more wine in the sideboard,' Bert called after her. 'Try the parsnip, Rosie.'

Waiting for Frank to let her in she shivered in the cold air, and tried to calm her misgivings.

Frank looked surprised, but led her to the kitchen where they sat on either side of the fire.

'Happy New Year, Frank.'

'Same to you, Rosie.'

'I've brought in a piece of Miriam's Christmas cake. Would you like some if I make a cup of tea?'

'Leave it in the pantry, I'll try it later on. I'm just not hungry now.'

She glanced at him, thinking, Ada's right. He does look miserable. 'How is your leg?'

'It's getting better. Doesn't hurt so much now.'

A few minutes later, embarrassed by the silence that had fallen between them, she jumped up.

'Your dad said to take a bottle of parsnip wine from the sideboard cupboard.

'Shall I get it?'

'No, I'll go.'

Resting her hand on the top of the sideboard she knelt down to look for the bottle. As she let go of the top her hand knocked against an ornament, which to her horror fell and shattered into pieces on the oilcloth. It's probably something Ada cherishes, she thought with a sinking heart, something I can't even replace. Picking up a large shard, and carefully tracing the curly gold lettering, she read 'A Present Fr – ' and knew without doubt that it was the remains of the vase she'd bought for Ada all those years ago. Frank had looked after her that day at Barry Island – but Frank had always looked after her. A sob rose in her throat, and tears streamed down her face, as she remembered that sunny day just months after Mama died. She saw herself wearing a black armband, seated in the charabanc with Teddy, while Ada nursed Albert in the seat behind, and kindly Bert stood on the pavement with his box Brownie trying to get them all in the picture.

'What is it, Rosie? What's wrong?' Frank had just reached her. In a moment his arms were about her. Then she was sobbing against him, uncertain whether her tears were for the motherless child that he'd befriended, or the lonely woman she'd become.

Suddenly Frank's arms tightened about her, and his lips sought hers hungrily. For a moment she tasted the salt of her own tears before losing herself in the wonder of his embrace. At last, unwillingly, she pulled away.

'What about Cynthia? Oh, Frank, I'm sorry.'

'You needn't be, Rosie,' he said, kissing her gently this time. 'Mam doesn't know yet, but Cynthia and I have decided not to see each other again. We talked about it before. It wasn't fair to her – it wouldn't have worked. When I kissed Cynthia it was you I was thinking of – it was always you – I couldn't go through with it. I nearly told you on Christmas Eve.'

She went into his arms again, and as his lips met hers they clung together. When at last he released her they looked at each other in wonder.

'I thought you'd never feel anything for me, Rosie.'

'And I thought I'd lost you to Cynthia. Oh, Frank, I'm so happy.'

They were sitting on the sofa holding hands, still marvelling at the love that had blossomed between them, when Ada and Bert returned.

As Frank explained about Cynthia, and how he and Rosie felt about each other, Ada smiled broadly. 'Always wanted this, I did – Bert will tell you. That Cynthia was a nice little girl, but she wasn't your type, our Frank.'

'There's a woman you are, Ada. Welcomed 'er with open arms you did at first, when you thought our Frank would be left on the shelf.' Bert was grinning from ear to ear.

'There's a soppy thing to say, Bert. It's only women that gets left on the shelf.' Ada clicked her tongue in disgust.

'I'll have to go,' Rosie said reluctantly. 'I wish I could stay and see the New Year in, but Beth will be in bed by now and Mother's on her own.'

'I'll walk you home, Rosie.'

'No, Frank! You should rest your leg.'

'Don't worry about that, it's improving all the time,' he said, as Ada handed him his coat.

'Happy New Year, everybody, I'll be thinking of you all at twelve o'clock.'

'Happy New Year, Rosie,' they chorused, kissing her warmly in turn.

Holding hands she and Frank walked slowly in the frosty night, their hearts full, the journey to The Laurels punctuated with stops while their arms went about each other.

'I don't think I'll tell my mother-in-law tonight, Frank,' she whispered, as he shone his torch on the path and they walked to the front door. Before they reached the porch the door opened and Mrs Cunningham peered into the darkness. 'Thank goodness you're back. I've been really worried, Rose. I thought you'd have been home ages ago—' Then she saw Frank and muttered, 'You'd better come in.'

In the brightly lit lounge she looked from one to the other

intently. 'Something's happened, hasn't it?' she said, and Rosie heard the fear in her voice.

'Frank and I are going to get engaged, Mother.'

There was silence for a moment. Then 'Well, I suppose I should congratulate you. You didn't wait very long, did you, Rose? If you get married, where does that leave me where Beth is concerned? I thought we were going to bring her up together.' Her voice was bitter.

'We were hoping for your blessing, Mrs Cunningham. I'll look after Rose and little Beth, too, don't you worry.'

Roy's mother had gone very pale. 'But I've brought her up since she was a tiny baby. I think I should be considered a little, don't you? She is my son's child. We'll have to discuss this properly when the time comes, young man. Anyway, an engagement doesn't mean a marriage right away, does it? I'm sure you both realise that it's far too soon for that.'

Chapter 27

The doodlebugs and V2s no longer terrorised London, but Mrs Cunningham didn't talk any more about the flat she was to have there when the war was finally over. Once, thinking to please her, Rosie had asked how it was getting on. Her mother-in-law's voice was full of self-pity as she'd answered, 'I expect you'd be pleased if I went to live in London, Rose. You were very glad for me to take Beth to safety during the air-raids, weren't you? I wonder if you've any idea what it was like for me burying myself away in the country all those years?'

Her love for Beth was unquestionable, and Rosie had tried to be patient. But several times lately, the last occasion that very morning, she had seen Roy's mother cwtching Beth tightly, the tears streaming down her cheeks. Rosie was worried, especially as Beth's little face had worn an expression of utter bewilderment.

An hour later, knowing it was time for Frank's lunch break, she made an excuse to go to Clifton Street, and taking a basket and her purse hurried from the house.

'Oh, Frank! What are we going to do?' she almost wailed, after telling him what had happened.

'What brought it on this time?'

'Looking in last night's *Echo* I was, at the adverts for houses for sale.'

Frank sighed. 'We'll have to think of something, Rosie, if we're to get married and have Beth with us. Knowing you, you'll blame yourself if Mrs Cunningham cracks up, although it won't be your fault. What happened to her plan to live in London? She'd have had to leave Beth then, wouldn't she?'

'Mother never speaks about the flat now, Frank. Not since she's known about us. Her idea was to have the two homes. Beth and I would be at The Laurels, the house always ready for her return. She'd have spent her time between London and Cardiff, probably taking Beth back for some of the school holidays.'

They'd reached the corner of Wesley Street and Rosie stopped. 'I'd better get back, Frank. I'm only supposed to be going to the shops.'

'What time shall I call for you tomorrow? About three be all right? Will you be up?'

'Yes I'll be up, see you then.' She was on the night-shift but tomorrow was Saturday, and the start of a long weekend off before starting the day shift on Monday.

Frank was back in Civvy Street, having been invalided out of the army with a small pension. For the last month he'd been working for his previous employers who'd had a good reputation for hand-crafted furniture before the war, and were now planning ahead for the day when utility furniture was a thing of the past.

Walking home she thought how understanding and patient Frank had been about Mrs Cunningham. He'd never knowingly hurt anyone. If only there was something they could do! Roy's mother had made it clear on more than one occasion that she thought they were in far too much of a hurry making plans to marry as soon as they'd found a place to live.

'This house is filled with memories for both of us, Rose,' she'd said one day, 'I shall treasure mine always.'

The remark was made pleasantly, but Rosie couldn't help noticing the slight emphasis on the words 'I' and 'mine', and it touched a sensitive nerve.

Were they in too much of a hurry? She'd asked herself the question over and over. Roy had been dead for almost three years. She had loved him dearly, and a part of her would always be his. She still felt a deep, warm gratitude for their mutual love, and she had a better understanding now of the way he'd often given in to his mother. Theirs had been a happy marriage. Perhaps at the beginning she had expected too much, a home of their own, new furniture – she'd wanted everything to be perfect. She thought of the endless window-shopping, and Roy's impatience to be married.

Frank's gentleness and understanding were his strength. He never lost his temper over Mrs Cunningham's behaviour. And he respected her memories of Roy. Frank was strong, and wise too, wise enough to know that they couldn't build their happiness on her mother-in-law's distress.

As the weeks went by Frank became a frequent visitor at The Laurels, making himself useful in many ways. He would carry the heavy bin from the garden to the front of the house, ready for the rubbish to be collected the next day, standing it beside the gatepost where the ornamental iron gate had been. Frank could repair almost anything and Mrs Cunningham began to rely on him. She was very appreciative of his help – it was so long since they'd had a man about the house – but if the word wedding was mentioned she would grow quiet, her lips coming together in a straight line, and she'd go round with a look on her face which said plainly, 'How could you do this to me after all I've done for you?'

'She'll come round, love,' Frank comforted her, 'she hasn't got used to the idea yet. But it's going to happen, Rosie. We are going to be married. We'll just have to wait until she realises that.'

He took her in his arms and held her close, and as her kisses answered his with mounting passion she thought bitterly, Why is there always a stumbling block? With Roy it had been her young brothers, and now there was her mother-in-law's attitude to contend with. When at last he released her she clung to him still, whispering, 'Oh Frank! Oh Frank, my love.' And he sighed deeply, saying, 'If you're going to kiss me like that, Rosie, I hope and pray she gets used to the idea very soon.'

They often looked at the property columns, but with no firm date for their wedding it took the edge off their enthusiasm.

Several times during February they went to look round different furniture stores. Rosie would hurry Frank past the windows and into the shop, saying, 'There'll be a lot more to see inside, love.' And Frank, remembering what she'd told him about window-shopping with Roy, would squeeze her hand understandingly.

The only snag about going in was that an assistant, his mind doubtless on his commission, would dart forward insisting on showing them around, losing interest as soon as they told him they couldn't buy anything yet.

'We ought to find a house first, Rosie, before we go looking for furniture,' Frank said. And she felt a twisting pain deep in her heart, remembering Roy saying the very same thing. 'After all, we know what the utility stuff looks like,' Frank continued, 'and we've got to apply for the coupons first anyway.'

One bleak day towards the end of the month Frank arrived at The Laurels unexpectedly during his normal working hours. Roy's mother had gone to town with Beth just after lunch and when he knocked Rosie had been adding Beetox to a meatless stew.

Frank couldn't hide his excitement at the news he had for her.

'Can you come to see a house right away, Rosie?'

'Where is it, Frank?'

He laughed. 'Do you remember when you were just a kid how you kept on and on about your grandma's house? Used to think it was a palace, I did. Hot water in the taps, a bathroom as big as our kitchen – and two lavatories, just imagine that! They didn't even have to go down the garden path with a coat over their heads when it was raining.'

Rosie's eyes widened. 'You mean the house is in Grandma's road?'

'The very same.'

With a cry of delight she flung her arms about him. Then her excitement faded.

'Oh, Frank! What's the use?'

'It's all right, love, I hadn't forgotten. There's nothing to stop us buying the house, is there? We'll be getting married soon, I hope, and it's a very reasonable price. All those years a bachelor—' he smiled at her— 'I've got quite a bit put by, I can put down a good deposit. But the first thing is to go and see it.'

At his words she felt excited again, and was just about to turn off the burner under the stew and put on her coat, when there was a knock at the door.

Opening it, she recognised the young man who stood there from the photograph on the sideboard in the dining room.

'Alun?'

'That's right. And you must be Rose.'

'Come in. Your mother is out with Beth. Sit by the fire, Alun, I'll make a cup of tea. They shouldn't be very long.'

Frank had stayed in the kitchen while she went to the door. He carried the tea tray through to the lounge and she introduced the two men.

Alun pulled a letter from his pocket. 'I've come to try and get to the bottom of this. Perhaps you can explain what Mother means by this letter, Rose? I don't understand it at all. After all the years she's been looking forward to having the flat with us, she now says she's going to stay at The Laurels. I managed to get a builder a few months ago – they're like gold dust since the blitz. Anyway the conversion's nearly finished so I wrote and asked if she'd like to come and choose the curtains and so on and she wrote back and said she wouldn't be leaving The Laurels after all. I was so angry at first, then I thought, There's something behind this, I'd better go to Cardiff and find out.'

'I know only too well what it's about, Alun. It's Beth. Frank and I plan to get married, though we haven't fixed a date yet. Mother's afraid she's going to lose Beth. It's nonsense, of course. Beth adores her.'

'When we find a house and get married, there'll always be a welcome for her there when she comes to Cardiff,' Frank said.

'But she's wanted this flat for years – she was talking about it even before the war.'

'She still wants it really, Alun. But she's been with Beth all those years in the country and she's afraid Beth will forget her.'

'Well, I've got some news for her. Christine is expecting a baby, Mother should be pleased about that. Mother and Christine are great friends.'

Hearing a key turn in the lock Rosie went into the hall. 'You've got a visitor, Mother.'

'Alun!' His mother was in his arms, and he was smiling at Beth.

'She's the image of Roy, isn't she? And to think I'd never met my sister-in-law or my niece. We were really disappointed when you had to cancel your honeymoon in London.'

'We have to go now,' said Rosie. 'It's been lovely meeting you,

Alun. Oh, and congratulations!' Turning to her mother-in-law she said, 'You must have lots to talk about. Shall we take Beth with us?'

'No, Rose, Alun would like to get to know her, I'm sure. You go on, I'll look after the stew.'

As they closed the door behind them, Frank said, 'If Alun can't persuade her, the thought of another grandchild might.'

She tucked her arm in his and they started down the road.

Frank's leg was improving, but they had to stop several times for him to rest. Fifteen minutes later, Rosie's heart beating fast with excitement, they turned into the road, and she could see the 'For Sale' notice about a dozen houses from Grandma's.

The house stuck out from its neighbours, the garden overgrown with weeds, its windows black with grime. But already she saw a smooth lawn with colourful flowerbeds, and crisp Nottingham lace curtains behind shining glass.

The door swung open revealing a hall exactly like Grandma's. Her mind, ignoring the dust that lay everywhere, saw instead the stairs covered in thick red carpet against which brass rods twinkled, and on the hall table, reflected in the gilt mirror, a bowl of hyacinths showing a promise of spring.

Rosie half expected Mabel to call her for hot chocolate, but it was Frank's voice coming from the kitchen that brought her out of her reverie, and when she stood in the doorway he cried enthusiastically, 'I'll make fitted cupboards all round, Rosie, and box in that sink – we could have two rows of shelves over there.'

Looking to where he was pointing she saw them filled with gleaming pans.

Frank promised to call at the estate agent's as soon as they opened, and they knocked on Grandma's door, longing to tell her about the house, disappointed when there was no answer.

Anxious to know what was happening back at The Laurels, Rosie decided to go home.

'I think you'd better go on your own, Rosie. It's a family thing, isn't it?'

'See you later then, Frank. I'll come down afterwards and let you know what happens. I'm so excited about the house, love, even if we may have to wait ages to move in.'

Back at The Laurels she could hardly believe the change in her mother-in-law.

'Christine's expecting a baby, Rose – isn't it wonderful after all the years of hoping?' Her cheeks were flushed and her eyes bright as she continued, 'It might even be twins, there's a history of twins in her family. I've been telling Beth she's to have a cousin, maybe cousins,' she added with a chuckle.

'Mother's coming up to see the flat next week,' said Alun. 'She'll stay a little while to supervise the finishing touches.'

'You'll be moving to London then, Mother?'

'Alun's convinced me I'm needed, and that I'm wrong to worry about Beth forgetting me. I'll be able to stay with you sometimes, like you said. And perhaps Beth can spend some of her school holidays with me. You go ahead with your plans, Rose. I'll be pleased to help in any way.'

Rosie decided not to tell Roy's mother that they'd just seen the house they wanted. I'll tell her next week, she thought, let her think we're taking her advice.

Mrs Cunningham was still away when they received the go-ahead from the estate agent's. That evening she and Frank went to the house to measure for curtains and carpets.

Upstairs they wrote down the measurements of the bathroom and the four bedrooms, the smallest of which was larger than any at Wesley Street. This room was at the back of the house over-looking the garden, and they were admiring the view, looking out at shrubs and flowerbeds now overgrown, when Frank said, 'Lovely this room would be for David. Nice and quiet for his studying.' His eyes were twinkling.

'Oh, Frank!' Rosie flung her arms about him and hugged him. She'd been going to ask about David, but was delighted that Frank had thought of it first.

'Don't tell him yet, Rosie,' Frank was saying. 'Let's give him a lovely surprise. I could make him a small desk with drawers to put his school books in. It would have to be made out of spare wood, but I think I could make a good job of it. And you can see to the curtains, and a nice rug—' She hugged him again, so tightly this time that he had to stop talking for lack of breath.

Armed with buckets and brushes Miriam and Ada joined her to scrub the pretty mosaic floor tiles until they came up in all the glory of their original colours, which took some time for they were laid through hall, breakfast room and kitchen. Frank spent most evenings decorating, becoming skilled at stippling a design, using a small round sponge and different-coloured paints to give the effect of patterned wallpaper.

Mrs Cunningham hadn't yet told Lizzie that she was going to sell The Laurels. Roy's mother got on very well with the cleaner, especially as Lizzie was careful to always keep her place with her. To Rosie Lizzie referred to her mother-in-law as the Missis, but Mrs Cunningham herself always received her full title.

Rosie often marvelled at the change in Lizzie. Her face had filled out over the last few years, and she was always neat and clean. It was as though the job and a little money of her own had given her self-respect. Rosie dreaded the day she had to tell her her services were no longer needed.

'I suppose we couldn't afford to have her, Frank? I know there's no need, I can easily cope with the cleaning myself – I'll be able to leave work to look after Beth very soon. But the job's made such a difference to Lizzie and the children.'

'We certainly couldn't manage the three mornings she does now, love. By the time we've bought the furniture our savings will be nearly gone.'

'Grandma's not as active as she was, and Aunty Mabel's always busy. I wonder—'

Frank smiled tenderly at her. 'It won't be your fault if Lizzie's out of work,' he said.

Rosie was thankful a few days later to give Lizzie the good news. She could do two mornings with Grandma Hughes, and one morning with Rosie, if she wanted, when her job finished with Mrs Cunningham.

The Laurels already had a buyer whenever Roy's mother was ready to sell. The Major's nephew was looking for a home, and liked the house very much.

Rosie's thoughts were on furnishing their new home. She was glad now that living with Roy's mother they'd never had anything of their own. The shops were full of utility furniture, and you had to fill in a form to obtain it. The craftsman in Frank probably wouldn't approve, but it looked quite nice, and would be a start. She had noticed the way David looked at her whenever the house was mentioned, and decided one day that she could keep the secret no longer.

'You'll be able to come with us as soon as we're settled in, David.'

He flung his arms about her, taking her breath away, then planted a smacking kiss on her cheek. When he sat down again his eyes were shining with happiness.

They both wanted a quiet wedding, and Miriam suggested a small family reception at number forty-two.

By the beginning of May it had become obvious that the war would end very soon, and in Wesley Street a collection began for a Victory party.

Rosie, waiting for Miriam to open the door one day, saw Lizzie James, book and pencil in hand, a few doors away.

'Leave it open, Miriam, Lizzie will be here in a minute, she must be collecting for the party.'

'She won't come here, Rosie – Oh! I might as well tell you. Collecting for a wedding present for you and Frank she is.'

'Lizzie collecting for us?' She couldn't keep the surprise from her voice.

Miriam laughed. 'She's a real fan of yours since she's been working for you, Rosie.'

For her wedding outfit Rosie chose a pale grey costume and frilly white crepe-de-Chine blouse; the wide shoulders and nipped-in waist of the jacket were flattering as well as fashionable. Beth and one of Frank's little nieces were to wear short pale blue satin dresses with circles of flowers in their hair.

On the Saturday before the wedding Mrs Cunningham returned from London with high hopes of moving into her flat by the beginning of the summer. Rosie met her at the station, and, as the tram passed the town shops, many of them were already festive with bunting and Union Jacks in anticipation of the news of final victory.

Suddenly Rosie was surprised to hear her mother-in-law say, 'I think now, Rose, that I was wrong to discourage you from marrying Frank. He really is a very nice young man. Beth being so fond of him it should be easy for her to adjust to her new life.'

'Thank you, Mother.' Rosie took her hand and squeezed it gently, knowing what it would have cost her to make that little speech.

When on Tuesday the eighth of May the Germans at last surrendered, flags miraculously appeared across Wesley Street, and plans were hurriedly made for a party and celebrations on the following day.

Rosie, on her way to make last-minute arrangements with Miriam for her wedding the next morning, found neighbours in little groups laughing and joking amid a general atmosphere of excitement and relief. Husbands still in their working clothes were high on steps and ladders decorating the houses with bunting and festooning lamp posts with red, white and blue streamers and paper flowers.

Everyone was in high spirits, and it took Rosie almost an hour to reach the front door where Miriam was waiting. As they entered the kitchen, a sudden thought wiped the smile from Rosie's face.

'Oh, Miriam! How are we going to manage if they block off the street for the party tomorrow?'

'Don't worry, love, that won't be until the afternoon. Your wedding is at ten thirty.'

On the table was the cake Miriam had made, the soya-flour marzipan flavoured with almond essence. On top were the decorations Ada had kept from her youngest daughter's wedding. Rosie smiled at the little figure of the bride dressed in flowing white lace, and the groom resplendent in tails. Still, it was the thought that counted.

It was early on Wednesday afternoon. The wedding breakfast

over, Frank had taken Mrs Cunningham home in his uncle's car. Beth was skipping in the garden waiting impatiently for the street party to begin. This evening she was to go back to The Laurels to spend a few more days with her grandmother before joining Rosie and Frank at the house, and David was to come to them the same day.

'I'll have to play the piano for the party, Rosie,' Frank said when he returned.

'Of course, Frank, it wouldn't be much of a party without music.'

So, as the street celebrations began, Frank and Bert wheeled the piano from the house on its protesting castors, and Frank began a medley of patriotic tunes.

Rosie, serving jelly and blancmange, suddenly stopped with a laden spoon halfway to a plate when she saw the banner suspended from a row of flags strung across the street.

HAPPY WEDDING DAY, ROSIE AND FRANK

She was filled with happiness. Glancing towards the piano where Ada, resplendent in her new dress of plum-coloured marocain, was turning the pages for Frank, she remembered Jan's glowing face that morning when she'd talked of Ernie coming home soon. And Bobby and Willie would be returning from the Middle East. Teddy, thank goodness, had never had to go.

On the surface the party seemed like the other street celebrations, the ones for King George V and Queen Mary's Jubilee, and King George VI's Coronation, but Rosie felt it was different, and it wasn't the fact that the butter was barely scraped on the bread, or that the sandwiches had very little filling. It was the realisation that Hitler was at last defeated, and the wonderful, optimistic feeling that tomorrow would be bright. As bright as the streets had been last night when all the lights went on for the first time in over five and a half years.

People had danced and sung until the small hours, leaving curtains undrawn and doors wide open, the light streaming out to brighten the already lamplit pavements.

The Victory party was almost over. The children had played musical chairs and run races. Now Ada was leading the singing of 'When the Lights Go On Again, All Over the World', her full rich voice as clear as if she sang alone.

Nearly an hour later, when the last strains of 'God Save the King' had faded away, someone started to sing 'Mae Hen Wlad Fy Nhad-Au' and the whole street, children and all, took up the words, and the few who didn't know them in Welsh sang 'Land of My Fathers' with the same patriotic fervour. When the last resounding *Gwlad!* had died away, the tidying up began.

Soon it was time for Beth to go to her grandmother. Rosie hugged her tightly, savouring the moment when the small arms were flung about her neck and a warm wet kiss was planted on her cheek.

'Ready young lady?' Frank gathered her into his arms and said something to make her giggle before taking her hand and going through the door. Amidst a chorus of goodbyes they walked up the street.

Later, Rosie and Frank walked home in the dusk. Frank was carrying the lovely cut-glass vase that Lizzie had so proudly presented from the neighbours. It had been wonderful to look round and see their smiling faces and to know that everyone of them wished her and Frank well. As Rosie thanked her warmly, Lizzie had started singing 'For She's a Jolly Good Fellow' and all the neighbours had joined in.

The evening had turned chilly. After supper Frank went up to the bedroom to put a match to the fire he'd already laid, and when she'd put the dishes away Rosie followed him.

The bedroom, with its pale cream walls and pink satin eiderdown, looked pretty in the soft light from the table lamp. When she'd switched it off she lay back with Frank's arm about her, watching the flames dancing on the ceiling. Suddenly they were blotted out as his lips came down on hers.

Much later, when she looked up at the ceiling again, the dancing flames had gone, leaving a pink glow that reflected her mood of warm contentment.

She saw the years stretching ahead, and the children they would have – brothers and sisters for Beth . . .

'Penny for your thoughts, love?' Frank said, drawing her into his arms once more.

When she told him, his lips sought hers again so that she no longer saw the fading reflection, but the glow within her remained strong, ready to be rekindled at a touch.